RAZORBILL

EARTH & SKY

MEGAN CREWE is the highly acclaimed author of several books and pieces of short fiction for young adults. Her first novel, *Give Up the Ghost*, was shortlisted for the Sunburst Award. *The Way We Fall*, the first instalment in Crewe's Fallen World trilogy, was published in 2012, and was shortlisted for the OLA White Pine Award. *Earth & Sky*, the first novel of her most recent series, received critical acclaim and was selected as a Top Ten Young Adult Fiction pick by the OLA.

EARTH & SKY

Megan Crewe

razor
bill

RAZORBILL
an imprint of Penguin Canada Books Inc., a Penguin Random House Company

Published by the Penguin Group
Penguin Canada Books Inc., 320 Front Street West, Toronto, Ontario M5V 3B6, Canada

Penguin Group (USA) LLC, 375 Hudson Street, New York, New York 10014, U.S.A.
Penguin Books Ltd, 80 Strand, London WC2R 0RL, England
Penguin Ireland, 25 St Stephen's Green, Dublin 2, Ireland (a division of Penguin Books Ltd)
Penguin Group (Australia), 707 Collins Street, Melbourne, Victoria 3008, Australia
(a division of Pearson Australia Group Pty Ltd)
Penguin Books India Pvt Ltd, 11 Community Centre, Panchsheel Park, New Delhi – 110 017, India
Penguin Group (NZ), 67 Apollo Drive, Rosedale, Auckland 0632, New Zealand
(a division of Pearson New Zealand Ltd)
Penguin Books (South Africa) (Pty) Ltd, 24 Sturdee Avenue, Rosebank, Johannesburg 2196, South
Africa

Penguin Books Ltd, Registered Offices: 80 Strand, London WC2R 0RL, England

Published in Razorbill hardcover by Penguin Canada Books Inc., 2014
Simultaneously published in the United States by Skyscape, New York

1 2 3 4 5 6 7 8 9 10 (RRD)

Manufactured in the U.S.A.

Interior design by Girl Friday Productions

LIBRARY AND ARCHIVES CANADA CATALOGUING IN PUBLICATION

Crewe, Megan, author
Earth & sky / Megan Crewe.

Originally published by Razorbill, 2014.
ISBN 978-0-14-319094-3 (pbk.)

I. Title. II. Title: Earth and sky.

PS8605.R482E27 2015   JC813'.6   C2015-900691-0

eBook ISBN 978-0-14-319316-6

Visit the Penguin Canada website at **www.penguin.ca**

Special and corporate bulk purchase rates available; please see
www.penguin.ca/corporatesales or call 1-800-810-3104.

To Deva, who made me want to write
a girl with a head full of numbers

1.

I'd like to think the courthouse won't be a problem. It's older than my house, older than our school. The mottled gray facade matches the overcast sky, dark stains creeping along the edges of the stone blocks and the grooves in the decorative columns. But I'm already tensing up, bracing against the uncertainty of a place I've never been before.

The rest of Ms. Vincent's law class gathers on the sidewalk outside the courthouse, a few final stragglers joining the crowd. Any second now, Ms. Vincent will turn up and we'll go in. I concentrate on the building. Eighteen windows: six across each of the three stories. Four fluted columns in front of the doorway. Five oak saplings spaced at equal distances on the short lawn beside the front steps. Smears of red and yellow dappling the once green leaves.

The tightness between my shoulders relaxes.

Jaeda's standing at the edge of the lawn in a hooded sweatshirt the same red as the leaves, bright against her brown-black skin. She looks like a catalog ad for "Fall's Hot Fashions." She's grinning at a joke Daniel just told—Daniel with his vintage bowler hat tipped low over his crinkled eyes. Three guys from the football team are mimicking moves from yesterday's game beyond him. One of the twins is tickling his girlfriend's neck with a twig. Next to me, Angela's pulling out her camera to snap a photo for the school paper. Nothing remotely abnormal.

A damp October breeze sweeps over us, and Angela shivers. "Why can't Vincent ever be on time?"

I glance at my watch. "She should be here soon." Ms. Vincent averages about seven minutes late, but twenty-three is her record. It's been fourteen since class technically started today.

"Someone should report her," Angela grumbles, tucking her chin behind the collar of her suede jacket. We both know she doesn't mean it. There's an unspoken agreement between everyone here, which I suspect exists in all of Ms. Vincent's classes: we'll cover for her when we need to. Because unlike most of the teachers who show up on time, when she is in class she makes us feel like we're learning things we'd actually want to know.

I'd assume my best friend's just grouchy because of the weather, but when she swipes her dark bangs to the side, a crease has formed between her eyebrows. I've known Angela since we were eight years old, and that crease means she's got some worry worming around inside her head. I glance away, deciding how to raise the subject, and that's when I notice the guy.

He's sitting off to the side of a bench on the other side of the street, mostly hidden behind a parked truck, but the instant my eyes slide over him, a sense of conviction jolts through me: *he shouldn't be there*. My pulse skitters and my mouth goes dry, my skin feverishly cold. A ringing echoes between my ears, insisting that the guy is *wrong, wrong, wrong*.

My coping mechanisms are so ingrained that even as part of me responds with *oh God, not again*, my hand is digging into the pocket of my jeans, finding the glass beads on my hemp bracelet. My fingers swivel each bead around the woven strings three times, in tandem with my silent mantra: *Three times three is nine. Three times nine is twenty-seven. Three times twenty-seven is eighty-one. Three times eighty-one* ...

There's a perfect dependability to math. No matter how many times you perform the same operation, the answer's always the same. As the factors expand out in their unshake-able pattern, my heartbeat steadies, the chill ebbs, and the *wrong* feeling fades away. Which it should, because the guy looks like a regular, nonthreatening human being.

He's gazing down at a book propped open on his lap, his black hair sloping jaggedly across his forehead, gray corduroy blazer open over a lettered T-shirt I can't read because of the truck. The corner of his mouth is quirked up as if he's read something funny. From his clothes and what I can see of his face, I'd guess he's in college. Maybe waiting for a friend who lives nearby before heading to campus.

I turn before he catches me staring, studying the courthouse again as the last ripples of *wrong*ness subside. Eighteen windows: six across each of the three stories. Four fluted columns.

One more mental disaster averted.

It's been a long time since a moment like that overwhelmed me, but the memories are as vivid as yesterday. The tremor of sobs in my throat, the frantic babbling. No matter how practiced I get, I know a total breakdown is just a slipup away.

The worst part—worse than the panic and the unpredictability of the feelings—is that no matter how intense or certain they get, or how much I want to react, there's never anything actually *wrong*. The feelings are unavoidable and unrelenting, and absolutely meaningless.

"Skylar," Angela says. "Earth to Sky!"

I blink and look back at her, smiling automatically. "Sorry. Thinking about the chemistry test."

The lie comes automatically too, but with a prick of guilt. It fits the image my friends have of me—*You know Skylar, always so focused, no wonder her brain needs to recharge sometimes!*—but I didn't become Skylar-the-cool-and-collected until middle school. One of the reasons Angela and I are friends is that she never blinked when every now and then in elementary school I'd randomly decide we needed to play somewhere else in the yard or go to a different store, or

I really didn't like that one song. Even the times I couldn't get away fast enough and the panic took over, she accepted my weak excuses and just seemed happy when I was okay again. She treated it like an odd but inoffensive allergic reaction I gradually grew out of. Except I haven't actually grown out of it. I've just gotten better at pretending.

"Like you'll have any trouble with the test," Angela says, rolling her eyes. "We have to go over the formulas again at lunch, okay? They always make sense when you're explaining them, and then an hour later, it's all a blank." She swipes her hand across her forehead dramatically, then perks up. "There she is!"

Ms. Vincent has just come around the corner, walking as quickly as the narrow heels of her ankle boots allow. She stops at the edge of our crowd, smoothing her windblown hair back into its usual auburn bob—the color I wish mine were instead of brown with a hint of orange.

"Yet another victory of public transportation over punctuality," she says, beaming at us. "Well, here we are. Let's head inside and see some law in action."

She leads us through the double doors like the captain of an invading brigade. A security officer does a quick check of our bags, and then we march up the stairs. My gaze snags on an empty corner on the first landing. *Wrong.* My hand is already in my pocket as the chill tingles over me, but the feeling's not as strong as it was with the guy outside. I only have to spin three beads on the bracelet before it's faded.

Twice in ten minutes. Sometimes I can go a whole day without one. What a great trip this is shaping up to be. I drag in a breath and zero in on Daniel's back ahead of me. On the shifting of his shoulders and the spot where his pale neck meets his sweater.

The sweater is forest green. I think it's his favorite. He wore it at least once every week last fall and winter. He wore it the second time we went out, the time when I said good-bye and bolted for my front door right when he was about to kiss me, because the stupid streetlight felt *wrong* and my mind scattered.

He was wearing it on the day, the week afterward, when I went up to him in the cafeteria and he talked to me like I was just some girl from class, and I knew there wasn't going to be another date.

It's a nice sweater, but I kind of hate it.

Jaeda's talking with the football guys now, which gives me a flicker of reassurance even though she and Daniel have been friends since sophomore year and never anything more. Even though I already had my chance.

Angela mock coughs and I jerk my gaze away, my cheeks warming. She smirks at me, knowing who I was looking at. But when I scrunch up my nose at her, she ducks her head, and that worry line creases the olive-brown skin of her forehead again. I'd almost forgotten.

Her mom's been pressuring her about her grades even more now that we're seniors, threatening to take away

Angela's camera if she doesn't get straight As. And Teyo, the guy she's been working up the courage to ask on a study date, just started seeing a freshman girl last week. Or it could be something she hasn't mentioned yet. Sometimes Angela likes to talk things out and sometimes she'd rather shrug them off.

"If I'm not allowed to worry about the chem test, you're not either," I say, keeping my tone light.

"Oh," she says, "it's not that. I swear I'm going to have an aneurysm over this Halloween dance. Two more people who were supposed to make decorations bailed on yesterday's meeting. So basically it's up to me and … me. Everyone'll know who to blame if it's a mess!"

I smile for real. This is a problem I can solve.

"I'll help," I said. "And I bet Bree will too."

"Really? I know you're not that into crafty stuff. And you two are busy with cross-country right now."

"It's not like that's all day. You just tell me what to do, and I'll do it. I know whatever you've got planned is going to look amazing."

"It really is!" she says. "You'll love it. I decided to go with an old-school theme, very gothic, but kind of golden-age-Hollywood glamorous too. You won't believe the awesome candelabras I got at Vintage Fleas, and Lisa found this velvet fabric for the tables, and …"

We spill out into a wide hallway on the third floor, beneath a ceiling edged with wooden beams. As we approach the doors at the other end, Ms. Vincent claps her hands together for our attention. Angela and I scoot closer, stopping by one of the arched windows that look down over the parking lot.

"In a couple minutes, we'll be invited inside to watch a few cases presented to the judge," Ms. Vincent says. "Remember, these aren't full trials with a jury and several witnesses and cross-examinations. With this type of case, it's mostly up to the judge—"

I never get to hear the rest of that sentence. Her voice is cut off by a hollow clunk that seems to come from right inside my ears.

And then the hallway explodes in a blaze of heat and light.

It smacks into me, my vision going white and my skin sizzling and my head aching as if someone's socked me with a brick. A siren call of WRONG, WRONG, WRONG blares over all that, drowning out every other sound.

I can't breathe. My legs wobble. I gulp for air and a squeak slips from my throat.

That noise brings me back. My fingers—they're clutching the window frame. Cool, polished wood. Two tiny nicks in the surface under my thumb. The tiled floor is firm beneath my feet, flat except for the crack at the edge of my right heel. I'm here, in the courthouse. It's not on fire. It hasn't blown apart.

The blaring wrongness recedes, just a little.

A hand touches my elbow. "Sky?" Angela says.

The hall is coming back into focus, but my thoughts keep spinning. Everyone around me is shifting and murmuring, in confusion or amusement. Like they don't care what just happened. How can they be so calm? We all just about blew up—

No. No we didn't. Sweat has broken over my skin, but I'm not even the slightest bit singed. There's no taste of ash or sulfur in my mouth, only the acidic flavor of panic. A flavor I know too well. I blink, and the world settles back into place. It was all in my head, like always. The blast, the light, the heat—none of it was real.

But the sense of *wrong*ness is still quivering through my body. I shove my hand into my pocket. The bracelet's beads are smooth against my fingertips. *Three times three is nine. Three times nine is twenty-seven.* Sixteen cars in the parking lot below. Five silver, four black, three red, three tan, one white.

"Are you all right, Skylar?" Ms. Vincent asks.

The feeling retreats further, but it doesn't leave. Why won't it let me go? I keep twisting the beads as I look up. Ms. Vincent is studying me, her brow furrowed. Almost everyone is staring. *Daniel* is staring. Embarrassment washes over me. I've been so good at staying in control and now …

I've never felt anything like that before—so vivid, so intense. What *was* that? I'm up to *3 times 59,049 is 177,147* and the *wrong*ness is still clinging on, humming through my mind.

But I didn't totally lose it. I can salvage this.

I draw myself up straighter and clear my throat.

"I'm okay," I say, and manage a laugh that's only a little hoarse. "I— There was a spider. A really big one. I might be slightly arachnophobic. Sorry, Ms. Vincent."

To my relief, several people giggle. They bought it. A couple of the girls near me take a step to the side, eyeing the wall nervously. Everyone else turns away. I want to think Daniel's gaze lingers a millisecond longer, a fraction more concerned than the others, but at the same time I want him to forget this ever happened.

Ms. Vincent hesitates, and then goes back to her introductory speech. *Wrong, wrong, wrong*, whispers the voice in the back of my head. Angela slings her arm around me, her shoulder bumping mine.

"Be real," she murmurs. "You need to sit down, or get some fresh air? Vincent will let us."

I look into her wide eyes, the coffee brown gaze I've known more than half my life. I could tell her. I've thought about it. She hasn't been fazed by anything I've thrown at her so far.

But my real is not her real. Those eyes didn't catch even a glimpse of what nearly knocked me off my feet. There is no way I can make that real to her. I wish it weren't real to me. I'd give anything to live in her world, the world everyone else lives in, where everything stays solid and definite and *right* when it should.

"Thanks," I say. "I'm okay."

The class moves toward the door, which has just opened. Angela gives me another searching look, then drops her arm. As we follow the crowd, I glance down the hall one last time. My steps falter.

He's there. The guy in the gray corduroy blazer, leaning against the wall by the stairwell we came up through. He's still got his book in his hand, examining the cover, but a tickle creeps up my spine, telling me that a second before I looked, he was watching us. When did he come up here?

"Everyone in?" Ms. Vincent calls. I pull my gaze away and walk through the doorway, leaving the guy behind.

2.

I put on my best fake normal through the rest of the field trip, through lunch and the chemistry test, smiling and nodding and tossing out comments when I need to, trying to pretend I'm not cracking apart. But I am. The whisper of *wrong*ness keeps running through my thoughts, with a dull throbbing in my head and shivers that race down to my toes. No matter how many times I twist the beads and multiply into the billions, it won't leave.

Why won't it leave?

When I sit down for dinner with my parents that evening, every question they direct at me, every time they say my name, the faint but unrelenting sense that none of this should be happening echoes through me. *Wrong, wrong, wrong.* My cheeks start to ache with the effort of holding that smile.

Nothing's wrong, I tell myself. *Nothing.*

The whisper ignores me.

It's never been like this before. The feelings might be random, but they've always passed in a minute or two since I learned how to control them. Even all those years ago, when I didn't know how and I'd sometimes fall apart, I just had to get away from whatever seemed to have triggered them and I'd be fine. But there's more than a mile between me and the courthouse, and my fingers are sore from gripping the beads, and I've cataloged every smudge on the windows and every lump in my potato salad. And none of it is working.

After dinner, I burn through my calculus homework. Normally I can lose myself in the neat rows of equations as they wind out across the graph paper, but my body keeps tensing, pulling me back. My pencil lead snaps twice.

I turn on my playlist of what my parents call "Golden Oldies" and repaint my nails my favorite shade of pearly pink. The melodies sound tinny to my ears. My hand trembles and dabs a splotch of polish on my knuckle.

I can't even take comfort in the crumbling leather-bound volume on Roman history I picked up last week at one of the vintage shops Angela and I frequent. Usually I find it soothing to read about people who lived so long ago, but still thought and acted totally human. So many catastrophes and so much turmoil across the centuries, and we're still here. I can imagine visiting the ruins someday, crossing the ground where all those earlier feet once walked, making my own mark.

Except today, that insistent murmur won't stop interrupting.

Wrong, wrong, wrong.

I close the book and lie down on my bed. Staring at the ceiling, I follow the edges of the glow-in-the-dark stars I put up when I was nine and never bothered to remove. My sight blurs. I swipe at my eyes, but the fear has already crept in.

Maybe it isn't going to stop this time. Maybe whatever's wrong with me, whatever bundle of nerves in my brain randomly misfires with those meaningless impulses, has finally gone completely haywire.

Back around the end of first grade, when the feelings escalated to once or twice a week and I shouted and cried about them every time because I didn't know what else to do and I didn't know they didn't matter, my parents took me to a psychologist. I'm sure she meant well. But whatever's wrong with me, she just made it worse. After the questions she asked about patterns and triggers, that I tried so hard to answer hoping she could make everything all right, the feelings started coming even more often. I was so afraid they'd end up haunting me every hour, every day, that I started forcing myself to conceal my distress as well as a seven-year-old could, to do my best to persuade her and my parents I was okay. Until I was faking it well enough that they decided I was recovering.

How are my parents going to feel when they find out I never did? If I don't get over this, if I just can't deal on my own anymore, I'll have to tell them. It hasn't even been a full day, and I'm already exhausted from holding back the panic.

I close my eyes, and visions of hospitals and lab coats swim through my mind. What if no one can fix me? I've paged through diagnostic manuals—I don't fit any typical form of any normal disorder. Maybe I'll just keep getting worse and worse. How am I going to travel across the world like this? How am I even going to manage college? My whole life—*everything* I want to do—

No. I can't think that way.

I push myself upright and go grab my laptop. There's one more thing that might distract me. I don't turn to this very often, because it's started to feel like an unhealthy indulgence. Noam ran away when I was five—I doubt I'd even recognize him if I saw him now. But if a little indulgence will keep me sane, I don't care how pointless it is.

I type a single word into the image search. "Crowd." For several long minutes, I scan photo after photo for my brother's face. Searching every corner, every shadow. As if maybe this time, after all this time, I'll discover where he took off to.

I don't, of course. But after I've worked through a few pages of results, the crushing terror has retreated enough that I can close the browser and start one of my Cary Grant movies playing. A little banter, a little eye candy. Daniel looks a bit like him.

While the images flicker across the screen, I sink back against my pillow. Sometime before the credits roll, exhaustion wins and I fall asleep.

• • •

The shrill beeping of my alarm yanks me back to consciousness the next morning. I groan and roll over, still tired. Then
I remember yesterday.

I lie still, waiting. My head's stopped throbbing. The
chant of *wrong*ness has gone silent.

I switch off the alarm and prop myself against the oak
headboard. My bedroom looks the same as always. Bookcase
stuffed with history and science books and classic novels.
Framed print of one of da Vinci's sketches beside it. Two
photos tacked to the wall over my desk: Angela and me at our
middle school graduation, taken by my mom; and Bree, Lisa,
Evan, and me grinning and brandishing marshmallow sticks
on our junior year camping trip, taken by Angela. I ease open
the drawer of my bedside table. Ten glass beads on my
bracelet. Three bottles of my favorite nail polish. One more
photograph, the top right corner creased: me perched on my
brother Noam's lap in a sea of wrapping paper, the Christmas
when I was four and he was fourteen.

Everything is as it should be. Everything is right.

A laugh stutters out of me. I don't know why it took that
feeling so long to fade, but I'm okay now. As okay as I've ever
been, anyway.

The spray of the shower has never felt quite so delicious.
Down in the kitchen, I take a weird enjoyment out of the
tinkling of the Bran Flakes falling into my bowl—so very

marvelously normal. Mom walks in, her hair, the same cinnamon brown as mine, swishing in its tight ponytail. She's wearing her work "uniform" of track pants, yellow T-shirt, and logo-ed hoodie that announces her position as a personal trainer at the Steel & Sweat Gym downtown.

"No cross-country practice today?" she asks.

"Practice is in the afternoon on Tuesdays," I remind her. "Coach has morning hall duty."

"Oh, right. You remind me when finals are scheduled, okay? I'll be there."

"I've got to place in sectionals first."

"You will." She squeezes my shoulder as she brushes past. "Think positive."

I wonder, like I do every time she recites that slogan, whether Mom really thinks positive about everything or whether, like me, she's just good at sounding positive no matter what's going on in her head. It's one of those things I wish I could ask, but don't. I've committed myself to being the kid my parents *don't* have to worry about, and I'd like to keep it that way as long as I can. Hopefully forever, if I don't have another attack like yesterday's.

After she's hopped into the car with Dad, whose office is just a few blocks away from the gym, I make my rounds, checking all the windows and the back door, flicking the latches open and closed three times so I'm satisfied that they're locked. Safe. Secure. It'd sound silly if I told anyone, but it helps clear my head for the day. Then I heft my backpack over my shoulder and head out.

The high school's only five minutes away, one of the reasons my parents picked this neighborhood. My gaze roves both sides of the street as I walk. Number 208 has a "For Sale" sign up that wasn't there before. A station wagon I don't recognize sits in the driveway of 175—a new purchase, or someone visiting. When I come around the corner, the sight of the concrete school building starts me ticking through my schedule. Calculus. English. Lunch: help Angela with dance decorations. Physics. Spanish. Cross-country practice until five. Tutoring Benjamin from five thirty to six thirty. Home for—

My thoughts and my feet jerk to a halt at the edge of the courtyard outside the main doors.

As usual, clusters of students are hanging out there, chatting and waving to friends. And standing on the far side of the wrought-iron fence near the bicycle rack is a guy I recognize, but not from school. A guy with jagged black hair and a gray corduroy blazer.

His face is tipped toward the sky, eyes closed, as if he's drinking in the sunlight shining on his golden-brown skin. *Wrong.* I shudder, and clutch my bracelet.

Why is he here? Yesterday was the first time I'd ever seen him. He looks young enough that I could believe he's a senior like me, but he doesn't go to this school. And he doesn't look like he's planning to join us, the way he's set himself off to the side, away from the bustle around the doors.

As I rotate the beads and the feeling fades, his lips curl into a slow, almost goofy smile. He lowers his head to study the passing students. Watching us, like he did in the courthouse. An echo of the imagined explosion washes over me, and my spine goes rigid.

I should walk right by like I usually would, like he's not even there. But the idea of going to my locker and then sitting down in class knowing he's out here, watching and waiting—for what?—makes my skin crawl.

This is pathetic. How could he possibly have anything to do with what went *wrong* at the courthouse yesterday, when I know that was a trick of my mind? He's probably just moved here, and this is his first day. His being at the courthouse was a coincidence—or he was supposed to join our class but was too shy. Which would explain why he's hanging back now too. I can prove it as easily as going over and talking to him.

Taking a deep breath, I amble along the edge of the courtyard. The shirt the guy is wearing under his blazer today is moss green, with a silver symbol like a sunburst on the chest. Dark-wash jeans, tan sneakers. A brown leather satchel hangs from his left shoulder. His hand rests on it, a little possessively, as if he's worried someone might try to steal it.

He's actually kind of cute, in a soulful hipster way that makes me picture him strumming a guitar on a coffeehouse stage. I reevaluate as I pass the bike rack: really freaking cute. Just standing there, he has a presence that makes the rest of the world around him seem somehow paler. My heart skips a beat.

As I reach the fence, his gaze passes over me without pausing, then jerks back. His eyes are a striking deep blue.

"Hey," I say, smiling. "Just starting today?"

He stares at me, tensed. For a second I think he's going to bolt. Then his stance relaxes. "Starting?" he asks.

"At the school," I say. "I haven't seen you around before. I'm Skylar."

"Oh," he says. The corner of his mouth curves up as if I've told a joke. "No, I'm not a student. Just visiting." His voice is smooth, with an inflection that sounds almost British, but also slightly muddied, as if English isn't his first language.

I raise my eyebrows. "So why are you visiting here?" Cannon Heights High is hardly a tourist destination.

"It's not important," he says, and then, casually, "You were at the courthouse the other day, weren't you?"

"I— Yeah."

"You were scared by a spider."

So he *was* watching us then. The back of my neck prickles.

"What were you doing *there*?" I ask.

This time, he outright ignores my question. "That was quite a reaction, for something as small as a spider." He steps right up to the fence, into my personal space, his presence suddenly feeling more intimidating than attractive. I scoot back.

"I really don't like spiders," I say, more sharply than I mean to.

He considers me, as if evaluating my answer. I should walk away. And then what? Tell the office there's a strange-but-not-necessarily-dangerous guy hanging out by the courtyard? Pretend he isn't here, surveying our school for some reason he won't explain?

Before I can decide, he seems to finish his evaluation. "All right," he says, as if it didn't really matter anyway. His attention drifts away, and his face brightens. I glance over my shoulder.

Jaeda's just ambled into the courtyard. Her hair is loose in a kinky halo around her head, and her skin is glowing as if it's been polished. The guy's mouth has curled back into that goofy grin I saw before. If he weren't making me nervous, I'd roll my eyes.

"Okay," I say, "so you're a stalker."

His gaze slides back to me, his expression blank, as if he didn't even hear me. All at once, anger rushes through me. So maybe my smile doesn't gleam quite as gorgeously as Jaeda's does, but I'm the one here in front of him; I'm the one talking to him. I'm the one who had to deal with the freaky panic attack he gave me yesterday and the even freakier hallucination afterward. All these stupid awful feelings I can't do anything about.

The vision of the hallway blasting apart tears through my mind, mingling with my current frustration, and before I've really thought about it, I'm adding, "Or what? You're deciding where to plant your bomb?"

I realize as I'm saying it how little sense it's going to make to someone not reading my mind. But all I want is a reaction. Still, I hardly expect him to flinch the way he does, his eyes widening. The anger drains out of me. Does he know what I'm talking about? Could it— Is that really why he was at the courthouse?

I still don't know why he's *here*. Or what he's got in that satchel.

I take another step back. "Never mind," I say. "I've got to get to class."

"Hold on," he says. "What do you mean, a bomb?"

"Nothing. Just babbling." I give him a smile I hope looks suitably sheepish and edge farther away, but he follows me along the fence to where it opens to the courtyard, and steps onto the cobblestones.

"No," he says, his voice eager. "Did you see something yesterday? The explosion— If you— Was there even really a spider?"

"Skylar!" a voice calls from behind me, and it's the most wonderful sound I've ever heard. Lisa and Evan are standing by the front doors. Lisa motions to me. "I need your help with the last question from the homework. Please?"

"I've got to go," I say to the could-be-bomber guy.

"Hey, wait!" he says, reaching for me, and I run for it. The warning bell dings, and the clusters of people in the court-yard swarm around me, carrying me along to the doors.

"Who was that you were talking to?" Lisa asks, nudging me as we head inside. "He was kind of cute."

Evan makes a pained face at his girlfriend, and I force out a laugh. That's what I'd thought.

"Just some guy," I say, risking a peek behind me. I can't even see him now.

But he's out there, he knows something about what I felt yesterday, and I have no idea what that means.

3.

Calculus is my favorite class, but the creeper outside has ruined it. I can't focus—my thoughts keep slipping back to him. How could he know about the explosion I imagined yesterday? Why is he at our school now?

The only thing I know for sure is, whatever he's up to, he didn't want to tell me. Which means it's probably something he realizes nobody would approve of.

There's no point in trying to concentrate with that idea niggling at me. As soon as Mr. Stahler's finished his opening spiel, I ask to go to the bathroom. Instead, I slip out one of the back doors and call the police on my cell phone. "There's a guy hanging around outside Cannon Heights High," I tell the officer who answers. "He looks suspicious, like he's trying to sell drugs or something."

I don't actually think this has anything to do with drugs, but I figure that detail will get them over here fast. The officer tells me someone will swing by, and when I hang up, a calm settles over me. If that guy really is trouble, I'm not equipped to deal with him, but the police should be. And even if he hasn't done anything illegal yet, maybe a little questioning will scare him off before he does.

My ploy seems to work; I don't catch a glimpse of the guy the rest of the school day. He's nowhere near the courtyard when Bree and I set out with the rest of the cross-country team after final bell. But as we run along the paths in the park, my gaze catches on people we pass. A shock of black hair here. A gray jacket there. Each time, my stomach flips before I register the rest. Pale face—too short—not him.

"You okay, Sky?" Bree asks after a while, tugging her frizzy ponytail tighter.

I hadn't realized my twitchiness was obvious. "Oh, yeah," I say. Automatic smile. "It's just been a long day."

"Tell me about it. You won't believe what Mack pulled in geography."

It's hard to talk much when you're running, so we fall back into the hush of regulated breaths. I wonder if Angela mentioned my little freak-out yesterday to Bree.

I have to stop letting it—and that guy—get to me.

I sink down into the steady rhythm of my strides. My arms swing, my lungs fill with that slow burn, my feet pound the asphalt. Left, right, left, right, one after the other, always the same. It carries me away.

By the time I've changed and set off for Benjamin's house, I'm not thinking about the guy or the courthouse or anything except the hour ahead. Ben grumbles a lot when we're working through his fifth-grade math homework, but sometimes, when I find the right words to make a concept click, this spark of awed understanding flashes across his face, like the curtains have been pulled back on the mysteries of the universe. I slog through the rest for those moments. There's nothing better than knowing I'm passing on the significance of numbers to someone else—the security in their certainty.

Today's tutoring session passes too quickly. I wave to Ben's mom as I head down the front walk. She returns the gesture before closing the door. Then I turn around, and my legs lock.

The guy in the corduroy jacket is standing on the sidewalk a couple houses down, satchel at his side, poised as if he's waiting for someone. He takes a step toward me when our eyes meet, and I realize he is. He's waiting for me.

My first impulse is to dash back to Ben's house, but if this guy is dangerous, I'd just be making them a target too. I back away along the sidewalk, tugging my cell phone out of my backpack.

"Hi," the guy says, in the sort of soothing tone people normally use on small children and the mentally infirm. "I just want to talk to you. I'm sorry if I scared you earlier." He spreads his arms, I guess to show that his hands are empty. If the gesture was meant to reassure me, it's wasted.

"You're scaring me *now*," I say. How did he know I'd be here? He must have been lurking around the school after practice and followed me. What does he want?

Is he trying to silence a witness? I don't even know what I witnessed yesterday. But he knows I reacted to something at the courthouse. Maybe he even figured out I called the police on him this morning.

My hand tightens around the phone. "If you don't get out of here, I'm dialing 9-1-1. It'll only take a second."

He pauses, about five feet away. "Whatever you saw yesterday," he says, "I didn't make that happen. All right? I was there to stop it. It's my job to protect people. I made sure the bomb was found in time so it didn't go off."

His job—to stop it? Doubt pricks me. That doesn't sound entirely implausible. Maybe I'm embarrassing myself, freaking out when he's just a young-looking undercover cop. He could have been hanging out by the school because he suspected someone from there was the real bomber.

Except now I'm thinking about this bomb as if it wasn't just a figment of my imagination.

He brought it up. Does that mean there really was one? How is that even possible?

"You did see something, didn't you?" he continues as I stand there frozen. "Something that scared you. The way you acted, I don't think it's the first time. I might know why that happens to you. That's the reason I came here. I think I can help."

"Help?" I repeat. His expression is earnest, but he could just be a good actor. I don't understand why a criminal would be following me around, but I don't see why a cop would be either.

He knows why … why I saw something that wasn't there? Why my brain panics at empty corners and streetlamps?

"Yes, I'd like to *help*," he says, emphasizing the word with a vigorous nod. "If you just tell me a little more, I can probably work out what's going on in your mind, and what you can do about it."

A jolt of hope pierces through my apprehension. Does that mean he can fix it? If he really does understand what's wrong with me, how to stop it from happening …

I'd never have to feel like I did yesterday again. I'd be able to stop worrying that next time I'll catch the feeling too late and completely break down.

I could let down my guard and just *live*.

"What's in your bag?" I ask, still clutching my phone.

His hand darts to the satchel with the same protectiveness I noticed this morning. The corner of his mouth turns up. "You think I've got a bomb in here?"

"I don't know," I say. "If you don't, why don't you show me what you do have?"

He hesitates, for just long enough that my thumb starts edging toward the Call button, and then he shrugs and pulls the satchel around in front of him. I brace myself as he unclips the buckles and lifts the flap.

"One volume of poetry," he says, retrieving the book he was reading at the courthouse. The title is written in what I think are Chinese characters. From his looks, I'd have guessed his background was Indian—or southern Italian, or even Hispanic, he's hard to pin down—but then, you don't need to be Chinese to read the language. He pops it back in.

"One bottle of orange juice. Wrapper from the sandwich I had for lunch. Pack of bubble gum. Pen. And this."

The last thing he presents is a parcel of shimmery black fabric, about the size of a folded blanket. He grips it at the top, which has the arc of a garment bag, and shakes it out. The fabric spills down like an oil slick, the bottom puddling by his feet. Even in the dimming sunlight, I can see the blurred shapes of the street reflected on its surface.

"What is that?"

"Difficult to explain," he says. "But I think we can agree it's not a bomb?"

"Yeah." I approach him, until I'm close enough to touch it. His hand tenses where he's holding it, but he doesn't stop me. The fabric feels silky under my fingers, and lighter than I expected, almost airy. I'm reflected on it now, a rippling silhouette.

My first thought, ridiculously, is that Angela would kill for Halloween tablecloths made out of this stuff. My second is that it's not like any kind of fabric I've seen or touched before. Even staring at it, I can't make out the slightest hint of a grain, the texture of the fibers. It's smooth as sheet plastic. But plastic couldn't move like this. Weird.

Then it occurs to me that, if the guy wanted to grab me, hurt me, he could do it right now. But he's just standing, waiting. Even without looking at him directly, I get that sensation again, that he's somehow more solid, more real, than the houses behind him, the sidewalk under our feet. The impact of his presence makes my breath catch.

It's not attraction or alarm or any other emotion I can identify. I don't have the warm, fluttery-stomach feeling that Daniel gives me, or the urge to run away. But it's something. A sign that he knows how to counteract all the *wrong*ness in my life?

When I drop my hand, he folds up the strange fabric and slips it into his satchel. He smiles as he offers his hand to me.

"Hi," he says. "I'm Win. You said your name is Skylar?"

"Yeah," I say. I accept his hand cautiously. He squeezes mine and lets it go.

"I saw a few coffee shops on the way here," he says, motioning to his right, toward the street I walked along on my way to Ben's house. "You pick the place, I'll buy you something to eat, and we'll talk?"

I waver. Mom and Dad will be expecting me for dinner soon, and Angela's supposed to come over later on to work out the last details of our English presentation. Still, I have a little time.

There's nothing he can to do to me in a public place, surrounded by other people, that he couldn't have already done if he wanted to. He could be playing some bizarre game with me, but I'll survive that. I might not survive passing up the chance to find out if he really does understand what's wrong with me, and how to fix it. I was an inch away from losing it completely yesterday. I'd give anything to never face that fear again.

"All right," I say. "Let's talk."

4.

Being willing to talk doesn't mean I'm throwing caution to the wind. I keep my phone in my hand as we head toward Michlin Street. Win eases my nerves by leaving a comfortable distance between us. There's a spring in his step, but he seems content to walk in silence. When we turn the corner, off the residential street and into the flow of evening shoppers and restaurant-goers, I return the phone to my bag. This neighborhood, an artsy strip just a little too far north to be considered downtown, is my home turf. Across the street, two couples are sitting on the brightly painted benches outside Pie Of Your Dreams, where the five of us—Angela, Bree, Lisa, Evan, and me—devoured an entire lemon meringue last weekend. Farther down the block stands the antique shop where I found my book of Roman history and Angela her Halloween candelabras. Win and I pass a chain coffee shop packed with college kids—pop tunes jangling through the doorway—and the hippy-chic vegetarian place Bree adores.

A "Help Wanted" sign is hanging in the window. I'll have to mention it to her.

Just beyond the thrift store where Angela buys most of her clothes, we reach an indie cafe with low armchairs and dark wood tables positioned by the front window. I'm not much of a coffee drinker—even a little caffeine gives me the jitters—but I've been in here a few times to grab a snack. Classic jazz is playing low in the background when we step inside. The rich scent of roasted coffee beans mingles with varnished wood and aged leather.

"Nice place," Win says, pausing to take it in. He tilts his head. "What musician is that?"

"Um, I'm not sure," I say. "The staff might know."

He nods and ambles over to the short line by the order counter. As I follow him, a broad man in a pinstriped suit turns abruptly from the pickup area. His elbow bumps my arm, and the dark liquid from his cup sloshes on the front of his shirt.

"Oh, for Christ's sake," he mutters. The younger man who's with him snatches the cup from him so he can dab at the expanding brown splotch with a napkin. The paper sops up some but not all of the stain. "I don't have time to go back for another shirt.".

"Sorry," I offer, even though he's the one who wasn't looking where he was going. He glances at me, and rolls his eyes heavenward before turning to his assistant.

"It'll make you seem more accessible to the audience," the younger man suggests. "Happens to everyone."

"Let's just get this over with. The tie mostly covers it …"

Their voices fade as they hurry toward the door.

"Problem?" Win asks when I join him in line.

"Just some grouch who thinks he's the center of the universe."

"I know a few of those." Win chuckles, and pulls a wallet out of his back pocket. "What'll you have?"

Not coffee, if I'm going to keep a clear head. "A small hot chocolate. And a peanut butter cookie. But you don't have to pay for me."

"I think I owe you, after the way I startled you."

"You don't have to pay for me," I say firmly. I don't like the idea that he might think I owe *him* after. I still don't even know who he is.

He accepts my declaration with a slight grimace, which vanishes as soon as the cashier asks for his order. We get our drinks and take a table in the corner, me scooting around back so I have a view across the shop all the way to the door. Win leans over his coffee and inhales the steam. A dreamy expression steals over his face. Then he raises the cup and takes a slow sip.

"I am never going to get tired of this stuff," he says. "Amazing what you can get out of a plant."

What *do* I know about this guy? He saves high school classes from bombs, he has the attention span of a guppy, and he moons over lattes.

"You wanted to talk," I remind him. "About seeing weird things?" I'd like to get to the *finding out whether he actually can help me* part of the conversation as quickly as possible. Even without coffee in my system, my body's humming with a mixture of excitement and anxiety.

"Yes." Win blinks out of his coffee reverie. "Sorry. Let me know if this sounds about right." He taps his finger against the table as if pointing out the elements in a diagram. "Every now and then, you go somewhere, or you see something, and you feel it doesn't make sense. It should have been different somehow. But there's no obvious reason why, and no one else seems to notice."

"Yeah," I say, staring at him. The way he explained it—I might not have phrased it quite that way—but that's exactly how it is. He grins, both with his mouth and those deep blue eyes. It's hard to stop staring. "How did you know?"

"I've experienced something similar. When did it start? Can you describe how it happens for you?"

I've spent so long keeping this part of myself under wraps that my throat closes up. But he knows—he really *knows*—without my having said anything. How much else does he know about the *wrong*ness? About how to make it stop?

The words spill out, faster than I intended. "I don't know—the first time I remember it getting bad was when I was around six. All of a sudden, I just feel that something's *wrong*. My whole body reacts, like a panic attack … Is that what it's like for you too?"

"Pretty much," Win says. "And they just happen whenever?"

"It seems like it. For a while, when I was little, I thought maybe I had some kind of sixth sense; that it was warning me. But there never is anything wrong. I had to learn how to calm myself down, or else my brain got totally derailed."

But if what he says is true—if there *was* a bomb—maybe the feelings aren't meaningless after all. Maybe I just didn't understand. You can't get much more wrong than being blown up.

"What calms you down?" Win asks, cocking his head.

It's amazing, being able to talk to someone about all this. Someone who gets it, who doesn't stare at me like I'm crazy. The urge to spill everything is overwhelming. I take a drink from my mug before I continue, to slow myself down. "Focusing on little details around me," I say. "And numbers. Numbers are good—three, especially. I have this bracelet; I multiply by threes with the beads."

"A bracelet."

"It's nothing magical." I tug it out of my pocket, but my body balks just shy of offering it to him.

Win eyes it. "It's too small for your wrist."

"When I first started doing the multiplying, I had this one my brother gave me, when I was a lot smaller. The hemp starts to fray after a while, so I've been restringing the beads, but it seemed … right to keep it the same size."

I run my finger over one of the beads. The dapples of blue and purple have been worn down by years of spinning, no longer as glossy as they were on that first bracelet. I remember how gleeful my five-year-old self was, knowing my big brother was making something just for me. Getting to pick out my favorite beads at the store, watching him weave the hemp strings. He never knew how much I was going to need it.

As with all my memories of Noam, the thought comes with a jab of guilt. An echo of another memory, the last one: his skinny form in the corner of my vision, waving from the doorway before disappearing forever.

My fingers have moved on to the third bead, the threes rattling out in my head, before I realize what I'm doing. Heat floods my cheeks. I didn't mean to give a demonstration. I shove the bracelet back into my pocket.

Win doesn't comment on my slip. "So there aren't any patterns to when you get the feelings?" he asks.

I pause. That's the sort of question my childhood therapist would have asked. "Not really. Except … I did start to notice, they mostly seem to come with things that are new, or somewhat recent. I've stopped going to current movies and picking up current books and even going to new places when I can avoid it. Somehow sticking to stuff that's older seems to help. What about you?"

"Something like that," Win says. "New things rather than old. That would fit. Have you gotten one of those feelings about anything recently? Other than the bomb, I mean?"

"I'm not sure," I say. "They're not exactly fun—I try to forget them as soon as they're over. But, this bomb—you said you were at the courthouse to make sure it didn't go off—so there really was a bomb? How did you know? Did the feelings tell you somehow?"

"The bomb's not important," Win says with a flippant gesture. "I took care of it. Are you sure you don't remember anything?"

"Why does it matter?"

"It could make a difference. Just think about it for a minute."

The hint of impatience in his voice sets me abruptly on edge. He's dodging my questions. I've told him so much, and other than his initial suggestions about what I've experienced, everything he's said has been vague, if not a total evasion. How can some *wrong*ness I noticed last week be more important than him stopping a building from exploding?

Maybe this was never about helping me. My stomach twists. Well, I don't know what he wants, and I don't see why I should have to figure it out if he's staying clammed up.

I take a bite of my cookie. Around us, friendly chatter carries through the coffee shop. Five junior-high girls whisper over their whipped-cream-topped mugs. A couple of middle-aged men discuss a video playing on one of their laptops. A barista is wiping down the table across from ours, her long brown hair swaying with the movement of her arm.

Everything is fine. Safe. Normal.

"So?" Win says.

"I told you," I say. "I don't really keep track. And I'm not okay with you asking all the questions and not answering mine. Who *are* you?"

"I *told* you," he says. "I'm Win." As if that really tells me anything. As if I'm the one being difficult. He sighs, cupping his hands around his coffee mug. "What if I say I'm a … a special investigator into these sorts of phenomena?"

With that hesitation in the middle of his sentence, he sounds like he's making up a story on the spot. "I'd say you'd have to do better than that. *What* phenomena? Do the feelings mean something? Where do they come from? You haven't explained anything."

"The problem with explaining it, well—"

His voice cuts off. His shoulders stiffen. Suddenly he's pushing back his chair and reaching for my hand. "We have to go."

Okay, this situation has gone right around the bend. "What?" I say. "I'm not—"

Then I lose track of my sentence, because beyond Win a new couple is walking into the cafe. At least, I think of them as a couple at first glance, because it's a man and a woman and they're about the same age: early thirties, I'd guess. But the second they step through the doorway, the woman pushes ahead with an air of authority. The man flanks her as they scan the interior of the shop. It's difficult to look away from her, she's so striking: tall and slim in her tan peacoat, with ice-pale skin and hair so blond it's almost white but somehow doesn't look bleached. But that's not what makes me go rigid.

I've been sitting across from Win long enough that I've tuned out the strange presence he has. Seeing the newcomers, it's like he's snapped back into focus. Because this couple has it too. The edges of their bodies are so definite, their coloring so vivid, they make the rest of the people around them, even the wall behind them, look faded in comparison.

Win turns to look. A word escapes his lips that's not part of any language I know, but it sounds distinctly like a curse. He jerks back around, grabbing my wrist.

"Come on. *Now*."

At the same moment, the pale woman's gaze meets mine across the room. A chill shoots through me. She makes a flicker of a gesture to her companion, her voice low but clear.

"That's the one."

5.

Win pulls at my arm, his back to the woman. Her gaze is still fixed on me. Her mouth curls into a sneer. She strides forward with predatory speed, and that's when my body wakes up and decides it's time to get out of there.

I slide off my chair. Win tugs me through the shop, his hand clamped around my wrist, his jaw tight. He's so obviously scared, it makes me even more terrified. I've never seen that woman before in my life—I'd remember that icy stare. How can she know me?

What does she want with me?

"Hey!" one of the baristas shouts as Win pushes the rear "Staff Only" door open. I glance behind just long enough to see the pale woman loping after us, her hand moving to a thin shape at her hip. My pulse skips and I scramble after Win. We rush through a narrow room packed with shelves of boxes and plastic-wrapped skids to the heavier door at the other end. Win shoves it and gives a huff of relief when it moves.

"Who—" I begin.

"Just come," he snaps. "Fast!"

The door is squeaking open behind us. I stumble into the alley. Win doesn't stop for a second. He swivels on his feet and drags me toward the street that's visible beyond the backs of the neighboring buildings. I keep pace, my wrist aching in his grip. Part of me wants to pull my arm away and part of me is worried he'd break the bones before he let go.

"We should be able to lose them out there," he says. Then the door we came out thumps again, and he lunges into a run.

I race after him, dodging the garbage spilling from an overflowing trash bin and splashing through a puddle. Footsteps are smacking the pavement behind us. Faster than ours. There's a twanging sound, like an out-of-tune guitar. Win swears again, yanking me to the side as a sliver of light crackles into the bars of a fire escape, so close the sparks singe my cheek.

My breath stutters, but I don't have time to wonder what the hell that was. The open space at the end of the alley is just a building-length away. I gulp air and lengthen my strides, my free arm pumping frantically. Win veers left and then right, and my foot skids on a crumpled plastic bag. There's another twang.

Pain slices up my left elbow, forcing a yelp from my throat. My muscles spasm and my feet tangle under me. Win hauls me upright, out onto the busy sidewalk.

The pain vanishes as we weave through the evening shoppers. For an instant, I'm relieved. Then I realize I can't feel my arm at all. It's gone numb from hand to shoulder, so numb I have to look down to make sure it's still there. When I try to move it, not a single fingertip wiggles. The arm might as well be hollow.

The shock sends a blur of tears into my eyes, but my feet keep running. Win bolts onto the road, and I follow. I don't know what else to do.

Tires screech. Someone yells at us. My arm bumps limply against my side, like a dead thing. Nausea bubbles up inside me. I swallow it down, training my mind on the simple act of setting my feet flat on the ground, one after the other.

I can't fall. Whatever might happen if that woman catches up with us has to be even worse than this.

We reach the opposite sidewalk just in time to dash around a bus pulling up at the corner. Win peeks over his shoulder and then turns sharply into a shop doorway beside us. He jerks my wrist, the one I can still feel, so I'll crouch with him behind the window display. I stare at the glossy objects lining the shelves around us for several seconds before my mind catches up. Shoes. We're in a shoe store.

"What …" I say, but I can't even figure out what question to ask.

Win holds a finger to my lips. He eases up to peer between the fur-trimmed boots lining the stand by the front window. His chest is heaving, an odd clicking sound coming with each breath. The woman trying on a pair of kitten heels by one of the benches goggles at us. A clerk is marching over.

"I don't know what you're doing," she says, "but—"

Win jumps up. "I apologize. We're leaving."

We are? I hurry after him as he sprints outside. "Quick," he says. "They'll realize we didn't run that way before very long. We need to get out of range."

He starts to jog back the way we came. My head jerks around, but there's no sign of the woman who was chasing us—the woman who *shot* at us. She must have run past the store. I trail after Win across the road, around the corner, and down a different street. My bad arm swings dully by my side.

In a minute, we've left most of the traffic behind. My skin prickles. We're surrounded by houses now. There's nowhere to hide if she finds us again.

"Where are we going?" I ask.

"It's not far," Win says. "She won't know to look for us there."

I'll take that for now. We jog down several more blocks and around another corner, until we reach a smaller commercial street and a squat, dun building with a sign declaring it the "Garden Inn." Win ducks inside and comes to a halt in the lobby. He sags against the wall, his hand pressed against his chest. A grayish cast clouds his skin. He's not just panting but wheezing now.

We haven't been running that fast. I'm hardly winded, and he looks reasonably fit.

"Are you going to be okay?" I say. "Do you have an inhaler or something?"

"I'm fine," he rasps. "Just need … a second. It's … the air's not …"

He trails off and doesn't continue. I stand there as he catches his breath. The balding man at the front desk studiously ignores us in favor of his wall-mounted TV. A tingling is creeping back into the skin around my shoulder and my thumb.

I prod the muscles. I still can't feel much, but I think the numbness is wearing off. Thank God. But there's an odd rough patch on the sleeve of my jacket. I look down at the sleeve, and slide it around.

My body stills. Just above my elbow is a mark about a half an inch thick and two inches long. Not a rip or a puncture. It looks as if the synthetic fibers have melted into a lumpy scar where the shot caught me.

What if she'd hit my back? My head?

What *was* that thing she shot me with? I check the skin underneath. It's smooth and unbroken. How is it possible for the same shot that melted my jacket to have left my skin unharmed, while numbing all my nerves? None of the laws of science I know will let me wrap my head around that.

Win pushes himself upright, looking less like he's going to die.

"This way," he says.

He wavers across the lobby to a doorway framed by faux marble. It's not until I've followed him into a hall lined with numbered doors and he pulls out a key that it occurs to me he's heading to a room here. A room he expects me to go into with him, alone.

I still know nothing about him other than his name, and the fact that he's associated with some very strange and violent people. He ran away from them, but that doesn't prove he's better than they are.

Win makes it a couple of steps farther before he notices I've stopped. "It's just a few more doors down," he says.

"I'm not going anywhere else until you tell me what's going on," I say. My shoulder twitches, a swath of feeling returning with pinpricks of pain.

"We can't talk about it in the middle of the hall," he says, managing to sound exasperated despite the continued hitching of his breath.

"Then I'm leaving," I say. "Maybe I shouldn't have gone with you in the first place. Why were those people chasing us? What have you gotten me mixed up in?"

"It was you they were looking for," he points out.

I remember that with perfect clarity: the moment the pale woman's gaze clashed with mine. *That's the one.* But I also remember how Win reacted before they'd even stepped in the door.

"You knew they were coming. You knew they were dangerous before they did anything. It's obviously got something to do with you."

"I know you'll be in even more trouble if you go out there and they find you again," he says.

"Then I'd better go to the cops," I say. "Maybe they can actually stop those people." The image of the pale woman flashes through my mind: her athletic speed, the confidence in her stride. I hesitate. "Unless those *were* some kind of cops."

"You know cops around here who use guns like that?" Win asks, raising an eyebrow as he nods to my arm. The flesh below my shoulder is still completely dead. I try to bend my elbow, and fail.

"I don't know," I say. "They could have all sorts of fancy weapons if it was the FBI, or some special army division."

"They're not FBI, or army, or anything like that," Win says. "And there isn't a police force on Earth that'll have any idea how to deal with them."

"And you do?" I say. "All you've done so far is ask me weird questions and make up stories about why you care. I'd rather take my chances with the cops."

His expression flickers. "You don't understand," he says.

No, I don't understand anything about him or what just happened. But I know I don't trust him, and he's all but admitted that woman is connected to him somehow. "You're right," I say, taking a step back. "But unless you feel like explaining for real …"

He looks at me, and then at the floor. Well, there's my answer. I turn and head back toward the lobby, not totally sure what I'm going to do once I get out there. My stomach's churning. Can 9-1-1 handle a situation like this?

I guess I'll have to find out.

I'm almost at the doorway when I hear Win's voice.

"Wait," he says. I glance back at him. His jaw is clenched tight and his eyes are bright with something that could be fear or excitement or both.

"I'll tell you," he says in a rush. "The real story this time, I promise. If you'll stay and listen. I *can* protect you from the people who chased us. And … I could use your help."

I pause. I don't know what the heck he thinks I can do for him, but he sounds like he means it.

He might be right about the cops. At least, if I'm going to them, it'd be better if I have some idea who those people are. Where to find them. What else they're capable of.

"I'm still not going into some locked room with you," I say.

Win considers. "I think there's a patio," he said, "on the roof. The woman who checked me in said something about breakfast there when the weather's good. How's that?"

If I don't like the look of it, I can always turn around. "Fine," I say. "Let's take the stairs."

I let him go first, so I can keep an eye on him. Pins and needles are jabbing into my wrist and down my upper arm. I can twitch my fingers and my thumb now. Progress.

Win's panting by the time we've climbed up all three flights, but he walks out onto the patio steadily enough. He sits down at one of the grimy plastic tables and motions to the chair across from him.

"You can stay closer to the door," he says. "And there's a fire escape over there"—he nods to a spot a few feet from the chair—"if that's not enough security."

If I needed to, I could obviously outrun him. I pull the chair out and sit, just out of reach. The autumn evening chill is settling in, damp and clammy. I shrug my jacket closer around me.

"Okay," I say. "Explain."

I expect him to launch straight into some elaborate story. Instead, he studies the tabletop with a frown. Then he raises his eyes.

"I wasn't lying to you because I wanted to," he says. "We're not supposed to tell anyone. Ever. That's the most important rule. But I think what we're trying to accomplish right now is more important than that rule. I think *you're* more important."

I have no idea what to make of that. Win rubs the back of his neck and sighs.

"The reason I was so tired just now," he says, "it's not because of a medical condition. It's because I'm not fully adjusted to the air here, or the gravity. There's more oxygen, and less pull, on my planet."

6.

O n your *planet*?"

This can't be real. I'm not really hearing this. But I am, and Win's looking at me with a twist to his lips like he knows how ridiculous it sounds—like he knows but he can't help it because it's true. Okay. So he's insane.

As I come to that conclusion, I'm already getting to my feet.

"No, wait," he says, lunging forward to grasp at me. When I flinch back, he holds his hand out beseechingly. "Let me tell you the whole thing. I'm not lying—I swear it. I can even prove it to you. Please."

I stand there, frozen. I don't want to listen to some long crazy story. But something crazy is going on, isn't it? Attendants come to drag him back to the psychiatric ward wouldn't carry strange melty-numbing weapons. And as I stare at him, I'm struck once more by the awful solidness of him: the way, when my attention's on him, the world around us starts to feel as filmy as tissue paper.

My hand slips into my pocket, thumb sliding over the beads. After a couple of turns, I can breathe again. But I don't sit back down.

"I'm waiting," I say.

"My planet," Win says quickly. "Kemya." He pronounces the *K* sound with a slight slur in the back of his throat, the part of his accent I couldn't place, which adds a disturbing edge of authenticity. "You could say we've been 'studying' Earth. Seeing how the people here deal with problems. Experimenting with possibilities."

"By stopping courthouses from being bombed and stalking high-school girls?" I say.

"I wasn't—" He stops, and seems to gather himself. "We have a type of … machine, that can create a special field. When we're inside the field, we can travel between the present and the past. Change events. Observe different outcomes."

He nods to the darkening sky. "The largest time field generator ever created is up there, hidden from your sensors and telescopes. It's holding in place a field that surrounds your entire planet. As if it's encased in a giant glass ball."

He runs a finger through the grime on the tabletop, drawing one circle that I guess is supposed to be Earth, and a dot that must be this generator thing hovering above it. Then a bigger circle, that stretches from the dot all the way around, engulfing the first circle completely. My chest tightens, as if it's me he's confined.

"There's a team of our scientists and Travelers working on an adjacent satellite up there," Win says, tapping the generator dot. "They keep the field running and monitor everything down here, and jump in when they have alterations to make that they think will be informative."

The words are so pat and technical it takes a moment for their full meaning to sink in.

"So you're telling me that you're an alien, *and* a time traveler," I say. "And you and other people from your … your planet, you've been playing around with things down here, messing with our lives?"

"*I* haven't," Win says. "I mean, not very much. I only just finished the training. But there are lots of other Travelers … and it's been going on for thousands of years. I don't—"

"Thousands of years?" I interrupt. The bottom of my stomach has dropped out. No. I need something—a flick of an eyelid, a tweak of a muscle—to tell me he's pulling my leg. But his expression is impenetrably serious.

It's too crazy to be true. There's no way.

"I don't like it either," Win says emphatically. "There's a group of us—we don't think it's right. We want to shut down the time field and stop the experimenting. To leave Earth alone." He runs his thumb over his drawing, smudging out the second circle, his "glass ball."

Well, if this weren't crazy, that's definitely the side I'd be on.

"That's why I'm here," he goes on. "We're looking for— The leader of our group, he designed a weapon that could destroy the generator, take down all the defenses. There are a lot. But he was almost caught by the Enforcers, our security division, people like the ones who chased us today. So he came down to Earth and hid the weapon from them, where the rest of us could retrieve it later to finish the job."

I don't know what to do other than play along. "Okay. And you think he hid it *here*?"

"No," Win says. "It's more complicated than that. The rest of the group, they're looking for Jeanant—our leader—in the past right now. But this is the time when he first came down, so I was assigned to stay here in case there was some sort of sign from when he arrived. I've been hopping from country to country, watching for anything unusual. I came to this city because I heard about the courthouse bombing."

"But it wasn't bombed," I say. "Not yet, anyway. You said you …"

He said he stopped it.

"I came and I watched, and I could tell pretty quickly the bomb had nothing to do with Jeanant," Win says. "But I've been waiting around for weeks—going through the same week, over and over—and I don't know what's happening with the others. We aren't supposed to be here at all, so our equipment is limited, especially communications. I'll be called in when they've succeeded, but that hasn't happened yet. I didn't know whether the Enforcers had caught on. Whether the others might be in danger. Then I saw your class, and … It was awful, afterward." He looks suddenly sick. Visions of ambulances, stretchers, smoke, and burned flesh pass through my head, and my own stomach clenches.

"I knew it would be so simple to go back and save all of you," he continues. "One little gesture to make up for a tiny bit of the harm the Travelers have done down here. And at the same time I could distract any Enforcers chasing the rest of the group. I didn't mean to let them get so close."

The sensation of burning heat and the blast of sound come back to me so vividly I taste ash in my mouth. So if I believe him, the hall really did explode, once. And then Win changed something so it didn't. And after …

After the explosion that didn't happen, everything felt *wrong* to me. Everywhere I went, everyone I talked to. For hours.

Maybe the problem wasn't with the entire world. Maybe what was *wrong* was me still being in it.

"When you watched, the first time …" I say. "We all died."

He nods.

The casual acknowledgment chokes me. I drag in the cool air. It's not true. It's just a story. How could it be true?

A story to cover *what*? What could possibly be worse than this?

"You came by the school this morning," I say. "You were still watching us." I remember the moment he lit up. "You were waiting for Jaeda?"

"Who?"

"Black hair, dark skin, very pretty …" I raise my eyebrows.

A flush spreads under his golden-brown skin. "Oh," he says. "It wasn't about her. I came back to see if the Enforcers had registered the change, started to investigate. And I'd noticed your reaction, when the explosion was supposed to happen, and thought it might be a good idea to observe you a little. I did notice—Jaeda?—the other day too. She has a … distinctive look. It was just good to see she was well."

Of course. "So I was right in the first place," I say. "You're a stalker."

"It wasn't like *that*," he protests. "I'd seen her for all of fifteen minutes. And I had a good reason to want to check on you."

I fold my arms over my chest, raising my chin. This is ridiculous. Nothing exploded, no one died, I'm fine. "I don't know why I was considering buying any of this," I say. "There are about a billion more plausible stories you could have told. Where's the proof you said you have? Is it just that I felt something weird yesterday?"

"No." He stands up and sets his satchel on the table. "I'll show you. You pick the time and place. If you could see anywhere, any time before now … where would you go?"

Right. This is a joke. My thoughts slip back to last night's reading. "Sure," I say. "Why not? Let's visit the Roman Coliseum. First century AD. When there are games on. Are you going to pull it out of that bag?"

"You could say that," he says as he opens the satchel. "We Travel in this."

He pulls out that bundle of shimmery not-quite fabric that fascinated me earlier and unfurls it. At a press of his fingers, there's a mechanical click, and a line splits down the middle so he can open it like an immense cape.

"Anywhere, any when," he says, a reverential tenderness in his tone and his grip on the cloth. "You're going to have to come inside, of course."

We're going to travel through time in a shiny tablecloth? This is the craziest part yet. I shake my head, a laugh sputtering out.

Win squares his shoulders. With a practiced snap of his wrists, he whirls the cloth around him. For an instant I'm watching his form disappear amid the folds of dark fabric.

And then, suddenly, I can't see him or the cloth at all.

My head whips around. The rooftop is empty except for the vacant tables and me. The wind teases my hair. Streetlights gleam in the distance. Where the hell did he go?

I'm heading over to check the fire escape when Win's voice emerges from the air where he was standing before.

"I'm right here."

The air parts, and the surface of the cloth shimmers back into sight. Only it doesn't look like a cape now, more like a narrow, arch-topped tent, a couple feet taller than Win and maybe four wide. Win's peering out at me between the flaps of its entrance, his mouth curved into a crooked grin as if daring me to try to explain *this* away.

I ... really don't have any rational way of explaining that. I blink, and the scene before me doesn't change. If this is crazy, then I'm crazy too.

Win tilts his head. "Are you going to come get your proof or not?"

My heart thuds. I could walk away and never stop wondering. Or I could take a leap. If his "proof" doesn't hold up, well, I'll know for sure none of this was true.

I step toward Win. He eases back to make room for me. I hesitate, and then push myself onward. The flap flutters down after I duck inside the sort-of tent, but it doesn't block the light. The pale outlines of the rooftop outside and the buildings beyond it swim on the inner walls.

Beside me, Win taps the fabric. It hums, and a wavering display lights up, presenting a series of dancing characters.

"So this thing is going to fly us through space and time?" Somehow it sounds even more absurd when I say it out loud.

Win skims through the data with his fingers hovering an inch from the display, his face intent in the reflected glow. "It's more bouncing," he says. "That glass ball I said the time field is like? We hit the inner surface and come back down. The field does most of the work."

With a satisfied sound, he pats the display with his palm. It vanishes.

"This cloth's an older model," he says. "The Traveling's not quite as smooth as—"

The rest of his sentence is cut off by a lurch. The shapes on the walls blur and my stomach jolts into my throat. We're rushing up and around, spinning and shuddering, as if we're trapped in some sort of manic elevator. The air shrieks. I close my eyes and clamp my jaw shut to keep from shrieking with it.

There's a tremor, and then we're plummeting. My hand gropes out and clutches the first solid thing it finds. My head's about to pull right off my neck. My lungs are squeezed tight.

We stop with a jerk. The shrieking fades from my ears, leaving only a faint ringing.

It's Win's elbow I'm clinging to. I open my eyes, and shut them again, fighting the urge to vomit. Okay. This is definitely not just a tablecloth.

"Sorry," Win says. "It's always awful the first time."

I draw air in and gradually expel it. The various parts of my body settle back into their proper places. I sneak a peek at him.

"It gets better?"

He cracks a smile. "Hard to say. But once you see where you can go, you stop caring."

Where you can go. I risk a look around. The walls are dark except for a rectangle of yellow light ahead of us. Indistinct figures ripple across it. I don't know where we are now, but it doesn't look like the rooftop.

"Ready?" Win asks.

I shouldn't have agreed to this if I weren't. "Ready," I say, without giving myself a chance to rethink it.

He draws open the cloth.

7.

The light hits me first, brilliant sun glancing off sand-strewn ground. The sluggish air wafts over me, tangy with sweat and something putridly metallic. Blood, I realize as my vision adjusts. Dark patches swim into focus just beyond the stone passageway that shelters Win and me. A figure in thin bronze armor dashes past the entrance, spear raised. Farther out across the arena, shapes of animals and men writhe and break apart. Shouts echo against the high walls, which are painted a beige and red that match the gore-splattered sand. Cheers rain down from above. Someone over our shadowy doorway is stomping their feet.

I gulp a breath. Grit prickles against the back of my mouth.

"The *Amphitheatrum Flavium*," Win intones beside me. "April 6, 81 AD."

It's warm—sweat is trickling down my back under my jacket. I reach past the flap of the cloth to touch the passage wall. The stone is rough under my fingers. Solid. Real.

How can it be real?

Less than thirty feet away, a rhinoceros charges into a cluster of gladiators, tossing one to the side with guts spilling from a gaping belly wound. Win grimaces. A dagger soars from beyond my view and strikes the rhino in the shoulder. A leopard stalks past, shooting a narrow glance into our doorway. I jerk back into the shelter of the cloth. As the leopard pads toward us, a rumbling starts somewhere down the passage behind us. We're trapped, surrounded by noise and violence and history.

"Take me back," I hear myself saying raggedly over the thudding of my heart. "I want to go back now."

The words are hardly out of my mouth when a shower of arrows flits through the air. One impales the leopard's haunches, another clatters against the stones, and a third is shooting straight toward us. I cringe against the side of the cloth as Win yanks the flaps together. There's a thunk and a patter as the arrow rebounds off the fabric. Too close. I squeeze my eyes shut.

"Take me back!"

We're already moving. That whirling, jostling feeling sweeps around us again. I press my arms around my head and count the frantic beats of my pulse.

We land with a quiver. The cloth's flaps part. A dusky light touches my face with a whisper of breeze, and I look up. The roof of the hotel is there to meet me.

I wobble out. The concrete feels firm beneath my feet. The air is cool and moist again.

But I can still see the gutted gladiator falling. Still taste the salty grit on my tongue. Still hear the hiss of the arrow that almost hit us.

I inhale, exhale, trying to flush the smell of pain and death from my lungs.

"We were really there," I say. "We traveled back in time."

"Yes," Win says. "Do you believe me now?"

As he folds up the cloth and slides it into his satchel, I sink onto one of the patio chairs, running my fingers through my sweat-dampened hair. Distantly, I notice I can bend my left arm now, though the elbow joint is still tingly.

I was just in Ancient Rome, 81 AD.

And what about the rest? Win has come from the planet of Kemya? Aliens have been altering Earth's history for centuries—millennia? They're looking down at us right now, at my planet in their goldfish bowl?

I died yesterday?

It's too much: too big, too awful. But I can't deny what just happened. That part of his story, at least, is real.

"Why are you showing me?" I ask. "Why did you want to talk to me at all?"

Win sits down across from me. "I think you can tell when the past has been shifted," he says. "The changes made during your lifetime, anyway. The feelings you told me about—some part of your mind is remembering experiencing things differently before the shift."

"*Why*?"

"I don't know," he admits. "I've heard that it's scientifically possible for shifts to have some effect on Earthlings who are particularly sensitive. It's unlikely you're the only one who's gone through this. But Travelers aren't supposed to interact with locals unless it's absolutely necessary. I don't think anyone before me has ever identified someone like you."

If he's right, then every *wrong* feeling, every panic attack that I convinced myself didn't mean anything … They were actually true. Something really was wrong.

The bench Win sat on, empty the first time I came to the courthouse. Some object once in the corner of the stairwell. The blast. *Shifted*. My life rewritten.

The whisper of *wrong, wrong, wrong* starts to echo in my head. Like it did all afternoon and evening yesterday. Telling me I'm not supposed to be here.

I'm supposed to be a vacant burned body lying in a morgue.

No. I look away from Win, across the patio. Seven tables. Four chairs around each except for three by that one in the corner. I'm here. I'm real. Yellow lights glinting in two windows of the apartment over the store across the street. A scrawny tabby cat stalking along the border of the neighboring roof.

Here. Real.

Alive.

"You see what this means," Win's saying. "If you can track the shifts, you can help us figure out where to go. Jeanant said he'd make little changes, some to distract the Enforcers and some only our group would know were meaningful, to lead us to his weapon. You can help us follow them."

Right. This isn't just about jumping through time. Follow a rebel from outer space. Find some alien weapon. Destroy a generator orbiting above my head.

"No," I say.

"It shouldn't even be that hard. If you just—"

"*No*." I bring my hands to my cheeks, holding the bracelet, feeling the clink of each bead's rotation against my skin. But my thoughts race on, threading back and forth too fast for me to keep up, and under everything else that little voice is still murmuring, *wrong, wrong, wrong*.

"You're not even supposed to be talking to me," I say.

"I'm not," he agrees, lowering his voice. "But all the ways we've hurt your people—all the ways our interference here has held back our people—it's because no one was brave enough to challenge our old assumptions. Jeanant wouldn't have gotten as far as he did if he'd kept toeing the line, and I don't know if the rest of us will either. Maybe we *need* you, if we're going to end this. Helping take down that generator could be the most important thing I do in my whole life. So if I need to break a few rules to make sure we finish this mission, then those rules have to be broken."

The determination in his voice is unmistakable. I have no idea what to believe. I can't absorb it all. I'm going to crash like a computer running too many operations at once.

"I need to go home," I say. My throat feels raw. "I'm late. My parents will be worried. I can't deal with any more right now."

"If you'd just think about it ..." Win says.

Like I'll be able to stop myself. "I need to go home," I repeat, getting up.

He stands with me, grasping my arm. "Will you at least— If you're ready to talk more tomorrow, will you meet me here? In the lobby? Before school, or after, whenever—"

"Okay!" I say, just to shut him up. "Okay."

Disappointment shows clearly on his face, as if he can tell I'm not sure I mean it. But I pull my arm back and walk away.

• • •

I'm halfway home when one awful thought pierces through the haze in my head.

Win's "Enforcers." Alien soldiers or not, they did find me at the coffee shop. He never said how. Could they find me again, now?

Whatever Win's involved in, he admitted he's broken the rules. How are they going to react if they find out he's not just told me, but *shown* me how he travels through time?

My fingers creep to the melted mark on my jacket. My gaze skitters along the darkened street. There's no sign of anyone following me. But if they're time travelers too, they'd have cloths like Win's, right? Which means they could appear out of nowhere, right in front of me, if they wanted.

My legs stall in the middle of the sidewalk. I want to be home so badly my bones ache with it, but maybe home isn't safe after all.

So where is? Back in the hotel with Win? No. They found me with him before.

I check my watch. Quarter to eight. Normally I'd be back from Ben's before seven. Mom and Dad will already be starting to fret. What are they going to think if I call them and make some weird excuse not to show up at all?

Picturing their anxious faces strengthens my resolve. I'm already screwed up enough over this—I'm not letting it mess up my parents' lives too. If that pale woman and her henchman show up at my house, I'll run to Win then. Not before.

I curl my fingers around my bracelet and walk on, timing the spinning of the beads and the beats of the multiplication tables with my steps.

When I reach my front door, I've managed to push back the jumble of Win-aliens-*wrong*-time machine-*wrong*-dead-*wrong*. It's not gone, but I think I can suppress it enough to act normal.

I catch the rustle of the living room curtain, and can guess that Dad was waiting there, watching for me. So as I open the door I'm already putting on a very honest guilty expression.

Dad's standing in the hall contemplating today's mail. He looks up as if he hadn't known I was outside, and Mom pokes her head around the kitchen doorway.

"Oh good," she says lightly, but I can see the tension sagging from her shoulders. "I was just about to call Benjamin's mother to see if she asked you to stay late."

"I'm sorry," I say, carefully tucking the melted strip on my sleeve out of sight as I hang up my jacket. "I ran into Bree on the way home, and she was upset about this guy, so we hung out and talked for a bit. I just realized I forgot to call when I got here."

"It's all right," Mom says. "You're seventeen—we should be glad you're home for dinner at all."

"You're here now," Dad says with his usual soft smile. "Let's eat."

"You didn't have to wait for me," I say as I follow him into the dining room.

"It's just my everything-in-the-fridge stew," Mom says. "The extra cooking time makes it even better."

But as we sit down around the table, a ghost sits with us. The memory we're all thinking about but avoiding mentioning: the night of waiting by windows and increasingly worried phone calls after my brother left with his knapsack and a promise to pick me up a Ring Pop at the convenience store, and never came home. I can see it in the quiver of Mom's hand as she ladles out the stew, in the way Dad stares at me for a moment as I pick up my spoon, as if he's not yet convinced I really am here.

So I put on my best carefree voice and tell them about Ms. Cavoy pulling me aside to compliment my physics project, about gluing black silk flowers for Angela's dance decor, about Bree and I breaking eighteen minutes on our three-mile run for the second time this week. Their daughter is happy, thriving; she isn't going anywhere. It's the best way I can make up for freaking them out: reminding them how much they don't have to worry about me.

The only time my performance falters is when Dad says, "You had that field trip to the courthouse yesterday, didn't you? You haven't told us about the cases you saw."

In an instant, I flash back to the courthouse hall—to the blast of light and the rush of heat. The echo of another past, where the explosion was real and lethal and I *wasn't* here right now. The past Win says was the real one, before he changed things.

This scene, the happy family around the table, would never have existed. Mom and Dad would have been grieving my death, the loss of their second child. My hand clenches my spoon.

"Um, I'm not sure if I'm supposed to talk about them," I say, which is thankfully true, because I barely remember anything from that morning except my panic. My voice cracks. I cover by stuffing a spoonful of stew into my mouth.

When I glance at the window, I half expect an icy stare to meet mine. There's nothing outside but darkness.

By the time we're clearing the table, the lingering tension has dissipated. Noam's ghost no longer seems to hover between us, though he lingers in my head. I load the dishwasher and start it running, and when Mom and Dad have settled on the couch to peruse the evening's TV offerings, I slip upstairs.

The bedroom between the master at the front of the house and mine at the back now serves as a guest bedroom/ workout space. It used to be Noam's. For years, I could push open this door and see his sketches tacked to the walls, the bright blue Converse sneakers he wore until the soles were falling off in their place of honor by the foot of his bed. Then one day Mom decided the waiting wasn't doing us any good. I came home from a weekend at my grandparents' house to find all of Noam's stuff packed into cardboard boxes.

She hasn't thrown any of it out. Most of the boxes are stacked in the attic, and a couple she keeps in what used to be his closet, beside the narrow shelving unit that holds her weights and exercise mat. I suspect she left them there so every now and then she and Dad can do what I'm about to do now.

I check the bedroom window first, confirming no alien gunslingers are lurking outside. Then I go to the closet and ease apart the flaps of the top box. There's a pile of Noam's sketchbooks, a box of acrylic paints, a huge Swiss Army knife he said he was going to use on camping trips. My hand is drawn to the worn baseball glove at the back. I pick it up. Sliding my hand inside, breathing the smell of old leather, I travel back through time the only way people are supposed to.

I was four when Noam decided he was going to try out for the baseball team. All his friends were. So they spent hours in the backyard throwing the ball back and forth, practicing pitches, then heading off to the park with the bat after Mom warned them not to break any windows.

One morning I got tired of just watching. Before his friends showed up, I grabbed his glove, marched into his room, and declared that I was going to play too. It seemed only natural to me that my big brother would humor me. He stood a few feet away in the yard and I held out the too-big glove and tried to snatch the ball when he tossed it to me. The first two times, it bounced off the rim and thumped onto the grass. I hated that ball. It wasn't fair.

Noam crouched down across from me and said, "Hey, third time's a charm!" And then he flipped the ball to me so gently it fell straight into the waiting glove. I remember laughing, it seemed so miraculous. "See," he said. "You can do anything."

Back in the present, I slip off the glove. So many emotions have welled up in my throat that I can't swallow.

Even after twelve years, it hurts. I don't know why he left. I can't imagine what could have been so bad here that he couldn't stay, that he'd clear out his bank account and take off and never speak to any of us again.

A thought sparks in the back of my head. I've wished so often that I could go back and ask him why he did it. If Win's special cloth could whisk us back two thousand years, twelve should hardly be a problem …

The images from the Coliseum fly up—blood, sand, a groan of agony, the hiss of an arrow—and my lungs constrict. I push the glove away. There's still so much I don't understand about Win and his story. And what would he want from me in exchange for a favor like that?

"Sky?"

Mom's come in. I close the box and turn around. "I just …" I say, but I don't know how to explain what I'm doing here.

"It's okay," she says. "Accepting Noam's gone doesn't mean we can't remember him."

I rub my thumb and finger together, bringing back the feel of worn leather. "He was a good brother," I said. "While he was here."

She smiles. "He was an *amazing* brother. You know, we don't mean to overreact when you're a little late or we're not sure where you are—"

"I know, Mom," I say. "It doesn't bother me."

She puts her arm around me and squeezes my shoulder, and I lean into her. A part of me wishes I could tell her everything, but most of me is glad she hasn't noticed anything's wrong. So I can pretend for a little longer that nothing is.

The doorbell rings, and Mom straightens up, her eyebrows rising. My heartbeat stutters before I remember.

"That'll be Angela," I say. "I forgot to tell you she was coming over—we've got an English presentation on *Hamlet* we have to work on."

"As long as she doesn't stay too late," Mom says with one last squeeze.

There's still a moment as I open the door when I find myself bracing for a pale sneer. My relief when I'm met with Angela's smiling face must be obvious.

"What's up?" she asks as she steps in.

"Not much," I say. "Just looking forward to getting this presentation over with." It's true enough. Angela's shy, but she can get into the performance element of it, even when it involves acting out Shakespeare's archaic vocabulary. I never stop feeling uncomfortable when the whole class is focused on me, every jitter and hesitation magnified.

"Well, I borrowed costumes I think Mr. Nebb will like from the drama department," Angela says, heading upstairs with me. "So all we have left to do is figure out what to say about how 'deep and meaningful' the scene is afterward. And practice."

"I wrote some notes …" I paw through the papers on my desk. When I turn around, Angela's sat down cross-legged by the end of the bed, looking up at the da Vinci print with an appreciative eye.

And I think: if I'd died in the explosion yesterday, she would have too. She and Daniel and Jaeda and everyone in Ms. Vincent's class. Wiped away like lines on a chalkboard.

I've been so distracted by the crazy, scary parts of Win's story that I've overlooked that. I haven't wanted to believe it; I haven't wanted to face it, but I know what I felt yesterday was something. Something big and awful.

Quite possibly we're only alive because of him. There must be a million other things he could have "shifted" to distract the Enforcers, and he chose to save us.

That could change, couldn't it? At any moment, without warning. A chill prickles over me. He said there were other Travelers. All it would take is one little tweak from someone else, somewhere out there, to set off a new chain of events in which I no longer exist. Any of us—me, Angela, my parents— could just disappear in the blink of an eye, without anyone knowing the difference.

"You okay?" Angela asks, and I snap out of it. She's watching me with that crease on her forehead, and I know it's for me this time.

"Yeah," I say, too quickly. "Here. There's this whole thing about the significance of the play within the play …"

I sit down next to her, rattling off the points I jotted down, but I'm only half there. The other half is picturing Win in that tacky motel, worrying about *his* friends, trying to make his own plans. Whoever he is, whatever he's really doing, he's the only one I know who has the slightest chance of protecting us. Of stopping these shifts.

And he thinks I can help him.

When I walk with Angela to the door an hour later, I only have a vague idea what we've decided on. I can't help glancing up at the sky as she heads down the street—at the few stars bright enough to pierce the city's glow. And maybe a satellite full of scientists from some distant planet poking at our world like we really are fish in a bowl. My chest clenches.

I'm scared it might all be true. I'm scared of what'll happen to us next if it is. Win took a risk on me, he said, because this supposed mission could be the most important thing he does in his whole life. If it's real, I can't think of anything more important that could happen in mine.

I *have* to go back and talk to him again tomorrow. For the first time ever, I might have the chance to set the *wrong-ness* right.

8.

I duck out the door at a quarter past seven the next morning. "Have a good run!" Dad calls from the kitchen.

I do, but not to the park for cross-country practice. I fall into a measured lope halfway down the block, letting the rhythm of my strides untangle my thoughts as I weave through the streets to the Garden Inn.

In the crisp dawn light, everything looks perfectly ordinary. Dry leaves drift across lawns; cars putter along the roads. I register the details automatically: blue sedan, gold sports car, gray truck with a ridge of rust along the back bumper. A folk tune tinkles from the open door of a cafe; a plane trails exhaust across the sky.

By the time I make it to the hotel, I half expect to discover it was all a dream. Then the front door opens and Win steps out onto the sidewalk. My gut lurches as the reality of the situation snaps back into place.

Win's hair is rumpled and his face looks worn, as if he's had as much trouble sleeping as I did. I told him I *might* come sometime today. Was he planning on waiting by the doors the whole time?

He wasn't kidding about how important this is to him, that much is obvious.

He smiles at me, relief shining through the weariness in his eyes, and I'm suddenly struck by how young he appears to be. He can't be more than a year or two older than I am. I can't imagine what it's like being on his side of this equation, stranded in time with vicious teched-up soldiers hunting him down.

"Thank you for coming," he says. "I'm sorry I upset you yesterday."

"It was a lot to take in," I say. "I'm still kind of freaked out."

"But you'll help?"

"I …" He doesn't beat around the bush, does he? "Look, I don't know how much of this to believe. I just know if people are messing with time, with what's happened in our lives, I want that to stop."

"And we'll stop it," Win says. His gaze darts up and down the street. "Do you trust me enough to come in now? We shouldn't risk anyone overhearing."

Right. Because even I'm not supposed to know.

He could have brought me anywhere, anytime when I stepped into his cloth with him last night. If what he wants from me was something he could take by force, he's had plenty of opportunities.

"Okay," I say, and follow him in.

As we cross the lobby, I remember stumbling in here yesterday, and the horrible sound of Win's wheezing. My hand rises to the melted streak on my jacket.

"Those people who came after us in the coffee shop," I say. "The Enforcers? Would they be able to figure out you're staying here? Or where I live, or go to school …"

"They'd have to spot us again," Win says. "It's a big city."

"But they knew where to look for us yesterday."

"Yes." Win pushes open the door to the hallway of rooms. "I think … we must have accidentally shifted something in the timeline around or in the coffee shop, and the scientists picked up on it."

I trace our path to the shop in my memory. "All we did was go in and buy a couple drinks. Would they be accessing the store records?"

"Unlikely. But there was that one man you talked to, wasn't there? The one who seemed angry."

"Yeah. He bumped into me and spilled coffee on his shirt." I hesitate. "And he said something about going in front of an audience. That could have been recorded. You think your scientists would notice something as small as a stain in a TV broadcast?"

Silly question, I guess, when it comes to people who can jump through two millennia in a matter of seconds. "The computers do most of the work," Win says. "Pixels to pixels, it'd be easy to catch."

"So how careful do I need to be?" I ask. "I mean, all sorts of things would have changed all over the city if a bomb that was supposed to go off didn't. But they managed to figure out that one little detail was important?"

Win stops at a doorway at the end of the hall and digs in his pocket for the key. "Ah, that's my fault," he says.

"What do you mean?"

"Well, what happened in the coffee shop would have been a *new* shift," he says. "When I stopped the bomber, that started one revised chain of events—one altered set of data. After waiting a few days, I jumped back to yesterday morning to see if the Enforcers had responded and to take another look at you. I didn't mean to shift anything else—I didn't know I'd end up talking to you. The accident in the coffee shop would have set off a new series of changes. Unfortunately it led them right to us. The Enforcers must have questioned that guy, found out how he got the stain and what you looked like." He pushes open the door. "But as long as I don't make any more shifts here, nothing else you do should stand out. It'll blend into that same chain. Hopefully I'll be moving on soon, and it's me they really want to catch."

"What about that jump to Rome yesterday?" I ask.

"They shouldn't be able to track the jumps themselves," he says. "Isis—she's our main tech person—put a scrambler on our time cloths. It's supposed to prevent any tracing."

"Okay." One less thing to worry about, I guess.

I ease into the room. A tidy row of clothes hangs in the closet alcove: a few pairs of jeans and several T-shirts and sweaters in a wide range of hues, from bright red to deep purple. Otherwise, it hardly feels as if anyone is staying here at all. The blue-and-green-striped comforter on the bed is already tightly tucked, the carpeted floor bare. The recycled air carries nothing but a hint of lavender air freshener. From what Win's said, he's been moving around so much—from place to place, and time to time—there mustn't be much point in getting settled.

Because he's not just the hipster college guy he looks like. He's part of the same freaky organization as the scientists we've been discussing.

Win motions me to the small glass-top table at the other end of the room. He grabs his satchel and sits down perpendicular to me, putting out his cloth. "It's very simple," he says. "Jeanant, the one who made the weapon and brought it here, he left a message for Thlo, who's like his second-in-command, that she'd receive if he didn't make it. To explain his plan, and where he would hide the weapon if we needed to retrieve it. It had to be vague, of course, because the Enforcers could have intercepted it, but she says he alluded to France and times of rebellion."

My mind slips back to my world history course a couple years back. "That doesn't really narrow it down. Just the first French revolution lasted a whole decade."

"I know," Win says. "That's why we didn't know exactly where to look. He gave a few other clues, and like I said before, he intended to make little shifts to help us find the right time and place, but he still has to be careful about it. If the Enforcers discover where to look first and find the weapon before us ..." He makes a gesture, pulling all his fingers into his palm and then flicking them outward like something bursting. "All his work would be lost. But that's how you can help. You've obviously read at least a little about French history before."

He lifts the biggest fold of the cloth up as if it's a laptop. When he squeezes the corners, it stays open like that. He speaks a low command in that unfamiliar language, and the display he used to program our destination yesterday glows on the lower half. He flicks through the data, his fingers manipulating the air above it as if weaving invisible strings, only occasionally touching the fabric. A faded white square comes into focus on the upper half, where the screen would be if it actually were a laptop and not a bunch of folded cloth.

My jaw's gone slack. I snap it shut as Win pushes the cloth-turned-computer toward me. The glowing outline of a traditional keyboard has formed on the lower half. The screen shows what looks like a normal browser window.

"If you could look up the sort of websites you might have visited before, try to remember if any of them gave you that odd feeling—the whole page, or even better, one specific part ..."

"Oh," I say, shaking off my shock. "Um, you remember I told you it's mostly new things that give me the feelings? You can't get 'old' on the Internet. I'm the weird one in my classes who goes to the library and looks up stuff in books."

"All right," Win says. "Then you could look at the books you read before. That would accomplish the same thing."

"Maybe." The whole point is that I read them because they *don't* give me the feelings. But it can't hurt to try. "And then what happens, if I find something?"

"You tell me, and it'll give me a head start on the trail Jeanant left," Win says. "As soon as we've got his weapon, we can leave, finish his mission to destroy the generator, and no one will be able to make any more shifts down here."

Looking at his multifunctional piece of cloth, I'm starting to find the idea of scientists from another planet more plausible. And he made his plan sound perfect. That's what starts the niggling doubt.

I don't really know which side he's on, do I? He sounded determined yesterday, sure, but maybe his mission isn't quite what he said. Maybe the Enforcers are the ones trying to stop his group from messing with Earth, and the rebels are the ones changing everything. The only shifts he's mentioned have been ones he or this Jeanant guy made. Who knows what he's really looking for during the French Revolution?

"Can you prove it?" I say, thinking back to our conversation last night.

"What?"

"Can you prove it?" I repeat. "That if I can point you to some spot in history, whatever you do there is going to help protect Earth? That that's really why you're here?"

Win looks genuinely startled, as if he can't imagine how anyone could think otherwise, but then, he also looks like a genuine human being while claiming to be an alien. "You still don't believe me," he says.

"I believe that you can travel through time," I say. "I believe that *someone*'s playing around with history. Why should I believe that running around in revolutionary France isn't just more of that?"

He opens his mouth, and closes it again. Then his face brightens. "I can show you," he says, grabbing the cloth-computer. "I can show you how much this matters to us—how committed we are to setting Earth free."

He tweaks something on the lower half of the computer, and the Internet browser disappears. "Everyone who joins our group watches this recording," he continues, a note of reverence creeping into his voice. "It's a— I suppose you could say a mission statement. From a speech Jeanant gave a couple years before he came here to see his plan through."

A clear image materializes on the screen. Win swivels it back toward me.

The recording is zoomed in on a man, catching him from the waist up, in front of a pale marbled background dotted with small indents. The angled edge of a shape I can't quite place—but somehow looks furniture-ish—bisects the lower right corner of the image. That and the thin, seamless but ripple-textured fabric of the shirt the guy's wearing give me the prickling sense that this could really be from another world, though the guy looks as human as Win does.

The guy—Jeanant, this leader Win's been talking about—appears to be no older than his midtwenties. His curly black hair drifts over the tops of his ears as he nods, the even light glowing off his bronze skin. But it's the way he stands that fixes my gaze on him. From the straightening of his shoulders to the tilt of his head, he exudes a firm purposefulness, as if he's exactly where he needs to be.

Then he starts to speak, in a low voice that carries through the cloth's invisible speakers in the choppy yet rolling syllables of what could be an alien language. After a second, a computerized English translation kicks in, its inflectionless tone blending into his voice.

"It doesn't matter where they were born, who their ancestors are, what's written in their genetic code," Jeanant says. "Every thinking, feeling conscious being deserves our respect. Every one of them deserves the chance to determine the course of his or her own life, without outside manipulation. Because no matter what some of us like to tell ourselves, they have their own minds with their own unique visions of the universe, that are just as valid and meaningful as anyone else's."

He punctuates his point with a sweep of his hands.

"Look at these people, and remember they could have been our friends," he says. "They could be our teachers, in a far better way than we use them now. But not until we make things right and release them from what's all but slavery. And we can. There may not be very many of us, but if we've learned anything from all our centuries of study, it's that a small group can make a difference. Again and again, across innumerable points of data, we've seen it happen. Every one of us in this room is valid and deserving too, and, working together, we can become something powerful. If we have the courage to take that chance, to question those who would keep us locked in the same old patterns, we can become something so incredible that we'll set all our lives on a completely different course—one we can be proud of. Can anyone here think of a better goal than that?"

His words reverberate through me. *No*, I think. That's what I've wanted more than anything, for as long as I can remember: to be powerful enough to fix all the inexplicable *wrongs* around me. To set my life on a new course without them.

The recording freezes in place. I manage to tear my eyes away. Win's staring at the screen as if Jeanant's speech has struck him just as deeply. I guess if there's any guy you'd follow across the universe, that's him. I'm not sure I've ever seen anyone so palpably *sure*, and so passionate in his assurance.

"What do you think now?" Win asks quietly.

I think if Win's helping Jeanant reach the goal he talked about, I'm all on board. I think the naked admiration on his face would be hard to fake. But I can't help asking, "So why are *you* here? Why is it so important to you that you came all this way?"

"I agree with him that it's wrong how we've treated this planet," Win says, folding up the cloth and pushing it into his satchel. "And … putting an end to the Traveling will help our people too. Back home, we don't have what you have here. The food—the trees—the sun! So much space …" He glances toward the window with obvious longing, and I remember my first glimpse of him at the school with his face turned toward the sky. "The way we live, it's not how people are meant to. I don't know how anyone can feel comfortable with it. Earth isn't a real home either, but here I can at least feel more like *myself*. What it should be like.

"At least I get to have this now and then," he goes on, "Everyone else, everyone who's not a Traveler—my parents, my brother, my friends—if things keep on the same way, they won't get to see or feel anything like this, ever. But when we destroy the time field generator, all the scientists up there will *have* to see it's time to focus on improving our situation on Kemya instead. So we can all have a world like this eventually."

I try to picture a planet without trees, without sun, without space. He makes his home sound horrible. Why would his scientists rather poke at us than fix the problems on their own planet, if it's that bad?

The question must look like skepticism on my face. Before I can ask it, Win adds hurriedly, "And there would be some immediate benefits, for me and my family. Thlo's going to have a lot of influence in the Council when this is over. If I've earned her respect, we'll have so many more options. We're not considered worthy of very much right now. I'm lucky they even let me into Traveler training—there's no way I'll advance very far unless I do something big enough for them to take me seriously."

He lowers his gaze, twisting the strap of his satchel between his hands. I wonder if he's embarrassed to admit his family's standing, or that his motives aren't entirely unselfish. The funny thing is, the admission shakes loose my last bit of doubt. He didn't have to tell me that. He could have pretended it was all big heroics. If he were pretending.

In a way we want the same thing. To live like people are supposed to, in a world that's *right*. I don't know what's happened to his planet that things are so bad there, but I know what it's like to feel at odds with your surroundings, to have nothing you can count on, and I can hear it echoed in his voice. I know I'd do just about anything to fix that.

"She'll be pretty impressed if you bring her this weapon all by yourself, yeah?"

"I'll say." He chuckles, and looks back up at me. "So you'll check the books to see if you notice anything?"

Saving the world by going to the library. It doesn't sound as grand as Jeanant's speech, but I'm not sure I'm ready to handle anything grand just yet.

"I guess I can give it a shot." I get up. "I can check the library after school today. Assuming your Enforcers don't zap me first."

It's an attempt at a joke, but it comes out flat. Mainly because I'm pretty sure the pale woman *will* zap me if she happens to spot me again.

As I turn to go, Win stands. "Wait," he says. "Here. You should take this."

He pulls off his blazer and pushes up the sleeve of his T-shirt. A thin silvery band is wrapped around his upper arm. It looks like solid metal, but when he tugs it, it splits apart into a long strip that wobbles like a piece of linguine. He offers it to me.

"Put it around your arm, or your ankle," he says. "If anyone who's not from Earth gets within about a hundred feet of you, it'll start vibrating, and it won't stop until they're farther away again. It's how I knew the Enforcers had arrived outside the coffee shop yesterday before we saw them. They'll be patrolling the city—this'll help you stay out of their way."

The material feels both soft as silk and firm as steel between my fingers. How is that even possible?

Aliens, I think, and for the first time, it's not followed by the urge to laugh. I can't think of another explanation that fits.

I slide the strip around my right ankle. As soon as the tips touch, they fuse together. The soft metal band lies smooth and still against my skin.

"It's not doing anything right now, and you're within a hundred feet," I point out as I pull my sock up over it.

"It's tuned to me," Win says with a little smile. "It wouldn't work very well if I was setting it off myself the whole time."

"Right." Because this is his—he gave it to me off his arm rather than offering a spare. Which means he probably doesn't have a spare. He did say he doesn't have a lot of equipment. I pause with my hands still by my ankle. "Don't *you* need it?"

"I can get away faster than you can, if the Enforcers find me," he says, patting his satchel. "And you could be the key to tracking Jeanant's clues—I wouldn't risk something happening to you. I'll be in here most of the time anyway."

Waiting for me to report back. Like it all rests on me. I straighten up. "Don't you have other jobs to do?"

"Not exactly. Mostly it's just keeping an eye on things: following the news broadcasts, scanning the Internet. Just in case."

"While everyone else is in France."

His shrug looks forced. "Someone needed to be here. I'm the newest recruit. That's the way it goes."

The newest recruit and, from what he said, one his people expect less of for some family-related reason. From the tension in his stance, I wonder if he suspects it's more the latter. "Well, thanks," I say, glancing down at my ankle.

Win lays his hand over mine, where I've rested it on the top of my chair. "Thank *you*," he says. "It's because of you I've got a chance at solving this."

A tingle passes over my skin. His hand is warm, but it's not only that. It feels, inexplicably, more *there*, more real, than the edge of the chair under my palm, than the sleeve of my jacket brushing my wrist. As if his fingers might sink right into mine.

The thought makes me twitch, and Win jerks back.

"It's okay," I say. "This is just all so weird still. There's something about you, and the Enforcers yesterday too. I guess it's an … alien thing."

He frowns. "What kind of 'alien thing'?"

"I don't know," I say, waving my hand dismissively. I feel awkward now, like I've just pointed out an ugly birthmark I was supposed to pretend not to notice. "You just look, and feel, like you're more here? More solid than everything else. It's not a big deal."

I'm ready to go, but the look on Win's face stops me.

"Oh," he says. "You can sense that too?"

A chill crawls up my back. "What? What is it?"

"One more reason it's important that we stop the shifts soon." He seems to search for the words. "You know … videotapes? Earthlings used to use those? And if you recorded footage from one to another, and then recorded a copy of that copy onto a third tape, and kept going— every time the video gets copied, it loses something. It starts to get fuzzy?"

"Yeah," I say, thinking of the static on my grandparents' home videos.

"It's kind of the same thing with time shifts," Win says. "Every time the world gets rewritten, the atoms, and their bonds, break down. So minutely you can't even measure it when it's just once or twice. But it's been building up for thousands of years. The balance is starting to tip—more earthquakes, more droughts, more disease, more instability in every way." His voice drops. "The fabric that holds life on this planet together is breaking apart."

9.

I leave Win and his hotel room behind as I head to school, but I can't shake the memory of his words. Morning mist lingers on the streets, hazing the city. I find myself touching things I pass—railings, telephone poles, tree trunks—to confirm that they're still real. To reassure myself with their solid surface under my fingers.

Win's people have supposedly been shifting our planet's history for thousands of years. It's held together this long. It's not as though we're all going to disintegrate with one more tweak.

But I can't help thinking of all the natural disasters that have hit the news in the last few years. Catastrophic climate change, new strains of flu, tsunamis and hurricanes. *The balance is starting to tip.* How fast will it tip all the way over, now that it's on the verge? Everything Win does, every shift his group of rebels makes, every ripple the Enforcers cause while trying to catch them, those are all one more rewrite, aren't they? I might have already relived this walk to school a dozen times, and not know it.

The idea makes me queasy. I reach into my pocket for my bracelet and spin through all ten beads. After I've finished, I keep holding it pressed against my palm, as if it can anchor me to this place. This now.

Maybe I can do more this time. More than escaping into my numbers and rituals and waiting for the unpleasantness to be over. I don't want to stand by and let the world fall apart.

And if Win's right and I can notice some clue in the past—if finding it for him means he and his group can put an end to all the shifts, all the rewrites, and the *wrong* feelings will go away—then once I've done this, I wouldn't have to pretend to be normal anymore. I'd just *be* normal.

My mind trips back to Jeanant's speech. *We can become something so incredible that we'll set all our lives on a completely different course ...*

I hope that's true.

The sight of heavier traffic up ahead jerks me back to the present. To get to school from the Garden Inn, I have to cross Michlin Street, where the Enforcers chased us yesterday.

I stick to the side streets until I'm five blocks past the cafe, and then dart across, peering up and down the road. No sign of the pale woman or her henchman. I head into the residential neighborhood on the other side and veer around another corner. As soon as the shops are out of view, I relax. Okay, home free!

I've taken two more steps when the band around my ankle starts to shiver.

I flinch, and then freeze in place. There's a man coming out of a house down the street with his preteen daughter, but it seems unlikely that Win's Enforcers would be traveling with kids. He said the range for the alarm was about a hundred feet. The alien, whoever it is, could be out of sight around an intersection or down a driveway.

My arm twitches where the pale woman shot me. What will they do to me if they see me again?

The band's vibration hits a higher pitch. I'm going to guess that means they're coming closer. I spin around. I don't know which way they're coming from. The trees and shrubs look far too exposed, but halfway down the block, I spot two cars parked close together near a garbage can left on the sidewalk.

I sprint over and duck between the cars. With a yank, I drag the bin in front of the gap between them. Now I've got cover on three sides, at least.

The quivering at my ankle has become a silent but frantic buzz. I crouch there between the bumpers, the sour smell of old garbage mixing with the oily scent of the cars. A gate creaks. An SUV rumbles by.

Brisk footsteps thump against the concrete, heading toward me.

I sink lower, clutching my bracelet. All I need is for them to walk right past me. Just walk on by, and everything will be fine.

The steps sound as if they're almost on top of me when they come to an abrupt halt. For a few seconds, there's only distant traffic noise.

I peek through the narrow space between the garbage can and the maroon sedan's fender, and my pulse stutters. It's the man who was with the pale woman yesterday—I'm almost sure of it. My attention was mostly on her, but he's wearing a similar peacoat, his navy blue. And he stands out against the lawn behind him as if he's in color and it's only black and white. Even if he's a different guy, I'm going to guess he's not human.

His head is turning, tracking something across the street. His hand slides under his coat to where I suspect his weapon is hidden. I tilt over just enough to see down the opposite sidewalk. A young woman with light brown hair is ambling along as her Yorkie sniffs the lawns.

I glance back at the man in time to see his expression shift from wariness to disappointment. His hand drops from his side. He thought she was someone he might need to shoot, but—

Someone tall, young, and female with light brown hair. I bite my lip. The woman is a little older than me, and her hair's longer and more ashy, but from a distance, considering he only caught a glimpse of me before, I can see how he wouldn't be sure.

They're definitely not just looking for Win.

I hunch down, my cheek against my knees. If the man looks over the garbage can …

His footsteps pass me, and then stop again. But it's only a quick pause before he's walking on. I stay there, in a tight little ball, as the sound of his steps fades away. The metal band's quivering dies down with them. After a minute, it goes still. I count out another sixty seconds before I peek over the trunk of the car in the direction the man went. He's gone.

I take a slightly roundabout route the rest of the way to school, jogging along the streets and then making a dash for the front doors. The alarm band doesn't shiver again. Inside, I lean against the wall and catch my breath. I feel as wrung out as if I did spend the last hour at cross-country practice.

It hasn't even been a whole hour yet. I wasn't with Win that long, and even after the close call with that Enforcer, I'm here twenty minutes early.

I kind of want to slip into the bathroom, shut myself in a stall, and just sit and breathe undisturbed for a while. But as I peel myself off the wall, my eyes catch on the sign down the hall above the library door.

The sooner I find what Win needs, the sooner he can move on with his mission—and take the Enforcers with him.

Pulling myself together, I head in and go straight to the history section. France. Times of rebellion. I can't remember exactly which ones I looked at for my essay. There are a few books that focus on the first, and best known, French

Revolution, and several others that cover the general period. I slide out one, and then another, flipping through them.

Nothing about these strikes me. Well, there's still the public library. I often go straight there for my research, because it has a much bigger collection.

And if I don't find anything there either? I can already imagine Win's face falling. He was so sure I could help. But maybe my sensitivity won't do us, or the world, any good after all. Maybe we'll both have to just keep standing by, waiting and hoping someone else can make it all better.

That possibility haunts me all the way to law class. It takes the puzzled look on Angela's face when I drop into the seat beside her to tug me out of my head.

"Everything okay, Sky?" she asks. "Bree told me you missed practice this morning."

My stomach clenches. Nothing is okay. And while Angela's taken plenty of my oddness in stride, I suspect time-traveling aliens would cross way over the line.

I look away. The football guys are bantering in the back of the room. Jaeda is watching them, her chin tucked into the wide collar of her turtleneck and her eyebrows raised in amusement. Daniel's sitting in his spot by the far wall, tapping the end of his pen against his lips as his neighbor points out something in the textbook.

At the sight of him, it hits me. Every *wrong* feeling I've had … It was a sign things had been different before. So that time, that time when he leaned in and the streetlamp freaked me out—there was another time when it didn't? When he kissed me? And then?

Who knows what could have happened, in that other version of my life?

Of course, the other version, without any shifts, would probably have involved all of us blowing up two days ago.

But we didn't. Nothing blew up, no one died, Daniel was never my boyfriend. This is the life I have now. And as far as anyone else knows, as far as Angela knows, it's the only life we've ever had.

I meet my best friend's eyes again. Even if I thought she'd believe me, why would I want her to feel as awful as I do, knowing what I do?

"I woke up with a headache," I lie, hating how easy it is. "It took a while for the painkillers to kick in. But I'm fine now."

That crease appears on her forehead. Before she can dig deeper, I grasp for a change of subject.

"So are you putting us to work again at lunch? The dance decorations are looking great so far."

"You really think so?" she says, brightening. "We're almost done. I want to get some amazing pictures on Friday."

"It's going to be awesome."

Our conversation is cut off when Ms. Vincent strides in, but I feel Angela eyeing me all through class, like she's checking for signs that I'm not okay after all. So I play the best *perfectly fine* I have in me. When all five of us gather in the art room during lunch hour, I laugh along with Lisa's dramatic tales of her twin brothers' latest mischief-making and Evan's dry asides. I cheer when Bree tells me how Rob from cross-country complimented her on a good run after practice, and join Angela in insisting she ask him out already. I glue more flowers and paint lightbulbs crimson as the air fills with tangy fumes.

But no matter how hard I try to lose myself in our chatter, I'm not totally there. Part of my mind is back with Win, listening to him explain how the fabric of the world is crumbling. When I cross my ankles, I notice the faint weight of the alarm band. How long will I make it before it starts shivering again?

"Lisa and Evan and I are heading over to Michlin Street to grab some pie," Bree tells me as we're leaving computer science, our last class of the day. "You want to come with?"

The memory of yesterday's frantic run flickers through my mind. "Oh," I say. "I— I have this lab report I really need to get done. I wish I could."

She gives me a little nudge. "You work too hard, you know. Take a break."

"I will," I say. "Tomorrow." Assuming the world's still in one piece then.

"I'm going to hold you to that," she warns me, smiling, before turning down the hall toward her locker.

Angela's holed up in the art room putting the finishing touches on her decorations, so I don't have to make excuses to anyone else before I hurry out. I speed walk all the way to the local library branch. Thankfully, wherever the Enforcers are right now, their paths don't cross mine. I dart past the library's double doors unmolested.

Inside, I meander past the rows of wooden tables and the staircase with its worn gray carpet. A couple of day-care attendants are herding a group of murmuring elementary-age kids toward the children's section. I scoot past them to the nonfiction area. The catalog numbers roll out across the yellowed labels as I venture into the deepening quiet between the shelves. Here's history … History of Europe … History of France. My hand stills over the plastic-sheathed spines.

None of them looks especially familiar. I know I paged through a lot of books trying to find good sources for my essay, hoping to get a couple that weren't too dry so I could actually enjoy reading them while I did my research. I brought a big stack of them over to one of the tables and evaluated them one by one, checking the table of contents, reading the first few pages …

My memory drifts back to the uneven pile of books, the quiet conversations around me, the rough cushion of the chair—and a sliver of panic jabs me. There. I was sitting there. A thin musty-smelling volume open in front of me, comfortingly old; a prick of betrayal when a string of words on a page jarred loose a chorus of *wrong, wrong, wrong*.

I stare at the books in front of me. There *was* something, then. A shift, the clue Win needs.

Which one was it? What if it's not here?

Some part of my brain obviously hasn't let go of that unanticipated betrayal by history, because as I step back, scanning the shelves, my gaze snags on a tall, thin spine, burgundy with white lettering. *The Further Revolutions of France.*

That one. I grabbed it, thinking it might be interesting to focus on the later, less-studied conflicts, on the ways the first revolution didn't actually solve all the problems the people hoped it would. My fingers clench before reaching for it.

I've never deliberately provoked a *wrong* feeling before. It's made a lot more sense to avoid them. Even though it's just some words on a page, even though I now have reason to believe that the feelings don't come from some flaw in my brain but a real perception, my skin's gone tight. I stalk away into a secluded corner in the midst of the stacks and sit on the floor, opening the book on my lap.

I skim the table of contents and flip to the introduction. My eyes dart straight to the second paragraph.

Though France's second and third revolutions are commonly identified as two separate events, it is clear that the July Revolution of 1830, the so-called Three Glorious Days, was in many ways a direct precursor to the …

The "Three" leaps out and smacks me in the gut. I blink, a ghost of my previous discomfort passing through me. It didn't feel like a betrayal just because history is usually safe. It felt like a betrayal because three is supposed to be my number, the number that drives the *wrong*ness away. But this time, *it* was wrong.

Because someone changed it.

I shake off my uneasiness and push myself to my feet. I have to show Win. Maybe this is all he needs.

I check out the book on autopilot, already counting the blocks to the Garden Inn in my head. I'm so focused on that, and on how I'll avoid the Enforcers if they're still patrolling, that the hand that touches my shoulder as I head out the door catches me completely by surprise. I whirl around, the book slipping in my hands so I have to clutch it to keep it from falling. And there is Win, grinning sheepishly at me.

"I didn't mean to startle you," he says. His gaze dips to the book, and his expression turns serious. "Is that it? You found something?"

He's standing right in my personal space, so close and *real* my lungs clench and I have to take a step back. "How did—have you been following me the whole time?"

"You said you would go to a library after your classes finished," he says. "I waited outside to see which one, but I didn't want to distract you. So you do have something?"

I guess he's not completely up on regular human etiquette, like how following girls around without telling them you're there is pretty creepy.

"I think so," I say, suddenly hesitant. I want to hear him exclaim that I've done it; that I've provided the missing piece that will ensure Earth's safety. But what if I haven't? What if it's just one more meaningless impulse? "I don't know if it's what you were looking for, but something's off."

A couple of guys bump past us coming out the door. Win motions for me to follow him. As I descend the steps, the alarm band shivers against my ankle. I stiffen.

"It's gone off," I say. "The alarm—"

"Just now?"

"Yes."

"Back, then." He grabs my wrist like he did in the coffee shop yesterday, tugging me through the library doors. A few steps over the threshold, the band's humming cuts out.

"It's stopped," I say, and he nods, not looking particularly reassured.

"We might be okay," he says, "but let's keep moving. Let me know if it goes off again. Does this place have another exit?"

"I think there's one on that side." I point.

We circle the checkout desk and duck around the stairs, and then push past a smaller door that leads onto a lawn dotted with stone checkers tables. We keep walking, on down the sidewalk. The alarm band stays still.

"Good?" Win asks. I nod. "What did you find?"

I'd almost forgotten. I pull the book from where I've been cradling it under my arm and open it to the right page. Win veers around a corner, and I hurry along beside him. "This," I say, tapping the sentence. "*Three Glorious Days*. The number feels wrong."

Win snatches the book from my hands, coming to a halt to stare at it. "The Three Glorious Days. Beginning July 27, 1830 AD. Paris. It's such a small detail—and not even part of the main revolutionary period—that must be why it's taking the others so long." He pauses, glances around, and starts walking again. "But that's all right. I can check it out myself."

"Can't you tell your friends so they can help?"

"Communication through time is difficult," he says. "And all our supplies we had to collect unofficially—inconspicuously. As I told you before, our equipment is limited. Isis set us up with devices that can signal between us, but the best those can do is drag everyone away from what they're doing to meet up and talk properly. For all I know, Thlo's already figured this part out and is way ahead, and I'd just be delaying them. I'm not calling them in until I have something concrete."

I glance at the book. "And I guess— You said there are 'official' Travelers making changes all the time too. We can't know that Jeanant's the one who did this."

"It's extremely likely it was him," Win says. "The regular Travelers shouldn't be shifting things that far back. There were a couple of mistakes, early on, where one little change altered centuries of history in ways no one intended, and there's no easy way to just set things back. So the scientists restrict the experiments to try to minimize the breadth of the impact. Nobody authorized would be making changes nearly two hundred years ago."

"But maybe I'm noticing something that was shifted way back then," I point out.

He shakes his head. "*You* should only be able to notice shifts that were made by Travelers working within your lifetime. Changes to things you already experienced once, that were then rewritten. A shift some Traveler made hundreds of years ago, it was already in place before you were born. You'd never know the difference with those. But Jeanant, he came here during your present, he's making changes now. This is almost definitely him."

The thought of thousands of years of shifts I haven't noticed, on top of the little ones I have, overwhelms me. It's a few seconds before I realize Win's still looking at me. Studying me, with a frank appreciation that makes my cheeks warm. He closes the book and hands it back to me, his grin returning. "You're amazing."

His fingers graze mine with that overwhelming *there-ness*, his eyes bright as he beams at me. My heart skips a beat.

Then he stops in his tracks, peering at the nearby houses as he swings his satchel around. The satchel that holds his time cloth.

Right. Because he's not some normal guy I met at school; he's an alien. An alien who's probably only pleased with me because I've been useful to him.

Anything that was enjoyable about that moment is swallowed up by my embarrassment.

Win doesn't seem to have noticed. He drums the top of the satchel, and then draws in a breath. His gaze slides back to meet mine.

"Skylar," he says. "I want you to come with me."

10.

I'm still a little off-balance, or I'd probably realize what Win means right away. "With you—to the hotel?" I say, and he laughs.

"To *France*," he says.

To France. To Paris, July 27, 1830.

I flash back to my first trip through time: the lurching, dizzying fall, the barrage of light and sound, sand and blood. My fingers drop to my pocket, pressing the bracelet's beads against my hip.

"I have to find the trail Jeanant left for us," Win is saying. "If we get there quickly enough, maybe you'll be able to sense what else he's done."

I'm already shaking my head. "I don't know if I can do that again."

"Of course you can," Win says. "It's really not so bad after the first time."

"But—there's going to be a revolution going on." Not just spears and arrows, but guns. Bullets flying. Bayonets stabbing.

"We won't jump right into the middle of it," Win says. "I'm not careless. We'll start at the beginning, before the fighting gets going, and keep away from the most dangerous areas. The cloth has all the information I'll need for that."

And what if Jeanant's trail leads us right into those dangerous areas?

"You don't really need me now, do you?" I point out. "You know where to go, you have his clues or whatever. You're trained for all this time-traveling stuff. I'll have no idea what I'm doing."

Win lets out a huff of a breath. "I know," he says. "But I'll be there to make sure you're okay. And I might still need you. If the others have spent the last few weeks searching and not even gotten this far—as far as you got me in just an afternoon—the rest of his trail might not be any easier to follow. I won't know until I get there. If we get there, and the clues are obvious, I can bring you right back."

He pauses, and points to the sky. "*They* wouldn't think any Earthling could do half as much against them as you've already done. They think they have everyone here completely under their control. But you've proven them wrong. Doesn't it feel good to … to know this time you're changing things for yourself instead of letting them shove you around?"

Remembering what he said this morning about getting *them* to take him seriously, I wonder how much he's talking for himself as well as me. But the thought of slipping away from those watchful eyes up there, of staging a goldfish rebellion, does give me a little thrill.

If it's really that easy for him to take me there and back … I guess from his perspective, it is. Step into the cloth, one second here, one second gone without a trace.

Like Noam.

My breath catches in my throat. If I go with Win, whisk away through time, it'll be just like Noam. Tonight would be that night all over again. Like Win just said, his companions have been searching for Jeanant's weapon for weeks. How long would it take us, even if my sensitivity helps? While my parents worry, and then panic, and maybe even start to mourn …

It'll kill them.

"It doesn't matter," I say. "I can't. I can't just take off and leave everyone wondering what's happened to me."

"They won't even know you've left," Win says, sounding amused now. "It's time traveling. No matter how long we're gone for, I can bring you back just a few seconds after we left when we're done."

Of course. I rub my temples. I'm in the habit of thinking time means something. For Win's people, it's nothing at all.

"It's not just for me, and for you," Win says. "It's for your whole *world*. As soon as we find that weapon, as soon as we can destroy the generator, every Earthling will be able to make their own decisions without anyone up there messing with their lives. And … Look, even if it turns out I need your help in France, if you decide you've had enough, I'll bring you back right away anyway. I swear it." He touches the center of his chest, and speaks a few choppy syllables in that slightly slurred alien tongue before switching to what I assume is a translation. "By my heart, by Kemya."

He could say anything right now. It's not as if I could make him bring me back home once we're across oceans and centuries; I can't operate the time cloth myself.

But he's right. Everyone I care about is at risk every second his scientists keep poking at us. What Win's asking, it's not just about an end to the *wrong* feelings and having a normal future for myself, it's making sure my parents and Angela and, hell, the very fabric of the planet still *have* a future. Isn't this what I've wanted my whole life—the answer to what was *wrong*, and a way to make it stop?

All that is being handed to me, and I'm too busy cowering at the thought of a past I've never seen to take it.

Locked in the same old patterns, Jeanant's voice echoes in my head. That's not what I want. The word pops out before I let myself change my mind.

"Okay."

"Wonderful," Win says with a smile, as if he knew I'd come around eventually, which somehow reassures me and gives me an uncomfortable twinge at the same time. He motions me down a shaded driveway between two houses. After checking that no one's in view, he pulls out the cloth.

A fresh anxiety washes over me. "We're going *now*?" I glance down at my bright purple jacket, my jeans. "Like this?" I suspect my outfit was not a common look in early modern France.

"No," Win agrees. "I have my Traveler clothes, but you'll need something else to blend in. Can we visit your house uninterrupted?"

"My parents will still be at work."

"Good. What's your address?" He shakes open the cloth, his smile widening. "We can be there in an instant."

• • •

The cloth gives a little jerk after Win enters the coordinates, but otherwise doesn't move. He frowns and taps the panel harder. I'm remembering what he said about it being an "older model" when there's a jolt. My stomach flips over. Then we're standing in my front hall.

"It's a lot easier when you're not going very far," Win says. So I guess I'm not just getting used to time travel really fast.

He studies the inside of the house as I lead him upstairs, eyeing the hardwood floor and the framed prints on the wall with what looks like equal fascination. He stops in the hall by the oil of a forest landscape Dad bought from a local painter, his hand hovering over it, tracing the sweep of the river.

"That scene's from a state park about an hour from here,"
I tell him. "We used to hike there when I was younger. It's
even prettier in the fall."

"Right, the reds and yellows would be striking. My dad
would love to be able to see it—for real, not just on a
recording. He always says the colors and textures aren't the
same when you can't …" His sudden enthusiasm trails off.
"He thinks too much about that sort of thing." He pulls
himself away, peering over the banister, and then takes in the
row of doors ahead of us. "You've always lived here?"

"Since I was two," I say.

"It's so big."

This is just a midsize three bedroom. What would he
make of the huge country homes in the suburbs, like the one
Bree's aunt owns?

"Houses on your planet aren't much like this?" I venture.

"No. We only have so much room to work with." He
shrugs. "We use it as efficiently as possible, though. And
when the scientists start focusing more on there than here,
it'll get better."

The question that tickled at me this morning rises up
again. "Why do your scientists care so much about experimenting on Earth anyway? Especially if there are things that
need fixing back on … on Kemya."

"A lot of reasons," Win says, stepping into my bedroom
when I open the door. "But the biggest one is selfishness. It's
going to take years, probably decades, before Kemya could be

anything like what you have here. The scientists, the Travelers, they get at least moments of enjoying a place that has open spaces, and fresh air, and … everything." The sweep of his arm takes in the painted forest, the house.

Coffee, I think. *Sun.*

"They don't want to give up that freedom for the time it would take to make a world like this back home," he goes on. "Someone else can do it—the next generation. But they've been saying that for dozens of generations. They convince everyone that it's for the best, for our safety, 'for the good of all Kemya,' when they probably haven't learned anything useful in *centuries—*"

He cuts himself off before his voice can keep rising. I don't see what playing with Earth's history could have to do with anyone else's safety, but the fear that spikes through me overshadows that curiosity.

"Are you sure they'll stop?" I ask. "They won't just build a new generator?"

"Jeanant thought it'd be too big a blow," Win says. "Thlo agrees. They'll lose all the history we've had access to before now—if you open a new field, you can only travel back to the point when *that* one started. And it'll shake everyone up. More people would want a change if it was obvious we had to make a decision."

I hope for both of us that he's right.

"I guess we'd better get a move on then," I say with forced cheer. "Here's my wardrobe."

The row of shirts and pants and scattered dresses in the closet is sorted across the spectrum of colors. Win flicks through them. He tugs out a white ankle-length sundress and a blue button-down blouse I haven't worn since my stint doing mailroom duty at Dad's office a couple summers ago.

"I think these would be the most suitable," he says. "We'll probably need to get them dirty so they don't look so new, though."

His gaze drops to my hands as he passes me the hangers. "And the locals might think your nail color's odd. Can you remove it quickly?"

With every second, the "trip" I'm about to take feels more real. I'm actually doing this. I clench my hand when it starts to tremble. "Five minutes?" I say, and he nods.

I sit down on the edge of the bed, grabbing the polish remover from the drawer of my bedside table. It jostles the Christmas photo of Noam and me. My gaze catches on it. Another past. Another time we could travel to, if Win agreed.

Maybe, when we're done … Maybe there'd be a chance?

The idea hovers in the back of my head as I get to work on my nails. Win examines the books lining my shelves, the photos on the wall. He rattles his knuckles against the wooden top of my desk as if appreciating the sound it makes. Then he pokes my laptop's touchpad, chuckling when the screen flickers on.

"Not quite up to your technical standards?" I say, thinking of his fantastic cloth computer.

"It's still impressive how much people have managed to accomplish here, in spite of everything," he says. "And how quickly too. So much changes in just a few years."

As I'm rubbing the polish off my last two fingers, he wanders over and peeks into the drawer. He picks up one of the bottles of nail polish, and then the second and the third.

"They're all the same color," he comments.

"It's the only one I use."

"Then why do you need three? Ah!" he continues before I can answer. "You said three is a meaningful number for you. You multiply by it."

"Yeah." I hesitate. I'm still not used to talking about this, about the rituals I've fallen into to get by. "I know it's strange. It just … feels best if I have three bottles. If one spills, and one breaks, I've still got another one. Third time's a charm and all that."

I push the drawer shut and pick up the dress. "So I guess I should change into this."

"Of course," Win says, not taking the hint. I raise my eyebrows at him.

"I need you to leave the room."

"Oh. Yes." His gaze skims my body and then jerks back to my face, his own flushing. I might mind the look, but it's nice to know he's humanlike enough to be embarrassed. "I have a few things to take care of at the hotel anyway."

As soon as he's stepped out, I pull on the dress and the shirt. My fingers fumble with the buttons. The outfit looks ridiculous with my running shoes, so I unearth my black lace-up winter boots, which might do a better job blending in with nineteenth-century Paris fashion. As long as no one stares too hard at my feet. I drag in a breath.

A knock on the door makes me jump. "Almost done?" Win asks.

He's already been to his hotel room, done whatever he needed to, and made it back. That's how little time I'll be gone for. Away and home again before Mom and Dad even leave work.

"You can come in," I say. I stop for a second in front of the mirror. My hair's gone all flyaway from the wind outside. I press it down.

"You'll want to wear something on your head, I think," Win says. He's changed too, out of his corduroy jacket and jeans into a loose shirt and slacks made of a canvaslike material, in a dun color that's just a shade lighter than his skin. Traveler clothes, he said. A little odd, but—no. Looking at them again, I can see they're totally modern. That seems like a strange choice for our destination, but I'm not going to argue.

"I don't have any hats that would fit in," I say.

"A shawl?"

"I have scarves."

"Good enough."

I hurry downstairs and grab the wider of my two scarves, a thin beige one, from the basket by the coatrack. By the time

I've dashed back up, Win has unfurled the cloth into its tent form in the middle of my bedroom. My heart starts to thud.

"Ready?" he asks briskly.

No.

"Wait." I snatch my jeans off the floor, pulling out my bracelet and, instinctively, my phone. No pockets on this dress. I pluck the small chocolate-brown leather purse Angela gave me last Christmas out of my closet and sling it over my shoulder, stuffing my phone and bracelet inside. The cool surface of the beads sends a whisper of confidence through me. I square my shoulders. "Ready."

Win ushers me into the cloth. The flaps slip shut, and the room outside fades into grayish outlines. The display swims into view. Win's hand skips over the figures.

"We'll go to the morning of the first day, and continue from there," he says. "The violence started later."

"Sounds good," I say. My voice comes out hoarse.

"It's probably better if you keep your eyes closed," Win says. "And, ah, you can hold on to me if you need to."

I inhale into the bottom of my lungs, and curl my fingers around the side of his shirt. The space is so close I can hear when he swallows.

"Here we go."

The time cloth heaves back and forth a few times before shooting upward. I squeeze my eyes shut, my teeth clenched so tightly my jaw aches. The shrieking of the air sounds more muted this time, but my stomach still churns as we whirl and plummet. When we jerk to a halt, I stumble into Win. A metallic taste is seeping through my mouth. I've bitten my tongue.

Win rests his hand lightly on my back. I open my eyes.

Shadows waver around a lit opening ahead of us, where I can make out a blur of movement through the cloth's wall. Shouts rattle through the fabric.

"We're in an alley," Win says, his voice low and even by my ear. "We'll want to step out quickly so no one notices us appearing out of nowhere."

"What are we going to do next?" I ask.

"Jeanant will have left some indication to direct us to the weapon," he says. "A small shift, or maybe a message of some sort. We'll have to look around. Stay close to me, and tell me as soon as you get one of those feelings—or if the alarm goes off. And try not to disrupt what's going on. We don't want to make any new shifts ourselves."

Or the Enforcers could track us down. I glance at my ankle, taking comfort in the stillness of the alarm band. "Got it."

Win reaches for the flaps, and I brace myself.

11.

We step forward together onto the alley's uneven cobblestones, into dry still air that holds a whiff of baking bread over an underlying tang of mildew and excrement. My nose wrinkles reflexively. Above the soot-mottled stone buildings that rise up on either side of us, the sky is brilliant blue, the sunlight painting sharp lines amid the shadows. Beyond the alley, men and women are strolling along the sidewalks in trim jackets and light pants, long-sleeved blouses and full skirts, despite the warmth of the morning. White bonnets shade the women's faces. I pull my scarf higher over my head, and breathe through my mouth as a more pungent gust of sewage smell wafts over us.

Hooves clip-clop against stone as a gentleman on horseback trots by. The pedestrians murmur to each other. Louder voices carry from beyond my view, rising and falling in words that sound vaguely reminiscent of my Spanish class. French is a related language—maybe I'll even be able to understand a little. I picked up Spanish and German quickly. Grammar's like a more convoluted form of math, nearly as dependable as numbers.

Win's whipped the cloth back into its folded shape with a few snaps of his fingers. When I glance at him, I'm struck by how well his clothing fits in: the brown shirt and pants are less fancy than what I see out there, but even though they looked completely normal back in my bedroom, here they somehow seem—oh. *Traveler* clothes. More weird alien tech, I guess, that lets him blend in anywhere.

He stuffs the cloth into his satchel and then cups my elbow, guiding me forward as if I'm a hesitant child. Which isn't far from how I feel. At least no one's shooting yet.

As we reach the edge of the street, the city engulfs me, thunderously real. The road before us ends at a low wall, beyond which I can make out the foamy waters of a wide river. Towering buildings of gray and beige blocks form a craggy line above the opposite bank. Beyond them rise the gabled roof and gray steeples of what is either a palace or an immense church. Notre Dame? Angela would know. Angela would kill to see this.

The shouts around us echo in my ears, mingling with the heavy breeze rising off the river. A woman's skirts rustle as she saunters by. The sun is baking my clothes and skin.

I'm here. I'm really here. I'm standing in the middle of nineteenth-century Paris—living, breathing history.

A wave of dizziness sweeps over me. I snap my attention back to the street, sucking in the dusty air and scanning the faces around us. Lips narrow and full, skin pale or flushed, wisps and curls of hair blond and brown and black—all strangers. Many of them openly staring at us, their expressions grim as they speak to each other in hushed voices.

Because we don't belong here.

My gut knots and a cold sweat breaks over my skin. I ball my hands into fists. I'm not going to wimp out already. I *can* do this. Win does it all the time, and it's not even his planet.

Several heads jerk around at a movement nearby. I follow their wary gazes to a cluster of men in blue-and-red uniforms, rifles at their shoulders, marching across a bridge that straddles the river on hulking stone supports. Soldiers.

Win isn't looking at them. "Let's see what this is all about," he says, tugging my elbow in the opposite direction. The city looms around me as I follow. Sights and sounds hit me from every direction: hostile gazes, hissed remarks, the sun slicing into my eyes. My vision blurs. I reach into my purse to grasp my bracelet.

Three times three is nine. Three times nine is twenty-seven.

My heartbeat evens out enough that I can focus again. Scattered men waving sheaves of paper are standing by the river wall, by the door of a bakery, by a hat shop window. Some are formally dressed, like the gentlemen ambling by, while others look more peasanty in loose white shirts and gray or tan slacks. They're hollering to each passerby, pushing the papers toward them. I guess Win thinks this might have something to do with Jeanant?

The guy closest to Win and me, barely more than a boy, catches my eye and scurries over. He holds out the creased pages from the top of his pile. It's a newspaper, with a bold headline ending in an exclamation point.

The boy says something, pointing to the article. A few strings of syllables sound familiar, but he's talking too quickly for me to pick out a single word. Another shudder of discomfort ripples through me.

Then Win jumps in. He answers the boy briefly, taking the paper, and seems to ask a few questions in mildly accented French. As I gape at him, I remember the book in Chinese he was carrying, the British lilt to his English, the job he's trained for. If you're going to be jumping through time all over Earth, I guess learning a few languages would be expected.

Win's grinning when he turns back to me. He says a few words in French before he catches himself and switches back to English, lowering his voice.

"In the last message Jeanant left for Thlo, explaining what he planned to do with his weapon if the Enforcers caught on to him before he could use it, he gave her two more details to help us follow his trail," he says. "Something about painting over a secret, and that we should 'watch the papers.' Apparently a law's just been passed here restricting the printing of newspapers. Dozens of the workers are protesting it today. They've been writing about all the problems with the current government, pressing people to action."

"That's one way to start a revolution. You think this is what Jeanant meant by 'papers'?"

"What else could it be? Come on! We should get as many different ones as we can. He must have left some sort of clue in one of them."

He strides down the street, accepting the newspapermen's offerings with a bob of his head. I can't speak to them at all, so I scrutinize our surroundings. I'm supposed to be helping, watching for *wrong*ness, for clues of another sort. But everything feels alien and out of reach. A whisper of uneasiness keeps coursing through me, like the one that dogged me for hours after the reversed explosion.

Nothing in the city or the people around me is *wrong*. Just me. They were living their lives long before anyone conceived of my existence. I don't fit here. I'm not even an intruder, just a speck of dust amid the towering buildings.

A dull buzzing fills my head. As I dash after Win, nausea surges up. I stumble, groping for my bracelet. My hand doesn't find the beads in time.

I double over, gagging. My throat burns, but nothing comes out. I swallow and shiver, wincing at the acid filling my mouth.

"Skylar?"

I manage to straighten up. Win's hovering in front of me, shielding me from the street.

"Are you all right? What's going on?"

There's a note of impatience under his concern. "What do you think's going on?" I say. "I'm not used to this, remember?"

"Of course I know that, but I didn't expect— Are you going to be all right?"

"Just let me …" I step back, pulling my gaze to the buildings overhead. My fingers close around the beads. Five more shops before the next cross street. A looping script spelling out the name of the restaurant beside us. A slight figure ducking past the green curtains over a third-story window. *Three times … Three times … Three times …*

Even if I'm not much more than a piece of dust here, all I have to do is float along and play by the rules of this time, this place. Isn't that what I've spent the last decade of my life doing: blending in? This is just a more intense version. I've managed to fool my classmates, my friends, my parents; I can handle this.

The queasiness slowly subsides. Win shifts from foot to foot, his gaze fixed on my face. His expression makes me think of a little boy worried he's broken a favorite toy. I guess I still don't look so good.

I still don't *feel* so good, but I'm okay enough to keep going.

"All right," I say. "I'm over it. What next?"

Win purses his lips. "Start looking at these," he instructs, passing his collection of newspapers over to me. "You don't have to understand them, just see if anything feels odd."

I study the headlines and the old-fashioned type beneath them as we wander on down the street. A few words with Spanish counterparts catch my eyes—*mal* and *mentir* and *colère*—and here and there one with an English equivalent, but otherwise the articles are a mess of letters to me. I skim each line, flipping pages, while Win accepts more papers. Having something small and concrete to focus on helps me tune out the wide, unwelcoming world around us. When a fresh wave of dizziness threatens, I already have the bracelet in my hand. I spin the beads, and the feeling draws back. There, I'm getting the hang of this.

I glance behind us after finishing my scan of the third newspaper, and tense. A couple of soldiers are striding our way. One is badgering the newspaper-holders they pass, but the other is eyeing Win. I tap Win's arm.

"*Merci!*" he says to the latest newspaperman, and tilts his head toward me.

"We've caught someone's attention," I whisper. Win looks over.

"Nothing from the alarm?"

I shake my head.

"Locals, then," he says, "but we're better off not risking a confrontation."

Setting his hand on the small of my back, he ushers me forward and around a corner. We scramble down the narrow street, ducking behind a small domed church. Win pauses and peeks around it. After a few moments, he nods.

"They haven't followed us," he says. "I'd imagine the soldiers here have more important things to worry about."

Not yet, it seems like. The increasingly narrow streets we continue down are quiet: every voice dampened, every movement restrained. Few people are outside at all, off the main strip. I glimpse faces here and there through greasy windowpanes. I'd pictured passionate shouts and cannon fire, figures stampeding through the streets. That must come later. It's building up to that, behind all those closed doors.

Or maybe that's just one more way I'm *wrong*.

A window creaks open overhead. I glance up in time to give a yelp of warning. A handful of rubbish rains down on us. Mainly on Win: carrot ends smacking his forehead and shoulder, a twist of wire tangling in his hair. Sharp laughter follows as he swipes them away. Two boys lean out of the fourth-floor apartment, one of them making a remark I can't understand. From the way Win's face hardens, I suspect it wasn't complimentary. He walks on, turning back to his newspaper, just as a third boy joins the others, holding what looks distinctly like a chamber pot.

"Win!" I dodge out of the way, pulling him with me, just as the reeking contents of the pot splatter the cobblestones. I grit my teeth against the urge to gag.

The boys jeer as we hustle around the next corner. I don't know why they decided to target us, but I will not let it get to me. I will focus on being grateful that I managed to avoid being splashed with bodily waste.

Staring down at the smudged print of the newspapers, I try to imagine the guy from Win's recording here. Jeanant, strolling along the riverside, evading trash in this warren of streets. Holding one of these newspapers with a glint of determination in his eyes. I get the feeling he'd have just laughed at those boys. *Every thinking, feeling conscious being deserves our respect.*

Sometimes it's hard even for me to remember that.

I rub my ink-stained fingers on the skirt of my dress, recalling Win's suggestion that my clothes will blend in better if they're dirty. Win's frowning at his own stack of papers.

"This all seems like the sort of rhetoric I'd have expected from the period," he says. "Interesting, but nothing stands out."

"Well, Jeanant couldn't make it too obvious, right?"

"No," Win agrees, with a weight in his voice that reminds me I'm supposed to be the solution to that problem. I examine my last paper, my heart sinking. What if my sense of *wrong-ness* doesn't even work in this time, other than to tell me how wrong it is that I'm here at all?

12.

We wander on, paging through the newspapers. I get the impression Win is moving without any particular destination in mind, just avoiding lingering anywhere we might draw attention. Down one street, we pass a couple of men in intense conversation. One of them jabs his finger upward, and the other sighs before offering a brief protest. Then the first catches sight of Win and me. His eyes narrow. All at once, he breaks into a low tirade, as if our presence has proven whatever point he was trying to make. I walk on, my eyes trained on my last newspaper.

Win's only partway through his pile, since he's actually reading the articles. He hands me a few of the ones he hasn't gotten to yet, and takes mine to give them a second look. I turn a page, and another. My gaze sticks on a name under a headline.

"How do you spell 'Jeanant'?" I ask.

"J-E-A-N-A-N-T," Win says. "It's unlikely he'd use his real name though … But we should probably keep an eye out for his code name, the one he'd have used when our group needed to communicate on public channels. Jeanant went by 'Meeth'—short for Prometheus."

Prometheus. I vaguely remember our unit on Greek mythology in elementary school. Prometheus was the guy who stole fire from the gods to give it to mortals, wasn't he? Like Jeanant bringing freedom from his people to us on Earth? It's fitting.

Curiosity nibbles at me as I study the article, which looks the same as all the others. No jab of *wrong*ness. "So what's your secret code name?" I ask. "Or is Win it?"

"No," Win says. "I didn't really choose mine. Someone else came up with it, as a joke, and it ended up sticking."

"Well, now I have to know."

The silence stretches. "It can't be *that* bad," I say.

He grimaces. "It's 'Pogo,'" he says. "Which is sort of short for Galápagos."

"Galápagos? Is that the joke?"

"Not exactly."

"So …"

"It was just Jule being Jule," he mutters. "He said I was 'practically bouncing up and down' when they first let me in on the mission."

My mouth twitches in amusement. "And what does Galápagos have to do with anything?"

"It's a long story," he says briskly. "Why are you asking about names? Did you see something?"

I point out the article. "Do you think this could be Jeanant? It's kind of like a mix between his name and the code name: 'Jean Manthe.'"

Win snatches the paper from me. "It could be."

His eyes light up as he reads the article. "It *must* be him," he says. "He uses a line that was in that message to Thlo: 'the theme of our cause.'"

I found the clue after all. "So what's he say?" I ask, leaning closer.

"He's sending a message to the 'true people' of Paris, that while they should fight for what they deserve, he hopes they'll take care not to 'destroy the very treasures that should be theirs'—the museums, the art ..."

"The other detail you said he mentioned—it was something about paint, wasn't it?"

"Exactly," Win says with a grin. "Where better to paint over something than in an art gallery? This article could be both a hint to us and a way of making sure the revolutionaries don't destroy what he's left."

"Where should we look first?" I say. "There are a lot of galleries in Paris, aren't there?"

"The Louvre existed in 1830," Win says. "It was converted into an art and history museum not long before now. That seems like our best chance. I think we're close already."

He turns right at the next intersection, and I follow, staring up at the buildings that are so tall and close I can only make out the very edge of their roofs. My scalp is sweating under the makeshift shawl. I swipe at a droplet running down the side of my face, and realize I've probably smudged newspaper ink across my cheek. Oh well. It'll fit my costume.

Nothing provokes that quiver of *wrong*ness. But then, my special sensitivity hasn't done anything for us here so far. We figured out our next destination from a name and information Win already knew. He didn't really need me.

I shake myself, feeling strangely deflated. It shouldn't matter. What matters is that we find where Jeanant left his weapon, one way or another.

Finally we come to the edge of a wide tree-lined boulevard. The structure on the other side of the street is so immense my first impression is that it's a castle. It lords over the road, as high as the several-story buildings we've been wandering amid, though the huge arched windows form only three rows across the stone face. Between the windows and along the roof, the stone is carved into fluted columns and cornices and figures human and divine. I itch to step closer, but the scene on the sidewalk out front stops me.

Soldiers in the same blue-and-red uniforms I saw on the bridge are gathered along the promenade by the building's foot. Some are patrolling, others hauling cannons or barrels, or rocks they're heaping into rough barricades along the sidewalk. One soldier heads across the road not far from where we stand, and I duck back into the shadows. One of Lisa's favorite phrases pops into my mind in her breezy voice:

Bad news up ahead! Somehow I suspect this would be enough to dull even her usual bravado.

"That's it," Win says, as if I hadn't figured it out. "The Louvre."

"How are we going to get past them?" I ask, jerking my chin toward the soldiers. They don't look as though they're planning to welcome visitors.

Win gives me an amused expression that's becoming familiar, and lifts the top of his satchel.

I roll my eyes at myself. "Of course."

"You don't see anything that seems even a bit off out there?" he asks.

I consider the building and the activity around it once more. The sight of all those rifles and cannons doesn't exactly soothe my jitters, but nothing stands out.

"No. Sorry."

"Well, anything painted will be inside. We can start by jumping forward to the end of this revolution. Jeanant could have placed what he wants us to find anytime during the three days, so that'll give us the best chance of getting there after him. If it looks like the locals have disturbed things inside, we can always work backward."

"Fine with me," I say.

Win directs me into the shelter of a doorway, out of view of the windows overhead. He whips the cloth around us. I lift my feet instinctively as the floor of the tentlike shape forms beneath them. Win flicks his fingers, and presses his hand against the data display.

The walls shudder. I stumble, and snatch at the back of Win's shirt. And the movement stops. We've Traveled less than a mile and no more than a couple days, after all.

Then Win pushes open the cloth, and my jaw goes slack.

The walls and floor of the vast hallway we've arrived in are lit with an amber afternoon glow, washing in from the few lofty windows nearby. Beside us, a ring of marble figures lounge on polished pedestals, carved in such detail I could have mistaken them for living people if they weren't so still and stony white. Beyond them, massive paintings line the walls. The curved ceiling looms some twenty feet above our heads, and it's a work in itself. Sculpted marble and glints of gold surround a scene of cherubs at play.

When I lower my gaze and step toward the paintings, the floor creaks softly. I don't recognize this image of a woman sitting by a pond, but the style makes me think of the Italian Renaissance. The canvas is taller than me and wider than I could reach with my arms spread. Standing in front of it, only the rippled texture of the brushstrokes stops me from feeling I could step right into the image. I've almost touched it before I realize and yank my hand back.

This is probably a masterpiece. Preserved from centuries ago for centuries to come.

And I'm here to see it, in the most famous museum in the world.

Angela would just about explode with artistic excitement. A pang of homesickness wobbles in my chest. I wish she were here, seeing it with me.

Maybe she will be, someday in the future I'm protecting right now. Assuming we can keep following Jeanant's trail to his weapon.

A sharp cracking sound echoes through the walls, and I flinch. Win is standing by one of the windows, staring outside.

Another shot crackles, somewhere in the distance, beyond the courtyard the window looks down into. The courtyard itself is empty, but past the wing of the museum opposite us, a stream of smoke is curling up toward the deep blue of the late-afternoon sky.

I've only heard cannon fire in movies, but the boom that reverberates through the glass a moment later makes me remember the weapons I saw the soldiers hauling. Those cannons were real. That smoke's from a real fire. It seems so distant, on the other side of the pane, but right now one of those stately buildings we passed just a few minutes and two days ago could be burning down. Real guns are being fired out there; real bodies are fleeing the flames, falling on the cobblestones. The gentlemen and women on the riverside street, the boys who pelted Win … people who already died long before I was born are dying again.

I walked among them for an hour or two, but I still have no idea what it was like for any of them, living here in this now. Instead I'm busy thinking of happy futures.

My throat's closed up. I force the words out. "Do you think we're safe in here?"

"It looks like Jeanant's appeal to save the art worked," Win says, tipping his head toward the vacant courtyard. "Let's go—we have a lot of ground to cover."

The sounds of the revolution dwindle when we head down the hall, until all I can hear is the tap of my boots and Win's shoes. I'm glad to leave it behind, but then I'm pricked by guilt. I was out there wrinkling my nose at the smells and cringing away from the muck, but I *can* leave. I can slip away into this museum and pretend this is some big vacation, and then I can jump back home, where there are no battles raging in the streets.

But I can't do anything about the violence out there. So as we walk farther, I let the sense of peace that emanates from the high ceilings and pale walls wash over me. I examine every relic we pass, absorbing lines and colors, expressions and gestures.

This is what humans have created, despite the shifts Win's people have made: things of beauty, things of meaning, even if most of the symbols and allusions go over my head. It's amazing.

We reach the end of one hall and wander through a series of smaller interconnected gallery rooms before emerging into another grand passageway. Win walks smoothly and efficiently, but when I glance at him, he's ogling the art as openly as I've been.

"You haven't been here before," I say.

He shakes his head. "There are a lot of places and periods on Earth," he says. "I've only seen a few. I wish we had time to really take this in."

He won't get the chance to later on, if his group succeeds and the generator is destroyed. I don't know why Earth's history would matter much to some alien race, but I can imagine how a person could find that freedom hard to let go of.

"You have your own art, don't you?" I say. "On your planet?"

"My dad creates pictures," he says hesitantly. "With paint. When he can afford it. He'd be overwhelmed by this place. It's not the same on Kemya—taking anything artistic seriously is discouraged, so there aren't really any traditions, any teachers to learn from. You'd find it hard to understand. There's a saying we have." He speaks in his native tongue, and then translates. "*If it doesn't build, then it breaks.* Making something that doesn't have an obvious use, it's considered wasteful, even destructive. What did we lose that we could have had if that person had applied him or herself to something more practical? It makes sense, of course. But I still wonder what we might make, if we had more opportunity."

Wow. With every new thing he tells me about Kemya, I like the place less. "Do you do anything … creative?" I can't help asking.

His mouth twists. "I copied my dad with the paint a little when I was young, because I wanted to do what he did. Before I knew exactly what people thought about that. Anyway, I didn't—"

He cuts himself off, and at the same moment I hear it. The faint rapping of footsteps somewhere behind us.

Win nudges me over to the wall, beside a display case holding a row of ornately etched pottery. The alarm band is calm against my ankle. "It can't be the Enforcers," I whisper.

"Probably a museum guard then," Win says. "Safer to be at work than out there. If he comes this way, I can take care of it."

The certainty under his flippant tone gives me pause. Does *he* have one of those awful numbing blasters?

The footsteps halt, then continue. We wait silently. There's a touch on my hand; Win's reached out, curling his fingers around mine. The *there*ness of the skin-to-skin contact sends an odd shiver up my arm, but it's comforting too. A very solid reminder that I'm not alone. I peek at him warily just as he looks away from me, his expression going distant while he listens.

After a minute, I'm sure the sound's getting fainter. In another, I can't hear the steps at all. Win steps away from the display case.

"Keep quiet," he murmurs to me, "and hopefully he'll never know we were here."

"What if Jeanant ran into a guard when *he* was here?" I ask softly as we continue down the hall.

"I'm sure Jeanant could handle that."

I frown. "What exactly would you or he—"

And then Win's gone. Vanished. Without a movement, without a sound—in the blink of an eye, except I haven't blinked.

My voice dies in my open mouth. I spin around, one way and the other, but there's not a single indication that seconds ago Win was standing there beside me.

13.

"Win?" I say, my hands clenched at my sides. It isn't like before, on the hotel roof, when all he did was step inside the time cloth. He didn't have it out—he didn't *do* anything. He just disappeared, right before my eyes.

I take a few steps forward, peering through the shadows. The hall is so quiet the thudding of my heart is deafening in my ears. Nothing stirs. The wide-open space that seemed so peaceful moments ago now feels horrifyingly lonely.

"Win, if this is some stupid joke …"

But as little as I know him, I find it hard to believe he'd suddenly start playing pranks when we could be mere minutes from stumbling on what he's spent weeks searching for.

Which means … something else snatched him away? A trap set by the Enforcers? Some other danger he didn't warn me about?

Oh God, what if he can't get back here? If he's trapped, if they take his cloth …

My skin goes cold as the full implications sink in. Without Win, *I'm* trapped. If he doesn't come back, I have no way to get home, ever.

I waver on my feet, hugging myself. "Win?" I call again, my voice shaking. "Win!"

No answer. I hurry back the way we came, not knowing what else to do. I can't go outside, into the smoke and the cannon fire. I don't belong here, and I feel that right down to my bones. I can't speak the language. I don't know anyone. It's a hundred years before the oldest people I've met will even be born.

Flashes of home flicker through my mind. Sitting with Mom and Dad at the dinner table. Joking with Angela and the others in the art room. What I wouldn't give to be there instead.

I skid to a halt outside the series of rooms we passed through, hugging myself tighter. "Win!" I shout.

There's a rattle of footsteps in the distance. Joy bursts in my chest as I whirl toward them, for all of the split second it takes before a voice carries with them. A thick, gravelly voice bellowing a demand in French.

The guard. I forgot about him. My legs lock. His footsteps are getting louder, running now. What kind of punishment was there in 1830 for breaking into a royal museum?

I duck through the interconnected rooms, searching for something large enough to hide behind. A second shout follows me, sounding as if the guard's already in the hall I just left. I dash through another doorway, and then, like a miracle, the voice I wanted to hear reaches me.

"Skylar? I'm over here!"

Relief hits me so hard my sight blurs. I run in the direction Win's yell came from, dodging stands and benches, through two, three, four more doorways. Win's just saying my name again when I burst into the gallery he's striding through.

He stops when he sees me, his mouth curved a little sheepishly and a matching relief in his deep blue eyes. I gulp air and swipe at the tears that have started to trickle down my face.

"Hey," Win says, sounding startled. He grips my shoulder, and his voice softens. "I wouldn't just leave you. I wasn't expecting that to happen."

Get it together, Skylar. I blink furiously, and a sharp command echoes from a nearby room.

"The guard," I murmur around the lump in my throat. "He heard me calling for you—he's coming this way."

Win's already yanking the cloth out of his satchel. He pulls it over us.

The room outside goes gray and hazy. I bite my lip, fighting to calm my rasping breaths. I'm okay now. I'm not lost, not trapped in the past.

Win takes my hand like he did before, squeezing it. I have to stop myself from clinging to his fingers. He must think I'm weak enough as it is.

The guard's footsteps approach. My shoulders hunch automatically, even though I know the cloth is keeping us invisible.

A thin man in a charcoal-gray uniform marches into the room. He scans it with narrowed eyes, drumming his fingers against his thigh just below his holstered pistol.

As the guard peers behind a statue in the corner, Win lets go of me to open his satchel. He pulls out a small blue-gray sphere about the size of a pea. When he slides his thumb over it, it gives a soft ping. Two flat edges materialize like wings. He brings it to his face and exhales over it. Then he propels it between the flaps of the cloth.

The sphere vanishes into the grayness on the other side. For several seconds, nothing happens. The guard mutters to himself and eyes the room one more time. Then a distinct pattering sound carries from off to our left, beyond the rooms he hasn't checked yet.

The guard spins around. He hurries through the doorway, bellowing a warning. His footsteps thunder across the floor, and gradually fade as he chases the fleeing noise.

Win peels open the time cloth, grinning. "That little piece of tech is what you'd probably call a distractor," he says, his voice low. "It'll make enough noise to keep him after it for a few hours, and never enter the same space we're in."

I'm a little impressed, but Win looks so impressed with himself I don't feel the need to mention it.

"What the hell happened?" I say. "How did you get over here?"

"I was, ah, *doxed*," Win says, heading back toward the hall where he disappeared. "We ran practice scenarios in training to prepare us to recognize the feeling when it's about to happen, but it comes on fast, and I guess I was distracted." His sheepish expression returns. "The time field doesn't allow certain types of paradoxes, like meeting someone from your future. It's as if we all carry around this big bubble of our present, whatever time it is for us outside the field, and if two bubbles clash"—he bounces his palms off each other—"whoever's from the later time gets bumped out of the way."

Suddenly I'm picturing Win as a goldfish floating around in our fishbowl Earth in a bubble of air. Colliding with another goldfish …

"So there's someone else here?" I say, my head whipping around. "One of your people? The alarm band didn't go off."

"I'd have been doxed before there was any chance of even hearing them," Win says. "Which is going to be a wider range than the alarm has." He pauses as we step out into the hall. "But you weren't."

"Obviously." I consider his explanation. "I've never been outside the field. Does that mean I don't have a 'bubble'?"

"Apparently not. We never discussed how Traveling would work for Earthlings, since Earthlings are never supposed to Travel." He stares down the hall, understanding dawning on his face. "There's a good chance it's Jeanant who doxed me. If he's here right now—if you can't get doxed—you could *talk* to him, find out everything we need to know!"

Before I can respond, he's tugging me toward the display case we hid behind earlier.

"How do you know it's him?" I ask.

"We know Jeanant was planning on being in here sometime in these three days. There's no reason any other Traveler should have been in the same place in that short a period of time."

He stops when we reach the case, just a few steps from where he disappeared before.

"I shouldn't go any farther," he says. "It is possible it's not him, so be careful. But hurry. I don't think Jeanant would stay here very long."

My mind hasn't quite caught up with this new development. "What do I do if it's not him?"

"Run back here. I won't move from this spot."

I hesitate, and Win grasps my arm. "Please," he says, turning the full force of those blue eyes on me. "You know how long it's taken us to get this far. If you can talk to him, we won't need to worry about decoding any more clues. You can get him to tell you exactly what we need to know. Say—say Thlo sent you. If he knows you're here for her, he'll explain everything."

And then this will be over, Win's group will have what they need, and I can return to the world I belong in.

"Okay," I say. "Just … don't move an inch."

He nods. "Go!"

I can feel his gaze following me as I jog down the hall. I'm about to do something he thought was impossible. Underneath my nervousness, excitement tingles through me.

I'm going to meet the guy from the recording. Talk to him, face to face. Show him that it's not just his people taking a stand for both our planets.

That thought emboldens me. I walk faster, past a series of paintings. A huge vase decorated with geometric patterns. A line of busts of presumably famous men. An intricately carved stone box that appears to be a coffin.

Halfway down the hall, the band around my ankle starts to quiver. A hundred feet. I slow. The quivering rises to a frantic vibration as I approach a wide doorway that leads into a side gallery.

Peeking through the entrance, I see only a large maroon-carpeted room filled with paintings. But there's another, smaller doorway on the other side. A faint scraping sound carries from it.

I pad across the room. The adjoining gallery is equally vacant, but the sound has gotten louder. Then, when I'm halfway to the next opening, it stops. Shoes tread lightly against the floor. I edge over to the doorway and peer beyond it.

It's him.

I recognize the guy from the recording in an instant. Jeanant. He's poised by the cushioned bench in the middle of the room, studying the paintings on the wall before him. A shading of stubble has darkened the bronze skin of his jaw, and a bluish smudge colors his right thumb, as if he got paint on it and couldn't wash it completely off. A top hat like the ones some of the gentlemen on the street are wearing is tipped over his curly black hair. He's dressed in one of their trim jackets over a shirt and pants identical to Win's Traveler clothes, but somehow he makes it look like a proper outfit instead of a bunch of random clothing thrown together. The assurance I saw on the screen, it wasn't just a performance. It's in him now, in his expression, the way he's standing, when he's unaware anyone's watching.

I gather myself and step through the doorway.

Jeanant's head snaps around. His dark brown eyes connect with mine, and the full impact of his presence hits me: the *there*ness that felt like attraction when I first stood close to Win, like terror when faced with the pale woman. I'm struck by the sense that we are exactly where we need to be—not just Jeanant, but me too.

His name catches in my throat. Before I can recover, he's turned, his composure regained, and lifted his hat to give me a slight bow. As he straightens up, he says something in that low, measured voice, something that sounds quite friendly although I have no idea what the words mean. Because he's talking in French. Of course. He'd assume anyone wandering around in here looking clueless has to be a local.

But even though I've interrupted him and as far as he knows I'm just an inconvenience, he's waiting patiently for me to respond.

"Jeanant?" I say. "I need to—"

The moment his name passes over my lips, I know I've made a mistake. His expression shutters. He flicks his hand toward his side. A sliver of cold jabs the center of my abdomen, making my sentence cut off with a gasp.

As he sweeps up the canvaslike bag on the bench and pulls out a familiar puddle of silky cloth, Jeanant says something in the lightly slurred tones of the alien language I've heard Win speak a few times. His voice is defiant.

He must think I'm an Enforcer, here to apprehend him. "No!" I cry. I try to step toward him, but the cold has seeped through my limbs, and my legs won't budge. "I'm not—"

He's already tossing the cloth around his body. His form vanishes amid its oily surface, which shimmers to reflect the room around us. "I'm a friend of Thlo's!" I force out, a second before the cold grips my jaw.

The cloth has vanished, and I can't do anything but stand there. Jeanant doesn't reemerge. I don't know if I got my last words out in time for him to hear.

I'm frozen solid. Win's too far away to hear me if I call out—if I could call out. My chest tightens, but I've hardly started to panic when a prickling creeps over my skin. My fingers and toes twitch. The paralysis is easing already.

Whatever Jeanant threw at me, it isn't half as powerful as the Enforcers' weapons. He wasn't trying to hurt me. Just to delay me, so he could get away.

I grimace inwardly. He was *right there* and I couldn't manage to say anything useful. I should have known he'd be worried about the Enforcers tracking him, just like Win. The whole reason Jeanant's here, hiding the weapon, is that they almost caught him already.

At the same time, that weird sense of purpose lingers inside me. I really am a part of this mission now. And if I get another chance to talk to Jeanant, I won't screw it up.

My gaze wanders the room as my body comes back to life. I'm sure that was paint on his thumb, but I don't see any message or hint that he's covered one up. There's no gleam of wet color anywhere.

The cold seeps out. I shake myself, rub my arms, and head back for Win.

14.

"Why didn't you explain it to him?" Win demands as we march down the hall to the room where I found Jeanant.

"He didn't give me the chance!" I say.

"I can't believe he was here, you talked to him, and we still—" He cuts himself off with a strangled huff.

Neither can I. But it's not like Win's in the best position to criticize. "You didn't exactly do much to prepare me," I point out. "'Go, hurry, get him talking!' I *tried*."

"Well, we'll have to try again," Win says, sounding like he's talking more to himself than to me. "Now that we know it can be done, we just have to find the right moment."

So I will get another chance. I let out a breath I hadn't realized I was holding. "You could come with me next time, so he knows I'm with your group, couldn't you?" I say as I motion him into the string of smaller gallery rooms. "I mean, I know that whole doxing thing happens if you're from two different times, but you're not *that* far in his future, are you? A few weeks?" My mind starts spinning, working through this warped physics equation. "You'd just have to find out where he was a few weeks after he first came to Earth, so your … bubbles would line up."

"Ah." Win clears his throat. "It's actually years."

I stop in the doorway and stare at him. "*Years*? But you said you'd only been waiting to hear from the others—I know you said it was a few weeks."

"And that's true," Win says slowly, as if I'm dense not to have figured this out on my own. "Thlo and I and the others, we've only been on Earth for about four weeks. But we couldn't race over here the second Jeanant disappeared. Thlo didn't even get his message, explaining what he'd done, until a long time after. He knew that as soon as the Enforcers realized he was responsible for the attempted attack, they'd start investigating anyone who'd been associated with him. If Thlo had been caught too, we couldn't have gotten anything done. So he programmed the message to transmit after there'd been plenty of time for suspicion to die down. And then—it's not easy to zip across the galaxy from Kemya to here. Especially when you're doing it without official permission. Putting the plan together, gathering equipment and supplies secretly, arranging a ship—it took a while."

My mind's spinning in a totally different way now. "So, wait, how many years are we talking?"

"Almost eleven by our sun," he says. "Which is something like seventeen for you."

"Jeanant's from seventeen years in the past? Then why—"

"No," Win says. "I told you before, Jeanant's present, the time when he came down to Earth, is the same as your present time—where I met you. *I* jumped back seventeen Earth years to get there."

Win is from my future. He could have seen me, seventeen years older?

No. Because I didn't have a future before Win came. I died in a courthouse bombing.

I press my hand against my forehead, as if that will still my thoughts. None of that matters now. I should focus on what's in front of me.

Two rows of ivory buttons on the bench's cushion. Three grooves running down each of the bowed legs. Two paintings on the wall across from me, seven there, where Jeanant was looking. Reds and greens, blues and yellows, in the rich tones of oil paint.

"Can we jump back a little earlier?" I venture when I feel steadier. "I could catch up with Jeanant when he first got to the museum."

"We've been wandering around for a while," Win says. "I doubt he arrived earlier than us. And two versions of you in the same building at the same time … It's just a bad idea. At least we know what room he picked. Tell me again what happened, what he was doing."

"I heard a scraping sound," I say. "When I got to this room, Jeanant was standing here, looking at that wall." I point. "I think he had blue paint on his hand."

Win moves onto the spot I indicated on the floor, frowning at the paintings. He crosses his arms in front of him, and I'm struck by the difference between him and the man who was standing there before. Win's frustration radiates off him, as if my failure has thrown all his plans for a loop, even though a half hour ago he had no idea it was even possible I might talk to Jeanant.

He's never had a solid plan of his own, has he? He's been willing to take risks, sure, but it's all been 'try this out and see where it takes us.' The mission itself, the idea of saving Earth, that was Jeanant's.

Because Jeanant's the first of his people to step up and actually *do* something about the time field. And even after he thought the Enforcers had caught up with him, he moved and spoke with such confidence, as if he'd face a whole army if he had to, and maybe come out on top. So much confidence I can still feel it echoing inside me.

We survived the Enforcers back home, the streets of Paris, the museum guard. We'll get through this too. For once in my life, I am not going to back down and hope I can wait out my problems.

"Do you see anything that looks like a clue?" I ask.

Win shakes his head. He eases closer, studying each of the pieces on the wall. There's a ship on a stormy sea, a shadowy forest, a woman reclining in the moonlight, a huntsman guiding his horse over a hedge, a family gathered by a flickering hearth, a portrait of a dour young man, and two ravens circling the moors. All of them have bits of blue here and there.

"I don't suppose any of them were signed by 'Jean Manthe'?" I say. The corner of Win's mouth twitches, as if he's not sure whether to smile or frown.

"Unfortunately not," he says. "And not by Jeanant or Meeth either …"

Meeth. The code name hangs in the air. I look at the images again, and the answer rushes to me. Win glances over, his eyes widening, at the same moment I turn to him.

"*Prometheus.*"

Bringing fire.

"I should have seen it right away," Win says a little breathlessly, reaching for the painting of the family by the hearth. "It's perfect. Only our group knows he went by that name. The Enforcers would never catch it."

He sets the picture on the floor and squats in front of it, running his fingers along the edge of the gold-trimmed frame. It creaks as he digs his fingers around a corner of the canvas, and I wince.

"You'll break it!" I say.

"For all we know it was destroyed before Jeanant added that article in the newspaper about protecting the art," Win says with a shrug. "I've got to see—here we go."

The corner pops out of the frame, and I notice that pressing against the paint has given Win's fingers the same bluish cast Jeanant's thumb had. But I can't help cringing as he yanks the canvas away. This could be a lost masterpiece, just now recovered.

Of course, it's a human masterpiece. Considering what Win said before about art and wastefulness, I guess even he doesn't see one Earth painting as much of a loss.

"I've got it!" he crows. He tugs something like a thin slab of plastic out from between the canvas and its backing. Embedded in the plastic-like material is a metal rectangle crisscrossed with silvery lines.

"What is it?" I ask. It hardly looks like a weapon capable of blowing up a massive satellite.

"A tech plate," Win says, grinning. "Either the guidance system or the processor, I'd bet, since those are the parts we'd have the most trouble constructing on our own when we rebuild the weapon. And ..." He taps the rows of tiny red characters printed along the edge of the slab. They remind me of the ones on the time cloth's display.

"These must be his directions to the next piece." His gaze darts over them, his body practically quivering with enthusiasm now. Seeing his face light up, part of me wants to be over there examining it with him. But that isn't enough to distract me from what he said.

"The *next* piece? I thought you just needed to find the one thing."

"Well, we need to find the weapon," Win says. "But Jeanant didn't risk putting all his faith in one hiding spot. In his last message to Thlo, he said he'd break up the most essential parts and spread them out between four different places and time periods. So even if the Enforcers stumble on one or two, hopefully we'll get enough to figure out the rest."

He says it in the same offhand manner he talked about ruining the painting. As if I should have known this all along. His earlier words come back to me: *We'll have to try again.*

He didn't mean here. He meant some other place, some other time. Another trip in the cloth—and another, and another—to more worlds I was never meant to be a part of. Worlds where nothing will be more *wrong* than me.

My stomach clenches. "So we've barely gotten started," I say. "You only asked if I'd come to France. You just assumed I'd follow you around wherever else you needed to go?"

"Well, I—" He looks up at me, and his voice falters. "You said you'd help."

"You made it sound like it was just this one place. Like we'd poke around in Paris a bit and then head home, no big deal."

His mouth opens. I can actually *see* him struggling to hold that innocent expression in place. It doesn't work. His gaze flicks away from me and back. And suddenly I understand.

"You knew I probably wouldn't come if you told me everything," I say. I was this shiny new shift-sensing tool he just had to bring with him, so he said what he thought would convince me and left out any other details that might have mattered. Who cares what I want if it gets the mission done?

"I was trying to keep things simple—"

"You *decided* not to tell me the whole truth."

And it worked. Here I am. With no way to get home unless he takes me.

My pulse has started thumping. I reach for my bracelet, for the comfort of numbers, but the thought of trying to pull myself together while he's sitting there watching me like I'm a freak show act just makes me feel more sick. Turning on my heel, I stalk out of the room.

"Skylar!" Win calls after me, but I ignore him. I march back to the wide hall, not stopping until I've reached one of the museum's tall windows.

This one offers a view over the city instead of the inner courtyard. The guns and cannons are momentarily silent, but a couple streams of smoke are still winding up toward the clouds over the carved stone rooftops.

I lean my forehead against the glass, absorbing the scene below as I rotate the beads. I can make out twelve scrawny trees along the side of the boulevard. Bright green foliage drifting in the breeze. Muddled patterns of soot or mud or some other dark liquid smeared across the cobblestones. A body in a red-and-blue uniform sprawled by the corner, unmoving.

What am I doing here?

The answer comes, unbidden, with the memory of the defiance on Jeanant's face as he spoke back against the Enforcers. I'm not just a passive variable in some alien fishbowl experiment. I'm fixing the world. I'm righting the *wrongs*.

I just can't help thinking I'd be doing a much better job of it with Jeanant as my guide.

I hear Win walking up behind me, but I don't bother to look over. He stops beside the window.

"I'm sorry," he says stiffly. "Meeting you, it was a chance I'd never have expected to get, a chance to make our mission so much easier. I didn't want to lose that. But I've never done anything like this before—bringing along an Earthling—I was never supposed to. I didn't know how much I should say."

"You think it's been easy for me?" I say. "At least you've done *some* of this before. I did want to help, and I know how important finding this weapon is to you, but it wasn't fair to ask me to make that decision without telling me what we were actually getting into."

"I know. I *am* sorry. And you know of it now: three more time periods, three more parts of the weapon." He leans back against the wall. At the edge of my vision, I see his head turn as he surveys the hall. His tone lightens. "It hasn't been all bad, has it? You did get a trip to Paris out of it. A Paris no one else you know will ever get to see."

Part of me wants to smack him, but a short laugh lurches out. "I guess so." I can't say I wish I hadn't seen this Paris. That it doesn't give me a little thrill to think that I might walk into the Louvre someday in my present, and be able to see how it's changed in the last two centuries.

"Do you want me to take you back?" Win asks.

I look at him then. His jaw is set, his mouth pressed into a flat line, as if he wishes he hadn't said that. But he did. Even though completing his mission could depend on the fact that I can talk to Jeanant, that I can sense the shifts.

In a way, that means more than anything else he's said the entire time I've known him.

The thought of home sends a wave of longing through me, but I force myself to pause. I parse out my anger, my sense of betrayal, the anxiety underneath. Nothing I've been through so far has been outright unbearable. My thumb runs over the bracelet's beads. I think I can handle more.

I don't think I can handle going back to living my old life, feeling every little shift and knowing what they mean, knowing Win's group is still struggling to stop them—struggling more because I gave up and let fear get the better of me. Jeanant's even more out of place than I am, a galaxy's length away from home and years apart from any of his own people, and he hasn't let that stop him.

I drag in a deep breath, trying to ease the jitters that rise up at the thought of leaping even farther into unfamiliar history. Maybe I'm not going to stop, but that doesn't mean I can't ask for something. "No," I say. "Not like that. But, before we go wherever and whenever we need to next—I think I'd feel better if you did take me home first, just for a few minutes. So I can … catch my breath." And regain my balance before my world's thrown out of whack all over again.

"And then you'd come with me?" Win says.

"And then I'd come with you," I agree. "We've still got my planet to save, don't we?"

He breaks into a smile. "Indeed we do."

15.

I settle myself in the corner of the window ledge. The hard stone braces me. "Do you know what our next stop will be?" I ask Win.

He holds up the slab of alien plastic. "Not yet," he says. "It's like his message to Thlo: kind of a riddle, in case the Enforcers get a hold of it. The first part isn't too hard. He says to take the number of years for that first message to reach us, and then repeat them two hundred and sixty-eight times since zero. Thlo's said that the message came exactly three and a half years after he disappeared, so—"

"938," I say automatically. Win blinks at me. "Numbers are my thing, remember? That's the year we need to go to? AD, I guess—that'd probably be what the 'since zero' means."

He gives me a slow smile. The smile that makes it hard to remember he's not a human boy, but an alien. "Definitely," he agrees. "The rest is more obscure, though. 'Where the little dragon scares off the big dragon. The sign will point at the sky.'"

"Dragons," I say. "So … somewhere in medieval Britain, then? That'd be the right time period."

"Actually," Win says with a patronizing air that obliterates any goodwill the smile bought him, "dragons are much more closely linked to many Asian cultures than they are to Europe. That's more likely what he was referring to."

I restrain myself from rolling my eyes. "Okay, can you get more specific? Asia's a big continent."

"Give me a second. There's something about that year …"

"Do you think it'll be another revolution?" I ask. "That's sort of Jeanant's theme, right? The line about the dragons does sound like some kind of uprising."

"Of course. That'll help narrow it down." He pulls out his time cloth and unfolds it into its laptop-like shape.

"You get Internet access here?" I say skeptically as he sets it on the ledge of the next window over.

"No," he says. "But there's plenty of information stored in the cloth itself. It's tricky to find anything *quickly*, sifting through all of it, but whatever we need to know, it's in here somewhere."

"What about the rest of your group?" I ask. "You have proof that you're on the right trail now. Shouldn't you let them know?"

He pauses, the glow of the display casting a greenish tint on his golden-brown skin. Then he shakes his head with a jerk. "No need yet. We're doing fine on our own. If we can catch up with Jeanant at the next location, we might be able to finish everything right there."

I don't see why having some extra help wouldn't still be a good thing, but right then a cannon booms outside the window, making the wall shudder. Win winces as I leap back. Someone is shooting right at the building.

"I expect this place will hold," Win remarks, turning back to the screen. Pulse skittering, I edge to my window and peer out, thinking I should suggest he do his information searching at my house.

The shadows across the street from the Louvre are lengthening as the sun sinks below the distant rooftops. I can't make out anyone moving between them. There's just a pair of birds circling each other against the sky, where one of the streams of smoke has faded into a wispy thread, and—

There's a new line of smoke snaking up between the other two, thick and gray. The instant my eyes catch it an uncomfortably familiar tremor of *wrong, wrong, wrong* pierces my mind. My skin goes clammy.

"Win," I say. "Win!"

"What?"

For a second, I can only press my finger against the glass as the *wrong*ness chokes me. My other hand fumbles for my bracelet. "There," I manage. "That smoke. I think something's shifted."

Win gazes past me. One of those alien curses falls from his mouth.

"That's the direction we came from," I say. "Did *we* make something—"

"If we were the ones who made it happen, you'd never have seen anything different," he says. "But maybe we shifted something else. The Enforcers must have picked up our trail somehow."

The words have only just left his mouth when the band around my ankle starts to shiver. "They're close!" I say, flinching away from the window.

Win dashes back to the cloth computer. "I've almost narrowed it down," he says. "Just give me a few seconds."

He flicks through the data on the display. I check both ends of the hall. The band's only vibrating lightly right now, but that could change at any moment.

"Can't we get out of here, and then you can finish looking? What if we don't *have* a few seconds?"

"If I stop, I'll have to start all over—there! The Bach Dang River." He reaches out to me with one hand, the other yanking the time cloth into its tentlike form. "Come on!"

My gaze slips past the window, and catches a movement outside. A pale figure flanked by two darker ones, marching across the boulevard toward our wing of the museum. The instant my eyes snag on them, the pale woman glances up at my window. Her barked command carries through the glass, and Win grasps my arm. I scramble with him beneath the folds of the cloth.

"She's outside—she saw me," I babble as the flaps fall shut.

"Well, in a moment we won't be here," Win says, swiping at the inner display. "Hold on."

I barely have time to wonder, *Hold on to what?* before the cloth jumps, and my stomach heaves with it. I stumble into Win, clapping my hand over my mouth to contain a surge of nausea. And then it's over.

Win swears under his breath and pokes at the display again. I stare through the translucent walls, and recognize the same wide hall of the Louvre, the row of busts, the high windows. We haven't moved more than ten feet.

"What—"

"Let me figure it out!" Win snaps.

The cloth lurches. I manage to keep my balance, but my head is spinning. The blurred outer walls of the museum rise around us. We've only Traveled into the courtyard.

An older model, Win said before, when the jumps were rough. Has it died? Win slams his hand against the display, but the cloth doesn't move at all this time. He leans forward, his head bowed, muttering something under his breath. It sounds almost like he's praying. I hug myself, braced for the pale woman to burst out of the doorway across from us. Maybe we should get out and run for it.

"You will work," Win growls at the display, as if he can intimidate the cloth into functioning properly. His fingers flit over the characters. And the world around us finally whisks away.

My eyes squeeze shut. The floor beneath me shudders and the air squeals. This must be what it's like to be tossed up in the middle of a hurricane. But at least it feels like we're actually going somewhere this time.

We come to ground with a jolt and a ringing in my ears. Only a dim light penetrates the fabric walls past the buildings looming close on either side, but the rumble of car traffic and the beat of a hip-hop tune filter in with it. Not the Louvre, or Paris, anymore. We've left the Enforcers far behind. I let out my breath.

"Third time's a charm," I murmur. "Where are we?"

Win consults the display. His stance relaxes. "Back in your city," he says. "The afternoon we left."

"Oh," I say. "I was thinking, like, my *house*, or …"

"I know," Win says. "But … I didn't expect the Enforcers to catch up with us that quickly."

"We must have made another shift at the museum, right?" I say, but even as the words are coming out, I frown. What shift could we have made that would have entered the Enforcers' records somehow? The only person we encountered was that guard, who didn't even see us. And yet the pale woman seemed to know exactly where—and when—to find us. "What else could it be?"

"I don't know," Win says, his voice tight. "They shouldn't be able to unscramble the signal on the cloths after what Isis did. We should be okay. I just thought it was better to take precautions. If they do figure out how to track us, jumping to your house would lead them straight there."

The thought of the pale woman standing at my front door sends a chill through me. "We can still go there; it's only a small chance," Win continues, but I shake my head.

"No." Seeing my room for a few minutes isn't worth even a tiny risk. This will have to do.

"Let me know when you're ready to move on," Win says. *Preferably soon*, I can tell he's thinking. With the idea of the Enforcers following us hanging over me, coming home isn't quite as comforting as I'd hoped.

"Why don't we dox the Enforcers, or them us?" I ask as we step out of the cloth into the alley.

"The group looking for me, they're from the same present I am," Win says. "Our timelines match up, for the most part. There's a little wiggle room: if it takes them half an hour to notice a shift we accidentally made, they can't show up there at the same moment we made the shift, or the half-hour difference in our 'bubbles' will push them away. Which is why they didn't show up the second we walked into the coffee shop the other day. And why we'll want to avoid staying anyplace for very long."

Right. I touch the backs of the buildings as we walk toward the street. The bricks and concrete are reassuringly real, but not *too* real. I peer out onto a shopping strip that's vaguely familiar. I think it's near Mom's gym … Ah! When I went in with her for Take Your Children to Work Day a few years back, we ate lunch at that cafe down the street. It had that Black Forest cake she swooned over.

The memory settles me more firmly into place. The people walking by are a blur of jeans and modern jackets, running shoes and stiletto heels, cell phones in hands or at ears. The air I breathe in is laced with exhaust and a salty-greasy smell from the fast food restaurant next to us. The tension in my chest eases slightly.

This is my world. Still here, just like it'll still be waiting after wherever we go next. I reach into my purse, curling my fingers around my phone. I could call Angela, or Lisa, or Bree—Mom or Dad, even—if I wanted to. But I don't know what I'd say, or if I might make some inadvertent shift that would definitely bring the Enforcers this way. Still, it's nice knowing I could.

Win shifts his weight from foot to foot in silent impatience. I only asked for a few minutes here, but now that I'm back, surrounded by the sights and smells and sounds that tell me I belong, the thought of leaving this all behind again is painful.

I could stay here after all. I could just walk away.

And leave Win to face the Enforcers alone. And go back on my word. *We've still got my planet to save.* Who knows if this city will even be here tomorrow if the other Travelers keep making their experimental shifts?

I press my hand against the side of the restaurant, letting the sense of my city wash over me. The sense of the world I'm defending. Then I turn back to Win.

"Okay," I say. "I'm ready." And this time I believe it.

We duck back into the shadows, and into the time cloth. As the folds close around me, I remember those first halting jumps when we were trying to leave the Louvre.

"They didn't do something to damage your cloth, did they?" I say.

"What?"

"The Enforcers. It didn't really jump the first couple times."

"Oh," Win says. "No, it was just being finicky. Like … a car stalling. I just had to get it going and then it was fine. We made it here, didn't we?"

I'd rather we'd made it with a brand-new, top-of-the-line time cloth that didn't stall. I'd guess that's what the Enforcers are working with. At least Win doesn't seem to think it's a problem that'll get worse.

He must already have programmed our next destination in, because he only has to tap the panel before we've lifted off. I'm almost relieved to feel the shaking, spinning motion that says we're really Traveling. Bracing myself, I squeeze down my nausea.

It feels like a while before we hit the ground. Trees stand around us, banding the sides of the tent.

"The hills over Vietnam's Bach Dang River, 938 AD," Win announces. "On the eve of the great rebellion. The battle takes place on the river, so whatever trail Jeanant's left us to the next part of the weapon, it's probably down there."

"Why didn't we go straight there?" I ask, and then realize the answer on my own. "Because if the Enforcers trace the jump, that would lead them right to us and Jeanant."

"They shouldn't be able to," Win says, like he did before. "Just a precaution. But we should still get moving."

He whips back the cloth to reveal a dirt road mottled with hoofprints and wheel ruts. The breeze is cool and damp, with a smell like the park back home just after a rain shower, but muskier. Win heads down the road, folding the cloth as he walks. My boots squelch through patches of gooey mud as I hurry to catch up. Massive ferns line the road around the mossy trunks of the broad-leaved trees, their twisting branches heavy with loops of vine. The buzz of insect life quavers around us. It presses in on me, and for a second I can't breathe. I curl my fingers into my palm, trying to bring back the feel of the buildings back home, then train my eyes on Win's satchel, on the rounded edges of the brass buckles, the scuffs on the smooth leather. The suffocating presence of the jungle recedes.

The road veers up a slope scattered with chunks of lichen-splotched rock. We're just nearing the top when twigs crackle somewhere behind us. I recoil, stepping toward the shelter of the trees. Win turns. No one's in sight, but a low thudding is carrying toward us. Like many sets of feet treading over the packed earth.

The alarm band around my ankle is still. "It's not your people," I say.

"Then that's most likely more of the army arriving," Win whispers. "Let's get out of the way. If they see us, we could shift something."

I was on board as soon as he said the word *army*. He squeezes through the heavy underbrush, me behind him, droplets of water dappling my shirt and dress. The jagged fronds scrape against my arms. As I push them away from my face, shivers slide over my fingers. I jerk my hands away.

Win has stopped. He grabs my wrist and tugs me down behind a particularly large fern.

The tramping sound is getting louder. From where we're crouched, I can make out slivers of the rutted road. There's no noise other than those footsteps and the insect hum.

Then they sweep into view: a stream of figures marching in rows four across, their plated armor and rounded helmets glinting, swords swaying at their hips. They stride past, perfectly in sync. Despite the muddy road, each soldier's uniform looks polished and clean.

Well, this appears to be a much more effective revolutionary force than the scattered locals we saw in Paris. Organized, disciplined. In a few minutes, they've tramped out of sight over the crest of the hill.

"They'll be going to join the battle that'll take place along the river in the next couple days," Win says quietly. "The Chinese army is coming to meet them, to put down the Vietnamese insurgents. But this time the Vietnamese are going to win their freedom."

He motions me onward through the jungle. "There might be more coming. We'll be safer staying off the road."

We weave between the trees and stumble onto a narrow trail running nearly parallel to the road. I study the back of Win's head, its slight bobbing in time with his strides, trying to imagine the massive databases he must have had access to on his home planet. Catalogs of thousands of years of history from all across Earth. I've never even heard of this battle. He knows so much more about my planet's history than I do, and I'm the one who lives here.

The one big question that's been gnawing at me rises up.

"Why did your people start doing this in the first place?" I say. "Studying Earth, experimenting … Your science is light-years ahead of ours; you don't care about art; you have to cross the galaxy just to get here—what did you all expect to learn from a bunch of humans?"

"Ah …" Win glances back at me, looking as if he's swallowed a fly. "That's pretty complicated."

"As if everything else you've told me wasn't? Try me."

There's silence as we haul ourselves up the steepest part of the hill, gripping the coils of vine and disturbing flowers that expel whiffs of a thick, cloying fragrance into the air.

Win's breath rasps with the effort, so loudly I start to worry the soldiers up ahead will hear it. He wobbles a little, but keeps going as the trail slants downward. Still not answering.

"Win," I say. "Why can't you just tell me? It's not like I'm ever going to give away your 'secrets'—no one would believe me if I tried."

"I don't see why it matters," he says.

"I want to understand why you did this to us," I say, and he grimaces.

"It's not a good story," he says. "No one really talks about it, except to remind ourselves … A long time ago, some of our people made an incredibly huge mistake. A mistake so big it destroyed our world."

"Just like that?"

He nods. "A new technology was introduced, and imple-mented widely, without quite as much testing as should have been done, and— Imagine if every nuclear plant on Earth simultaneously melted down and then exploded, multiplied by a hundred. We had just enough warning to evacuate some people to what you'd call a space station that was orbiting the planet before the atmosphere below was completely poisoned."

"Oh," I say, a trickle of horror running through me. *Every nuclear plant times a hundred.*

"We've all lived on that space station ever since," he goes on. "Expanding and improving it as necessary. And suppos-edly making plans for moving on. When the disaster happened, our scientists had already been scouting out planets to establish a colony on. But then, after the accident, everyone was scared of rushing in too quickly and making another mistake, losing the little we'd managed to hold on to. You have to understand, in the beginning—it was the fate of our entire people at stake. Once we set a course, we were only going to get one chance."

"Earth was one of those planets?" I venture. "To *colonize*—"

"Obviously that didn't happen," he says quickly. "They wanted to run a few experiments somewhere, to see what sort of challenges we might face, and how the inhabitants might deal with it. Use a time field so we could have them do things over, and check what factors influenced the outcome. They picked Earth. The original idea was that they'd run a relatively brief series of tests and then move in, but after a few years of trials and Traveling, the scientists started noticing discrepancies in the readings. They realized the shifts were degrading the planet."

Ah. "You didn't want a planet that was already starting to fall apart," I say. It was good enough for the Travelers to escape to and play around with, but not good enough to be a home.

There's no way I want Win's people moving in with us, but it hurts anyway. The thought that they used us and would keep using us until we're not fit for anything except being thrown away. How long will it take after we've stopped them for the world to recover?

"We should have ended it a long time ago," Win says. "I know that. Lots of us know. It's just, the scientists, especially the ones doing the time work, they're respected, and they like the way things are. And when you've been so cautious for so long, it's hard to even think about doing something risky. No one knows what will be waiting for us on another planet."

"But you're all stuck in that space station—you said the people who aren't Travelers never leave at all."

"We've gotten by for so long that way, no one knows any different. Most people don't see any need to hurry." He pauses. "But Jeanant, and Thlo, they suspect the longer we keep delaying, the more likely it is the station's engines will fail when we finally do leave orbit."

The breeze licks under my scarf, the cool moisture it carries making the wool cling to my neck. "So they'll put us through hell, destroy *our* planet, and maybe even screw up your own people's chances, just to avoid a little risk."

"You'd understand better if you grew up there," Win says. "But I hate it too."

The trail curves around a spire of craggy rock jutting from the soil, and as we come around it, the trees fall back, giving us a glimpse of the land below: a wide blue river snaking through the jungle, sandy banks shimmering in the sunlight piercing the gathering clouds. The circular walls of a town stand farther to our left, brown roofs rising into sharp peaks.

Win draws in a breath, gazing at the view. The awe on his face is almost painful to look at. It chokes off my anger. It makes sense now, his comments about the lack of room, about trees and sun. He doesn't even have an *outside* where he's from.

He turns and hurries on. My vision seems to ripple as I follow. The trail narrows, the jungle pressing closer, and then slants more steeply downward.

My feet skid on the slick soil. I grip the branches of a nearby sapling to catch my balance. The feel of the moist bark sends a shudder through my fingers. The trees drown out the view, trunks and vines and leaves twice as big as my head crowding around me. I hold out my hands, snatching at stems, twigs. They seem to slip through my grasp. My skin is too thin.

I shake my head, but the sensation lingers: the world around me expanding and contracting as if I've stumbled into a fun-house mirror maze. My legs wobble, and I cling to a fern, feeling as though my hands are about to pass right through it.

It's not like Paris. Or maybe it is, just … more.

A thousand years of shifting, of distortion and degradation, that the atoms making up my body have experienced and this jungle hasn't.

Ahead of me, Win still stands out against the jungle with his alien presence, but I have to stare to see it. Because it's not that I'm fading, only that this past world is more solid than the one I was in before.

I fumble in my purse for my bracelet as I scramble on down the trail, trying to count the points on the leaves, the pebbles on the ground. Everything I look at echoes that solid *there*ness back at me. The jungle sways, or maybe it's me.

The smooth surface of the beads meets my fingertips as my heel lands on a loose rock. I don't even have a chance to catch my balance before my feet are shooting out from under me.

16.

I grope for something to steady myself. My free hand finds only air. I hit the ground hip first, a yelp jolting from my throat.

Saplings and shrubs claw at me as I tumble down the hillside. My ankle bangs against a tree trunk and pain stabs up my leg. I roll over, flailing until my fingers catch a loop of vine. My arm wrenches, but I jerk to a stop. I drag in a breath, my heart and head pounding.

"Skylar!" Pebbles skitter as Win scrambles down the trail. He comes to a stop by my left and picks his way over. "Are you all right?"

"I don't know." My shoulder throbs as I prop myself up on my hands. My ankle, the one that hit the tree trunk, is radiating a stinging pain. The tongue of my boot is bent to the side, and a wide scrape runs from my anklebone halfway up my calf. Blood's beading on the raw skin.

I wiggle my foot, and the pain stings only a little deeper. I think I should be able to walk. Just won't be running any races today.

"It doesn't look that bad," Win says hopefully.

Too bad the rest of me still feels like crap. I glance up, and the jungle presses in with a rush of dizziness. I close my eyes. Then I realize what's really wrong with my ankle.

"The alarm band!" I twist around, searching the damp soil beside me. It must have been scraped off by the impact. I peer through the trees, trying to figure out which one my ankle hit. They blur together.

Win's gone still. "It came off? But then— Here." He tosses down a small pad of tan fabric that he's taken from his satchel. "Put that on the wound. I'll look for the band."

He clambers up the slope without waiting to see if I caught the pad, shoving aside stems and fronds to scan the ground. I'd be annoyed if I didn't want so badly to get up there and help him look. I pick up the square of fabric and set it over the bloodiest part of the scrape. The second I apply pressure, the pad seems to fuse with my leg. The line between its edge and my skin smooths away. I flinch, and then reach to poke at it. I can't even feel the edge. How am I ever supposed to take it *off*?

Above me on the slope, Win swears.

"Isn't it there?" I say.

"It might have … disintegrated," he replies, wrenching aside another sapling. "Traveler tech is programmed to do that in Earth's atmosphere, in certain conditions, to make sure nothing's left behind accidentally that the locals could study. Your fall could have set something off."

My stomach sinks. "So we'll have no warning if the Enforcers show up."

He shakes his head.

That ... isn't good. My thoughts are still swimming in my head as if it's full of water. I reach for my purse, panic flashing through me when I see the flap's open. But both my phone and my bracelet are still tucked inside. I drag the bracelet out and hold it against my palm, sliding my fingers over the beads. Slowly, the weight of history recedes.

"Well, you said it isn't likely they could be tracing our jumps, right?" I say. "We'll just need to be even more careful about shifts than we were in Paris."

"We'll have to manage," Win agrees. "Can you stand up?"

I grasp a low branch and haul myself upright. My ankle twinges, but not too badly. Why do I feel so weak? I swallow. My mouth tastes like dust.

The last time I had a drink was a thousand years from now.

"We should have brought canteens," I say as Win edges back to me, a weak attempt at a joke.

"What?" Win says. "Oh. I do have— Come on, you can drink while we're walking."

He reaches into his satchel as we pick our way back to the trail, and hands me a narrow bottle of blue-tinted liquid. By the time I figure out how to open its oddly pointed cap, my hands are shaking. I bring the bottle to my lips. The liquid is cool and faintly sweet. As it slides down my throat, my thoughts sharpen. The residual dizziness fades away.

"Traveling takes a lot out of you," Win says. "You should probably eat something too. Here."

He trades me a plastic packet for the bottle. I'm expecting some sort of exotic alien snack, but it's just standard Earth trail mix: peanuts and almonds and dried fruit. I guess to Win, *this* is an exotic snack. I pop a few handfuls in my mouth. When I look around, the *there*ness of the jungle only feels half as imposing.

The ground starts to even out as we shuffle on. The sun glints here and there through the gray haze of the clouds, but the air's so damp my clothes are chilly against my skin. The hem of my dress snags on thorns and twigs, dirt stains mingling with the ink.

As I stuff the half-finished bag of trail mix into my purse, Win holds out his hand to bring us to a halt. "Pull your scarf up over your face," he says. "We're already going to stand out more than I'd like. I think we'll be safest if we stay out of the locals' way completely."

I'm fine with that. I pull the folds of my scarf over my nose, my breath making the air beneath the fabric even more humid.

The trail peters out into the dense vegetation. We creep on to the jungle's edge.

"Jeanant should have left another hint, like he did with the newspapers in Paris," Win says. "'The sign will point at the sky,' the message said. As soon as you see anything that feels odd …"

As if I need a reminder of my function here.

A smattering of trees dots the grassy ground ahead of us, leading to a well-trampled road. On the other side, the grass gives way to alternating stretches of marsh and rocky yellow beach, slanting down toward dark greenish water. The river is so wide it looks more like a lake, though its surface ripples with the current. A wash of misty air drifts off of it.

On a nearby span of beach, several dozen men are gathered, hunched over long poles of bamboo. Conical straw hats shade their faces as they slice at the ends of the poles with carving knives, cutting them into points. They all move with the same sort of steady, efficient rhythm as the soldiers who passed us before, not a word exchanged between them. A heap of already-carved poles lies by the side of the road.

"That's how they'll beat the Chinese," Win murmurs to me eagerly. "They fix those poles in the river, just beneath the surface, and lure the enemy ships onto them. Brilliant strategy. It lets them kill or capture most of their opponents, including the prince leading them, while losing few of their own soldiers. I saw satellite footage once, but … it's different being right here."

The way he's staring at the workers, talking about them as if this battle is being put on for his entertainment, makes my skin tighten. When he looks at me, raising his eyebrows as if to share the excitement, I have to glance away.

"When's the Chinese army coming?"

"They arrive tomorrow. These will be the last preparations. And then everyone here will be free to rule themselves for the first time in hundreds of years."

Despite my discomfort, those words strike a chord in me. If these people can defeat a larger power with good tactics and some well-placed pieces of wood, it's not so insane to think Win and I—and Jeanant—can beat the Enforcers, is it?

A scraping sound at our right draws my attention. A figure slides into view amid the vegetation: a boy, no more than nine or ten years old I'd guess, scrambling down from a branch he must have been perched on. His straw hat dangles against his back. He peers around him with wide eyes, and his gaze finds me. His mouth drops open.

Win mutters a curse as the kid darts toward the beach. "Let's get going," he says. "Before anyone comes investigating." He pulls me back into the thicker tangle of the jungle. The boy's chattering voice filters through the trees. We push on as quickly as we can, wading around clumps of fern. I keep glancing back, but no one seems to be following us. That doesn't mean the boy seeing us didn't shift something, though.

"With all your special Traveler tech, no one thought of inventing something that'd make the locals see you as someone like them?" I ask.

Win stops, panting. "Someone did, actually," he says. "There are devices that project over the face ... but we only managed to get our hands on a few of those. The others have them. I wasn't supposed to be going anywhere it'd be that hard to blend in."

I guess in my present day, he could have pretended to be a tourist just about anywhere and no one would have blinked.

We stand still for a minute, waiting and listening, but all I hear is his rasping breath and the leaves hissing in the rising wind. Win motions me back toward the river. We slink along until we can make out the road again.

Back the way we came, the workers are still bent over their poles. The boy is puttering along the grassy strip between the jungle and the road, scanning the jungle's depths, scowling in a way that looks both sulky and determined. I've seen a similar expression on Benjamin's face when he's tackling a new math concept he hasn't quite wrapped his head around.

I guess the adults felt finishing their preparations was more important than following up on some kid's story about two strangers in the woods. And now he's searching for more proof. Trying to be a hero. Even though I don't want him to succeed, I feel a twinge of sympathy.

"Nothing yet?" Win says.

"Nothing seems off."

We continue through the jungle, staying close enough to the fringes to keep an eye on the road and the riverbank beyond. Another squad of soldiers marches past, followed by a line of donkeys pulling carts laden with piles of those bamboo poles. My ankle starts to ache in dull protest. There are a lot of things pointing at the thickly clouded sky: trees, rooftops, the distant hills. But everything looks perfectly normal.

Just like in Paris. The only thing my special sensitivity found us in Paris was the sign that the Enforcers had arrived. It didn't help us follow Jeanant's clues at all. I bite my lip.

We come to a stop about thirty feet from the first buildings around the town.

"Well, I don't think we should try to go right into town," Win says after an awkward silence. "In this atmosphere, they won't be welcoming to foreigners. It'd be almost inevitable that we shift something noticeable. But I suppose—"

He's interrupted by a patter on the leaves above us. Rain sprinkles down on our heads. I step closer to the nearest tree, wiping the moisture from my face. Win grins. He spreads his arms and lifts his chin as if welcoming the weather. It occurs to me that space stations wouldn't have rain. This might be the first time he's ever felt it.

The patter picks up, from a rattling to a drumbeat. Before I have time to call out to Win, we're in the midst of an all-out deluge. The rain rips past the leaves and thunders over us. Chuckling, Win rushes to my side. He pulls the time cloth into its tent shape around us, and the rain fades into a heavy warbling against the fabric sides.

I swipe at my dripping hair. My shirt's dripping too—my dress, my boots—everything's soaked. The fringe of my scarf is sending a steady trickle over my face. I peel it off my hair and sling it over my shoulders, shivering. I haven't been this soaked since Lisa dared Bree and I to run a mile during the first big thunderstorm the summer after freshman year, and at least then we had a house to duck back into and towels to wrap ourselves in.

The world outside has gone watery, as if we're standing under an umbrella in the middle of a waterfall. Win brings up the data panel on the wall. "We could jump forward to this afternoon, or tomorrow morning. See if we can pick up the trail then. Jeanant might not have gotten here yet." He's still smiling.

"We still won't know where to look," I say, crossing my arms over my chest. I picture Jeanant as I saw him in the gallery, and try to imagine him here. Where would he go—what would he use?

I have no idea. And even if I find him again, what are the chances he'll think I'm worth talking to now? I must look like a drowned rat. A drowned, battered, muddy rat. At least I don't remotely resemble any Enforcer I've seen. Though I wouldn't mind having one of those peacoats right now.

A sputter of laughter escapes me at the thought. Win turns.

"What?"

"Oh, nothing," I say. "Other than I could use a towel and a change of clothes, and the Enforcers could be five feet away right now and we'd have no idea, and are we even sure this definitely is the right place? Maybe Jeanant's first message was delivered too late, and we're supposed to be in a completely different century."

"Hey," Win says, touching my shoulder. "We're on the right track. I'm sure of it. The numbers, the line about the dragons, it all fits together. We've managed to stay ahead of the Enforcers so far. I've kept you safe, haven't I?"

I nod.

"So you don't have to worry."

I want to believe him. He holds my gaze, his deep blue eyes completely earnest, and my shivers ease. "Okay," I say.

He pauses, his eyes not leaving mine. His smile comes back, softer now. "I'm not going to let anything happen to you."

His hand rises to brush a few stray strands of damp hair from my cheek. At the contact of his skin against mine, my awareness narrows, away from the frightening world outside to the small space between us inside the walls of the tent. The tingling realness of his fingertips. They linger, his thumb grazing the line of my cheekbone.

I open my mouth, meaning to argue or just to break the sudden charge in the air between us, but his fingers trace down my jaw to the side of my neck, sending a totally different sort of shiver through me, and I can't even breathe. I sway into his touch instinctively, just as he leans in and kisses me.

17.

I've only been kissed by two other boys: Evan, during one of those silly party games in junior high, which was just awkward, and my boyfriend in tenth grade, who was always on the slobbery and grope-y side, which is part of the reason he was only my boyfriend for two months.

Win's kiss is both more practiced and more polite. A question, not a demand. But the touch of his mouth against mine sends a sizzle of electricity through my nerves, so real and *there* it knocks all the sense from my head. My fingers have curled into his shirt and my lips are parting before my mind has quite registered what's happening. Win must take that as an answer, because he eases closer, deepening the kiss. Hispresenceradiatesaroundme,softskinandwarmbreathand—

He pulls back in what feels like the middle of things, with a shaky inhalation. Not far back, because I'm still clutching his shirt. His hand falls to rest on my wrist, and I let go, blinking at him, my mouth still partly open. I snap it shut as

my momentary daze starts to clear. That was— I don't even—
My thoughts are still scrambled, and he's watching me again,
with a studied intentness. An intentness that makes my body
tense, though I can't explain why.

"Well," I say, fumbling for words. "What was that about?"

"I, ah …" He drops his gaze briefly before giving me a
sheepish smile. "Sorry. I was wondering what it would be like."

At first I'm too muddled to get it. Why exactly is he
apologizing? And what *what* would be like? I don't believe
for a second that's the first time he's kissed someone.

Then his thumb, so strangely solid, skims the back of my
wrist, and it clicks. He's looking at me like he did when he
was getting me to tell him about my sense of the shifts. Like
when I found the change in the history book. Full of awe and
scientific *curiosity*.

He's never even talked to an Earthling before. Of course
he's never kissed one.

I flinch, yanking my hand away. Would I even have
kissed him back if I hadn't been overwhelmed by the alien
realness of him? It was a stupid automatic reaction, and I
gave in to it like a kid in the throes of a desperate crush. I'm
not sure how much I even *like* him. Anger surges up, more
than I knew I had in me.

"I'm not here for you to experiment on," I bite out.

Win's expression freezes guiltily for an instant before he
starts to protest, and that tells me all I need to know.

"What? I—"

"I'm not. Your. Experiment," I say, jabbing at the air between us so he has to step back. The anger makes me feel a lot stronger than the uncertainties that were suffocating me a few minutes ago. "I'm a person, with thoughts and feelings that matter just as much as yours do, even if your people have time fields and galaxy-crossing spaceships and all sorts of technology I can't even imagine. I am *trying* to help you, and you still think it's fine to treat me like I'm a toy, the same way all of you have been playing around with everyone on Earth for so long. And I. Am. Sick of it."

"I didn't mean …" Win begins, and doesn't seem to know how to finish. He looks a little sick himself. Good.

"That's the problem," I say. "You didn't mean it. You just wanted to see 'what it would be like.' Well, congratulations, now you know."

He reaches out as if to grasp my arm, as if he can pull forgiveness out of me, and all the times he's grabbed me before, tugged me down streets and through buildings— through the jungle we're in right now—flash through my mind. My stomach turns. I've known all along that I'm just a tool to him. But some part of me believed he was starting to respect me at least a little, to see me as more than a *wrong*ness detector and a wide-eyed simpleton he could show off to.

I dodge him, angling toward the front of the tent. "Don't touch me," I say. "Don't *ever* touch me again." He's still too close. I can't stand being stuck in this cramped space with him, not after what just happened.

I push aside the flaps and duck out. The rain has lightened to a drizzle, dappling my cheeks and my uncovered hair. I reach for my scarf instinctively, and my eyes catch on something pale moving through the deeper jungle.

The figure stalking through the brush is far enough away that she disappears here and there between the trunks and ferns. She's wearing a loose, dark brown costume that covers her from her feet to the top of her head, and her face appears to have the same tan coloring as the locals. It's only her hand that gives her away. A flicker of ice-pale fingers as she holds up something in her palm to consult it.

The woman from the cafe—the Enforcer. My heart stutters.

Then Win comes bursting out of the time cloth, snapping it down against his arm. "Skylar, it's not—" he says, and the woman's head whips up. She lunges forward, her hand dipping to the weapon at her hip, and I spin toward Win.

"The Enforcers," I blurt out with a frantic gesture.

Win flings the cloth out before my words have died in the air, his hand darting to the data panel as the translucent walls form around us. A glint slices through the air. The tent shudders and crackles. But it still moves. We whirl up toward the sky.

The cloth jars to a stop beside a lone stilted house near the side of the road. The river shimmers in the distance, past the sprawl of a rice paddy. The sky has turned clear. My arms ache from hugging my chest, but I can't quite bear to let go.

"Is this where we want to be?" I ask.

"It's the next morning," Win says without glancing up from the display. "Let me find a better spot."

With a lurch and a blink, we've leapt back into the jungle. Win looks around to make sure we're alone, and then nods curtly at the flaps. "We should get some distance from here. It's possible they found us because that kid seeing us shifted something. But for them to keep following us so closely … Maybe they really have figured out how to decode Isis's scrambling to trace our jumps."

Oh. Oh crap.

I hug myself more tightly as we hurry around a thicket of bamboo and through a cluster of massive waxy-leaved plants. The wet skirt of my dress sticks to my legs, hampering my steps over the uneven ground. And the two jumps, though short, have messed with my sense of balance. My foot slips on a lump of moss, and I almost trip. Win's hand shoots out. He jerks it back, just shy of my elbow, as I catch myself.

Don't ever *touch me again.*

I don't want to think about that moment right now. I don't want to talk about it. I just want to make sure I don't get shot by that freaky woman or her colleagues. So I pretend I didn't notice his slip, and he doesn't mention it. We walk on as if nothing has changed.

The jungle around me looms, pressing in. I reach into my purse and grip my bracelet. *Three times three is nine. Three times nine is twenty-seven.* Clusters of five feathery leaves around yellow berries on the bush we're passing. Two scrapes on the bark of that tree.

Win's face is turned ahead, but I can feel him scrutinizing me from the corner of his eye. "I'm fine," I say.

I'm not going to die here. We're going to stay one step ahead of the Enforcers, and then I'll be home, safe and well, before anyone even knows I'm gone.

A chorus of shouts carries through the trees up ahead. We pick up our pace, pushing to the edge of the jungle. There, on the road along the river, lines of men are jogging by, some in armor, many in simple shirts and pants. They're scooping up poles from the heaps we saw being made yesterday and hurrying on toward the town, where the bows of a row of slender ships curve out from the water.

"It's starting," Win says.

"You don't think we're supposed to be right out on the river where the battle is, do you?" I ask. How could Jeanant hide something there? But the rebellion is beginning and they're all leaving, and I don't see any hint to guide us.

"I doubt it," Win says. "But when most of them are off in the boats, it'll be safer for us to investigate the town."

Which would be great, if we'd gotten any idea what we're looking for. "What exactly did the message from the Louvre say again?"

He takes the slab of plastic out of his satchel. "'Repeat the years for my first message to reach you two hundred and sixty-eight times since zero, to the place where a little dragon scares off the big dragon. The sign will point at the sky.'"

As he says the last words, one more group of soldiers strides past, hefting the remaining poles. Their carved tips bob toward the sky. My breath catches.

"The poles!" I say. "They're the key to winning the battle, right? And you said they put them in the river, pointing up?"

"But …" Win edges forward, watching the men march down the road. The sand is marked with the lines of the poles, but none remain. The first few boats are casting off from the shore. "He wouldn't put something we're meant to find *in* the river. There'd be too much risk of losing it."

I turn Jeanant's words over in my head. Imagine him saying them in his smooth, careful voice. "Maybe we're too late," I say. "He said the sign *will* point at the sky—that could mean it won't be pointing yet, but it will in the future. We were supposed to find it before they went off with the poles."

Win's eyes light up. "That makes sense. All we need to do is jump back an hour or two!"

He ducks behind a broad trunk, unfurling the time cloth. I move as close to him as I can while leaving a little space between us. The ground hiccups beneath me, my stomach flips, and we're there, in the paler light of the just-risen sun.

Several heaps of poles lie at intervals along the road. We creep closer. "Does anything look odd about any of the poles to you?" Win asks. "It'll be difficult for us to examine every one without being noticed."

I squint at the heap, but they all look the same. "Let's check the others. There has to be something." Or maybe I'm wrong, and the clue has nothing to do with the poles after all.

We examine the next pile, and the next, each bringing us closer to the town. I scan the jungle, but there's no sign that the pale woman's followed us. Yet. I miss the soothing coil of the alarm band around my ankle.

A faint tramping sound reaches my ears. Another squad of soldiers has come into view on the road toward town, maybe a quarter mile away.

"Quick, before they get here," Win says. He hurries over to study a heap of poles laid on the edge of a patch of marsh. A flicker of color catches my eye. I glance back at the soldiers, judge them at least a few minutes distant, and dart across the road.

It's just a thin scrap of cloth. A scrap dyed three colors— red, purple, and yellow—caught in a crack near the point of a pole at the bottom of the pile, as if it ripped off someone's clothes.

"What?" Win says.

"It's nothing," I say, but I can't quite pull my gaze away. There's *something* about it … I narrow my eyes, staring at the scrap as hard as I can, and it prickles over me. A twinge of that alien *there*ness, as if the fabric is slightly more real than the pole it's caught on.

"That one!" I correct myself, pointing. The soldiers are close enough now that I can hear a question voiced from one to another. I grasp the end of the pole. It only slides out a few inches at my heave. The footsteps behind us speed up to a run.

Damn. As I yank the pole again, Win dives in beside me, grabbing it just below my hands. A few of the other poles clatter over each other, but we wrench ours most of the way out. With one last jerk, it's free.

"Let's go!" Win says. We race across the road, clutching the pole between us.

A thin shout pierces the air. A boy, the one who saw us yesterday I think, is perched in one of the trees by the edge of the jungle. He points to us, calling out, as we crash into the underbrush. All we can do is keep running. Win tugs the pole from my hands, levering it under his arm so we don't have to balance it between us. My ankle starts to throb, but I just push myself faster.

I check behind us once, as we veer around a rotting log, and catch a glimpse of a conical hat in the streaks of sunlight that penetrate the foliage overhead. But only one. When I look again, a minute or two later, there's no sign anyone's chased us this far into the jungle. Either we've lost them, or they decided it wasn't worth pursuing us for one pole out of hundreds.

Win's pulled the loose collar of his shirt up over his mouth—to muffle the rattle of his increasingly ragged breaths, I realize. In spite of it, I can hear the click in his throat. Finally, when my own lungs are starting to ache, he stops. He leans against a boulder, the pole braced against the ground, rasping as he recovers from the run.

Now that I can take a closer look at it, I notice a ring of shallow scratches around the middle of the pole. I lean in. The shapes look like those alien characters. "Here," I say. Win pulls the pole to him.

"Is that it?" I ask. "Jeanant left another message?"

He nods, but his forehead has furrowed. "I think they're directions," he says. "They're not very specific. But it's definitely Jeanant. We're supposed to travel over water and into"—he pauses the way he always does when he's having trouble translating—"a dark that stays deep no matter how brightly the sun is shining."

"That's it?"

"It's the last line from one of his poems. But it referred to the space station—he was talking about the inner passages, the maintenance tunnels."

Why am I not surprised the guy who spoke so eloquently in that recording was also writing poetry in the midst of planning his rebellion?

"Did the people here build underground tunnels?" I say. "Or maybe … There could be caves."

"Those are the most likely possibilities." Win leans the pole against the boulder. "How did you know this was the one?"

"That piece of cloth," I say, motioning to it. "I think Jeanant must have left it. It doesn't feel *wrong* exactly, but it's a little more … real. Like you, and him, and the Enforcers." I pause. "But that's something I notice because of my 'sensitivity,' isn't it? He didn't know you'd have someone like me helping you—how did he expect your group to find it?"

Win slides the scrap out of the crack it was stuck in. It's only the length of his forefinger and about as wide. He rubs it between his fingertips. "It must be something Thlo would have known the significance of. She's the one he was counting on following him here. He didn't know who else she'd bring with him. It's a good thing I had you."

He shoots me a grin, for just a second before it falters and his eyes dart away. As if he thinks he's not even allowed to smile at me. The gesture sets my teeth on edge. I just want him to treat me like an equal, not some puppet for him to use. Why is that so hard?

Turning away, he pulls out the time cloth. The wavering lines that he brings up on the display look vaguely like a topographic map overlaid by a glowing grid. Win motions toward one point, and the lines there enlarge.

"There's a network of caves in the side of the hills we came down from," he says. "As well as on the other side of the river. I suppose we should start here, only take another jump if we have to."

"But if he said we have to go over water—"

"There's a stream, here," Win says, tracing the line. "That could be what he meant. Let's find out."

18.

We set off again, Win in the lead. Soon, the pale gray face of a cliff looms above the treetops. Shoulders of rock poke through the underbrush.

The cliff face is spotted with openings, many far above our heads. Between them, vines and bushes and even trees creep across the wider outcroppings, as if the stone is dappled with pockets of jungle. We follow it, examining the shadowy gaps. How are we supposed to know which one Jeanant used?

Then I spot it. Scratched beside a large curved opening, a symbol like a burst of flame.

Prometheus.

"Hey," Win says, staring at it. He's only taken two steps when he jerks to a halt and stumbles backward. His breath hitches.

"What?" I say, bracing myself for some unseen enemy. But Win's shaking his head with a sudden smile.

"I caught it that time," he says. "If I'd kept going, I'd have been doxed. Someone's nearby."

"Jeanant?" He must have placed that thread not long ago. I could get my second chance.

"I hope so," Win says. "There's no way for me to know for sure. Are you … okay to try talking to him again?"

"Yeah," I say, though my nerves have gone jittery. I will *not* screw things up this time. "I'll mention Thlo right away."

"Good. And be careful, in case it's not him. If it is, once he realizes you're with our group, you shouldn't have to explain very much. We need to get all the parts of the weapon. Maybe he has them on him and he can just give them to you; maybe he can tell you directly where we need to go. He should know the best way to proceed."

"All right." Just present myself and let Jeanant figure out the rest. Shouldn't be that hard.

"I'll wait right here," Win says, ducking into the shelter of a tree.

The cave entrance is several feet wide and high, with a tangle of ferns and saplings stretching along a ledge just above it. A series of boulders rambles away from its right side in a jagged line. Just a few feet within the opening, the shadows blend into total darkness. I square my shoulders and head inside.

The daylight behind me fades quickly, the air between the rocky walls cooling with a faintly chalky smell. My damp clothes chill my skin.

The passage narrows, until I can touch both sides with my arms outstretched. My sense of the space ahead has faded into hazy gray impressions. I hesitate, then remember the phone in my purse.

I pull it out and turn it on. The glow of the screen glints off the ripples in the cave floor and the dribbles of moisture sliding down the rough walls. My wallpaper photo beams at me—the one Evan snapped of Angela, Bree, and Lisa, and me, our faces sunlit and fingers raised in victory signs in front of the biggest roller coaster at the amusement park we trekked out to this August. The roller coaster I made myself go on with the rest of them, even though the jolts and scares of the rides echo the panic of the *wrong* feelings.

I'm doing this—tramping across centuries and continents, holding myself together—for them. So there will be more summers and more amusement parks and more goofy photos. So we're all safe.

The reminder steadies me. I walk on, holding the screen close to my side. There's nothing ahead but blackness. I've been moving forward another minute or two when a light flickers in its midst.

I freeze. The light flickers again, and settles into a faint glow. I switch off my phone, setting my feet down as softly as I can manage. As I draw nearer, the cave splits into two passages, the glimmer down the one to my left. I continue toward it.

The glow is hitting the wall at a bend in the passage, emanating from somewhere beyond that turn. I'm just a few feet away when a figure steps out to meet me.

The light only catches the side of his face, but even as I squeak in shock, I recognize Jeanant. He's still wearing his Traveler clothes, but his head is bare, his black curls tied back from his face and a thin gray cloak replacing the Parisian jacket at his shoulders. His eyes narrow as he peers at me in the darkness.

"I know Thlo," I blurt out. "I'm not with the Enforcers. I'm trying to help you."

The tension in his stance has relaxed before I'm finished the first sentence. He smiles, giving me an echo of the feeling I had when I met him in the Louvre. The certainty that we're doing something *right* here.

"I know," he says warmly. "I heard you just as I was leaving Paris, but I didn't think it was safe to return. Any change in the order of my plans is risky. I hope you can understand why I assumed the worst."

"It's okay," I say. "I should have explained right away."

He eases forward. His gaze hasn't left my face once. There's a sort of wonder in his expression.

"I've been trying to understand why, if Thlo realized what I meant to do and followed me immediately, she wouldn't have met me herself," he says, and pauses. "But she didn't come immediately, did she?"

I shake my head. "It's all gone the way you planned. The first message—"

"Wait," he interrupts, holding up his hand. "I shouldn't have asked. It's my future. I don't want to test the limits of the time field. Either one of us could be doxed."

"*I'm* not really from your future," I admit. "I'm from here. From Earth."

His eyes widen, but the admiration in them only deepens. Not a hint of Win's clinical curiosity. My nervousness washes out of me.

"I wondered," he says. "That's why you've been able to reach me, and the others haven't, I assume?"

"Yes," I say. "We've been following your instructions. Not always quickly, but …"

"But you're here," he says. "Would you come into the light? I have to be sure you're real."

He moves around the corner of the passage, toward the source of the glow. I follow him into a wide alcove, where the canvas bag he was carrying at the Louvre lies on the cave floor beside a square object a little thicker than my thumb, which is shining with an artificial light.

"Completely real," I say. My confusion must show in my voice, because his smile turns wry.

"It's been several days, and the Enforcers haven't been far behind, so I haven't had much chance for sleep. An apparition arriving to tell me that everything I've worked for is coming to fruition—it's exactly the sort of hallucination my mind would want to conjure up right now."

Here in the brighter light, I can see the signs of strain. The creases around his mouth, the slightly ashen cast to his bronze skin, that I'm not sure were there in Paris. What was just a few hours for me was obviously much more for him. Just how long has he been jumping through time, distracting and evading the Enforcers while waiting for the safest moments to hide the parts of his weapon?

"I'm really here," I say. "And we're going to make sure your plan works. *I'm* going to make sure it works."

A drop of icy water falls from the cave ceiling, sending a shock of cold through my scalp. I wipe it away with a shiver, and Jeanant's eyebrows rise.

"Your clothes are wet. You must be freezing."

Before he's finished speaking, he's unclasping his cloak. He wraps it around me, securing it at the base of my throat. The fabric is so thin I can barely feel its weight, but the chill recedes everywhere it touches.

"You don't have to give me this," I protest, even though I'm already pulling it closer around me.

"You need it more than I do," he says. "At least I was prepared for this trip. There's no way you could have been. I'm glad Thlo trusted you. She's brilliant, but she wasn't always as open-minded as Earth's people deserve. It must be so difficult for you to understand what my people have done to your planet, and yet you've come all this way to help me.

You're from northeastern America, I'd guess, from your accent? And your clothes—early twenty-first century?"

"Right on both counts," I say.

"Thlo approached you at random … ?" He halts, looking chagrined. "I haven't asked your name."

"It's Skylar," I say. "And, no, not exactly." It seems too complicated to try to explain Win's situation, so I skip that part. "I was noticing the shifts. It turns out I'm sensitive to when the past's been changed. And your group, um, noticed that I was noticing."

"So you've always felt something wasn't right," Jeanant says, and I nod. His voice softens. "To live with a sense you had no way of understanding—and to fight with us, now that you do know—that sort of bravery doesn't come very often. Thank you."

I should be the one thanking him. Jeanant's shown more respect for me in the last five minutes than Win has the entire time I've been around him. I wonder how Jeanant got to the place where he stopped seeing us as test subjects and recognized we were people too.

"And now I need to apologize again, for rambling," Jeanant goes on. "It's been so good, to *talk* to someone properly. You've come to meet me for a reason."

"Yes," I say. "We tried to find you again so you can tell me how we can finish this."

"You've done perfectly so far," he says. "I've no doubt now we *will* finish it. I just want you to know I wish I'd gotten here sooner. I wish someone had thought to do this before me."

"It isn't your fault," I protest.

"Everyone on Kemya is at fault for this terrible situation," he says. "And it's my fault I didn't plan my moves carefully enough to take my shot at the generator, or this would already be over, and you and Thlo and the others would never have had to be in more danger." His mouth twists, and he draws himself up straighter, with that now familiar confidence. "I'm going to do everything in my power to ensure I don't make a second mistake. Which means, as much as I wish we could talk longer—"

He cuts himself off, his head jerking toward the open passage behind me. His hand leaps to a spot on his upper arm, where the outline of a thin band shows faintly through his shirt. "They're here."

He scoops up his bag and the glowing square in one smooth movement. As he motions me deeper into the alcove, he dulls the light against his palm. "Stay here while I lead them the other way," he murmurs. "As soon as they see I'm gone, they'll follow me."

No, he can't go, not yet. "The weapon," I whisper. "The parts. If you have them, you can give them to me—"

"I've already left the second part in the wall," he says. He presses something small and flat into my hand. "When you hear that the Enforcers are gone, twist the corner of this. It'll help you find the spot. And after you'll have to go not far from your region of America, just before blood is spilled where the trees were laid low. That should be all Thlo needs to hear. Be careful."

I snatch after him as he pushes away from me, but I miss his sleeve by an inch. He rushes toward the passage, little more than a lean silhouette in the dimmed light, and I open my mouth to call his name. Then the clatter of footsteps carries from the distant end of the cave. My voice catches. The Enforcers. A group from his time, it must be, or he'd dox them like he does Win. If I shout, I'll bring them right to us.

I flatten myself against the wall. Jeanant's feet thud against the stone as he races away. Someone yells, and the other steps speed up to a run. The dimmed glow of Jeanant's light fades away completely. A twanging quavers through the air, and I wince.

But they must have missed, or maybe they shot after Jeanant had already whisked away in his time cloth. Through the pitch dark, a few muttered sentences in the alien language drift down the passage: annoyed, not triumphant. Someone sighs. And then there's no sound at all.

I wait as the silence stretches on, until I can't stand the blackness any longer. Then I fumble with the token Jeanant placed in my hand. One of the corners bends when I press it. I twist, and light sprays from its surface.

It's just like the square he was carrying. The alcove feels more eerie now that I'm alone in it. The warmth of Jeanant's cloak gives me only a small comfort.

I probably should have given it back to him. But there wasn't time. There wasn't even time to get all the information from him I think Win wanted. *Before blood is spilled where the trees were laid low.* I have no idea what that means. Maybe Win will. Jeanant said it would be all we needed. I guess he'll leave the other two parts there for us, with whatever instructions he didn't have time to give me now. He might not have had the remaining parts on hand.

There's still the one he said he left here. I step back, examining the cave wall, then running my fingers over it. Finally, about halfway down, they catch on a crease that wobbles. Digging at it with my nails, I pry a chunk of the rock free.

There. Another slab of that alien plastic, about as long and wide as my forearm, lies in the crevice I've opened up. I pull it out. A rectangle of metal much like the first Win found, but twice as large, is embedded inside it amid lines of etched characters. It's come with another message.

I tuck the slab under my arm as I creep back down the passage. The entrance is a bright speck in the distance. I hurry toward it, wondering where Jeanant is now. If this place with the trees is the answer, if his role in the mission will be finished there, will he be able to go home? I know he hasn't made it back to Kemya in Win's present. If he had, he could have told all this to Thlo himself instead of leaving clues.

Seventeen years in the future, Win said. Seventeen years before his group and Jeanant can meet without doxing. Surely the Enforcers will give up their chase before then?

The darkness falls away, the vague shapes of leaves and tree trunks coming into focus beyond the cave entrance. I jog the last short distance, eager to be out in the sun.

The space beneath the tree where Win was going to wait is empty. I swivel, just outside the cave opening. He's nowhere.

The Enforcers, I tell myself, clamping down on panic. The ones who came from Jeanant's time. They'd have doxed Win, or he'd have felt them coming and moved out of range. Now that they're gone, he'll be making his way back here. I just have to wait.

A crimson bird with absurdly long tail feathers flutters down onto one of the boulders in their jagged row beside me. A branch creaks. And then an out-of-tune twang hums through the air from somewhere to my right.

I flinch around. Someone's crashing through the brush— there's a hollered command. I throw myself in the opposite direction, toward the line of boulders. My shoulder jars against one as I scramble behind it, and there's another shout. Twigs crackle underfoot, far too close. I crouch down, trying to listen over the thundering of my heartbeat. Was I seen?

A brittle voice calls out in words I don't understand. It's the pale woman's voice. I stiffen. I don't know if she's trying to talk to me, or her companions. She says something else, but still in the alternately staccato and slurred syllables of their alien language.

The slab Jeanant left weighs heavy in my lap. I can't let her get this.

I peer around me. There's a rustle in the bushes a few feet away, near the mouth of the cave. The point of a straw hat and a childish face show through the broad leaves. A pair of frightened eyes stare at me, and then flick back to the area in front of the cave. Where I guess the pale woman is standing.

It's the boy who followed us before. We didn't lose him after all. He must have staked out the cave after he saw me go in, determined to get his proof of our treachery. He couldn't have expected it to turn out like this. And I can tell he doesn't have any more of an idea how to escape than I do.

Then another voice rings out, from somewhere farther away. "Why don't you let us leave peacefully? We haven't done anything wrong."

It's Win. I swallow the cry of relief that rises in my throat.

"Stay where you are," he continues. "I'll go."

He's talking in English. Just to be sure I'll recognize his voice, or because he wants me to understand what he's saying? Did he mean that last instruction for me? Stay where I am. He'll go … to me? Considering he's the one with the time cloth, that sounds like a reasonable plan.

As long as the pale woman doesn't get to me first. "We will apprehend you," she says, switching languages automatically at Win's lead. Her accent is thicker, breaking the words into sharp fragments. "It will be as easy, or difficult, as you decide. I would prefer to bring you both back alive, but we only need one."

She sounds nearer than before. I adjust my weight over my knees, so I can propel myself forward if I need to run. Glancing over at the boy, I raise a finger to my lips, hoping he'll understand the gesture. But he isn't even looking at me. His face is rigid with fear.

"I'd prefer none," Win retorts. He sounds almost as if he's above us. I stare in the direction his voice seemed to come from, and glimpse a flicker of golden-brown skin amid the tangle of vine-strung saplings on the ledge over the cave.

"If you truly meant to protect this planet, you would let us remove you," the woman says, her steps crunching closer. "You are playing with history here as much as anyone else."

Leaves ripple over the cave entrance. Win's almost at the edge of the ridge above the boy's head. But he's still too far away, and the woman sounds as though she's just steps from reaching me. I ease forward, readying myself to dash to meet him, and the boy's gaze darts up.

He must see Win creeping toward him. A yelp bursts from his mouth. *He* bolts, out of the brush, toward the shelter of the cave. Straight into the pale woman's line of sight.

My arm flies out, as if there's any chance of me stopping him. He's past me, bare feet skittering on the rock-strewn ground. I leap up just as that awful twang splits the air. A stream of energy slams into the boy's legs, and he topples onto his hands and knees.

"It's a local," a man is saying, on the other side of the clearing. "He saw us." The pale woman, standing just a few feet from the cave, is already flicking a switch on her weapon.

"I know," she snaps, and pulls the trigger before my protest reaches my lips.

This shot doesn't just twang, it shrieks. The blast rams into the boy's head, sending a shudder through his body as he slumps to the ground. The side of his face is blackened, his left eye nothing more than a cinder, his skin crackled like overheated plastic. He doesn't so much as twitch again.

I register that in the second it takes the pale woman to whirl toward me. Win leaps from the underbrush at the base of the cliff, racing across the last few feet between us.

"No!" I try to say as he flings the time cloth around us, but my throat is so hoarse I can barely hear myself. Our surroundings spin away in a blur of color and the wailing of the wind.

19.

The cloth lurches around me. The image of the boy's charred body shudders with it, imprinted on the back of my eyelids. Shudders, then slumps. Shudders, then slumps. Alive, and then, in an instant, completely extinguished.

Burnt to a crisp. Bile rises in my throat. She didn't even think about it. He was a local. He saw their tech. She killed him.

She wouldn't have been there at all if it weren't for Win and me. *He* was only there because he followed us. Where was he supposed to be, that day, before we came?

"Skylar," Win is saying. The air outside the cloth has stopped screaming. "Skylar, we're okay now. We made it."

"He's dead," I say, trembling. "He's dead because of us."

"What?" Win says. "The kid? That's what the Enforcers do. That one woman, Kurra, I've heard stories about her. Apparently she has an even more brutal streak than the others."

You are playing with history here as much as anyone else, she said.

I train my gaze on the blurred landscape beyond the cloth, trying to escape the thoughts rushing through my head. But it's true. True with a *wrong*ness that peals right through me. He wasn't just a kid. He was part of history. Not just on that day, but the next—and the next week, and the next year, and on and on.

"One Earthling's life, it doesn't mean anything to them," Win's saying. "Even one Kemyate life doesn't matter that much. Which is why we have to—"

"But it's not just him," I interrupt. "He wouldn't have died before, because we wouldn't have been there for him to follow—he would have grown up and had his own kids and those kids would have had kids and … A thousand years. A thousand years of generations and all those people are gone. They're gone because of *us*."

Hundreds of faces, lives, vanished into oblivion with one shriek of Kurra's blaster. Snuffed out down the long chain of history as easily as hitting a Delete key. I sink down on the floor of the time-cloth tent.

"Skylar, you don't know that," Win says, but he sounds less certain now. "He could have died that afternoon, in the battle, or tomorrow, or the day after, some other way. It could be hardly any difference at all."

"Or maybe it's a huge difference," I say. "Maybe—maybe he, or one of his descendants, grew up to be some brilliant leader, or scientist, or—" The possible immensity of it overwhelms me. All it takes is the loss of one person somewhere along one influential family tree, and it's not just hundreds but billions of lives rewritten. The siren call of *wrong, wrong, wrong* blares in my ears. I cover my face, but I can't shut it out. I can't shut it out because it's coming from inside me.

"It's not your fault," Win says, standing over me. "There wasn't anything you could do. Kurra killed him, not us. And we have to move, Skylar. If they're tracing us, we have to get away from this spot before they decode the signal."

I shake my head and it just spins more. The words keep falling out. "I should have known. I should have noticed he was still following us, made him leave. I should have seen …"

Win sucks in a breath with what sounds like a growl. A flick of his hand brings up the glowing data panel.

I stare at my knees, Jeanant's plastic slab pressed against my abdomen, as the world outside blurs and returns. Blurs and returns. Day, night, buildings, countryside. Each lurch makes my gut clench tighter. It doesn't matter how many jumps we make, how far we go across space and time. The boy will still be lying there dead in the mouth of a cave near the Bach Dang River, sometime in 938 AD. I don't know if a single one of the worlds outside looks like the one that was mine. I don't know if I can ever go back to the exact time and place I called home. It could be completely different now.

The idea crawls under my skin and squeezes around my lungs, and I can't sit still any longer. Win's reaching for the display once more as I rock onto my feet.

"Stop," I say. "That's enough. Just stop."

I don't wait to see if he listens. I shove Jeanant's slab toward him and stagger between the flaps.

I burst out onto an expanse of rolling hills, knee-deep in grass. The thick blades hiss as I stumble through them. Splotches of clouds dot the sky, *one, two, three, four*—my heart is pounding so hard my arms are shaking—the line of a wooden fence breaks the sea of grass on the hill beyond this one. Dark evergreen forest sprawling in the distance. An acid burn in the back of my throat. Three red-roofed buildings in a row along the knoll to my left. Five horses grazing in the pasture beside them. One black, two chestnut, two dappled gray. I still can't breathe.

My bracelet is in my hand. I don't remember taking it out. I don't even remember starting the cycle of threes, but my thumb is already on the fourth bead, my lips moving along with the predictable methodical story of the numbers: *3 times 243 is 729. 3 times 729 is 2,187.* It's not enough to quiet the noise in my head. My fingers twist the beads harder. And then there's a snap, a loosening, and the warm glass slips from my grip.

I snatch at it too late. One of the hemp strings broke. I broke it. I stop and spin around, ready to paw at the grass, and almost bump heads with Win. He's crouching down amid the blades. I didn't realize he was behind me.

"Here," he says, holding up his hand. He's plucked up the lost bead, white splotched with turquoise. I take it and look at the bracelet. I can't tie the bead back on, not in any way that'll hold. It'll have to wait until I get home and can weave a whole new bracelet. *If* I ever get home—*if* that home bears any resemblance to the one I left—

Win straightens up and touches my shoulder. The gentle contact interrupts my thoughts on the verge of their panicked downward spiral.

I told him not to touch me. But he isn't pushing or tugging or maneuvering me this time. He's just there, his palm sending a little extra warmth through the fabric of Jeanant's cloak.

"I think all those jumps one right after another will confuse the signals a bit," he says. "And I was picking isolated spots so it's unlikely we'll shift anything noticeable. But if they've found a way to break Isis's scramble, Kurra and the other Enforcers could still follow us here. We should get out of sight. There was a building that looked empty on the other side of the hill. Can you make it there?"

The killing blast from Kurra's gun shrieks through my memory again, and my hand clenches around the bracelet. This wide-open landscape is only making me feel more lost. Walls, solid and secure—that sounds good.

"Okay," I say.

We climb back the way we came. "There," Win says, pointing, when we've reached the crest of the hill. Near the neatly spaced trees of an orchard stands a rough wooden shack, its door hanging loose on its hinges. I nod, and we scramble down toward it.

The shack has clearly been abandoned by whomever it belonged to. Streaks of dirt crust the one small window, and the door's hinges are coated with rust. One corner of the roof has collapsed, giving us a splintery view of the dimming sky outside. But the walls are sturdy enough to hide us from view.

Win sits down on a span of mossy wood that looks like it might once have held a mattress, positioning himself so he can see the hill we arrived on through the murky window. The hill where the Enforcers will arrive if they track us here. I drop onto the floor. The boards are damp and smell like rot, but the discomfort helps hold me in place. In this now. Away from fractured images of death and destroyed ancestries and—

"It isn't your fault," Win says, his gaze flicking from me to the window and back again. "I didn't know that kid was following us either, and I was the one outside the cave. I was the one who startled him and made him run."

"I saw him hiding there. If I'd said something, gotten him to leave quietly before they noticed him …"

"What could you have said? He wouldn't have understood you!"

He's right. I know that. But the guilt is clamped tightly around my chest. "I could have found a way. If I'd been paying enough attention, seen everything I needed to—"

"Skylar—"

"You can't tell me I couldn't have done anything!" I burst out. "I was there. And I didn't stop it. Just like—"

A surge of emotion, tangled regret and grief and anger, rushes up inside me. My voice falters. *Just like with Noam.* That was what I was going to say. But this has nothing to do with Noam.

Except somehow it does. Somehow that much older anguish has swallowed up everything else I was feeling, as if it was the same all along.

"Just like?" Win prompts.

"It doesn't make sense," I say. "It was a totally different situation. I just— My brother, Noam. He ran away when I was five. I was sitting there watching TV and he walked away with his knapsack and all the money he had saved in the bank, and I had no idea he wasn't just going to the convenience store. It doesn't matter."

Win pauses. His gaze darts to the window and back, reminding me that we're not really safe here. But he doesn't move. "Maybe it does," he says carefully. "If it's like what happened to that kid, if that's why you're so upset, I think it matters."

"I'm upset because someone *died*," I snap before I can catch myself.

"I know," he says. "But it seems like there's more than that."

"I guess." I rub my forehead. "Do we really have time to get into this?"

"Do you really think you can handle going back out there right now?" Win asks, gesturing toward the doorway.

I look at the slice of pasture beyond the slanted door. A shiver runs through me. There's so much that could be *wrong* that I can't even see yet—

I grip the bracelet. "No," I manage. "Okay. Noam." I refocus my thoughts on that time, the afternoon when he ran off, the evening of worry, the growing realization over the next few weeks that he was never coming home. "When he left, I knew I should have noticed that something was wrong. If I had, maybe I could have said something that would have changed his mind. Maybe he thought I didn't even care that he was leaving."

"Or maybe it didn't make a difference," Win says. "He'd already made up his mind. I think it *is* like the kid in the cave. There probably wasn't anything you could have done."

"I had enough chances to notice," I say. My throat is raw. I've never said this much about Noam to anyone, hardly even let myself think it; but now that I've started, it feels like I'll choke if I don't get it out. "I talked to him when he was walking me to our grandparents' house after school, and I saw him answer his phone when I was getting my snack. But when he was heading out, when he told me he'd grab me something at the store and then said good-bye, I didn't even look at him.

All I cared about was a stupid TV show. Three chances, and I didn't take the last one. I lost it, and he never came back."

"Third time's a charm," Win says.

"What?" I glance up at him.

"You've said that before," he says. "And three—that's your special number. That's the one you multiply with, when you're upset. Right?"

Oh. "I never really thought about that. It was … Noam's the one who always said that. I got it from him."

I never thought about it because I'd been trying so hard to get past my guilt over Noam, but hearing Win put it together, it's obvious. Three times. Three chances. A connection I never made, because I wasn't multiplying back then. Was I even getting the *wrong* feelings, before Noam left? I frown, reaching back toward my first memory of *wrong*ness. My second day of school in the first grade, less than six months later. Something about a tree in the corner of the playground. I cried through recess and couldn't tell the teacher why.

Win said I notice the shifts because I'm more sensitive than most people. But I wasn't always. I *started* noticing.

A moment flashes back to me: my five-year-old self standing in Noam's bedroom, hands balled into fists, swearing to myself that I'll pay more attention from now on, to everything. With the warped childish hope that it would magically compensate for whatever mistake I'd made and bring Noam back. If I could just catch every detail the way I should have that day, from then on, forever and ever …

"It all goes back to him," I say, breathless. "I thought if I just paid more attention to everything around me, I could stop something that awful from happening again. And after that, the feelings started."

And got worse. Every jab of *wrong*ness made me more desperate to be aware, to see what was wrong, which just made me more sensitive to the shifts. I created my own dysfunction.

"If you think about it, it's a good thing," Win points out. "If you didn't notice the shifts, you wouldn't have been able to help us."

"I know," I say. "But it's not good in a lot of ways too. A normal person would have been sad about that boy dying, and angry at that woman for killing him, without having a panic attack of guilt over it, right? How much danger did I put us in just now?"

And it isn't going to stop. Every time we've jumped to a new era, it's almost overwhelmed me. I lost the alarm band, our protection from the Enforcers, because of it. And after what we just saw, just the thought of Traveling anywhere else gives me a jolt of terror.

"We got out," Win says. "We're okay." He checks the window. "Still okay."

"What if it happens again?" I say. "You know it was at least partly because of us that boy died. We can't let anyone else get hurt."

"We're doing the best we can," Win says. "We're trying to stop something horribly huge. We might not be able to avoid changing a few small things along the way, but we're changing things for the better too."

A life that might have led to a vast chain of other lives doesn't feel so small to me. "We couldn't go back, make sure he didn't follow us … ?"

"The more we interfere with the locals, the more shifts we'll end up making," Win says. "We'd just be increasing the consequences."

Of course. I had my chance and now it's gone. Just like with Noam.

At least with the boy, I know exactly what happened, where things went wrong. With Noam, it's the uncertainty that's hardest to take. No one thought he was the type to run away. The police never managed to track him down. It was like he vanished into thin air.

My heart stops. Wait. That's possible, isn't it? I disappeared into thin air just hours ago, in Win's time cloth. Why couldn't Noam have disappeared the exact same way?

It fits so seamlessly I'm struck dumb. Maybe it really is my fault Noam left—maybe I'm the one who took him. I don't know why I would have, but what other time traveler would think Noam was important enough to steal him away? Maybe it'll be clear when I get there. But this is the only thing that's made sense in twelve years of wondering. A perfect circle, beginning with Noam's disappearance and leading me back to him again as the means of bringing him home.

"You look like you've had an idea," Win says, offering a tentative smile.

I bite my lip to keep from grinning. I can do it. I already did, right? I'll go get Noam, and bring him—somewhere safe, until I'm done Traveling with Win—and then we'll decide what to do next.

But I have a feeling Win isn't going to like this plan. I exhale slowly. I don't have to ask for it all at once. I can just ask for the favor I was already thinking of when I first saw how far his time cloth could take us.

"I want to see my brother," I say. "I want to go back to the day he ran away. So I know for sure what happened."

Win's smile falls. "Won't that make you feel worse?"

"No. I think it'll actually help me cope better. The not knowing, that's what really messed with my head." And once we're there, Win will go along with whatever I do. Because Noam's already disappeared, so he must. Right?

"I don't know," Win starts.

"I don't want long," I say, breaking in. "I've done everything you've asked me to do so far. I'm just asking *you* for this one thing."

"But, Jeanant ..." He lifts the flap of his satchel to look at the two slabs now wedged inside. "You did talk to him? What about the rest of the weapon? What did he say we should do?"

"He told me where we need to go," I say. *Where the trees were laid low.* Presumably the message on the second slab will fill in the rest. My fingers drift up to the hem of Jeanant's cloak. *He* understood how hard this journey has been for me. I think he'd see why I need to do this. If finally knowing Noam's okay will mean I can help Win finish this mission without another breakdown, it's better for everyone.

Win's watching my hand on the cloak. "He gave you that," he says. It's hard to tell whether he means it as a statement or a question.

"I was cold," I say. "He said I needed it more than he did. Look, Win, even if you don't get why this is important to me, can't you just believe me that it is? If you want me to be your tool, I'll do a lot better job if I'm sane."

His shoulders stiffen. He gives the window one last glance. "You don't have to say it like that," he says, his voice rough. "We'll go. It's only fair. What's the date?"

20.

Win has the time cloth set us down several blocks from my grandparents' house, to give us some distance if the Enforcers trace the jump. We hurry out into a chilly Friday afternoon in early March, three months before my sixth birthday. Other than the smattering of snowflakes drifting down around us, nothing's moving. It feels as if I've stepped into a memory where the world is frozen, immutable.

Five-year-old me will have just sat down at the kitchen table while my grandmother pours me a glass of apple juice. Noam will have ducked into the spare bedroom with his cell phone. In about five more minutes, I'll be curled up on the couch watching cartoon antics while he heads out past the faded blue door, and never returns.

But he will. I just have to make it happen.

Win's staring up at the sky, blinking as errant snowflakes stick to his eyelashes. His mouth has curled into a wondering smile. No snow on a space station either. I let him meander, picking up my pace as we turn onto my grandparents' street. Only three short blocks away now. It's hard to believe Noam's so close, after so long.

"Wait—Skylar!" Win says, but I keep walking. This time it's my mission, not—

Smack. The sensation crashes into me from head to toe, like I've slammed into a concrete wall—or a concrete wall speeding at two hundred miles an hour has slammed into me. I stumble, my forehead aching and my ears ringing, every joint shuddering as if I've jolted a dozen funny bones all over my body at the same time. The startled noise I make sticks in my throat. I press my hand against the side of my head, my nerves jangling, fighting to stay upright.

My eyes creep open, and my balance wavers. Where am I? This isn't— No, wait, it's the right street. Just … a few blocks more distant than I was a moment ago. There's Win, somehow ahead of me, jogging back toward me.

The word comes to me: doxed. So this is what it feels like. I don't want to do that again. Tiny pricks of pain are still sparking in the strangest places: the roots of my teeth, the bases of my fingernails. Fixing my consciousness in the still, cold world. This isn't just a memory. This is a real place, a real present, even if it's one that's also my past.

"I tried to tell you," Win says as he reaches me, panting.

"Yeah," I say, rubbing the last of the tingles from my arms under Jeanant's cloak. "I wasn't thinking. I've gotten used to not having one of your 'bubbles.'"

"Your younger self is in that house, isn't she?" Win says. "Meeting yourself is the biggest paradox there is."

"Well, let's get back there, as close as we can," I say. "Noam will leave soon, and I don't know which way he's going to go."

We're almost at the spot where I was doxed when a figure emerges onto the sidewalk up ahead. A figure in black jeans and a navy hooded jacket I recognize immediately. He veers across the street toward us, taking the usual route to the convenience store. Well, if I'm right, he never intended to go anywhere else.

Noam turns the corner, too close to the house for me to follow him directly. I'll have to cut him off farther down. "We'll go around," I say to Win, and lope over to the street parallel to the one Noam's on. As I jog on, Win quickly falls behind, his breath ragged. That's fine. It means he'll have less chance to interfere.

I round the block. A moment later, Noam comes into view up ahead. I slow to a brisk walk.

"Noam!"

He flinches before he turns around. Which is weird, but I don't have time to wonder about it, because in that time I've covered the last short distance between us, and I'm staring at my brother's face for the first time in twelve years.

He looks oddly young. I'm the same height as him, a disorienting perspective, and I don't remember quite so many freckles marking his pale skin, or the way he cocks his head as if trying to give the impression of toughness. But it's really him. I have to restrain myself from reaching to touch him.

"Yeah?" he says, his brow knitting.

I open my mouth, and stop. For some reason I thought the right words would come to me in the moment. Because they must have before. Instead, I'm tongue-tied. Win's footsteps thud around the corner behind me. I have to spit something out before he messes this up.

"Noam," I say, "this is going to be hard to understand, but I need you to listen to me. It's me. I'm—"

The second I try to voice my name, my throat contracts and my lungs clench, as if all the air has been sucked out of the space around me. A sharp prickling races along my jaw and down my chest. I gasp, and snap my mouth shut.

Noam's eyes dart away from me and back again. "Are you okay? Who *are* you?"

I suck in a breath. "I know this'll sound crazy, but I'm—"

The feeling shocks through me again, my bones wobbling with it, and this time I know without a doubt that if I push just a smidgeon farther, I'll find myself doxed across the city. Damn it, damn it, damn it.

"Hey!" Win rasps, almost here, and I blurt out the first thing that pops into my head.

"Don't go, Noam. Don't run away. If you come with me, I can make sure everything's all right."

His stare becomes incredulous. "What are you talking about?" he says. "Why would I *run away*? Who the hell are you?"

"Sorry," Win forces out as he catches up, grabbing me by the elbow. "She doesn't know what she's saying—she's not well. You go on ahead with whatever you were doing."

He starts to drag me away, and the protest bursts from my lips automatically. "No! Noam—you have to see—" My fingers fumble before I manage to open my purse. "Look!"

I hold out the bracelet. Noam was already starting to walk away, but he stopped at my movement. He's looking at it.

"You recognize the beads, don't you?" I say. "I had to restring them, but they're still the same."

The words have barely left my mouth before Win's wrenched my hand back. "That's enough," he says in a low voice. And then, louder, for Noam's benefit, "You need to stop bothering this guy. Come on, it's time to go."

Noam's gaze lifts to meet mine, and just for an instant, I see something like recognition in his eyes.

Then he's shaking his head. "I don't know what's going on with you two, but I can't deal with this right now. I'm sorry." Gripping the strap of his knapsack, he rushes across the street.

I move to run after him, and Win's hand tightens around my elbow. I spin around to face him.

"What are you *doing*?" he says before I can speak. "Weren't you just complaining about changing the past? What do you think's going to happen when you're talking to your brother like that?"

"I'm not trying to change anything," I say. "I'm trying to do what must have already happened. You heard him. He isn't going to run away. I must have taken him somewhere. With you, in the time cloth."

Win blinks at me, and suddenly the logic that made perfect sense to me minutes ago seems shaky. His expression softens into what looks like pity. My gut twists.

"It doesn't work like that, Skylar," he says. "Haven't you seen? You can't feel the effects of a shift you haven't created yet. If there was a time when your brother hadn't disappeared, because you weren't going to meet me for twelve more years, we wouldn't have met in the first place, because you wouldn't have been noticing shifts and I wouldn't have noticed you. So you couldn't have taken him away. He's always been gone."

"But …" He releases my arm, and I rub my forehead. Noam is hurrying out of view, still headed toward the store. I can't let him get too far out of my sight. I start to walk after him. Win sticks close by my side.

"It doesn't ever work that way?" I say weakly. "You never see something because of a change you're going to make later?"

"The idea that time is static and anything that's going to happen has already happened—it's a nice thought," Win says.

"But it's from your movies and books, not actual science. If it *were* really that way, there wouldn't be any shifts for you to sense, because everything would always have been the same."

I understand what he's saying, logically. But the idea that Noam disappeared through time with me felt so *right*. And just now, he sounded like he honestly had no idea why I'd accuse him of being about to run away.

"You knew you were going to do this when you convinced me to bring you here," Win says. "But you didn't tell me."

"Like that's so different from all the things you didn't bother to tell me before whisking me across hundreds of years?" I respond.

He scowls at me. "At least *I* knew what I was doing."

"Yeah, well …" My annoyance fades as quickly as it rose up. He has a point. I just don't want to admit it. "He's my brother. I've spent all this time wondering where he is, beating myself up for missing the signs—I thought I saw a chance to sort it all out, so I took it. I still don't understand. If *I* don't take him away, and he didn't mean to leave … what happened to him?"

Win sighs. "Look," he says as we reach the commercial strip with the convenience store on the corner. "I have a brother too. If *he* disappeared, and I didn't know how or why … I don't think I'd deal so well with that either. We're here now. The plan was supposed to be to find out what happens to him. I take it you still want to?"

Something inside me balks. "What could have stopped him from coming home? What if …"

I don't know how to finish that sentence. All I have is a vague feeling of dread.

"We can find out, or we can leave," Win says, with a gentleness I hadn't expected. "You just have to promise not to get involved. Hopefully that little conversation didn't shift anything recordable."

Fear washes over me, before I remind myself that if Noam disappeared before I ever Traveled here, then it can't be anything I've done now that caused it. If I had nothing to do with it, neither did the Enforcers.

"If something is going to happen to him—if he's going to disappear anyway, *couldn't* we take him away instead?" I ask. "I mean, that wouldn't even change anything, really, right? He'll be gone either way."

"And what do you think we could do with him if we take him?" Win says.

I hadn't really thought it through before. I just assumed the solution would come to me the way I assumed the right words would. "We could bring him back to my present." Even as I say it, I know how ridiculous it sounds. "Although … okay, he'd still be fifteen, and that would be really weird, and probably shift a whole lot of things."

Win nods. "And the Enforcers aren't going to ignore some story about a boy who disappears and returns twelve years later the exact same age."

There has to be *something* I can do. But I can't make a plan before I know exactly what happens.

"Okay," I say. "We'll just watch and see. I have to know."

There's no sign of Noam through the convenience store window. When I look up, I spot him stepping away from the bank building halfway up the block. Stuffing a handful of bills into his knapsack.

My heart sinks. His savings. What's he going to buy with $650, if he's not leaving town?

Noam hurries off in the opposite direction. After a few minutes, he reaches the park where in my present I do cross-country practice. He heads down one of the paths branching away from the road. When we reach the edge of the park, he's waiting by a bench under a broad oak tree. The memory flashes through me: running there beside Bree, the swish of her ponytail, the thump of our feet. I jerk myself back behind the public restroom when Noam turns our way.

"What do you think he's doing here?" Win murmurs beside me.

"I have no idea."

I hug Jeanant's cloak, trying to ignore the snowflakes speckling my face. A few minutes later, a guy who looks vaguely familiar slinks into view. I lean forward as far as I dare.

"Hey Darryl," Noam calls. Ah. Darryl: Noam's friend who mostly hung out at the house when Noam's other friends, the baseball guys, weren't around. I remember Mom and Dad discussing him in a way that gave me the impression they didn't like him very much.

Darryl veers over to join Noam. "You've got it?" he says, and when Noam nods, he ducks his head, swiping a hand over his lank blond hair. "I didn't know who else to call," I think he says.

Noam makes a couple comments, his voice so low all I catch is something about a "stupid idea." I itch to move closer, but Darryl keeps glancing around. And as soon as he notices me coming over, Noam will too.

After a final brief exchange, they fall silent, Noam kicking at the frost coating the grass, Darryl checking his phone. Finally, an old Miata with patchy red paint pulls up to the curb across from them. Darryl's back goes rigid.

A couple guys who look about my age lumber out of the car. The shorter one has his chest puffed out inside his white training jacket, like he's trying to compensate for his babyish cheeks and the zits speckling his jaw.

"All right, let's go," Babyface says with affected gruffness.

"Go where?" Darryl asks.

"We're not talking about this here, retard. Come on, we're taking a drive."

"But I thought—"

"You do remember that you're stuck in the same school as us for the rest of the year, right?" Babyface says. "I can make all those days really, really miserable if I want."

Darryl's face falls. Noam looks uncertain, but he shrugs. "Let's get this over with." He marches over to the car. Darryl hesitates, and then follows.

As Noam reaches for the car door, I step forward automatically, my pulse thudding. Win holds out his arm in front of me.

"We're just watching," he reminds me, leaning close. "But we can follow them. All right?"

I tense as they climb into the backseat. Despite Win's words, I have the urge to run out there, to interrupt the situation somehow. But the *somehow* stops me. What, try to drag Noam out of the car? Like that's going to do anything other than make me look even crazier than I already have. I still don't understand what's going on. Those guys are just high-school kids too—how bad could this possibly be?

"So, marshlands?" the taller guy says to Babyface as they reach the sidewalk.

Babyface nods, a grin I don't like at all creeping across his face. "Yeah."

They hop in the front of the car. I bite back a protest as the doors slam shut. The engine guns. Then the Miata roars away from the sidewalk, away from us.

21.

D o you know those guys?" Win asks.

"No," I say, tearing my gaze from the spot where the car turned out of view. "You said we can follow them?"

"We can beat them to wherever they're going. What's the marshlands?"

"It's a sort of nature reserve along the coastline, just east of the city," I say. There isn't much going on out there at this time of year. Which maybe is the point. "It's pretty big ... but there's only one road that runs along it. We could watch for them there and see where they turn off."

"All right," Win says. "Just remember, if we have to stay in the spot we've jumped to, to avoid being seen, the Enforcers could show up almost on top of us. Then we'll *have* to leave, no matter what else is going on."

"I know."

He pulls the time cloth around us. The characters flash by on the data display. After a moment, he nods, and his hand twitches toward me as if to rest on my back, the way he's steadied me before. I scoot out of reach automatically. He jerks back, his mouth tightening.

Part of me wants to say it's fine, to take his hand and let the tension still hovering between us release. He did bring me here; he's doing this because I asked. But he hasn't apologized, for *anything*: for the experimental kiss, for the patronizing comments, for dragging me around like a puppy on a leash. For all I know, he really is only agreeing to this because he's worried about keeping his Jeanant communication tool in working order.

I hug Jeanant's cloak around me instead. "Let's go."

Win presses the panel. The cloth sways—my gut lurches—and deposits us across the street from the park.

Win frowns. I close my eyes as he swipes at the panel some more. The cloth hums faintly and the air inside shivers. "Come on," Win murmurs, poking something on the opposite wall. "Wake up!"

When he smacks the panel again, the floor lifts and the world spins. I open my eyes to a four-lane highway that stretches out ahead of us. We've landed on the gravel shoulder.

To our right, clumps of reeds and bulrushes hiss as the breeze tickles over them between the hunched trees. The snow has picked up, tiny flakes pirouetting down and dissolving on the moist ground. In the distance, I can make out the gray shimmer of open water, the same shade as the clouded sky.

As I expected, no one's out here today. Too cold and dreary.

"If they drive past us, can we just Travel after them?" I ask. "How closely can we follow?"

"The navigation system is coordinate-based," Win says. "But I can estimate from where we are now and give a distance and a direction. As long as the cloth behaves, I should be able to keep them in sight."

I ease my weight from one foot to the other, trying to be patient. Trying not to worry that they'll never make it here in the first place. Finally, a glint of red appears on the road coming out of the city. I wince as the Miata whips past us, just a couple feet away. It zips on down the road, passing the blue sign of the nature center where I've been on school trips.

"Here we go," Win says.

We jump—again and again—always behind the car but close enough to keep it in view. I've just caught my balance for the fifth time when the Miata pulls over, off the shoulder onto a sheltered strip of grass between two clusters of pine trees.

I rest my hands on the wall. From where we're standing, I can identify Noam's jacket as he steps out of the car with the other three guys. Babyface and his tall friend motion Noam and Darryl toward the marsh beyond the trees. I can't hear a single thing they're saying.

"Can we get closer?"

"Let's see ..." Win's fingers dart over the panel. We shudder to a halt on a patch of earth matted with fallen reeds, some twenty feet from where the two older boys are now facing my brother and Darryl.

"All right," Babyface says. "Where is it?"

Noam opens his knapsack. "I've got six hundred and fifty."

"And I've got another eighty," Darryl says, pulling a thin wad from his pocket.

The tall guy guffaws. Babyface folds his arms over his chest and jerks his chin toward Darryl. "That's hardly a third of what that weed you stole cost us, limpdick."

Oh God. So that's what this is about. It's just like Noam to be here trying to help his friend out of some massive screwup—a massive screwup it sounds like he told Darryl was a stupid idea at the time.

"Even worse than we thought!" the tall guy crows. "Time to teach them a lesson."

"This is just to start," Darryl says in a rush. "I told you, I need more time to get the rest."

"Yeah, like you've gotten so much already? You're hiding behind your friend here like the pussy you are." Babyface turns with an awkward sort of swagger, groping for something behind him under his jacket. His inflection changes, as if he's rehearsed the next lines. "You need to learn some respect. Maybe this'll help you see how serious we are."

He pulls out a pistol. Darryl flinches, and Noam takes a step back, dropping the knapsack and holding his hands in the air. I stop breathing.

"Get down on your knees!" Babyface says, waving the gun while the tall guy jitters with excitement.

"Look," Noam says, his face pale, "you don't have to—"

"I'm going to do what I want," Babyface says. "I'm the boss here." He fumbles with the pistol with unpracticed hands, but I hear a click I can only assume is the safety coming off. "Go on! Down!"

There's no way I can see this scenario ending well. My hand leaps toward the flaps, but Win blocks me. "Just watching," he says, his voice strained.

"We can't let this happen!" I protest. "We have to stop them."

"I swear, I'm going to get the rest for you soon," Darryl is sniveling.

He reaches pleadingly toward Babyface, who smacks his hand away with the gun. Noam's shoulders tense. "Not good enough," Babyface says. "Tomorrow. You've got junk at home you can sell, yeah? TV, computer. You wanted to keep that stuff, you shouldn't have messed with mine."

"We can't just appear in front of them out of nowhere," Win says. "And we can't change what's going to happen without shifting who knows how many other things—"

Darryl snuffles and wipes at his nose. "I don't know where— Maybe this weekend? You have to—"

"I don't care!" I say, trying to shove past Win, at the same moment Babyface raises the hand with the gun.

"I don't *have* to do anything for you," he says, and smacks Darryl across the face with the side of the pistol. "You should have thought of that before you decided to try to pull one over on me, asswipe."

As he starts to swing his hand again, Noam lunges forward.

"Stop it!" he says. "He said he'll do it, he just—"

A cry slips from my throat, but it doesn't make any difference. Babyface tries to shove Noam off, but Noam catches his arm, yanking it down. And the sharp crack of a gunshot echoes across the marsh.

"No!"

As Noam slumps, I squirm away from Win to scrabble at the flaps of the cloth. "No, no, no, no, no." The word breaks from my throat, over and over. My fingers slide along smooth fabric that hardens at my touch. The cloth has turned seamless, impenetrable.

"Let me out!" I say, spinning around. Win grips me by the arms.

"You can't," he says. "You just can't, Skylar."

"I don't *care*. Whatever you did—let me out!"

I batter him with my fists, and he releases me. But the time cloth doesn't. I throw myself at the translucent wall, a shock of pain spiking through my shoulder, but it doesn't even tremble.

I have to get out of here. I have to go to him.

But I can't.

All I can do is watch as Darryl cringes away from Noam's motionless form. As Babyface drops the gun, eyes bulging and jaw gone slack, and his tall friend jabbers something about how pissed his dad is going to be. As Noam just lies there, his head lolled to the side, his eyes unblinking. Babyface tests a toe against Noam's ribs, and jerks his foot back as red streaks over the blue of Noam's jacket.

"Is he really … ?" the tall friend says.

"Looks like," Babyface says shakily.

"Oh hell," Darryl moans. "Oh hell. He's—call the hospital! The police! We have to—"

"Shut up!" Babyface snaps. "You idiot. Doctors aren't going to help him. He's dead. And you bring the police in and—and we'll both say you're the one who had the gun."

"We can't just *leave* him," Darryl says, and clamps his mouth shut when Babyface glares at him.

"No one has to know," the tall friend says. "Right? We just … don't tell anyone. We can put him in the water."

Babyface rubs the side of his face. "All right. All right. Not like we can do anything else for him. Right?" He directs the last at Darryl, before bending to pick up the dropped gun.

Darryl stares at it, blanching. "Yeah," he gasps. "Yeah, sure, whatever you say."

I bang my fist against the cloth and yell, but whatever Win has done makes the fabric swallow up our sounds too. Through a blur of tears, I see Babyface and his friend heave Noam up by his wrists and ankles and carry him to deeper water. Bile rises in my throat, and I have to look away. So I only hear them stomp back across the squishy ground, heft a couple rocks from near one of the trees, and carry them to set them on Noam's body with a faint splash. And then another, and another. When I look again, they're staring at the spot where Noam's disappeared into the marsh.

Babyface shudders. Then he turns to Darryl. "You open your mouth about this to anyone, and you'll wish you were the one down there."

Darryl nods, his eyes red-rimmed. The tall friend grabs Noam's knapsack. Darryl stumbles after them. On the other side of the trees, the car doors creak. The red Miata lurches onto the road and roars away. And only then Win touches the panel and frees me.

The flaps peel open. I tumble out, falling calf deep into the frigid marsh water. My stomach rolls. I double over, puking what was left of the trail mix into a patch of weeds. I gag and sputter, and propel myself forward, thrashing through the bulrushes to the spot where Noam fell.

Nothing's left of him but a splatter of blood already leaching into the wet soil. I crawl out next to it, but I'm no longer sure exactly where the boys sank him. Shivers rack my body, and the tears start again. I cover my face, my hands gritty with dirt against my skin. The sobs wrench through my chest as if they're pulling my guts right out of me.

All this time … All this time I felt hurt and betrayed and even *angry* at him. And he was only trying to help a friend. A friend who wasn't really a friend at all, dragging Noam into this. Why couldn't they have shot *Darryl*? Why did Noam have to care so much?

After a while, my sobs ease off, but there's still a painful hitch in my lungs with every breath. Win is standing off to the side, his Traveler pants soaked to the knees. The breeze licks over us with a fresh gust of snow. I pull my legs to my chest.

"Now you know," Win says quietly. "It wasn't your fault. You couldn't have stopped it from happening no matter how much you were paying attention."

I have the urge to argue, but he's right. I can't imagine anything five-year-old me could have said to stop Noam from heading out the door this afternoon on his mission to protect his friend. But there are still so many ways it could have gone differently. If Noam had just given Darryl the money and left before the other guys showed up. If they'd refused to get in the car. If the guy—the *kid*—with the gun hadn't wanted so badly to show how tough he could be. If Noam hadn't tried to shield Darryl from the beating. If the gun had been pointing just a few inches to the side.

So many chances for Noam to have lived.

"We have to go back," I say, rocking to keep warm. "Earlier today … or yesterday … I have to convince him not to go meet Darryl."

"You can't," Win says.

Of course he'd say that. "Why not?" I demand. With more strength than I thought I had left, I push myself onto my feet so I can look him in the eyes. "As long as I show up sometime when the younger me isn't around, there won't be any doxing. I'll think of something to say that'll work. I know one human life doesn't seem important to *you*, but I can't just let him die. Not like that."

"It is important to me," Win says. "But that doesn't change—" He stops and shakes his head. "You're upset— You must be freezing— Let's just—"

I'm gearing up to declare I'm not leaving this place until he's agreed to let me do what I need to do, when my gaze slips past him and snags on the air near the shoulder of the road behind him. The air that is wavering with the translucent outline of a huge metallic cone, several times as large as Win's time-cloth tent and yet somehow almost familiar …

"What?" Win says at the look on my face, at the same moment as the outline shimmers away. He couldn't have seen it anyway, I realize; it's my sensitivity again. But he seems to figure out what my reaction must mean. He bites out a curse, yanking open the time cloth.

Which is a good thing, because the cone's not gone. As Win throws the cloth over us, an opening parts in the seemingly empty air where it stood. Four figures charge out. A blaster glints in a raised hand. Before I can manage more than a squeak of alarm, Win's fingers flick, and we're hurtling away from Noam's final resting place.

We make three jerky leaps before landing in an unfamiliar city, but I'm reeling so much I hardly notice. "What— What was that?" I manage to say.

"You saw the carrier?" Win asks, his hand hovering over the panel.

"I saw something. Big ... like an upside-down cone." I gesture, and Win nods.

"When the Enforcers need to work in groups and bring equipment, they use the carriers to Travel," he says. "Less maneuverable than the cloths, but more room." He frowns at the glowing characters. Then he closes his eyes, pressing his palm against his forehead as if he's got a headache.

The motion brings me back to the scene we just witnessed. The baby-faced guy hitting Darryl across the head with the gun. And everything after. The horror swells back up. One clear thought pierces the haze in my mind.

"It doesn't matter," I say. "We're going back. I'm going to save Noam."

22.

My legs wobble, and Win reaches to steady me. I'd pull back, but suddenly I'm not sure I can support my own weight. He keeps his hand on the side of my arm, tentatively.

"Skylar," he says, his voice as raw as I feel, "I know how much this means to you. But we've got the Enforcers just a few steps behind us. No one saw us at the marsh. For them to have found us there, they *have* to have broken Isis's protections on the cloth's signal. There's no doubt they're tracking us directly. And we're exhausted, and wet, and cold, so neither of us is going to be thinking clearly right now. The past will still be there in a couple hours. Let's find somewhere safe—safer—and give ourselves a chance to take all of this in, and then we'll talk about it. I promise."

I don't like it, but he's making sense. My head feels as wobbly as my legs. I swallow, noticing the ashy dryness of my mouth. "Okay. Okay. Do you have more of that blue water stuff?"

Win's posture relaxes. "Sure."

He hands me one of the bottles, and I gulp from it as he skims through the data. "Ah," he says. "I think this should work. Give us a good head start, anyway."

We jump once more, landing in an alley across from a long white building with streams of people heading in and out of its doors in the midafternoon sun. "Los Angeles," Win announces. "Union Station."

And then a yellow light starts to flash behind the cloth's display with an electronic ping. Win stiffens.

"What is it?" I ask.

It takes him a few seconds to answer, as if he's hoping the flashing will stop and he won't have to say. "That's the power indicator," he says, sounding twice as tired as before. "Traveling takes a lot of energy. The cloths can only make so many trips before they need to be recharged."

My damp clothes suddenly feel colder. "So it's dying?"

"This is just the early warning. We'll get at least a few more trips out of it. I'd guess four or five jumps … more if most of them are short. We'll be all right."

In an ideal situation, we won't even need that many. One back to save Noam. One to follow the instructions Jeanant gave me and grab the last two parts of the weapon. One to bring them back to Win's companions. But it doesn't leave much room for error. Or escape, if Kurra catches up with us.

The drink has cleared my head a little, but it's still hard to focus. "So what do we do?"

Win drags in a breath. "We keep going," he says. "And we only jump when we have to. I was already planning on that, since each jump gives the Enforcers another chance to trace us, so I guess it doesn't change much. Come on."

We step out. Win leads the way across the street and through the station entrance to the ticket office. I glimpse the date on a computerized screen: it's the Sunday before I met Win.

Somewhere across the country, there's another me who hasn't seen any of this yet. I wince away from the thought.

"We're taking a train?" I say.

"It'll let us get some distance quickly," Win says. "Give us some time to rest and talk while staying on the move. I've got enough American cash left to buy a long trip."

"And they won't figure out what we did—check the ticket records or something?"

"I'll buy another ticket, going another direction, first. That'll be the shift they catch—the first one. Anything after, they won't know it's us and not just a ripple."

I stick close to him, trying not to sway, as he books the fake ticket and then a private sleeper room on the next cross-country train. It's leaving in just a few minutes. We rush through the crowd to the platform and scramble on board.

Our room's down a narrow hall toward the back of the train. The bunks haven't been pulled out yet. I collapse into the long padded seat, Win sinking down across from me. A whistle sounds. The motor hums. With a hitch, the train begins to whir along the track.

I slouch in the seat, gazing out the window but not really registering anything beyond the glass. My head tips forward. And before I notice what's happening, exhaustion has carried me away.

I wake up with a start at a screech of metal wheels against the tracks. Win's still sitting next to me, his head tilted against the seat, his eyes closed. Outside the train window, dusk is falling. I've been out for hours. How could I have slept, when—

It was already late afternoon when I left with Win from my present time. Between France, Vietnam, and my own past, I've been on my feet until what's the equivalent of well into the next morning. Even if I'd been sitting at home the whole time, I'd have had trouble staying awake.

My stomach growls. I pull the half-full bag of trail mix from my purse and scoop a few handfuls into my mouth. It takes the edge off the pangs.

My mind flickers back to the marshlands. To the scene that played out just a few hours and twelve years ago, before my eyes. My gut clenches. I set aside the rest of the trail mix.

What's Darryl doing now, in this present? How has he managed to live with himself all this time? And those guys, Babyface and his friend: have they felt even a speck of guilt?

Shapes and colors flash past the window. I see Noam's pale, determined face, the swing of an arm, the water rippling around a bloodstained jacket. After a few minutes, I pull down the shade, but the beige blankness gives me no comfort. I start picturing that shimmering cone—the carrier, Win called it—appearing beside the train tracks, the Enforcers spilling out. I wouldn't even know …

I push the shade back up. There's nothing but scattered industrial buildings and stretches of yellowed grass passing by outside. Win said we didn't have to worry. But my pulse keeps jumping.

Even though nothing feels *wrong*, I dig out my bracelet, careful to avoid unraveling the hemp string further where it snapped. The remaining beads rotate under my fingers, and the threes roll out through my head. The pattern holds me in place, here in the small cabin with the whir of the train's wheels against the tracks and the plasticky smell of recycled air, but it doesn't calm me. My nerves are still twitching, my muscles tight.

I can't do it anymore: just get through it, wait for the worst of the emotions to pass. No matter how many times I turn the beads, no matter how many cycles of three I multiply, Noam will still be dead.

Win said we could talk when we were somewhere safer, when we'd had time to think. I don't know where we're going to find a safer spot, and I've done enough thinking.

"Win?" I say.

He raises his head. I ready myself. I have to lay it all out as clearly as possible, not giving him any room to argue.

"I know we can't just take Noam the way I thought," I say. "But we don't have to. All we have to do is make some little tweak to stop him from ending up in the marshlands in the first place. I couldn't seem to talk to him properly about the future, but … maybe if I write him a letter without too many details, give it to him when he's leaving school—I could tell him when Darryl calls him, it'll be a prank, he should ignore him and just stay at the house. And if he goes anyway, can't we just, like, grab him for half an hour until the guys have gone off with Darryl and there's no way for them to take Noam too? We don't even have to get anyone else involved— the police, my parents—it'd just be Noam's life we're changing."

Win's mouth twists. "You're talking about reversing someone's death. Of course that's going to impact other people."

"Well, after," I say. "But—you reversed the deaths of my whole class the other day, just to distract the Enforcers. Jeanant's been making all kinds of minor changes to distract them too, right? It's not like they're going to know this one is significant. And even if they check it out, we won't stick around for them to catch us."

"I didn't mean that," Win says. "I meant *you*. If your brother doesn't disappear, your past will be completely different."

"What?" I say. "That's a problem? I'll get to grow up with the brother I was supposed to have. He'll get to finish high school and college and meet a girl he wants to marry and do all the other things he should have gotten to do. My parents won't have to spend all that time wondering what they did to drive him away. I won't be so torn up with guilt that I …"

I falter. I forgot that part of the equation. What made me seek out the answer to Noam's disappearance to begin with. To know what happened, to know he was okay, so I could get my head on straight.

"If he doesn't disappear, I won't get obsessed with paying attention to details," I say. "I won't notice the shifts."

My mind trips backward down the long line of freak-outs and awkward moments and excuses that have been an unshakeable part of my existence until now. What would my life have been like, rewritten without that? What would it be with Noam in it?

Win's voice brings me back. "If you don't notice the shifts, I won't notice you. We'll never talk."

Oh. Of course. "I won't be able to help you follow Jeanant's messages," I say. "I wouldn't even be here right now." This room, this window, this seat, the rocking of the train's motion, all erased from my life, even though it feels so real right now. The idea makes me dizzy.

Who will *I* be, without the twelve years of guilt and compulsions?

But trading the certainty of what I have for Noam, for my parents, for a normal life—it's not even a question.

"So what?" I say. "Maybe you won't get to run off to Paris and start collecting parts of the weapon, but Thlo and the rest of your group should figure it out eventually, shouldn't they? You don't *need* me, I just … hurried things along."

"We don't know that," Win says. "If things happened differently, the Enforcers might catch the others, or me, before we make it that far. And even if it would have worked out if I never met you, I *did*, Skylar, and now you and me and Jeanant and the parts he left for us to find, the parts we've already collected, they're all tangled up together. You've been interacting with people from all different eras, with Travelers from different presents. If we yank you out of the timeline it might not snap back into place perfectly. Things could just slip out of existence."

I stare at him. "Is that something that actually happens? Or are you just making that up because you don't want to do it?"

"It's happened," Win says flatly. "Not very often, but— you've heard of cases where planes or boats just disappear and are never found? Even people? Sometimes that's some mistake in our calculations, too many overlapping shifts in the same area at once. No one has any idea how many objects too insignificant to draw notice might have vanished due to some small margin of error. You erase and rewrite parts of the world enough times, and bits and pieces end up getting written out."

I remember the metaphor he used before: a recording of a recording of a recording. The video getting grainier, the sound more fuzzy, with every copy. Until some details, some words, you can't make out at all anymore. I pull my legs onto the seat, hugging them through the clammy fabric of my dress.

"You really think the messages, or the parts of the weapon, could just … stop existing? Or …"

Even people, he said. Me? Win? Jeanant?

"I don't know," Win says. "But what we've been doing, it's so uncontrolled compared to any official shift. And taking you out of it would be just about the biggest shift anyone's ever made. I have no idea what could happen."

He looks down at his hands. "I understand why you want to save your brother. I'm sorry. I wish we could, but I can't agree to do it when it would mean risking *everything*."

The reason I'm here at all. Jeanant's plan to destroy the time field generator. Possibly the only chance we have to free Earth from Kemya's control—the only chance that's come in thousands of years. I know, I *know*, you can't remove one figure in an equation without making the whole sequence void.

I won't care, if I go back and protect Noam and my life is written over. I won't have any more of a clue than anyone else that the world around me is being shifted and experimented with on a daily basis. I could shrug off Jeanant's sacrifices and Win's and the fate of every other person on this planet, so my family and I can live in happy ignorance.

I feel awful just thinking about it. And yet some part of me still finds the possibility appealing.

"It's not fair," I say, knowing how childish that sounds. "Why is it so easy to end some kid's life, but saving someone, we can't do that?"

"I'm sorry," Win says again.

I press my face against my knees, squeezing my eyes shut. Fresh tears start to well behind my eyelids. I was right there, I saw Noam, I talked to him. How can helping him be so out of reach?

"There isn't any way?" I ask without raising my head. "There's no Traveler loophole you haven't mentioned?"

I don't expect him to answer. Win's silent for what feels like a long time, as the tracks rattle beneath us and the conductor announces the next stop approaching. Then he says, "Maybe there's something."

I jerk upright. "What?"

"I don't know exactly how we would work it," he says slowly. "But once something is outside the time field, shifts can't affect it. As soon as we have the parts of the weapon off the planet, back on our ship, it doesn't matter what happens here on Earth, we'll still have them. So then, in theory, you could go back and help your brother survive without us losing anything."

"So we'd just have to get the last two pieces, and then we could do it?"

"I can't promise you it'll work," Win says. "The logistics could be complicated, and … Thlo would have to agree. But I'd try."

Try. That doesn't feel like quite enough—to keep going, leaving Noam farther and farther behind, without a definite plan to go back for him. I should be overjoyed that there might be a way after all, but the hope that bubbled up inside me starts to deflate. Maybe I'm just too tired for talk of logistics and complications. I rub my eyes.

"I want you to know," Win says, and pauses. He fixes me with that deep blue gaze, his face so weary I wonder if he slept at all. It occurs to me that no matter what he's done, no matter how he's treated me, an awful lot of what we've been through has been new and unsettling to him too. That it's not just me who's struggling with uncertainty.

"You don't have to be here helping with Jeanant and the weapon if you don't want to," he goes on. "You've done so much already. What I said before—that I'd bring you home, if you wanted me to—that still stands. If this is getting to be too much, I'll take you back, and you can have that time to think through what you want to do, while I go get the last two parts. And then I'll come get you, and we can sort out this thing with your brother, if it's possible."

Home. The thought sends a pang of longing through me. To curl up on my familiar bed, surrounded by my familiar things.

Will it still be familiar? I'd almost forgotten the fear that clutched me after the boy died by the caves. My past didn't seem to have changed that much, but all I really know is that my brother and I still went to my grandparents' house after school that day, and he still disappeared. What about my parents? My friends? What if I shifted something while we were following Noam?

"If you just tell me where Jeanant said we needed to go," Win is saying, "I can finish the rest myself."

"He said …" I pause, trying to remember his exact words. It was less than a day ago I spoke to Jeanant in the cave, but it feels like weeks. "We're supposed to go somewhere close to my region of the States—'just before blood is spilled where the trees were laid low.'"

Win frowns. "'Where the trees were laid low?' That's it?"

"He seemed to think it was all we'd need to know. But, there was a message on the weapon part he left in the cave too."

I watch Win as he digs in his satchel for the second slab of alien plastic. This mission has become mine as much as his. But—he's right, I've already helped more than either of us expected. I've gotten him one step away from the end. There might not even be anything else I can do, where he's going next. Maybe I'll just get in the way, and it'll be better for both of us if I go home now.

Of course, he could also decide his loophole is too risky and not come back for me at all. Not only would I not be able to save Noam, I'd never know whether Win even succeeded. Whether the shifts are going to end.

"'Remember when we talked about the ones who came first, losing their lives to those who came later, because of

greed on one side of them and inaction on the other,'" Win
says, reading from the slab. "'Revisit the irony and the tragedy.
Start by following the path of anger.'" He turns it over,
searching for more writing. "I don't know what that means.
'The irony and the tragedy.' I've heard Thlo use that expression before. I guess she'd know what he's referring to."

"Jeanant thought I was working with Thlo," I say.
"Because that's what you told me to tell him."

"Well, if it's supposed to be close to where you live, that
narrows it down," Win says. "You must know some of the
local history—does any of this, the trees, the greed and
inaction, ah, ring a bell?"

"Maybe …" I try to think back to my US history course,
but the names and dates have blurred. "The thing about
'those who came first and later,' it could mean the Native
Americans and the European settlers. But I'm not sure what
he means about the different sides."

Win digs out the time cloth. "I can try to look it up. I
don't know how easy it'll be to find with information that
vague, though."

As he unfolds the cloth, I have the sense of time slipping
away from me. As soon as he finds it, I'm going to have to
make a decision about where to go.

The answer Win needs was probably in my history
textbook somewhere—but I don't have that anymore.
Although …

"Wait," I say, and Win looks up. "My friend, Lisa, she's taking US history this year because she had scheduling conflicts before. They cover the stuff about the Native Americans right at the start. If we went back, to my present, I could ask her about it." Lisa's not the most academic one in our group, but even if she doesn't remember . . . "And I can look at her textbook to see if anything feels *wrong*. That worked with France."

A trip home will buy me more time to decide. It'll be easier once I know what's waiting for me there.

"That did," Win says. He hesitates. "And then you'll want to stay there, in your time?"

"I don't know," I admit. "I'm still figuring that out."

"Well, let's go," Win says more brightly. "It sounds like that's more likely to work than me sifting through thousands of years of history for mentions of trees."

23.

The cloth pings again when Win pulls it into its tent form in the cramped space of the train cabin. The light behind the panel flickers its warning. I pause. "Are you sure it's okay—making an extra jump when the power's low?"

Win's already flicking through the data. "It's not that far and barely any time. We'll want to be careful where we land, though."

I shudder at the thought of the Enforcers tracing us to my friends. "Right." I glance down at myself, at the ink- and mud-stained dress still clinging damply to my legs. God knows what my face and hair look like. "I should probably go home and clean up."

Win nods. "I'll set us down close to my hotel and we'll walk from there. If the Enforcers have determined I was staying there, they'll assume that's where we were going and look there first."

"Smart," I say, but I'm not sure he even hears the compliment. The cloth lifts off at that moment with a squeal of wind. My breath catches, my gut flips, and I open my eyes to a wrenchingly familiar street. A few blocks from the Garden Inn, less than ten minutes from the house I've spent most of my life in, if we hurry.

I duck out, almost afraid to look around me in the clear afternoon light. But nothing my gaze slides over feels *wrong*. The brick houses, the tiny lawns, the sapling trees with their sprigs of autumn foliage—they all look exactly as I remember. A coil of tension I hadn't even registered inside me starts to loosen.

"How long is it since we left here?" I ask Win as we head down the street, taking the first corner so we'll be out of view if the Enforcers catch up. "I mean, in present time?"

"About ten minutes," Win says.

Still at least an hour before I'd have to worry about my parents getting home, then. I walk even faster. We've taken another turn, onto my street with just a couple blocks left to cover, when a digitized melody emanates from my side.

Win's head jerks around as I fumble to open my purse. "My phone," I say, tugging it out. The call display tells me it's Angela.

"Hey," I say, bringing the phone to my ear. It's a struggle to sound normal. "What's up?"

"Not much," Angela says in her usual cheerful tone. It feels like years since I last heard her voice. "I'm still at school, working away. Do you remember where you and Bree stashed the painted lightbulbs? I've looked all over the art room. Maybe I'm going blind."

Painted lightbulbs … Right. 'This' afternoon, at lunchtime. And centuries and centuries ago. Where *did* we put them? I press the heel of my hand against my temple. I should be able to remember details like this—I would, if there weren't so many other crazy memories crowding in between then and now.

"I think—" A red plastic tub, slid onto a shelf. "Check the cabinet in the corner by the pottery wheel."

There's a shuffling sound as Angela makes her way over, and the creak of a door opening. "Aha!" she says. "I figured I could count on you. Thanks! I promise not to badger you about dance stuff ever again."

"It's okay," I say. And then, remembering the main reason I'm here, "Lisa's not there with you, is she?"

"No," Angela says. "Weren't she and Evan and Bree heading over to Pie Of Your Dreams? I figured you were with them."

"Oh," I say, my cheeks warming. By Angela's time, that was only half an hour ago. I must sound like a basket case. "Yeah, I had an errand to run, I guess I got so distracted I forgot she mentioned it. Well, I should let you get back to decorating. It's going to be great, Ang."

"You know it," she says. "See you tomorrow!"

Tomorrow. I roll the word around in my head as I drop the phone back into my purse. It feels like a foreign concept now.

We come to a stop in front of my house. An ache spreads through my chest. I left my keys in my school bag in my bedroom, but the spare is where it should be, under the false bottom of the mailbox. I push open the door.

The hall looks the same, and the stairs, and my room with the comforter slightly rumpled where I sat to wipe off my nail polish; my jeans slung over the side of my laundry basket. I let out a breath like a laugh.

"I'll get changed and wash quickly, and then I'll go see Lisa," I say to Win. "Wait downstairs?"

His nod seems hesitant, but he goes without a word. I dig through my closet, trying to decide what to put on. Something that's not too weird for me to be wearing here, but not too weird if I Travel on with Win either … That possibility is feeling more distant with every second I spend breathing the familiar ocean scent of Mom's fabric softener.

In the end I pull out a slightly rumpled peasant skirt Angela encouraged me to buy but that's never felt quite like my style, and a plain T-shirt. Jeanant's cloak can disguise my upper half if I leave this time period again. I peel the cloak off and find the fabric's so thin that if I fold it tightly, I can squeeze it into my purse. I carry the rest of the clothes into the bathroom, so I can clean up before I get dressed.

The face that stares back at me in the mirror is wan and mottled with dirt. A reed tip is tangled in my hair. The memory blinks back: Noam sprawled on the marsh ground, his hair limp against the matted grass. The blood. His jacket, turning so red …

I press my palms against my forehead. Not going to think about it. Not going to think about the slimy texture of the reed—like the ones I pushed past as I slogged through the marsh—as I untangle it. Not going to *feel* all that over again. I'm going to make it right as soon as I can, and then that death won't matter.

Funny how it seems like some huge tragedy has happened, when nothing's actually changed. What I saw has been reality all along. I just didn't know.

Somehow, that's the thought that breaks me. I drop down onto the tiled floor, balling my scarf against my face in an attempt to smother my tears. They hitch out of me in little gasps.

It's been twelve years. In this time, right now, my present, Noam's been dead and tossed away like a piece of litter for twelve whole years. Not wandering in a crowd somewhere. Not living a distant but happy life. Not living at all.

And I was there, and I couldn't stop it.

But I will. I will. I repeat that to myself, and the sobs slow. I have to pull myself together and find out the information Win needs, and then I'll have my chance.

I sway back to my feet and peel off my clothes, splashing water on my face and into my armpits. No time for a shower. I'm pretty sure Lisa had history today. If I can catch her and the others at Pie Of Your Dreams, I can ask her and check her textbook if I need to and this will all be done.

Hair combed and fresh clothes on, I grab a piece of paper and a pen off my desk to shove into my purse, in case I need to note a bunch of details. Then I hurry downstairs. Win's sitting on the leather couch, running his fingers back and forth over the arm, his mouth bent into a crooked smile.

No leather on his space station either? It must be strange, getting such pleasure out of all these things I take for granted. The thought sends a tickle almost like affection through me. When he looks up, I'm hit by a clashing of memories: the guilt on his face after the experimental kiss, the gentleness of his hand steadying me after Noam …

I have other things to focus on right now. "Okay," I say. "Let's solve this riddle."

We walk in silence toward Michlin Street, sticking to less-trafficked side streets. Win's gaze never stops roving around us, but there's no sign of the Enforcers so far. When we turn onto the main strip in the midst of the afternoon shoppers, the brightly painted sign of the pie shop standing out a block and a half away across the street, I stop.

"You can't be, like, hanging around," I say, feeling suddenly awkward. "Lisa and Evan saw you at school yesterday. I don't want to have to make up a story about that too."

Win shrugs. "Not a problem." He glances longingly at the cafe where we first talked, but I guess stopping by there when the Enforcers have already pegged it once is too big a risk.

Instead he gestures to the furniture shop we just passed. "I'll browse around in there until you're done."

"Okay," I say, but my legs balk again when I make to leave. I can't help asking, "You will wait? You won't leave without talking to me?"

He touches the center of his chest and says that short phrase in his own tongue he used when swearing he'd take me home if I'd asked him to, back when he first invited me on this journey. "I promise I'll be here."

He kept that first promise. I offer a small smile, and turn.

"Skylar," he says before I can go, his voice low. He pauses until I look at him. "I— I had a teacher once, one of the veteran Travelers, who oversaw the last segment of our studies. Just about every lesson, he'd go into this little lecture about how we couldn't expect Earthlings to live up to Kemyate standards, that the shifting had made them defective, they just didn't have the same kind of thought or emotion … But I don't think he must have spent much time down here. Or maybe he never really paid attention."

He's still holding my gaze, like it's important to him that I understand. I don't know how to respond, but the words sink into me like a balm. If this is the closest he can bring himself to apologizing, I'll take it.

"Thanks," I say. He gives me a nod and I head to meet my friends.

I weave along the busy sidewalk, surrounded by shops and cafes I've walked past or been in dozens of times. The

"Help Wanted" sign is still there in the window of the vegetarian restaurant. The chain coffee shop is blaring another pop tune. The yoga studio across the street—

The sign flickers before my eyes, as if an afterimage is laid over it. A logo with two stylized figures instead of one. A shiver of *wrong*ness passes through me, but when I blink, both the shiver and the afterimage fade away.

That was … odd.

I amble on, across the street and past Vintage Fleas. My gaze catches on the window display. I stumble, then stop. There … there used to be—I can almost see it—an old phonograph with a mahogany box—in that spot, right there—

No. It's a '70s-style lamp with a fringed shade. Hasn't that always been there? I rub my eyes, and the lamp remains, but so does the sense that I glimpsed something else.

"Sky!" a voice calls. I look up to see Lisa beckoning me from the doorway of Pie Of Your Dreams. "Hey!"

"Hey, Lisa." I hurry over, trying to push my uneasiness away. Inside, Bree and Evan are sitting a table right at the front of the shop.

"I saw you from the window," Lisa says, gesturing as she drops back into her seat next to the glass. I sink into the extra chair.

"I thought you had a lab report to do," Bree says.

Right. The excuse I gave. I put on my best embarrassed face. "I realized after I got home it's due the class after next. Didn't want to miss out on pie if I didn't have to!"

"You want the rest of my pecan?" she asks, nudging her plate with its half-finished slice toward me. "They cut the pieces so big—I think my stomach'll explode if I eat any more."

"It's good for you—puts meat on your bones," Lisa says with a wink, motioning between Bree's thin frame and her own much curvier body. Bree rolls her eyes, but she's grinning.

"Thanks," I say, scooping up a bite. My own stomach's grumbling again at the smell of sugary pecans.

"We were discussing winter break plans," Lisa informs me as I gulp down a few sticky-sweet mouthfuls. "I think we can convince our parents that a road trip down to Miami Beach would be good for our souls. Evan just wants to do another ski trip."

"You know what they're going to think of if we bring up Miami," Evan protests. "Partying, drinking, drugs. It just takes one paranoid parent to shut the whole thing down. And then they'll be suspicious no matter what else we suggest. If you start too big you screw it all up."

"What I want to know is: is there something you've been getting up to that we don't know about, Evan?" Bree asks, arching her eyebrows. "Because my mom would trust me not to do anything too stupid."

Evan grumbles about some parents being more open-minded than others, Lisa shoulders him playfully, Bree shakes her head with a smile and a rustle of her frizzy curls, and I … just sit there. I should be able to jump into the conversation, spin off the joke, offer my own opinion. But somehow even right there with them, I feel slightly out of sync. As if they're a few beats ahead of me and I can't catch up. My last forkful of pie has turned gluey in my mouth.

I swallow it down, forcing a grin so I at least look like I'm participating. It must be that question nagging in the back of my head, for a mission none of my friends have the slightest clue about. If I can just get the answer, take the pressure off, maybe I'll be able to relax.

Just before blood is spilled where the trees were laid low ... The ones who came first, losing their lives to those who came later, because of greed on one side of them and inaction on the other.

"Lisa," I say quickly when there's a break in the banter. "In US history—you've been covering the battles with the Native Americans?"

Bree gives me an odd look. "Yeah," Lisa says. "Why?"

"I, um, this is going to sound a little weird, but I figured it might have come up," I say. "Was there an incident where some Native Americans had a problem with two different groups of settlers at the same time? Pressure from both sides? Maybe something to do with trees being cut down?"

Lisa giggles. "Okay, that does sound weird. Where did *that* come from?"

I motion vaguely. "I was reading this book—it referenced it, but without any details—I was just wondering what it was talking about."

"And I'm sure Lisa was paying sooo much attention in class," Bree says teasingly. But Lisa's expression has gone thoughtful.

"I think there was a thing about the Native Americans being between two sides," she says. "We watched this documentary a couple weeks ago—and then we had a big discussion about the different alliances. The British were supposed to be helping the Native Americans against the American soldiers taking their land. But then there was this battle where the Native Americans came to ask for protection at some British fort, and the British said no way."

Greed and inaction … "That sounds like it," I say, my heart leaping.

"I don't remember anything about trees being cut down, though," she says with a shrug.

"It might not have been cut down, I guess. Just that they'd fallen."

"Oh, that. . . Maybe the name of the battle was something about fallen trees? Because there was a storm that knocked a bunch down where they were fighting or something."

"You remember where it was?" I ask. "The battle?"

She laughs. "We didn't talk about it *that* much."

Bree is still watching me, her eyebrows slightly raised. "You could probably look it up now if you need to know more, right?"

"Yeah," I say, pulling myself back. That should give us enough detail for Win to find the right battle in his time-cloth computer.

"And now back to more important topics," Lisa says, leaning toward Evan. "How can we make this beach trip happen?"

As they talk about sun and sand, my mind slips to an imagined battlefield: trees laid low by a storm, Native soldiers fighting Americans, the British watching at a distance …

Guns firing. Blood spilling. Bodies crumpling.

If anything, I feel even more detached from the others now. Here I am, hanging out with my friends as if nothing's wrong in the world—as if Jeanant isn't racing through the past trying to save our planet, as if some new shift couldn't rewrite all our lives at any instant. My skin tightens.

"What about you, Skylar?" Bree says, breaking through my thoughts. "What do you think? We're going to have to work together on this."

"Yeah," I manage. "Ah, maybe if we picked a different beach that's not right by Miami?"

"But still close enough that we could drive over there to party a little," Bree says, and jabs her finger in the air. "Genius!"

What does Miami matter when the atoms around us are disintegrating? Bree's comment pulls up an echo of Jeanant's words from the recording: *Working together … we can become something so incredible that we'll set all our lives on a completely different course.* I was a part of *that*, of fixing myself, fixing this whole world.

But like Win said, I've contributed lots already. Why can't I count that as enough risks taken, and just enjoy the fact that I got home safe?

Lisa lets out a low whistle, looking out the front window. "Whoa. I've never seen anyone bleach their hair that light and still make it look natural."

I follow her gaze, and my back goes rigid. It's Kurra. With her white-blond hair mostly covered by her hood, stalking down the sidewalk past the pie shop. She probably would have seen me if she'd glanced in the window—I'm only five feet back from the glass. But she's focused on a metallic square in her slim hand.

"Maybe it is natural," Evan's saying. "She could be an albino."

Kurra glances up briefly, looking down the street, and picks her pace up to a jog. Toward the store where I left Win. In a second, she's passed out of view.

"Don't albinos have pink eyes?" Lisa says. "Hers looked gray."

My lungs constrict. Win has no way of knowing she's coming for him without his alarm band. And any second one of her colleagues could come by and notice me. Me here with Bree and Lisa and Evan, who are oblivious to the danger— easy collateral damage.

I've jeopardized everyone around me, and everything I've been trying to help Win accomplish, for a little comfort I couldn't even enjoy.

"I think that's mice with the pink eyes," Bree says, and I push back my chair.

"Sorry, guys," I say. "I've—ah—I just remembered, there was something I promised my mom I'd take care of before she got home—"

They're staring at me, but that no longer matters. I wave my hand with a tight smile, and rush outside.

24.

I hesitate when I reach the sidewalk, drawing back toward the shop's doorway. Kurra's partway down the next block now, almost at the furniture store where Win said he'd wait. She pauses amid the flow of pedestrians, and then strides on past it. I assumed she was tracking him somehow, but maybe he found a way to throw her off.

Or maybe he's gone?

My chest clenches tighter. The moment Kurra disappears around the next corner, I sprint down the street. I burst into the furniture shop, breathless. A young couple is meandering amid the coffee tables. Two employees with name tags are murmuring near the counter, the older one scowling as though he's rebuking the younger. Win's nowhere to be seen.

Did he leave the second I walked out? Maybe he decided, with my meltdowns and demands, it was more trouble than it was worth to keep me around.

Even as the fear jolts through me, I'm already discounting it. I remember the way he said his promise, the way he held my gaze. Whatever else I might criticize him for, he hasn't ever gone back on his word.

So where is he?

The older employee saunters away, leaving the younger to do a circuit of the store. I hurry over to him.

"Excuse me," I say. "Did you see a guy in here, black hair, brown clothes, carrying a—"

The young man's mouth twists. "Are you with him? When you see him, tell him fire exits are for emergencies only. And he's lucky that chair he knocked over didn't break."

My gaze darts to a small sign at the back of the store, over the outline of a doorway. He ran out the back. Like in the coffee shop the other day. He must have been watching from the front windows, and seen Kurra or one of her colleagues coming.

"Thanks!" I say, and dart out. I circle the block and duck down the alley past the backs of the stores.

Win isn't there either, but I didn't expect him to be. He said something, when the Enforcers chased us before, about getting "out of range." If Kurra's tracking him, I'd guess her tech works something like the alarm band. It didn't direct her to me, so it must be picking up his … alienness. She probably needs to be close to pick him up. In which case he'd have tried to get some distance.

I edge down the alley toward the back of the furniture store. He wouldn't have gone anywhere the Enforcers might already know about, like the coffee shop or the hotel. And he wouldn't have risked leading them back to my house. But I can't just hang around here hoping he's able to double back— one of the Enforcers could show up anytime.

A splotch of color catches my eye on the pavement outside the door: a small splatter of blue liquid. A shade of blue I recognize from Win's drinking bottle. I stop, and test it with the toe of my boot. It streaks at my touch. Fresh.

I hustle farther down the alley. Another tiny splash has hit the edge of the laundromat by the street. He's left me a trail. So he went to the right, from here.

I poke my head out to check for Enforcers, and then jog down the street. I'm starting to think I made a mistake, that it was a coincidence, when I spot a third speckling of blue on the sidewalk, in a line like he was running to cross the street when he spilled it. On the opposite curb, a little more. I jog on.

Farther down, a streak of blue dapples the front step of a hulking brick building. I take in the boarded lower windows, the battered "For Sale" sign, the empty socket where the doorknob should have been. It looks abandoned. He went in there—to hide? The building is several stories high, so maybe he thought he could get enough distance from the street to avoid the Enforcers' tracking that way.

Any doubt vanishes when a face appears in a fifth-floor window. Win raises his hand to me with a tense smile, and waves me up. A grin breaks across my face as I nod. He's fine.

I hurry across the street and nudge open the knobless door. It gives a soft creak, and then there's a whisper behind me, so faint I might have missed it if I weren't already on edge. I glance back.

The air is shimmering on the sidewalk just outside the door. I flinch, and scramble behind a dusty reception desk just as Kurra emerges from a time cloth outside.

I crouch there, heart thudding. She marches straight in, past me, toward something at the left. A stairwell. Her footsteps clatter up the stairs.

Crap. I stand up, wavering on my feet. She's figured out Win is here—somehow. Maybe they have better tech than even Win realized. And now she's between me and him. I dart a look toward the door, but for all I know there are more Enforcers waiting outside.

Win saw me come in. If I head toward him, maybe he can evade Kurra and reach me like he did by the caves.

I creep to the stairwell through a wide room floored with cheap tiles and scattered with the remains of an office area: a few laminate desks and plastic chairs, a tipped-over cubicle divider, a scrawl of crimson spray paint on the wall. Given the broken door, we're obviously not the first people to have made illicit use of the space. Inching up the stairs, I can't hear Kurra above me. She must have already gone out onto one of the upper floors.

If I'm lucky, she didn't know exactly which one Win's on, and I can sneak right past her to him.

I steal up toward the fifth floor as quickly and quietly as I can manage. I've just passed the second-floor landing when a yell carries from above. Another voice responds, too muffled for me to decipher. I push myself onward, breath held. There's another exchange, and then a sound I'd recognize anywhere. The out-of-tune twang of an Enforcer's weapon, piercing the air.

I freeze. Another shout reaches me, loud enough that I can make out the words.

"You're supposed to be protecting Kemya," Win's saying. "Why aren't you there instead of worrying about what happens on Earth?"

His voice is ragged, as if it's taking all the effort he has in him just to project it. He's already tired out—from the recent run here, from evading Kurra, and maybe her colleagues too. Why is he talking at all? His voice is going to draw them right to …

Oh. It's for me. To draw *me* to him. I swallow thickly. He's putting himself in even more danger so I can find him.

Kurra's stilted voice yells back. "Why are *you* worrying about what happens here?" She pauses. "You're almost surrounded. I can see you—just a little dot on my screen. You may as well give yourself up."

I edge up the stairs. Her screen—her tracking device. But she still doesn't know I'm here. She probably doesn't even suspect the girl she's seen him with is human. Traveling with me is forbidden, after all. I guess that's one small advantage.

"You're giving up your life for people who are just shadows," Kurra says. "Why do they deserve your loyalty more than Kemya?"

"We're the ones who made them this way," Win says. "What we did to them, what we're still doing—it isn't right."

"Most of Kemya would disagree with you," Kurra retorts. Her voice is coming from somewhere across the fourth floor. She must have caught Win on his way down to meet me.

Neither Win nor she nor any other Enforcer is in sight from the fourth-floor landing. There's a lot more furniture here than below. A mess of gray desks and dividers blocks off my view of most of the room. Whatever company owned the building must have gone under, and decided it'd cost more to haul out the furniture than leave it. I squeeze between two dividers pushed at awkward angles to each other, straining my ears and my eyes in the dim light.

"They haven't been here," Win says, somewhere to my left. "They don't understand. If they did ..." His voice quavers, and cuts off. My stomach flips over in the time it takes for him to find it again. "No one back home would want their lives controlled this way."

I veer toward him, staying crouched and setting my feet carefully amid the bits of glass from a shattered desktop. My ankle, the one I injured in Vietnam, twinges.

Kurra gives a hoarse chuckle. "You don't think we have our lives controlled, one way or another, on Kemya? Have you made every choice in your life perfectly freely?" Her voice bounces off the walls, the low ceiling, but I think it's more to my right. Good. I can still hope to get to him first.

"It's not the same," Win says.

I skirt a tipped-over desk and step across a scattering of faded printouts in what seems to be the middle of the room. Several of them are stained with splotches of yellow. The scent of old cat urine hangs in the air.

"No," Kurra agrees. "Because Earth *belongs* to us. The colonists who volunteered to settle on this insignificant planet knew what that meant. All you're doing is defiling their sacrifice."

What? I halt in midstep, catching my balance against the cracked seat of a chair.

"Maybe the original colonists agreed to participate," Win says. "But their descendants weren't given a choice. Why should these people keep paying for the decisions their ancestors made hundreds of generations ago?"

The original colonists ... Hundreds of generations ago ... He can't really mean—

I scoot around a table. Footsteps rasp somewhere nearby. Kurra, or one of her companions?

Her reply rings out so clearly she can't be more than ten feet away. "All of us live with what *our* ancestors did to Kemya. We keep paying for their mistakes. At least the first Earthlings came by choice and not through a careless accident."

I don't want to hear any more of this. I force myself to keep going. I have to find Win. There's nothing else that matters right now.

Two dividers bent toward each other form a narrow passage. I slip down it. Win's voice comes from just up ahead. "So we lost one choice, and they only got one."

"I'm protecting my people; that is all I need to know," Kurra returns.

I creep forward a few more steps. There's a rasp of indrawn breath, and Win's voice wavers out one more time, from what sounds like just the other side of the divider next to me.

"And I'm protecting *all* our people."

I don't let myself think about anything else—about what he's saying, what she said, what it means. We have to get out of here. My lips part, but in the same moment papers crinkle on the floor behind me. Too close. They'll hear me.

I reach out and rap my knuckles lightly against the plasticky surface of the divider. One, two, three. If they hear that, hopefully they'll think it's Win.

"Skylar?" Win whispers.

Again: one, two, three. I hesitate with my hand against the wall. The person behind me treads closer.

"Stay where you are!" a male voice snaps. The man I saw with Kurra before barges around the table into the makeshift passage. I scramble away with a yelp, eyes fixed on the weapon in his hand. The air blurs between us. Win tosses back the time cloth and whips a metallic marble from his hand.

It explodes in the Enforcer's face with a shower of sparks. He winces, arms flying up, and the blaster twangs. Its bolt of light crackles against the unlit fluorescent panels in the ceiling, sending a shower of plastic shards down on us. One slices across my forehead.

The man keeps coming. Win lurches into me, spinning us around and pulling the cloth over us. The Enforcer is wiping his eyes, raising his weapon, as the derelict office dims and washes away like paint in the rain.

The cloth whirs and shrieks and deposits us in front of a row of pale houses with red roofs. I catch just a glimpse before we shudder away again amid an increasingly frantic series of pings. Win's fingers dart over the data panel. He lets go of me to squeeze his other hand against his side. The flickering yellow light turns the dark patch on his shirt a deep orange.

He's bleeding. Blood down his side, trickling over his hand.

25.

The cloth heaves to the ground, and Win staggers. I catch him as he turns back to the display.

"Win, you have to stop! You're hurt."

He's panting. It wasn't just fatigue I heard in his voice before, it was pain. "I'll be fine," he says. "Just a cut. Stupid glass."

His hand slips, and I see what he means. A thick chunk, its edge glitteringly sharp, is protruding through a tear in his shirt from the flesh just below his ribs. The shot I heard on my way up the stairs, or an earlier one, must have caught one of the glass desks when he was near it. Blood is welling up around the chunk, soaking into the waist of his pants now. Nausea washes over me.

"You're not fine! We have you to get to a hospital. You need someone to look after that *now*."

He's shaking his head. The idiot. He'd let himself bleed to death in front of me if he could. He almost did, wandering around that office with Kurra following him when he could have jumped away. I push between him and the data panel, digging Jeanant's cloak from my purse.

"At a hospital ... records ... they could track us," he mumbles as I try to wrap the thin fabric around his abdomen. He looks down at his side. At his bloody fingers. A gasp sputters out of him. "That doesn't look so great. Okay."

"I don't care where we go," I say. "As long as it's someplace you can get help."

He's still staring at the wound. I nudge his hand away and hold the cloak in place. Blood immediately begins to seep through the fabric, but it's something.

"She's going to be mad," Win says shakily. "Well ... she was already going to be mad. And the cloth ..."

I don't know what he's talking about. He reaches past me to tap the panel.

"Where are we going?" I ask.

"Somewhere good," he says. "Everything'll be fixed. I promise."

It's night where we touch down, on a cobblestone road lined with squat wooden buildings. The windows are dark, but the light of the near-full moon catches on puddles and moist patches on the stones. The smell of rot tinges the air. I grab the time cloth from Win as he tries to stuff it into his satchel one-handed. His other hand is clamped to his side, over the expanding red splotch on the cloak, and I don't want him moving it.

"Where do we go from here?" I murmur.

Win jerks his head toward the end of the street and starts walking, a hitch in every step. His jaw is clenched. He swerves around the corner at the first cross street and heads down a narrower road. When his knees wobble, I grasp his elbow. His lips twist into a grimace. He keeps going, with my grip steadying him, past a courtyard and around a stable. But his steps are slowing to a hobble.

"Just a little farther," he rasps. "Couldn't let the Enforcers trace us too close."

If I were strong enough, I'd carry him the rest of the way. As it is, I'm scared to get any closer—scared of bumping that slice of glass deeper into his side. My hold on his arm tightens as we scramble over a particularly uneven section of road. He stops, his gaze drifting, and then pushes onward.

"There," he says.

We edge around the back of a house, and pause at a small wooden door in what appears to be a shed. The knob looks ordinary to me, but Win does something with it, pushes one spot and tugs another, spins it and jiggles it, and somewhere inside a bolt grates open. He shoves the door wide and lurches away from me, down the flight of stone steps on the other side.

"Close it behind you," he mumbles. I do, bracing myself for the darkness, but the instant the door clicks into the frame, the deadbolt shoots over of its own accord, and a faint streak of artificial light flickers down the slanted ceiling.

Win's already made it to the bottom of the stairs, where there's another door almost identical to the one above. Only this one doesn't even have a knob. He slides his fingernails along an indent in the middle, and flips open a thin flap in the wood to reveal a black metallic square. Clearing his throat, he presses his thumb against the square.

At the short phrase he says in his alien language, the door emits a quiet hum, followed by a sound like a sigh. Then it glides back into the wall. Win staggers on into the room on the other side.

I hurry after him. The door whispers shut behind me, so swiftly I flinch. The second it's closed, three bright lights blaze on above our heads.

The room is smaller than my bedroom at home, and windowless, with a set of narrow bunks built into one wall, two wide cabinets on the other, and a spindly chair mounted on a large silvery cube at the opposite end from the door. Even though the place feels unlived in, there's a fresh tang in the air and no hint of dust. Everything—the seamless mattresses on the bunks, the chair, the tiled floor—has the hard sheen of metal in muted shades of gray, peach, and brown. But the surface beneath my feet gives like linoleum, and when I set my hand on the edge of the upper bunk, the frame offers the warmer, slightly gritty texture of plastic, as if it's some synthesis of steel and polyethylene. Which I guess it could be.

Win motions vaguely around him. "Safe house. Only for total, absolute emergencies. There's supplies. Take anything you want." He limps over to the chair and sinks into it with a wince, reaching behind its arm.

There must be a control there I can't see, because a moment later a shimmering glow flows out of the block at the chair's base, cocooning him. It seems to condense at the spot above his wound. He peels away the cloak with a shudder and tips his head back, closing his eyes.

Through the ragged gap in Win's shirt, I can see the rough edges of broken skin, the blood seeping out around the jutting chunk of glass. His body looks so fragile. Fragile, and human. Human skin ripped back from human flesh, human blood coursing from human veins.

Colonists. Ancestors.

The memory of the conversation I overheard weighs on me. But I can't ask him about it now.

As the glow continues to pool over the wound, the slice of glass starts to crumble and then wisp away, as if the light is somehow consuming it. Win's blood bubbles up more quickly as the obstruction dissolves. I step toward him, afraid something's gone wrong, but a second later the bleeding slows. His skin creeps over the exposed flesh. The glow intensifies, so bright it stings my eyes. When I look again, as the light dims, Win's abdomen is smooth and whole again. Even the blood on his clothes has been whisked away.

Win keeps lying there, completely still and silent except for the stutter of his breath in his chest. The glow wavers and swirls, I suppose healing whatever was injured on the inside. I sit down on the lower bunk, watching. The minutes drag on.

What if he was too hurt for it to completely heal him? My fingers itch, and I reach into my purse for my bracelet, but the slick surface of the beads gives me none of their usual reassurance. To distract myself, I get up and walk over to the cabinets.

The first door opens to reveal six shelves, two stacked with bottles like the ones Win was carrying in his satchel, but tinted green instead of blue, and the others holding boxes stuffed with sandwich-size packets that feel waxy to my touch. Win said I could take anything, but who knows what's in there?

The bottles seem safer. I pick up one and twist the lid open. The liquid fizzes lightly as I tip the bottle to my lips. I sip tentatively, then take a few deeper gulps, washing the traces of soured pecan pie from my mouth. The liquid has the same sweet taste as the blue stuff, but a prickle of some sort of spice as well—like cinnamon, but not quite.

I lower the bottle, feeling my heartbeat slow, my muscles relaxing. Maybe there's something in there other than water and flavoring.

My newfound calm doesn't stop me from jumping at an unexpected rustle. "Hey," Win says softly, straightening up in the chair. The glow has dissipated. He twists at the torso, and then leans forward to rest his elbows on his knees, his body tilted a little to the left as if his right side is still tender. Then he sneezes, twice.

"Are you okay?" I ask.

"Yes," he says. His voice is faint, but nowhere near as wretched as when he was bleeding all over himself. "You know, I think somewhere in all this Traveling, I caught a— what do you call it?—a cold." He sniffs experimentally, and chuckles. "We're inoculated against everything serious, but even we haven't come up with a proper vaccine for an ever-mutating virus. The one thing the med seat can't cure."

"Not much good then, is it?" I say without thinking, and Win outright laughs. He pinches the bridge of his nose.

"Well, it fixed everything else." He tips a little farther, and then pushes himself upright, his eyes suddenly intense. "You talked to your friend? Did she help you figure out Jeanant's message?"

After what he just went through, he still cares more about the mission than anything else. He'd rather die than fail, I think with a twinge. Even though it's my planet we're saving. He's risked so much more than I have, and I was ready to step away.

"There was a battle," I say. "Between the American settlers and the Natives, near a British fort, somewhere a bunch of trees had fallen because of a storm. The name probably has something to do with that—with fallen trees."

"That's enough," he says, a smile crossing his face. "And Jeanant said he'd leave the last two parts for us there?"

"He didn't really have time to go into detail," I say. "But when I asked him to give me everything we needed, he told me to go there."

"That must be his plan, then. Hand me the cloth? I should be able to find the exact date easily now."

I pick up the cloth where I left it in a heap on the bunk. When I turn, Win bends his head to cough, looking so tired despite his relief that I'm afraid he's going to topple off the chair. So … vulnerable.

So human.

I stare at his face. Following the shape of his jaw, the angle of his brow, the curve of his cheeks. I never questioned it, just assumed it was a disguise. But he never looked fake, or felt it, or—in that moment, in the rain—*tasted* anything but real.

Win glances up at me. His forehead furrows when he catches my stare. Exactly as a human's would.

"It's true, isn't it?" I say.

The furrow deepens. "What?"

"I heard your conversation with Kurra," I say. "Most of it, anyway. About … colonists from Kemya coming to Earth?"

"Ah," he says, and his head droops again. "I forgot you didn't know."

My fingers tense around the time cloth. "Well, I don't," I say. "You didn't *tell* me."

"You seemed so disoriented already, when I was explaining why we came here," he says. "And it doesn't really matter. When the time field's destroyed, when Kemya has no business with Earth anymore, it may as well not be true. We'll be two separate peoples."

"But we're not," I say. "We're— You're—"

He nods, with a shamed curl to his lips. Every time he forms another distinctly human expression, my awareness of it prickles deeper.

"The story I told you before was true," he says. "Except there wasn't any fully sentient species on Earth when we discovered it. All the plants and animals you know, yes, some quite similar to what we had on Kemya, but ... no people. And we needed people down here to participate in the experiments, to test our survival strategies, to make sure that even if all the tech we had stopped functioning before the rest of us landed, or if we crashed, or anything else that could go wrong, we could still survive. To try out different techniques and different situations, to see what worked best. It was going to be our only chance to do things right ..."

"So you sent some of your people down."

"A few hundred Kemyates volunteered. I don't know how much they were told—it's usually glossed over when we talk about our history; everything's about their valiant sacrifice. You heard the way Kurra thinks about it. They were sent down with no tech, no way of communicating with the scientists above, prepared to face the worst and let their experiences guide the rest of us. But they must have assumed that after a decade or two, everyone else would follow. Once we were confident we could handle any problem the planet presented."

He pauses, his expression miserable. I know the rest: "But then your experiments started screwing up Earth, and it wasn't good enough for the rest of you anymore." I should be horrified, but mostly I'm numb. The idea refuses to sink in.

"And the people we'd left down here, they had children, and their children had children, and they slowly lost the story of where they came from," Win says. "You can see echoes of it, in some of the myths …"

We're all just aliens who forgot we were aliens. I start to laugh, but it catches in my throat. No. Not aliens. Humans who didn't know we didn't belong on Earth.

"There are fossils," I say. "I know archeologists have found— There are remains in our evolutionary tree, going back *millions* of years."

Win shrugs. "Faked. Like I said, there was already some similarity between the species here and what we had on Kemya. The scientists planted missing links when they noticed you were looking. To see how you'd react. To erase any lingering doubt. I'm not totally sure."

"But …"

What argument do I have that defeats the vast reach of Kemyate technology? These are people who can leap through time, travel across galaxies, heal a near-fatal wound with light. Why shouldn't they be able to make a skull read as millions of years old?

"I know it's awful," Win says. "I can't even explain how everyone just kept going along with it for so long ..."

"You don't really think we're part of your people anymore," I say. The way he talked to me when we first met. The way Kurra talked about us. *Shadows.* "Because we've been fading away, just like our history. Because of what you've done to us."

What they did to us not as aliens looking down on some less advanced species, the way Earth scientists poke at rats, which was horrible enough. They conducted their experiments and played with our lives as one set of human beings manipulating another. The figures I've imagined up there, staring down into their goldfish bowl from orbit, think and feel almost the same ways I do. And somehow they could do this.

"It's easy to see other people as hardly people at all when you're watching them from a distance," Win says quietly. "When they live so differently from you. When you've been trained since you were born to think of them as something apart. Earthlings do it all the time, to each other. How many of your wars have been fought because one group of you decided you had the right to conquer another group, to enslave them or slaughter them?"

How many of those wars were started because of Kemyate interference? I want to ask. But the question dies before I open my mouth. I watched the revolutionaries in France, the soldiers in Vietnam, the boys lording their power over Noam and Darryl in the marsh. Humans have always known how to hurt each other. Maybe we've been nudged in new directions from time to time, but no one forced war or oppression, genocide or terrorism, on us.

"A few of us are trying to make it right, at least," Win adds. He rubs his face.

"Is it really going to be all right?" I ask. "You'll blow up the time field generator, and then what—find some shiny new planet to explore while we're left here?" I grope for a concept that could apply—restitution? Compensation?—but the scope of the injury done to this world is so immense it's hard to comprehend. I'm scared to ask how long it'll take for us to bounce back. Thousands more years?

Win's lifted his gaze. "I just know that it'll be better for you if the time field is gone. Does it make that much of a difference that we're not as alien as I let you think? Would you have decided to stay home and not help if you'd known?"

It makes a huge difference. Just the sight of him strikes me with a jab of betrayal. Because he's one of them, part of this setup ... And not. It all started so long ago. He didn't have any more choice in how his people first came to Earth than I did.

He's right too. I'd still be here. The Traveling, the great experiment, it still needs to be stopped.

"*Did* you want to stay home?" Win says suddenly. "There wasn't really a chance to ask when you came to meet me, back in your city. I can still bring you back, now that I'm ..." He gestures at his healed side.

"No," I say. "I decided I want to keep going. To see this through to the end, to make sure you get all the pieces of the weapon. So I know, for sure, it's over." I pause. "And I would still have been here, even if I'd known. I just wish you'd told me before."

"I'm sorry," he says. "I— I think it's mostly that I didn't want to see you look at me the way you are right now."

I bite my lip, closing my eyes. The shock keeps reverberating through me. I've got nothing left to say.

The silence stretches between us. There's a whisper of fabric as Win eases out of the chair.

"You're hurt," he says. "Your forehead …"

I reach up, finding the spot where the shattered office light hit me. A sticky line of congealing blood just below my hairline. It stings at my touch. I'd been so worried about Win as we fled that I hardly noticed it before.

"I'm sorry," Win says again, his voice dropping. "I thought I could avoid the Enforcers completely if I moved fast enough—I didn't mean to lead you straight to them. I would have gone back for you, if you hadn't found the trail I left."

"What were you thinking?" I say, abruptly angry. "They were shooting at you—you were bleeding to death—you should have gotten out of there."

The look he gives me is bewildered, as if I've suggested he should have scared the Enforcers away by dancing a jig. "*You* were there. I didn't know how close you were. I didn't know how quickly they'd leave if I did. I couldn't just abandon you there with them."

Except he could have. It would have been easy. But his regret over my little scratch is so palpable, I can't bring myself to say that.

"I'm fine," I say instead. "It's nothing."

"I have another …" He bends down, lurches, and grabs his satchel. With a shaky hand, he fishes out a patch like the one he gave me for my ankle. "It's my last one," he says apologetically, "but there's probably a few more here I can take, just in case." He raises his hands toward me, and then hesitates. "Can I?"

I nod and dip my head, tugging my hair aside. My words from earlier echo in my memory: *Don't* ever *touch me again*. I shut my eyes as his fingers brush across my temple, patting the bandage in place. The contact is actually soothing. A more recent image rises up: Win stalking through the maze of desks and dividers, trying to find me before Kurra did, so focused on my safety he didn't even notice how deeply the glass had cut him. He didn't even know if I'd found his answer. But he'd promised to wait. He'd promised not to leave without me.

"Thank you," I say as he lowers his hands.

He gives me a tight little smile. Then he sneezes, and stumbles, and I have to catch his shoulder to stop him from falling over.

"You're supposed to rest, after the med seat," he mutters. "I'll be all right, though. But the cloth … If we're going to Travel again, we should charge it."

He takes the time cloth from me and crouches down, rocking on his feet. A tiny glinting string unhooks from a spot near the top of the arch. He pokes it into a similarly sized hole by the base of the cabinet. Then, as if he can't help it, he leans forward so his head rests against the cabinet door, holding him up.

"It'll take hours to charge fully. But we just need a bit. And then we can go."

"Then you *should* rest," I say. "You obviously need it. Do you think— Are we really safe here?"

"For a while," he says. "This is a general safe house, but Thlo was able to covertly set aside a period of time, and Isis put another scrambling code on it … But we know now the Enforcers can break those with enough effort. I'll just rest a little." He wavers to his feet and makes it the few steps to the bunks before collapsing on the lower one.

"As much as you need," I say. It took the Enforcers days to start tracing Win, after he caught their attention stopping the courthouse bombing. Surely we have at least a few hours here. I sink down on the floor beside the bed, propping myself against the side of the bunks. "You sleep. I'll watch for … for anything wrong."

He nods against the mattress. His hand shifts toward me restlessly.

"Skylar," he mumbles. "You're not just a tool."

I glance over at him, but his eyes are shut. A slow breath rasps over his parted lips. He looks so deeply asleep I wonder if I just imagined him speaking. I have the urge to take that outstretched hand and squeeze it, but that might wake him up.

He's not just a lackey in this rebel group either. He deserves every bit of the respect he's trying to earn. Sick and tired and exhausted—but nothing's stopped him from working toward their cause.

From keeping his promise to protect me.

It wasn't right, how he treated me at first. But he hasn't only been thinking of his mission. The risks he took, the danger he put himself in just an hour ago—that was for me. So I could decide whether I wanted to go with him. So the Enforcers wouldn't hurt me the way they'd already hurt him. Watching his sleeping form, I feel a little tug inside, as if whatever injury he did to me has been stitched back together with a thread of forgiveness.

As the minutes slip by, the lights in the ceiling dim. I pull my knees in toward my chest and clasp my hands in front of them. My stomach pangs, and my ankle pulses with a muted ache, but I ignore both. After a while, my own eyelids drift down. I jerk them up. Someone has to keep watch.

I get up and look through the cabinets again. Drink some more of the greenish water that smooths the jitters from my nerves. Prod the other packets, and decide I'm not quite curious enough yet to risk opening one.

In the second cabinet, the one I hadn't checked before, there are bundles of folded Traveler clothes, packets of the alien bandages, and other bits and pieces I don't recognize. I pull out one of the shirts, holding it to myself. About the right size. If we're going a few centuries into America's past, this'll probably look better than my modern T-shirt. I pull it over my head.

When I sit back by the bunks, I pick up my purse and reach for the bracelet instinctively. My fingers graze the folded paper I stuck inside for note-taking. Didn't need to use it after all.

Maybe it can serve another purpose. One more stop, and then hopefully I can go back to save Noam. I need to figure out what to write to him; what he'd believe.

I pull out the pen and the paper, setting the latter on the floor. *Noam,* I write. The *m* wobbles. I stop, staring at the blank page, and bite the end of the pen. *When you get home, Darryl's going to call you. He's going to sound upset, but it's just a joke. A prank he's pulling on you.*

Is that enough? If I try to explain how I know this, I'll probably just end up sounding sketchy.

I'm composing the next sentence in my head when footsteps thud outside the door.

26.

The lights overhead flash brighter as I jump up. "Win," I whisper, grasping his shoulder. "Win!"

Win flinches awake, rolling off the bunk onto his feet. As he teeters, swiping at his eyes, I shove my partly written note into my purse and reach for the time cloth. And the inner door hisses open.

The guy who strides in comes to a halt just inside, the door wisping shut behind him. His eyebrows rise. The comment he makes in Kemyate sounds amused. I pause, still crouched by the cloth on the floor. Win's tensed, but he's just glowering at the guy, his expression more pained than frightened.

Do they know each other? The guy doesn't look much older than Win. He's a couple inches taller, well built, with a sheen of black hair, and he's wearing similar Traveler clothes.

"What are you doing here?" Win asks, his voice as stiff as his posture.

"Thlo set the safe house to send a signal if someone used it during this time," the guy replies, following the switch to English with a nearly perfect American accent. At the mention of that familiar name, my frantic heartbeat slows to something closer to its usual pace. "She asked me to check in." He chuckles, his teeth flashing white against his dark skin. "So you managed to get yourself into trouble even in the twenty-first century, *Dar*win?"

Darwin? Oh. Win—Darwin. Our code name conversation comes back to me. "Galápagos," I murmur, and the newcomer's gaze flicks to me. His eyes narrow, and the jaunty tone vanishes. He snaps out a question, back in their shared language.

Win's flushed. "*She* is Skylar," he says. He covers a sneeze, and moves a little in front of me as if to shield me. "And it's thanks to her I've been doing your job for you, Jule."

The guy—Jule—launches into what sounds like the start of a rant, throwing his arm in the air. Win's hands clench at his sides. He cuts Jule off before the other guy's gotten very far.

"If you want to argue about it, speak in English so she knows what's going on too," he says. "I'm not talking about it otherwise."

Jule's eyes flash, and in that second he looks almost as dangerous as Kurra. Then he sighs and steps over to lean against the bunks, folding his arms across his chest.

"How much have you told her?"

"She knows everything," Win says. "She needed to."

"I'm not going to give away your secrets," I say. Jule's gaze darts to me and back to Win.

"I think you'd better explain this directly to Thlo," he says. He reaches behind him to a leather bag a little larger than Win's satchel and pulls out a time cloth of his own.

Win's shaking his head. "You don't get it. We've tracked down almost every part of the weapon, Jule. We've only got one more place to go."

"Sure you do," Jule says. "*You*'ve managed to track down the meaning of Jeanant's messages with some Earthling girl while the rest of us are still deciphering the first detail. I knew growing up with that rotter family of yours left you soft-brained, but hell. Did you sniff too much of your dad's paint fumes before you left?"

"No, and I can think a lot better than some coaster who lets his grandfather's accomplishments do his work for him," Win retorts. "Look. What do you think this is?"

He pulls one of Jeanant's plastic slabs from his satchel, holding it close enough for Jule to read the characters etched along it. When Jule reaches for it, he jerks it back. "Just look."

Jule's expression transforms from skeptical to startled in a way I find immensely gratifying after how snarky he's been with Win. I straighten up as he steps closer.

"You really did it," Jule says in a low voice, and laughs. "How the hell …"

"It was Skylar," Win says, motioning to me. "You know we talked in training about how there were probably Earthlings sensitive enough to be disturbed by the shifts— she's one of them. She figured out exactly where Jeanant went in France, then helped me follow the signs after that. It's because of her we have almost everything we need, and we know where to go next, where to get the rest, so we can finish the mission and go home."

"It was still stupid, Win," Jule says. "You know the rules are there for a reason. We have to bring this to Thlo. She's the one who should decide."

"So the rules are more important to you than getting the weapon?" I ask.

He looks at me, a little more thoughtful this time, and his mouth quirks into half a smile. "It's nothing personal, Earthling. Most of us know there's a good reason to follow the safety precautions." He hesitates, and his gaze slides to Win again. His smile disappears. "Unless you were planning on following the standard protocol for data compromisation."

Standard protocol? Win looks puzzled for all of a second before his golden-brown skin goes greenish. "Of course not!" he bites out.

"What's—" I start to ask, and then it hits me. Data compromisation. *It's a local. He saw us.* Kurra's blast. My stomach flips over. "Win …"

"Before anyone hurts you, they'd have to kill me first," Win says, more threatening than I've ever heard him, but his arm trembles where he's clutching the plastic slab. Abruptly, I remember the way he evaded the subject of contacting the others, letting them know what we were doing, when I brought it up before. I thought the excuses were pride, his need to prove himself. But if standard protocol is eliminating any Earthling who sees a Traveler in action ... maybe he wasn't avoiding the subject because his reasons not to contact them were selfish. Maybe he just didn't want to tell me that he was afraid of what the others might want to do to me, if they knew.

I touch Win's back, wanting to express somehow that I'm with him.

Jule rolls his eyes, but his discomfort shows in the dampening of his voice. "I'm not saying *I* think that's a good plan."

"And Thlo?" Win says. "What would she think?"

"I'm pretty sure she's smart enough to come up with a few alternatives," Jule replies, but I don't find his tone completely convincing.

Apparently Win doesn't either. "I can make sure of that if we go get the rest of the weapon first. Once we have everything, there's no mission to jeopardize."

"I can't let you do that," Jule says. "You expect me to go back to Thlo and tell her I let you run off with some Earthling? Or to lie to her?"

"It's for Thlo too," I say. "The Enforcers—they've managed to track our time cloth. If we jump to wherever Thlo and the others are, we'll be leading the Enforcers straight to them."

"Then we'll go in mine," Jule says, still addressing Win.

"It'll only hold two," Win says. "We can't just leave Skylar here."

"It's as safe a place as any, for her and us. As long as … She's from the twenty-first? You did check what she's carrying, right?"

"What?"

Jule turns to me. "What's in that purse?"

I inch back, my hands tightening around it. "Nothing important."

"Right." He steps forward as if to take it, and Win shoves in front of him. Jule raises his arm to elbow Win to the side. Win's braced himself for a fight, but Jule is bigger, and probably stronger, and Win was half dead a couple hours ago.

"Stop it!" I say, and thrust my purse toward Jule. He backs off of Win immediately, accepting the purse with surprising grace.

"Thank you," he says. Then he fishes inside, pulls out my phone, and tosses it on the floor.

"Hey!" I cry, but he's already smashing it under his heel. He gives the screen a few good stomps, until the glass is splintered and the shell cracked, the insides spilling out. Then he scoops it up and shoves the mangled pieces through what looked like a vent low in the wall. There's an electric sizzle. I guess I'm never seeing that phone again.

"You didn't have to do that," Win protests.

"If you want her to stay alive, *you* should have," Jule says, wiping his hands together and handing my purse back to me. "Don't you know what these twenty-first-century types are like? Calls and texts and photos and video—who knows what she's already recorded that'd get us in trouble?"

It hadn't occurred to me to try, but I realize he's right. I kept telling Win it didn't matter what I knew because no one would believe me. But if I had pictures, video footage, hard evidence—that could be another story.

I glance at the vent, my fingers twitching. But if giving up my phone will convince the rest of Win's group I'm safe, I can deal.

"All right," Jule says. "Let's go."

"We're not—" Win starts, and the wail of a siren cuts him off.

I wince as it blares through the room again. The lights overhead flash yellow. Win ducks past me to grab the time cloth, tugging free the thread that was charging it.

"Not so safe," he says to Jule. "Skylar told you, they've been tracing us." He hesitates. "We have to go. But we could switch cloths. You could make a few jumps in ours, lead the Enforcers on a chase, while Skylar and I go get the rest of the weapon, and then we can all meet back at the agreed spot."

For a second, Jule looks as though he's considering it. But then that second becomes two, and three, and his face hardens. I can see his answer there. Win touches my arm.

"Forget it," he says. He rushes past Jule to the entrance, and I dash after him. Jule spins around, grabbing at Win as the door gasps open. He's not fast enough. We flee up the steps. Win scrabbles at the outer door and it swings open too. I slam it back in Jule's face before racing after Win into the street.

Win lists to one side, and then motions me across a square with a small, silent fountain. We've almost reached the shadows of the carriage house on the other side, Jule's footsteps thundering after us, when Kurra stalks around the side of the building.

Win skids to a stop, swaying, as her weapon jerks up. He whips out the time cloth. There's a shout behind us—Jule?—and Kurra's head twitches to the left, and, without thinking, just reacting on panic, I swing my purse at her gun hand with as much force as I can manage.

It knocks the blaster off-target. But Kurra's other hand snatches at the purse strap. She yanks me toward her. Win pulls the cloth around us as I yank back, and the strap snaps.

"No!" My bracelet—Noam's beads—

The purse disappears through the flaps. I almost lunge after it, but Win's arm is around me, with a rasp in my ear. "*Skylar.*"

I catch myself just before I stumble out. The cloth lurches, and the night, the rain-slick cobblestones, Jule, and Kurra all jolt away.

27.

Win coughs, loud enough that I can hear him over the shrieking of the air outside. He stumbles when we touch down, catching himself against the wall of the time-cloth tent. The daylight streaking in from outside reveals a feverish flush that's risen under his skin. He clears his throat.

The loss of the purse—and my bracelet—is still wrenching through me, but my concern overwhelms it.

"Are you okay?" I ask. What if the little sleep he got wasn't enough? What if the confrontation with Jule and that short run were too much for him? He might be bleeding again, inside, and I'd never know.

Win sniffs, and says, "I'll be all right. It's mostly just the cold now. It was fascinating for a moment, but I think I'm ready for it to be over."

I have to catch my smile at the flippant irritation in his voice. Okay, so he's not dying. "Good luck with that," I say. "It'll probably be at least a week before it's gone."

He looks so stricken, I can't help laughing. So much for scientific curiosity.

"If Earthlings can survive that long, I suppose I can too," he says, the corner of his mouth curving up. He leans forward, peering beyond the cloth. We're on a grassy meadow, glinting modern buildings peeking over the tops of the nearby trees. "I didn't have time to put much thought into our destination. I suppose we should find that battle before Kurra catches up with us again."

"That guy, Jule, do you think he's going to come after us?"

"He can't," Win says brightly. "He has no idea where we're going. And no one in our group has tracing tech like the Enforcers do. We won't see him again unless we want to."

I guess there are some benefits to a lack of supplies. Jule doesn't strike the same terror in me that Kurra does, but he wasn't exactly pleasant to be around either.

"Thanks," I say. "For … defending me with him."

Win glances at me. "You're just as much a part of this mission as the rest of us now," he says. "You deserve to be able to see it through. And … I meant what I said to him. *No one* is going to hurt you, no matter what I have to do."

Though his hand quivers where he's holding it by the data panel, there's a determined light in his eyes. He's sick, and he's obviously still weak, but in that moment I have no doubt he'll get us through this. An odd warmth spreads through my chest.

"Thanks," I say again. It doesn't seem like enough, but I can't think of any other words that are right. I touch the back of his shoulder, gently, like I did when he shielded me from Jule. A soft smile touches his lips. He reaches out to rest his hand on my shoulder in return. This time I have no urge to flinch away.

"All we have to do is pull this last bit off, and you'll be safe for good," he says. He turns back to the display. "Americans and Natives, British fort, fallen trees, right?"

"Yep," I say. "And somewhere in the northeast."

He flicks through the glowing characters. "Ah," he says after a bit, with a noise of approval. "There we go. The Battle of Fallen Timbers. Ohio, near Fort Miamis. August 20, 1794 AD."

• • •

When we step out into the Ohio forest, the blanket of humid heat that washes over us is a shock. It fills my lungs and congeals against my skin. Only pale sunlight drifts through the bright green foliage of the trees. As we look around, a sluggish breeze passes over us, not lively enough to cool the sweat already beading on my skin. I long to peel off the Traveler shirt I put on over my own, but I'm sure I'll look out of place in my T-shirt.

"The Native soldiers will engage with the Americans in about an hour," Win says, repeating the information the cloth's display gave him. "That should give us time to locate the spot Jeanant meant for us to find before 'blood is spilled where the trees were laid low.' The fallen trees are over that way"—he waves—"at the edge of a river. And that way"— another wave—"is Fort Miamis. Where the Natives will run when they're overwhelmed, and be refused shelter."

It's not like the other periods Jeanant picked. In France, in Vietnam, the underdog was going to win, drive back the people trying to oppress them. This battle … The Natives are going to be beaten, and beaten again and again all across the country, until they give up their claim to almost all the land they once considered home.

Maybe Jeanant wanted to remind his followers of that too. That standing up to a greater power isn't always easy, and you don't always win.

The thought casts a gloom over my spirits. I hug myself despite the heat. "Which way do you think we should go?"

"The message says, 'Follow the path of anger.' Sounds like a lot of people around here are going to be angry." Win frowns. "Maybe the fort? I'd be pretty upset if my allies turned their backs on me."

"We might as well check it out," I say.

We start off, picking our way between the narrow tree trunks. Only a few shrubs and patches of grass sprout here and there amid the dead leaves coating the ground. Win wheezes a little after we clamber over a log, but the terrain isn't too rough. This forest is a lot less dense than the jungle in Vietnam. It reminds me of the state park my parents and I used to visit—the one from the painting Win admired.

Because, like Jeanant said, this place is pretty close to my part of the country. For all I know, I could run into my own ancestors here—or Bree's, or Lisa's … or almost any of my classmates' or neighbors', really.

My heart skips a beat. What if we do? What if we do, and we shift something here? What will *that* do to my present? Angela should be safe—her parents were born in the Philippines—but I don't know about anyone else. Could I accidentally write someone out of existence? My friends? Noam? *Me*?

I yank my thoughts back to the world around me. My fingers itch for the bracelet I no longer have. I curl them into the folds of my skirt.

Five woodpecker holes dotting the trunk of that maple. Crisscrossing roots forming triangles and pentagons in the dirt.

I'm here *for* all those people, the people whose lives are connected to this place. Here to protect them from shifts, not make new ones. I have to focus on that.

Win slows and points to a stretch of cleared land up ahead. We creep toward the edge of the clearing.

In the middle of the field stands an earthen rampart, surrounded by a low shadow I realize is a trench. It's bordered by the pale tips of pointed stakes. The sight of them jerks me back to the workers carving their bamboo poles along the Bach Dang River. I blink, and the heaped blockades of dirt and rock on the Paris streets flash through my mind.

There are other soldiers standing behind this rampart, along the wooden walls of the fort. The rising sun is glinting off their tall, black helmets and the muzzles of their rifles. The light catches in my eyes, and thousands of years of history collide. Booming cannon fire, the sizzle of Kurra's blaster, the crackle of a pistol in a marsh.

Everywhere we go, every when, it's so much the same.

I grip the branch next to me, absorbing the dips and ridges and whorls in the bark. We're almost done. Just a little further, and then I can go back to living in one place, in one time. And I'll know no one else is wandering around changing our history either.

"Fort Miamis?" I make myself say.

Win nods. "Doesn't look like it'd be easy to get inside, or even to get close. I don't think Jeanant would pick a place where we'd be so likely to be seen. Do you notice anything about it?"

I squint at the ditch, at the soldiers patrolling the walls, and shake my head.

"Well, let's look a little closer, and then we'll move on." He steps forward to skirt a cluster of bushes.

Apparently the sentries have already spotted us despite our sheltered position. The second Win moves into clearer view, a rifle twitches and a shot thunders across the field. Win throws himself backward, and I leap to help him. The bullet thuds into the trunk of an alder just a few feet away. We scramble deeper into the forest.

"So friendly," Win says with a cough.

"I guess we'd better avoid them completely," I say. I don't know why the soldiers would be shooting at us. I guess we must look a little strange in this clothing—or the two of us together, me pale and Win darker—or they might have caught something we said about getting in the fort and taken it as a threat.

It's easy to see other people as hardly people at all when you're watching them from a distance.

"To the fallen trees, then," Win says, motioning to our left.

We head off, the dry leaves crackling under our feet. "We don't want to rush in there," Win goes on. "The Native army will be waiting right near the place where the storm hit the trees, expecting the debris to slow the American army down."

"And they probably won't be any more friendly than those soldiers," I finish for him. I get that Jeanant had a theme he was trying to emphasize, but I can't help thinking his people, himself, me, this whole mission, would have been safer if he weren't constantly sending us into battlefields. Maybe the chaos makes it easier to cover up shifts, and offers more action to distract the Enforcers chasing him. Still, we'd be a lot more likely to get through it alive and carry out his plan if he'd decided to hide the weapon parts somewhere and some*when* more peaceful.

"Do you think …" I start, glancing around, and my voice trails off. Something about the trees—the angle of a branch, the flicker of a leaf?—sends a ripple of *wrong*ness through me. My gut knots.

"What?" Win says.

"I think something's been shifted," I say. "I don't know what. Over there."

I point, the *wrong*ness shivering over my skin. A chill rises through me.

I have to keep it together without the beads, my usual trick. I close my eyes, picturing Noam sitting down on the couch with five-year-old me at our grandparents' house instead of heading out the door. Picturing the generator orbiting above us exploding in a burst of flame.

The feeling recedes.

Win cocks his head. "Do you think it's Jeanant or the Enforcers?"

"I don't know."

He starts off in the direction I indicated, and I trail behind him. We've only made it a few steps when a figure moves into view between the trees up ahead. No, three figures: three people in brown Traveler clothes that almost blend into the trunks, heading our way. I catch a flicker of ice-pale skin amid the shadows, and bite my tongue.

Win's already pulling his satchel open, a curse on his breath. Kurra darts forward, waving her companions along with one hand while raising the slim black shape of her blaster. I scoot close to Win as he tosses the time cloth around us. The Enforcers fade into a haze of motion beyond the tent walls.

Just as Win brings up the display, a horribly familiar twang reaches my ears. A jolt of light sparks against the tent wall, right in front of me. I yelp, and the cloth heaves. Win swears again as it hits the ground.

I swivel. We're still in the forest. All I can see is the wavering forms of trees around us, but twigs are snapping underfoot somewhere nearby. Win smacks the panel, smacks it again, and the cloth doesn't move another inch.

"Win?" I say shakily.

"It's going to take a few minutes for the circuits to realign," he says, looking pained. "I'm sorry. It gave us about seventy feet, but we'll have to—"

Back where the snapping sounded, a sharp voice rings out, with a word I don't recognize and yet can clearly understand. It's a call to action.

Win grabs my hand. "Run!"

He drags the cloth down and dashes forward, and my feet follow him automatically. We crash through the underbrush, duck beneath a low-hanging branch, and dodge around a mossy heap of stones. Win's breath rasps. He's squeezing his arm against his side, the side where he was bleeding just a few hours ago. It must be hurting him. He keeps running, weaving us back and forth so it'll be harder for the Enforcers to get a clear shot, but I'm pulling ahead of him.

I can't hear our pursuers over the sound of our feet, but I don't dare look back. My ankle is starting to throb, and it's taking all my focus to keep my strides steady. The thick air burns my throat. Win trips on a root and I haul him upright. He makes a sound as if he's trying to speak, but it's lost in his heaving breaths.

We swerve past a thicket of saplings. The cloth Win didn't have time to fold streams over his arm. We can't stop until we're sure it'll work—as soon as we do we're easy targets again.

I spot an immense oak ahead of us, wide enough to give us both shelter for a moment to check the cloth. Another twang sings out behind us, followed by the hiss of sizzling sap. Win jerks me to the right. We leap a shallow creak and veer around a birch. My ankle wobbles under me. I grit my teeth, tugging Win toward the oak. I think a flicker of acknowledgment crosses his face. My hand tightens on his forearm.

And then I'm holding nothing but air. My fingers spasm, and I stumble. Lurching around, I find myself alone amid the trees.

No, not alone. In the distance, a hooded figure is charging toward me. Kurra narrows her icy eyes and raises her weapon. I whirl around. Five more feet to the oak. That's all I need.

The out-of-tune twang splits the air as I dart away, and my foot kicks out from under me. I throw out my arms to break my fall, tumbling into a patch of weeds at the base of the oak's trunk. A jolt of pain shoots up my calf from my already sore ankle. And then there's nothing. No pain. No feeling at all. As if my leg now ends at the knee.

28.

I roll onto my back and scuttle away crab-like, dragging my numb foot. It bumps over the uneven ground, sending odd shocks up to my thigh. Kurra stalks toward me through the brush, slower now. She's lowered her blaster to her side.

She hit my leg on purpose. Why? She pauses to scan the forest around us, and I remember: she's aware I'm not alone. She doesn't know where Win's gone either. She may even suspect there are others besides Win and me. If she kills me right away, she won't be able to ask. Somehow I don't think she plans to make it a polite interview.

One of the other Enforcers calls out a question from behind her, and she sends him off to survey the area with a flick of her arm. Then she focuses her attention back on me.

I shove myself backward, groping for anything I can use to shield myself, to try to fend Kurra off. Her blaster jerks up, and she barks a command in the Kemyate language that given her expression probably means, "Stop or I'll shoot." My body locks up, my arms quivering.

I'm a sitting duck. There's no shelter I can get to, crippled like this, before she could zap me ten more times. But I still have three working limbs. If she gets close enough, I'll have to try—

Close enough.

Kurra stalks through the trees toward me, flicking something out of her sleeve into her free hand, and my mind fixes on that one thought. Win disappeared—Win was doxed. Because someone from another time must be nearby. If that someone is still there, the same thing will happen to Kurra, won't it? If she comes just a little closer.

I will myself to hold still and wait, ignoring the cramping of my shoulders. Kurra stops by a birch tree. The birch tree Win and I ran past? She's almost at the spot.

But instead of continuing toward me, she stays where she is, about fifteen feet away. Eyeing whatever she pulled from her sleeve, and then me. Her cold gaze penetrates my skin. Her mouth tenses, lines forming like spidery cracks in the marble-pale skin around her lips.

She says something else, a string of syllables that could be a question. I stare back at her. Her hand drops, revealing the metallic square she's holding. Its face swims with faint ripples of light. She makes a scoffing sound in her throat, a mix of surprise and horror.

"*Earthling*," she says—not the casual way Jule used the term, but like a slur. That's when I understand. The thing in her hand, it must be the device she was using to track Win in the office building. Whatever she said a moment ago, it was a test, to confirm what she couldn't believe her eyes were telling her.

"The impudence," she goes on, the staccato rhythm of her accented English fracturing the word. "Your 'friend,' whoever he is—when the Council hears—" She shakes her head. Her gun arm steadies.

Standard protocol, I think, and my lungs clench. But she doesn't shoot. She must still want to know what I can tell her about Win.

Which gives me time. I have to make her move closer— and fast, so she doesn't notice the doxing feeling in time to catch herself. I need something to provoke her.

My fingers dig into the dirt, grounding me. "That screen of yours is defective, then? Or maybe your eyes are? Since when do Earthlings Travel?"

She takes one step toward me. "Since our feeble revolutionaries outdid themselves in dishonor, it seems," she sneers. "You're not Kemyate. I should have known when I first saw you."

"Maybe you're not as smart as you think," I snap over the thudding of my heart. "I knew you were a monster the moment I saw you."

Another step. Her lips curl in disgust. "Feeble words. Who else is with you?"

"No one," I say. Did they see Jule near the safe house?

"There is someone," she says, slowly and firmly. "Who is Noam?"

I freeze, my mouth falling open. How can she— Where did she get his name?

Kurra smirks at my discomfort. "You were writing a message to him. He—or she—is another one of your 'friends'? Tell me about him and maybe you will live a little longer."

Oh God. The letter I started. It was in my purse—the purse Kurra grabbed. Of course they looked through it.

"He's no one," I say. "He's nothing to do with this."

She shrugs. "You will tell me."

I can't let them go after Noam. After everything that's already happened to him …

I can't protect him unless I get out of this.

My mind trips back to the conversation I overheard between her and Win. Her disgust with Earth. My anger at what her people have done to us. I clutch on to that, feed it into my voice. "Don't you have better things to do? Or did you screw up on Kemya so badly that they gave you no choice and sent you off to chase shadows?"

Her face tightens. "You know nothing."

"I know this shadow's outrun you for days," I shoot back. "You're obviously not half as good at this 'job' as you think you are."

"I will not listen—" She tries to interrupt, but I just shout louder.

"No wonder you got assigned here! The Council must know you're just as defective as this planet."

"Enough!" Kurra snarls, her thumb flicking over a switch on her blaster. She springs forward, and the image of the boy crumpling by the cave flickers behind my eyes. My arms flail back instinctively, my heel jamming into the soil to propel me away, toward the oak, as if that can save me now. My head flinches down, anticipating that awful twang—

And there's silence. Not even the sound of her steps.

I look up. The forest around me is empty. Something like a whimper rushes out of me. It worked. She's gone.

The straining muscles in my arms give out. I flop down on my back. Overhead, the leaves stir in the humid air.

I don't have time to celebrate. Kurra will be twice as angry now, and she knows where I am. I need to get moving.

Twisting around, I spot a large stick lying by a bush several feet away. With my lame-crab-walk, I scoot over to it and test it with my hands. Sturdy enough, I think.

I prop it against the ground as a lever and haul myself upright. My body sways as I pull my half-numb leg under me. It's still a dead weight, except for a prickling ache that's creeping up my nerves from my ankle. If it wasn't fully sprained before, I'm pretty sure it is now.

How long did it take the numbness to wear off last time? Forty-five minutes? An hour? I don't have that long. I rotate, scanning the forest. I don't know where Win was doxed to. But I know we were running in this direction when it happened. Which means if Jeanant's around, if he's the one who doxed Win, I should go that way to find him. If I have the rest of the weapon with me when I make it back to Win, we can leave the Enforcers behind forever.

Using the stick as a cane, I hobble past the oak. It's impossible for me to walk quietly with my foot dragging, so I concentrate on speed. I need to find Jeanant before he leaves if I'm going to know where he's hidden the other two weapon parts. And … it would be so *good* to see him one more time, to feel the surge of certainty his presence brings.

The sunlight glints brighter up ahead. After several more lurching steps, I realize the trees are thinning. The distant warble of running water reaches my ears. I push myself toward it, faster, and a figure steps out from behind a nearby tree. A man with coppery skin and long dark hair, a rifle tucked against his arm. I jerk to a halt.

Of course. Win said the Native American army would be waiting near the river.

The soldier's gaze skims over me, holding mine for just a second before darting away. I glance across the landscape behind him, but I can't see any of his companions. Either they're well disguised or farther away. Maybe he's a scout, posted on the fringes of the ambush, ready to give the alarm.

I hold out my arms, balancing my weight on my good leg, in a gesture I hope conveys I'm unarmed and intend no harm. I'm coming from the direction opposite the American force they're expecting, and I'm a teenage girl with an obvious injury. Let that buy me a little sympathy.

The man's forehead has furrowed. "Where have you come from?" he demands in a low voice, striding toward me. "Where are you going?"

"I— The fort—" I blurt out. I don't have the accent, but if he believes I'm with the British, then technically I'm on his side. "I went out yesterday and got lost. I'm trying to find my way back."

He looks skeptical. "The fort is there," he says, gesturing past my arm with his rifle. "Go. It is not good for you to be here."

There's nothing I can do except pretend to follow his directions. "Thank you," I say, with honest gratitude. I'm glad just not to be shot at.

He nods sternly, waiting to make sure I leave. I turn and limp off toward the fort, counting each awkward step until I can't hear the water anymore. When I look around, I can't see the scout either. I hope I've come far enough that he won't notice me changing course. Turning, I set off parallel to where the river must be.

Somewhere over there are the trees laid low that Jeanant talked about, uprooted trunks and splintered branches left in a storm's wake. Where blood will be spilled. That man I just met, he could be dead by the end of the day.

When we talked about battles like this in class, I remember the teacher, our textbook, making them sound like great victories for America, the winning of this land for ourselves. But it's hard for me to see that man as an enemy. Right now I can imagine all too clearly what it's like to find out the world you thought was yours isn't after all, that there are people with more power than you ever dreamed of and they'll happily squash you with it.

Maybe he should have shot me. He's as human as I am, and he has far more right to be here. He's just protecting his people, like I've been trying to protect mine. Why shouldn't he want to protect them from me? I've brought Enforcers here; I might be messing with history at this very moment. Any additional tragedy that happens here will be because of Win and me. Our fault for getting in the way.

And Jeanant's, I guess, for leading us here. The thought makes me uncomfortable, but I can't deny it. Why couldn't he have made his instructions clearer?

I'm not even sure I'm going in the right direction now. I pause, scanning the forest. As long as I'm close to him, Kurra and her colleagues can't come near me. So maybe what I need to do is bring him to me.

"Jeanant?" I call, trying to pitch my voice to carry, but not so loud the soldiers by the river will hear. There's nothing. I risk raising my voice a little more. "Jeanant?"

When there's no response after several seconds, I shuffle on, watching carefully in case my call has brought someone I don't want heading my way.

A branch creaks somewhere to my left. I duck down, scrambling behind a shrub that dangles clumps of bright red berries. I peer between the spindly twigs. A pebble rattles. Then I catch a glimpse of black curls and bronze skin amid the trees.

I heave myself back onto my feet, a grin splitting my face. Jeanant halts at the movement, and then matches my smile with his own. But the warmth in his face isn't enough to cover the dark circles under his eyes or the way he tips toward the tree next to him as if he needs it to catch his balance.

"Jeanant," I say, hurrying over to him. "What's wrong?"

"Nothing," he says. "I'm glad it's you, Skylar. I didn't know if I would see you again."

He reaches toward me, reminding me of that moment in the cave where he thought I might be a hallucination. There's a bare patch along his jaw that I realize is one of those alien bandages, hiding some injury. He looks thinner than I remember—his cheekbones harsher, his dark eyes more stark. How long has it been for him since we last met?

I clasp his hand between mine. The contact of his skin sends a tingle of determination through me. "I'm here," I say. "Still completely real."

His posture relaxes, back into his usual self-assured stance. The ache that was forming in my chest eases too. After everything he's done for my planet, for *me*, it's nice to think that my presence offers him a little comfort.

"Someone hurt you," he says, frowning and gesturing to my makeshift cane, my leg.

"It was— It doesn't matter. I'm all right," I say. I have the urge to spill my fears—the boy by the cave, Noam and Kurra, the fragile surface of history we're walking on right now—but I can't bear to add to the weariness still obvious in his eyes, behind his concern. He's been carrying a burden much larger than mine.

And now I can relieve him of it.

"The rest of the weapon," I say. "Where is it? We weren't totally sure what you meant, about the 'path of anger' and all that."

"Oh," he says. "I had thought Thlo would remember."

"Well, it's complicated. Have you already hidden the parts? Do you have them on you?"

Jeanant gives me another smile, but this one's smaller, sadder. "I was placing the third—but only the third. You know there is one more after this?"

"But don't you have it now?" I say. "You knew we would come here— You told me— If you just give me them both, this will all be finished."

He pauses. "I understand why you were thinking that. I've thought about it a lot, since I last saw you. But I can't risk giving you everything."

29.

For a second, I can only stare at Jeanant. "What do you mean? Isn't it more risky the *longer* it takes us to find them?"

"I've done all this before," he says, in that even, reasonable tone. "Before Thlo came and she found you and you found me. If I do something differently now, the whole chain could unravel."

I shake my head. "No. It was your message that brought Thlo here—the message you've already programmed to be sent, right?"

"But there are so many other factors. Too many variables I can't predict or control. If I don't follow the same path, I can't be sure I won't give something away that will lead the Enforcers to the rest of the group. And anything could happen with the locals … I only know the steps I planned already worked, so the only guarantee I have is if I follow them as closely as possible."

I comprehend what he's saying, but at the same time, I can't accept it. "I'm right *here*," I protest. "What if the next place we go to, some local *kills* me, or the guy I'm Traveling with, or Thlo, before we get to the last part?"

"I don't want that to happen," he says quietly. "But all I have is what I know: that what I planned before was right. I have nothing else to hold on to, Skylar."

I hear it in his voice then, under the forced calm. He's as scared as I am. Scared of shifting the path he took. Scared of rewriting everything that's happened into a much more unhappy ending.

What happened to the guy from the recording, the guy who talked about taking chances, breaking out of old patterns—about working together to do something incredible?

"You're not doing this alone now," I say. "You have to let us be a part of that plan, so we can make sure the weapon's safe. Isn't that worth the risk?"

"You haven't seen …" Jeanant says. "The line between success and failure is so thin. After that mistake when I was approaching the field generator—the Enforcers could have blasted my ship to bits before I made it into the atmosphere. It was the difference of a second."

"But you got that second. You *did* make it." Anger I hadn't realized was there bubbles up. "Do you even know how much you're risking if you keep making more shifts, leaving this trail for us to follow?"

My present, my future, the world I know.

"It's all in the plan," Jeanant says, but a plea's come into his voice. "I decided exactly what I would do before I came, in case I had to escape down here: the details that would be noticeable but superficial. I promise you, I've been as careful as I could while balancing covering my tracks and protecting the weapon. We've done far too much damage to Earth already." His hand brushes the side of my arm and drops away. "I'm so sorry for that. And so glad to have had the chance to talk to you—it's made the time between so much more bearable. Please, would you tell Thlo something for me? Tell her when she has the weapon reconstructed, to make absolutely sure the moment is right before she strikes."

There's a finality in his words that makes my gut twist. "Why can't you tell her yourself? Where are you going to go, when you've finished hiding the weapon? You just have to wait until your present is the same as hers—I know that's a long time—but then she can find *you*."

That small sad smile comes back. "That can't happen."

"Why not?"

"Skylar," he says, "I don't want to talk about this. Just tell Thlo what I said. You don't need to worry about me."

Are there any words more guaranteed to make a person worry?

"*What*?" I say. "What's going to happen? Why don't you think you can meet her?"

He sighs, and closes his eyes. "I knew how this was going to end when I left Kemya," he says. "I'm ready for it. If I'd managed to destroy the generator, the Enforcers would have destroyed my ship immediately after. As it is, they'll have destroyed it as soon as I jumped down here, so I have no way to safely leave until Thlo arrives. I can't expect to outrun the Enforcers for years. And I can't let them take me back to interrogate me—no one's strong enough to hold out forever. I can't let them pry the others' names, the plan, from my mind. So I have to make sure, when the time comes, that I die rather than let them take me."

He says it so matter-of-factly that a lump fills my throat. "No," I say. He can't mean it. Is the future really that inevitable? Or is he sure the same way he's sure he can't break from his plan and end his mission now?

I grasp his hand again, squeezing it tight. Trying to remind him that this moment is just as real as his plan, as the fears in his head.

"Please," I say. "Take the chance. Let me have the rest of the weapon, and tell *me* a place to meet you, in my time. I'll bring the parts to Thlo, and then I'll go home, and I'll come find you. I'll help you, as much as you need. It can end that way instead."

If he says yes, I swear I'll make it happen.

For a second, I think he might change his mind. A glimmer lights behind his eyes that could be hope. He opens his mouth, and then jerks his hand away to clap it against the side of his arm. Against the outline of the alarm band he's still wearing.

"They've caught up with me," he says.

Before I can speak, he pushes me toward the shelter of a thicket. "Wait here," he says urgently. "You'll find the part, where I intended—over the hill, by the log—it'll all follow the same plan. I have to, Skylar. For Kemya. For Earth. I'm not going to let you down."

But you are, I want to say. *You are, right now.* But he's already hustling away.

As I lean against the brambles, the slow burn of anger swells inside me. He's so busy trying to be noble and stoic, he can't see how he's screwing up his own plan. Leaving the vaguest of messages, so even the woman who knew him best was stumped for weeks. Deciding he'd rather *die* than take the chance of finishing this now. He says he hates what his people have done to Earth, but he's acting a lot like the rest of them, isn't he? Too afraid of making mistakes, of deviating one inch from the available data, even when his stubbornness could mean we'll never find the rest of the weapon. It's not just his life on the line, but mine, and Win's, and Thlo's, and Jule's—everyone who's come here following him. Who believed that stuff he said about working together and setting off on new courses.

My grip tightens around my makeshift cane. I'm going to *make* him see …

I straighten up, and grass rustles underfoot somewhere behind me. I flinch back down.

A moment later, two people move into view, mostly hidden in the depths of the forest. They both have short dark hair, which lets me hope briefly that they might be just more Native American scouts. But they veer closer to me as they stride past, and the sunlight catches off the fabric of their clothes. That plain canvaslike material all the Traveler outfits are made of.

One of them, a woman, turns her head toward me. I stiffen, but her gaze passes by the thicket without pausing.

These must be the Enforcers that set off Jeanant's alarm band—the ones chasing him from his present. They're heading the same way he went. I suck in a breath, watching as they're swallowed up by the forest again. He got a good head start. He's probably already whisked away.

Taking the last piece of the weapon with him.

The thought of having to do this—the deciphering of his clues, the fumbling with the locals, the jarring sense of being out of my time—yet again sends a fresh burst of frustration through me. Then I remember the look on his face when I thought he was going to agree to my proposition.

He doesn't want to die. He doesn't want it to be this hard. But he honestly doesn't see any other way. I'm sure, remembering the way he talked in the recording, that he meant everything he said back then. That doesn't change the fact that he's the product of an alien culture that's been content to sit back and wait for thousands of years rather than risk making a new home. That he's been alone and constantly dogged and hasn't had anything solid to cling to for days, maybe weeks, except the path he laid out for himself. I'm not sure I'd even still be sane, if it were me.

It's amazing he made it this far.

The Enforcers seem to have moved safely out of hearing. I haul myself to my feet, testing my stunned leg. My knee bends, and a shock of pain sears up it. My toes are tingly, but everything from the ball of my foot to the top of my calf is still numb.

I hate being this helpless.

I can make out a short slope scattered with saplings up ahead. That must be the hill Jeanant meant.

As I turn toward it, the still air breaks with a twang and a crackle. A yell carries from beyond the hill, a brief sentence in that alien language. My heart stops. It's Jeanant's voice.

Before I've thought it through, I'm hobbling toward the slope as quickly as my off-kilter legs will take me. Have they hit him, or did he manage to get away? Why was he still here?

I've just hit the base of the slope when a woman's voice reaches my ears. I halt, worried about the sound of my steps. There's a thick fir tree ahead, at what appears to be the crest of the hill. I pad up to it, setting my stick and my feet as gently as I can, and crouch down, leaning against its low, needle-heavy branches. The pungent green smell fills my lungs. My breath catches.

The slope dips down several feet from the base of the fir, into a small glade surrounded by birches and maples. The grass shines in the early sunlight, dappled with delicate purple flowers. It would be a beautiful scene, if Jeanant weren't sprawled in the middle of it. One of his legs is stretched out in front of him at an awkward angle and his bag—the one that holds his time cloth—lies a few feet beyond the reach of his splayed arm.

The two Enforcers I saw earlier stand over him, aiming their blasters at him. Jeanant pushes himself a little more upright, and I can tell from the way his leg slides on the ground that he can't move it. And now they're speaking to him, first the woman, then the man, in Kemyate, their voices harsh.

Jeanant gazes back at them. His handsome face looks even more worn than a few minutes ago, but his eyes are defiant, his chin steady, as if *he's* the one in control of the situation. I swallow thickly. How can that unshakeable confidence save him now? They've got him.

He says something to them, with an odd twist to his body—turning away from the slope, as if he's trying to subtly direct their attention elsewhere. My gaze slips away from him to the edge of the glade, just below me. A fallen tree lies on the forest floor there. Its jagged edges are crumbling, the peeling bark splotched with lichen. A bed of dead leaves coats the ground beside it. Except in one spot, near the middle of the trunk, where it looks as if they've been swept to the side to clear the soil.

Because they have been. Understanding hits me with a sickening jolt. *By the log.* The dirt in that spot looks churned up, as if someone dug into it and then covered the hole. Someone who didn't have time to smooth the leaves back over that spot to hide it.

He's still here because he wasn't finished. If he hadn't been so stubborn …

The male Enforcer glances around the clearing. If they start checking the area, it won't be long before they find the log and that'll be it. They'll have the part, and I'll lose both that one and the one it was meant to lead to. Everything Jeanant's done, everything Win and I have done, it might be for nothing.

I'm edging forward before I notice and yank myself back. I can't barge in there—I'll just end up shot again, hauled off for questioning. That won't help Jeanant.

I have to distract the Enforcers somehow, give him a chance to grab his cloth. Then they'll follow him, and I can get to the weapon part.

I paw the ground, my fingers closing around a rock the size of my palm. The woman Enforcer is still talking to Jeanant, her voice rising. Jeanant shakes his head. I grip the rock, wind back my arm, and hurl it.

It patters into a bush maybe twenty feet away. The Enforcers pause, not taking their eyes off Jeanant. When there's no further sound, they seem to decide it wasn't important. The woman snaps out another demand.

The Native scout. He and the army he's with, they're not far behind me. If I could convince them that the Americans are arriving, that they're *here*, and send them charging in … It might almost be true. Win said the battle would start in an hour, and that was a while ago. The American force can't be far off.

But they weren't supposed to be met by a charge of Native soldiers right now. If I disrupt the ambush, change the timing of the battle, how will that affect the outcome? Who wins? Who dies? If there's one young man out there who's supposed to father a line that stretches all the way to my present—one wrong step and I'm killing all those people, people I *know*—

My thoughts scramble and scatter. *Wrong*. The sweat freezes on my skin.

It hasn't happened yet. I haven't done it, everyone's still safe. I'm going to keep them that way, like I promised myself I would.

Before I can come up with an alternate strategy, the woman below makes a comment that sounds decisive. The Enforcers step toward Jeanant, their blasters pointed at his arms.

To numb them too. So he has no way to struggle, so they can carry him back to Kemya, helpless, for that interrogation he was terrified to face.

My hand shoots out, as if I can stop them from here. In the same moment, though he's looking toward the opposite end of the glade, Jeanant calls my name.

"Skylar!" he yells, so loud it sends a sparrow bursting out of a nearby tree. "Careful!"

The Enforcers' gazes twitch away, as if they expect to see the person he's talking to. And using their momentary distraction, Jeanant lunges.

He grabs the man by the hand, the hand holding the blaster, reaching for something on the base of the gun. There's an instant when I see how perfectly it could play out—he'll swivel the gun, blast the woman, turn it on its owner, and leap away. *Yes.*

Except he doesn't.

The man jerks back with a shout, but he's not fast enough. A hollow click echoes through the glade, and Jeanant tugs the man's hand toward his head. A streak of light burns into my vision, shattering against Jeanant's temple.

His body shudders. Then his arms sag back against the grass. His head lolls, revealing a blotch of seared-black skin. His eyes, the eyes that blazed with so much purpose just a few seconds ago, stare blankly at the sky.

30.

Jeanant's voice—my name—is still ringing in my ears. I stare at him, as if he might roll over, snatch up his time cloth, and leap away. But he doesn't. His body lies there, still and limp, as the Enforcer whose blaster he grabbed kneels down and presses a small device against Jeanant's neck. The man straightens up, sounding upset as he reports the result to the woman. She snaps something at him, and they bicker back and forth. Over who's at fault? How they'll explain this?

And Jeanant doesn't move. Doesn't blink. Doesn't breathe.

I press my hand to my mouth. My eyes have flooded. He called out to me, and I didn't—

He couldn't have known I was watching, though. His gaze never once stopped on my tree. *Careful,* he said. He wasn't crying for help. It was a warning, knowing I was probably close enough to hear. And a distraction, to buy himself a moment to go for the blaster.

He *had* the blaster. Why didn't he try to escape?

I close my eyes, my mind replaying the scene. His hands on the blaster, while the Enforcer still gripped it. The woman beside him already starting to react.

It was only a slim chance. For him to have hit the woman well enough to disable her, to have managed to wrestle the blaster completely away from the man and shoot him too, before one of them stopped him … Only a slim chance, when it was the only chance he had to prevent himself from being taken for interrogation. I can already imagine him reasoning through his options, just as he tried to reason with me all of ten minutes ago, and deciding the risk of being forced to give up Thlo and the others and ruining everything was greater than the risk of losing just a couple parts of his weapon.

His words echo back to me. *I knew how this was going to end when I left Kemya.* He was so sure this was his fate, one way or another. And maybe he hoped if he were dead, the Enforcers would be too focused on that to search the area and find the part by the log.

If so, he was wrong. As I smear my tears across the sleeve of my borrowed Traveler shirt, the Enforcers stop arguing. The man pats down Jeanant's clothes while the woman digs through his bag. She pulls out a gray cylinder about the length and width of my forearm with an exclamation. I can tell from the widening of the man's eyes that it must be the last part of the weapon. Damn it.

The woman tucks the cylinder into a wide pouch at her hip. Then she starts to circle Jeanant's body, scanning the ground, the trees. With each rotation, she moves closer to the edge of the glade. Closer to the log and its disturbed patch of earth.

My body goes rigid. I can't let them take another part of the weapon. If they get that one too, Jeanant might have given up his life for nothing. I don't know if the two parts we've already collected will be enough.

A sense of resolve rushes through me. I'm still working with him, even if he only ever saw himself as alone.

Just a few trees and a couple of bushes dot the slope between me and the log. There isn't enough cover for me to sneak down there without the Enforcers seeing me. I need them to leave.

My thoughts dart back to the idea I had a few moments ago, before Jeanant's shout and the blast. The Native American army. If I send them this way, the Enforcers will have to clear out, at least for long enough that I can dig up whatever Jeanant buried.

The man steps away from Jeanant's body, and the woman barks what sounds like an order at him as she continues her ever-widening circuit of the glade. There's no time to think—I have to do this *now*.

My leg aches as I turn around. Grasping my walking stick, I shuffle back down the slope. While I was crouched there, the numbness faded a bit more. With every step, a sharp tingle shoots up from my ankle. But as soon as I think I'm out of hearing, I push myself into a lopsided jog, shoving myself along with the stick, gritting my teeth against the pain. A fresh layer of sweat beads on my skin.

It wasn't that far from here that I spoke to the Native scout, was it? I veer toward the river, trying not to wonder how close the American soldiers are now, how big a catastrophe I'll cause by drawing the Native army out of their ambush. The image of a mass of chaotic figures, slashing and shooting, swims up through my mind.

Wrong.

Panic slices through me. I pause, my chest heaving.

If I screw this up—if someone dies who shouldn't—if I rewrite the family tree of every person in both armies—

And if I don't?

I wanted to believe I could save everyone. Not let one more person die. But I was as wrong as Jeanant thinking he could bring about some perfect outcome if he just held all the variables perfectly in place. Life doesn't work that way. After everything I've seen in the last couple days, I can say pretty definitively that life is messy, and inexact, and unfair, full of so many variables I could never take half of them into account. It's terrifying, but thinking otherwise is just deluding yourself.

If Jeanant had just given me the rest of the weapon when I first met up with him here, he wouldn't be lying there dead in the glade. I wouldn't be risking the lives of everyone in my present, or risking my own life if I run into Kurra again. He was so sure his way was the best way, the only way. I think he was wrong about that too.

There was no *careful* enough to protect him. And maybe there isn't a careful enough to protect me, or my family and friends. The shift I make now could wipe me out of existence. I could be killing dozens of people I know. But if I don't do this, Win's people could decide to wipe out billions at any moment, as long as the time field is in place. Everything will be *wrong* until the world itself falls apart, whether I'm around to feel it or not.

Jeanant's speech is still true even if he faltered from it. So *I* will take this chance.

My pulse evens out as I hurry on. I turn my head, absorbing shape, color, leaves, bark, and there—

A face. I stop. The scout I saw before is standing at his post by the same tree. He frowns when our gazes meet. My voice catches.

What I'm about to do, it's not just chess pieces moved around on a board. The people in this present matter too. This is a human being whose life I'm planning to alter.

A human being whose brow is knitting as he jerks his chin toward the forest beyond us.

"What are you doing here again?" he says roughly. "Go on. This is a dangerous place."

"It's dangerous for you too," I say, before I realize I'm going to speak. I remember Win's comments about the battle.

About the Native force nearly defeated, turning to their allies, turned away. "There's so many of them coming—so many of you could be killed."

"We know," he says. "They will kill us either way. Better to die standing up. We will stand here as long as we can. Now go!"

He steps forward, reaching as if to propel me in the direction of the fort. I wobble backward. And I realize this is his choice too. His choice to be here at all, defending his people.

From anyone who threatens them.

"What if I saw some—if I saw Americans, soldiers, heading this way?" I say.

He grabs my wrist, so tight the bones pinch. "Soldiers? Where?"

"Over there." I wave my stick. The image of the armies hurtling together flickers behind my eyes, making my heart thump. I clamp down on my panic.

Wait. It doesn't have to be like that. Just because I'm taking this chance doesn't mean I should throw everything to the wind. The Enforcers are as human as this man and his colleagues. It isn't going to take a whole army to overwhelm them.

"There's just two," I add quickly. "I think they wanted to … to spy on you and report to the others. You just need a few people to scare them off."

He hesitates, probably wondering if this is some elaborate trick. The Enforcers could already have found that spot by the log, be digging out that last part of the weapon. If I'm doing this, we have to go. So I blurt out one more thing.

"I think they've killed one of your men."

It's almost true. I know what side of this battle Jeanant would have been on.

The scout's fingers squeeze my wrist, and then he releases me, pushing my arm away. For one wrenching moment I think it's a dismissal. He hefts his rifle.

"Two?"

I nod. He turns and calls something quietly through the trees. Four more men with rifles emerge a short distance away. The scout motions them to join him with a few words of explanation in a language I don't know. The other men stare at me. One of them purses his lips toward me and says something that doesn't sound kind, but my scout cuts him off with a brusque retort.

"I'll show you," I say, hoping that will get us moving, and start toward the slope.

After a few lurching steps, I hear them following. They slip past me, their expressions dour, making less noise between the five of them than I do on my own. It feels like no time at all before I spot the hill with the bristling fir at its peak. My stomach flips over.

I'm really doing this. No turning back.

"Over there," I whisper, indicating the slope. The scout draws his companions together for a brief discussion. Then they creep to and up the hill, rifles ready. I trail behind.

The Native soldiers pause at the top of the slope for no more than a second. Then the scout hollers, and they charge down the hill. Rifle fire crackles. I cringe, suddenly terrified I'll hear that awful twang.

It doesn't come. The soldiers' feet pound into the glade. The Enforcers must be fleeing.

This is my chance.

I scramble up the slope, reaching the fir just in time to see the last of the Native soldiers racing into the forest on the other side of the glade. There's no sign of the Enforcers. Jeanant's body is still sprawled on the grass. Seeing him again, so limp and vacant, makes my legs lock up. I force myself onward.

I'm halfway down to the log when another shot peals out, and the stutter of answering fire echoes through the forest. Not the twanging sizzle of the Enforcers' blasters. Regular gunfire.

I stop, peering across the glade. The Americans? Were they already that close? And I sent the Native soldiers straight into their ranks.

Rifle shots rattle between the trees. I bite my lip. There's no way I can protect them now. I can only finish my own mission.

I skitter the rest of the way down through the dead leaves and pebbles, stumbling to a halt by the log. The patch of cleared dirt looks exactly the same as before. The Enforcers hadn't found it yet, then. Exhaling shakily, I drop to my knees. I may only have a minute before they decide it's safe to return.

Soil clogs my fingernails as I claw at the dirt. My nose and mouth prickle with the earthy smell of decay. I scoop aside handful after handful. Then my fingers jar against a hard surface.

Another sputter of gunfire reaches my ears, closer now. I grope along the hard edge of the object I've started to unearth. Working my thumb around its corner, I manage to wiggle it free.

It's another slab of that plastic-like material, but this one is dirt brown instead of clear. And bigger, about the same size as my calculus textbook, with a seam around the top that suggests it can be opened.

Hoofbeats thunder over the ground somewhere in the forest, far too near for comfort. I heft the box under my arm. Someone shouts, another gun crackles, and a voice cries out.

I did what I had to do, I remind myself as I stagger back up the slope. But in that moment the throbbing of my ankle is nothing compared to the guilt searing through my chest.

The shots are echoing through the forest in quick succession now, mingled with bellows and groans and the occasional anxious whinny. I don't know if the battle was supposed to start now anyway; I don't know how much I've thrown history out of order. I just know if one of those bullets finds me before I deliver this box, there'll be no good to balance out the harm I may have done. So I run as fast as my ankle allows, the bark of my walking stick scratching my palm.

Any second now, even if no one shoots *me*, one shift, one new death, could unravel my family's entire thread through history. Will I just disappear if that happens?

I have to find Win first. That's all I can worry about now.

The sounds of the battle recede until I can hardly hear them over my pounding heart. My foot has just crunched down on a twig when it occurs to me that it's not just Win I need to be watching for. Kurra and her band of Enforcers are still lurking here. Now that I've left Jeanant and his Enforcers behind, I can't count on them being doxed.

I slow down, scanning the forest. The faint rifle fire and shouts behind me won't cover the sound of my passage. I set my feet around the sticks and looser pebbles, avoiding the shrubs that would scrape against my clothes.

Where would Win have gone, to find me after he was doxed? Where would he think I'd look for him?

The fort. That's the only real landmark we saw together. It's as good a possibility as any.

My gaze catches on an ivy-draped tree that feels familiar. I pad toward it. Now that I'm not racing headlong but taking in the landscape around me, other details I must have absorbed emerge: a crumbling stump, a moss-coated boulder, a bush sprouting pale yellow flowers.

The trail of fragmented memories leads me on a rambling path through the forest. After a couple of minutes, I spot the impression of a boot heel in a soft patch of dirt, pointing in the opposite direction. Mine, it looks like. It must be from when we were running away from Kurra—which was also away from the fort. I'm going the right way, then.

As I limp on, the humidity presses in with the day's rising heat. The surface of the box slides in my damp grasp. At this rate, I'll drop it if I have to run again. I glance down at myself. With a little wiggling, I work the box over my chest between the Traveler shirt and the T-shirt underneath. I tuck the bottom of the T-shirt up around the box and the bottom of the Traveler shirt into the tight waist of my skirt. It's uncomfortable, but it seems secure enough.

A few minutes' walk later, I glimpse the roof of the fort through the foliage ahead. I pause, thinking of how the British soldiers greeted us last time. Win wouldn't have gone close enough for them to see him. Where would he wait, if he's here? If I call out to him, Kurra's as likely to hear me as he is.

I hobble around the edge of the clearing, taking in every fluttering leaf, every bird's chirp, as if one of them holds a clue. I'm just following the curve around the north end of the field when a sharp voice cuts through the air.

Kurra. I duck down, swiveling to try to determine which direction it's coming from. She's speaking in Kemyate, so low or distant I probably wouldn't be able to make out most of the words even if I understood the language.

I see one of her companions before I see her: a sturdily built man with tan skin and chestnut hair braided at his neck.

I scoot behind the base of a birch's trunk. He turns away from me, gesturing to someone out of view.

Kurra speaks again. I'm so used to her threats, it's odd to hear her sound so ... cajoling. But if her comments are directed at Win, he doesn't respond.

They seem to be moving away from me. Does that mean Win's over there too? If Kurra's tracking him again, I should follow. I creep forward from one tree to the next. Then the man I can see spins on his heel. I duck behind a maple.

Kurra's voice reaches me again, louder now. Footsteps crackle closer, then stop. I can only pick up a hint of the whispered conversation that follows. They walk on. I think they're coming toward me now.

I dare to lean an inch past the side of the tree. My pulse stutters. I can see three Enforcers now, Kurra in the middle. They're coming toward the fort after all.

As I watch, they veer at a slight angle. Slowly but surely, they walk past my hiding spot, leaving me behind.

My gaze drifts up over their heads, and every muscle in my body tenses.

Win's standing on the wide branch of a chestnut tree, maybe twenty feet away and at least the same distance above us. He's poised against the trunk, half hidden by the leaves, his brown clothes blending into the bark, the cowl neck pulled up to cover his dark hair. I might not have noticed him at all if not for the oily splotch of the time cloth clutched in his hand.

His head dips, following the movements of the Enforcers below. They're between us now, heading straight for him. They must be tracking him on that screen.

I ease myself upright and wave my arm, but Win's focus doesn't waver from the Enforcers. He doesn't know I'm here. I can't get his attention without drawing their attention too.

Why doesn't he jump away? He's got the time cloth right there ...

But how long has he been doing that—jumping from hiding spot to hiding spot with Kurra on his tail? Maybe she shot the cloth again, and it's malfunctioning. Maybe the power's nearly drained again. There are all sorts of reasons he could be stuck there. Waiting for me.

Win's legs quaver. He braces himself, his eyes closing. Fear grips me. He's sick, he was all but mortally wounded just a few hours ago, and now he must be even more exhausted.

Kurra hesitates, just a few feet from his tree, frowning at her hand. *Go on*, I think at her. *Keep moving.* She turns, studying the ground. At any moment she's going to look up.

She murmurs something to the Enforcer with the braided hair, and one of Win's feet slips.

He throws out his hand to a smaller branch nearby, catching his balance, but his shoe rasps against the bark. The branch he's grabbed creaks. Kurra's head snaps around, her gun hand flying up to follow her gaze.

No.

I can't watch this happen. Not again.

I'm sprinting forward before that thought has even fully formed, my walking stick tossed aside. The pain radiating up my leg brings tears to my eyes, but I don't care. Win would probably tell me to stay where I am, that it's too dangerous to interfere, but I don't care about that either. I am not a shadow; I'm a human being who's spent the last two days fighting to liberate my planet, and I am not letting it end like this.

The other Enforcers whip around to face me, and Kurra's attention jerks away from Win. She sidesteps, her blaster swinging down, but I'm already hurtling toward her with all the strength in my body. I crash into her. The twang sings past my ear.

One of the other Enforcers hisses a curse. Kurra rams her elbow into my side, squirming out from under me. I try to dodge her as the third Enforcer aims his weapon. I'm too slow. A streak of light sizzles into my shoulder. I stagger, numbness clawing through my chest.

That's it, I think blankly. As I gasp for breath, Kurra snatches my elbow and brings her blaster to my head.

And then she's stumbling to the side as Win shoves past her with a sweep of his time cloth. I fling myself at him, and he tugs the cloth over me. Kurra gives a cry, her pale eyes wild. She jabs out with her blaster. But this time Win's already hit the panel.

As the muzzle sparks, her furious face and the rest of the forest whirl away.

31.

The world outside the cloth comes into focus and dissolves again as Win raps his fingers against the data panel. The yellow light of the power warning flashes around us. I gulp and sputter. Though my ankle's on fire, my legs are still holding me up. But a broad swath of flesh, from the base of my chin down across the right side of my torso and along my arm, is numb. It feels as if there's a gaping hole in the front of my body. A gaping hole where my vital organs should be.

"You can still breathe," Win shouts over the shrieking of the wind. "Everything inside you is still working, even if you can't tell. Just try not to think about it."

Easier said than done. I suck air into the back of my throat, but I can't feel it moving down to my lungs. Somehow, a moment later, an exhalation rushes out. I close my eyes, trying to let it happen automatically. Listening to my pulse thumping in my ears, a confirmation that my heart's continued beating.

The shrieking stops and the cloth goes still. "Skylar?" Win rasps. My eyes pop open.

We've landed in a dim stairwell. I make myself step out of the cloth after Win. He heads down the stairs and I follow, clutching the railing. We pass three flights and then duck out into a darkened hall. My foot brushes a sheet of plastic crumpled in the corner.

Open doorframes line the hall. Win ducks through one of them, and I limp after. The space on the other side appears to be a vacant condo apartment: bare white walls, marble countertops in the open-concept kitchen, tall steel-edged windows looking out over a concrete balcony that doesn't yet have a railing.

"They're just finishing up this place—no one's moved in yet, and the workers will all have gone home for the day," Win says, wheezing. He peels down his cowl and rolls it back into his shirt collar, fumbling with it as if he can't get his hands to work quite right. He coughs a couple of times against his elbow.

"You found Jeanant?" he asks. "Before you found me again?"

I nod, not quite trusting myself to speak.

He shakes his head with a rough laugh. "I can't believe we pulled that off."

I guess we did. Not perfectly, not without … loss, but our mission's over.

There's nothing left to do.

The enormity of it overwhelms me. I hobble forward, toward the late-afternoon sun shining bright in the blue sky beyond the windows. The warmth tingles over every part of me except that numb hollow around my core. When I reach out to touch the glass, the box lodged inside my shirt pokes the still-awake skin over my stomach. One-handed, I tug at the Traveler shirt until I can pull the box out. Bits of the dirt it was buried in cling to my fingers.

Win will bring the parts to Thlo, and hopefully these three will be enough for their group to destroy the time field. We'll have set everyone's lives across two planets on a completely different course.

Incredible.

The word resonates in my head in Jeanant's voice. The smell of the forest lingers on the box, on my clothes, loamy and damp. Taking me back to Jeanant's last cry, to his body sprawled in the glade.

"That's the third part Jeanant left," I say. My voice is thick, and not just because I can't feel my vocal cords.

Win takes the box, runs his thumb along the seam, and frowns. "Just the third? But—"

"He didn't want to change any detail from his original plan," I say. "He said— He said that if he shifted something by giving us the rest of the weapon all at once, he might throw something off and alter the chain of events. Make it so the Enforcers from his time caught Thlo, or she'd miss his message or … I tried to convince him."

I thought I almost had. But … what if he'd been right after all? Did the Enforcers catch up with him finally, force his hand, because of those small moments when his path on Earth was changed: the moments he lingered with me? Maybe in some previous past, when I died in the courthouse, Jeanant dashed away the second after he hid each part, placed his last offering uninterrupted, and lived on at least a little while longer.

Of course, in that other past, maybe Thlo and Win and the others would never have completely deciphered Jeanant's all too careful clues, never kept ahead of the Enforcers, never have finished his mission. I don't know. I can't know. There might not have been any good way for his journey to end.

I fold my working arm across my chest. This is what mattered to Jeanant the most: this moment right now. Getting as many of the parts as he could into our hands. He would rather have died for this than lived without accomplishing it—I know *that*.

Win looks at the object I've given him, and then at me. In that instant, he looks so tired, I'm afraid his legs won't hold.

"We're not done," he says.

"We are," I say, and pause when my voice breaks. "Jeanant's— The Enforcers from his time, they caught him. He made them kill him so they couldn't take him for interrogation. He's dead. They found the last part, the one he was still carrying. We have everything we can get."

"Oh. *Oh.* You saw— Are you all right?"

The worry in his deep blue eyes isn't the analytical consideration or anxious impatience I've gotten used to, only honest concern. He isn't freaking out that we lost the last part or demanding to know why I didn't do better. He just wants to be sure I'm okay. Somehow that makes me *feel* almost okay, for the first time since that argument with Jeanant in the forest.

"Yeah," I say. "I mean, I wish I could have stopped it. I wish we hadn't lost anything. But … it is what it is, right?"

"Yes. It must have been hard, to even get this. I'm sorry I couldn't have helped more." He slides the box into his satchel. "There's a good chance the three will be enough. Thlo and Isis will have a better idea, once they take a look. It's time we go talk with them. I'm sure Jule has already filled Thlo in on the basics." He grimaces. "I just wanted to work out what we're going to say about going back for your brother first. Assuming you still want to."

Noam. My plan: going back to that day, finding him at school, the note …

The note.

Kurra's voice comes back to me, the intensity in her cold eyes. *Who is Noam?* My fingers clench where the purse used to hang.

"Win," I say in a rush. "Kurra knew— I'd started writing my note to Noam, when we were in the safe house— It was in my purse— She asked me who he was. What if they've already gone back looking for him?"

"Whoa," Win says. "How much did she know? What did you say in the note?"

"I don't remember. I'd only just started. The only thing she mentioned was his name."

"Last name too or just first name? The year? *Your* name?"

I shake my head. "Just 'Noam,' and I was starting to tell him about Darryl …"

"Then he's fine," Win says firmly. "How many Noams do you think there must be across the history of this planet? They don't have anywhere near enough to lead them to him. We didn't shift anything while we were there, no one even saw us except for him. There's no way they could determine …"

He trails off, and the realization hits me. The way it all connects, like one long line of factors in the cruelest of equations.

"There's no way, unless I go back," I say stiffly. "Suddenly a boy who died stays alive. That would have to show up on their monitoring. A boy named Noam."

Win lowers his eyes. "We could distract from it by making another shift first," he says. "Try to hide it as a ripple like we did with the train ticket. But … they'll be searching for that name. Investigating any shifts associated with it. Especially in the time periods they've traced us to before. It'd be hard for them to miss."

The acknowledgment seems so final. Almost inevitable. Of course I can change every past there is except the one that matters most.

"What would they do, after they noticed?" I have to ask.

"They'd look into his background, his family, his friends," Win says. "They'd find records of you."

"And Kurra would recognize me."

"Maybe not. If you shifted everything, so you weren't ever here with me … I think it'd depend on whether she was inside or outside the time field when you did it. But she'll have sent up reports. The Enforcers will still know Noam was significant. And they'll have a description of the girl I was Traveling with."

"They'd kill us, wouldn't they?" I murmur. "They'd kill Noam, to set things back the way they were before, and then they'd kill me, because they wouldn't know I'm never going to meet you after all. I can save him, and they'll just murder him all over again."

A choked laugh jerks out of me. I cover my mouth. It's like they've already killed him. The instant Kurra snapped my purse from my shoulder, she killed any chance I had of saving Noam.

He was already dead. And maybe it was wrong of me to want to make a shift for no one's benefit but his, mine, and my family's. Maybe I was selfish not to have cared what other consequences there might be. It doesn't matter now. This risk is too great, weighing the lives of all the people connected to him who are still alive against a boy who's been gone for years. There's no choice here.

I sink down onto the floor, leaning my back against the window. The sun beams over my hair. The skin around the edges of my frozen core is starting to tingle. I stare blankly at the wall. So that's it. Despite everything I managed to accomplish, I couldn't save the two people I most wanted to.

"If there was a way ..." Win says.

"I know," I say, before he can go on. I honestly believe he'd do whatever he could to help me, if it were possible. "But there isn't. I guess you might as well take me back to my time." Back to find out what else might have shifted, after the other history I just meddled with. *I* might not even be there. We might arrive only for me to blink out of reality the second my life aligns with its proper present.

I hug my knees. Well, I'm going to have to find out eventually.

"You could even tell Thlo you realized Jule was right and you shouldn't have brought me with you, that you took me back before you went for the third part," I go on when Win doesn't speak. "Maybe she'll be less upset then? You can show off how much of their work you managed to do for them, without me there to distract things."

"You wouldn't be a distraction," Win says. "You're an equal part of this. More than equal. I wouldn't have gotten anywhere without you."

"No one else needs to see it that way."

"You really think I'd take credit for everything you did?"

I shrug. Why shouldn't he? Earning his companions' respect is a lot more important to him than to me.

Win crouches down and rests his hand over mine. Solid and warm, and with a sense of sureness that abruptly reminds me of Jeanant. I look up at him. His face wavers through the tears that have collected in my eyes. But I can still see his expression, so serious it hurts to hold his gaze. He swallows audibly.

"Skylar," he says, weighting every word with raw sincerity, "the way I treated you, in the beginning— The way I talked to you— What I *did*, without considering how you'd feel— I didn't have half as much respect for you as I should have. It was wrong of me. I could make a lot of excuses, but that's not the point. The point is I was stupid, and I'm sorry. So sorry. You've been … you've been spectacular."

After all this time, I'd stopped hoping for a real apology. I'd assumed we'd put it to rest without that.

Win's mouth twists, painfully, and I realize I haven't responded: he thinks it wasn't enough, that I'm still angry. And any part of me that might have been melts.

"Okay," I say. "Just don't let it happen again."

A little smile creeps across my lips, the best I can manage right now. There are things to smile for, in spite of everything.

Win catches the smile, and returns it, twice as wide. As I hold his deep blue gaze, something in my chest flutters. Something that feels more real than the skipped heartbeats he gave me when we first met, when I wasn't used to the alien *there*ness of him. When I didn't really know him.

"I think you should meet them, Thlo and the others," he says. "They already know you exist. And … you were the one who talked to Jeanant. Thlo will probably have questions."

The flutter fades as my mind trips back to his conversation with Jule about "standard protocol."

"How angry is she going to be?" I ask.

Win hesitates. "Honestly," he says, "I'm not completely sure how she would have reacted if she'd found out what was happening in the middle of things. But we're done now. If I try to hide you away, that'll make Thlo think there's something to be suspicious of—and she'll know your name and what time period I'd have met you in, and Jule would recognize your face. If she wanted to find you, she could. If we just go to her, she'll see she doesn't need to worry. That after everything, you can be trusted. And the safest thing for all of us will be for you to go back to your life as if nothing ever changed, so the Enforcers never realize who you were."

Part of me balks. But what he's saying makes sense. And Jeanant trusted this woman, believed in her. He wouldn't have, if she were cruel enough to see eliminating me as a reasonable solution, would he?

"Also," Win says, a little sheepishly, "there is a practical concern. I'm not completely sure the cloth has enough power left for two more trips."

What else is new? If I weren't so shell-shocked, I'd roll my eyes. "Well, when you put it that way, it sounds like a great idea."

Win laughs and helps me to my feet.

• • •

When the time cloth lands in the place Win says was arranged for the rebels to meet up—"Isis has it set so only people with the right code can Travel in," he assures me. "That'll slow the Enforcers down"—I'm expecting something like the inside of the safe house. Instead, the room is oddly normal looking by Earth standards. It has the feel of a posh modern office space: about the size of the first floor of my house, with a cluster of boxy sofas and armchairs at one end and a long table surrounded by matching ebony chairs at the other. The pale hardwood we step out onto is slick with polish. The only windows are angled skylights built into the high ceiling, casting splotches of sunlight across the floor.

I sink onto the arm of one of the sofas, resting my ankle, as Win folds his cloth. Nervous anticipation tickles under my skin. The numbness has faded enough that I can feel my chest rising and falling again, the tiny hitch in the back of my throat. Even after everything I've seen, I don't feel quite ready for this.

"You'd better leave the Traveler shirt here," Win says. "Can't bring any of our tech back with you."

"How many people will be showing up?" I ask as I pull it off over my T-shirt. I drop it onto the sofa.

"Five," Win says. "Assuming everyone's all right. Thlo, Jule, Isis, Pavel, and Mako."

He edges closer to me at the swish of fabric behind us. As we turn, two figures emerge from a time cloth that's shimmered into sight in the middle of the room.

One of them is Jule. He glowers at Win for a moment before sprawling across one of the chairs. "Well, this should be interesting. I hope you've got a good story worked out, *Dar*win."

Win's back has gone rigid, but he ignores the other boy. He tips his head to the curvaceous woman who stepped out beside Jule. "Hey, Ice."

Her smile cracks a dimple in her dusky cheek as she tugs a bonnet off her crimson-streaked hair, which is coiled into a frizzy bun. Part of blending in, I guess ... Were they still searching France?

"Win," she replies, returning his nod. Her hazel eyes flick over me and seem to judge me as no threat. I wonder how much of the story Jule told her.

With a rustle, the flaps of two more time cloths split open nearby, one right after the other. A lanky woman with caramel hair and skin, who looks to be in her late thirties, and a similarly aged, slightly pudgy man with a grim expression emerge from the first. Mako and Pavel, I presume. Because the woman who strides out from the cloth beside them can't be anyone but Thlo.

Despite her short stature, every part of her, from the briskness of her steps to the firmness of her square jaw, emanates strength. Like all the Kemyates I've met, she doesn't neatly match any Earth ethnicity: at one angle her face looks

Chinese, at another South American. Her smooth black hair is slicked away from her face in short waves flecked with gray. Only that and a few fine lines around her eyes and the corners of her mouth give away that she's much older than her companions. Her eyes themselves, a brown so deep they're almost black, settle on me immediately.

"This is Skylar," Win says before anyone else can speak. He steps between them and me as he covers a cough. In that moment, under the weight of those five stares, I'm inexpressibly grateful for his attempt at protection. "I don't know what Jule said, but she—"

"Win," Thlo interrupts. She doesn't even look at him; her gaze is still fixed on me. Her tone is so measured in its gentleness it makes me shiver. "She can't be here. She isn't part of this conversation. Isis, Pavel." She adds a command in Kemyate.

The woman Win called "Ice" and the older man move toward me. I draw back against the sofa. Win throws out his arm to block them. "No," he says. "She deserves to be here. We wouldn't have any of the weapon if it weren't for her. We wouldn't know what Jeanant wanted. She's *talked* to him."

Those last four words are the ones that break Thlo's careful composure. A flicker of surprise darts across her face, and is gone.

Win didn't mention that part to Jule.

"Wait," she says, just as calmly as before. Pavel and Isis halt in their tracks.

"It's true," I force out before she can change her mind. "I've talked to Jeanant. And there was something he wanted me to tell you." It seems like a cheap way in, but I'm having trouble focusing under Thlo's gaze, so frankly assessing I want to crawl away inside my skin.

Win has yanked open his satchel. He takes out the smaller tech plate embedded in its rectangle of plastic and offers it to Thlo.

"It was in the Louvre, hidden in a painting, during the July Revolution," he says.

Thlo studies it, and hands it to Isis. "Guidance system," Isis reports, her eyes widening as she takes it in.

"What else?" Thlo says.

He hands her the second tech plate, which Isis identifies as a processor. And then the box. Thlo opens it carefully, a few last bits of forest dirt sprinkling on the floor. She draws out a makeshift book of bound pages with a shiny texture, the surface of the ones I can see etched with figures and mechanical diagrams.

"The schematics," Isis murmurs, her eyebrows lifting even higher. Her hands tremble as she flips through it. She makes a breathless explanation in her own language.

"The fourth—we weren't able to retrieve," Win says. "The Enforcers caught Jeanant before he could place it."

"I saw it," I put in. "If it helps, to figure out what you're missing."

But Thlo seems to have paused over Win's last sentence. "They— I think you'd better start from the beginning."

So Win describes how he discovered my abilities— glossing over the way his impatience caught the Enforcers' notice—and our Travels together, up to our final escape from Kurra. Jule snorts once, at the mention of the trip to the Coliseum, but after that it seems to take all his concentration just to avoid looking impressed. No one else makes a sound.

In the face of their awe, Win's posture straightens, his voice becoming more and more confident, even though he has to stop a couple of times to sneeze. He leaves spaces for me to fill in the parts of the story only I know, which I do as succinctly as possible. I stumble a little when it comes to the final bit, summarizing my argument with Jeanant. And then his death.

"He didn't want to take any chance the Enforcers would be able to interrogate him," I explain haltingly. "Protecting all of you—he told me that was the most important thing. It must have been more important to him than losing that last part."

"What was it, the one they took?" Isis asks.

"It was a sort of tube, about this big." I gesture.

Isis glances to Thlo, pointing to something in the book of blueprints. "I bet that was the beam's fuel. He wouldn't have needed much, but he was using ..." She says a word I don't understand. "It'll be difficult, but we can probably find a way to get more."

Thlo nods, still silent. She takes each of the weapon parts again in turn, reading the messages etched on their casings. At the third, her eyes soften.

"'We all started in one place,'" she murmurs. "'Some stayed, and some struck out for new ground. Those who follow after always want to take what those before them have built.'"

"'Visit the crocodile's day by the spiderweb'?" Mako reads from beside her, when Thlo halts.

"Algeria, 2157 BC by the Earth calendar," Thlo elaborates. "It's the first place we Traveled to as colleagues."

We all started in one place. I can hear Jeanant's voice in the words. He wasn't just talking about the last location—he was talking about Kemya and Earth.

Thlo sets the box aside. She steps closer to me, taking my chin in her hand. I have to resist the urge to flinch away. For several seconds, she just holds my gaze, as if she can read my intentions there. I can't help blinking, but I manage not to look away.

"I won't tell anyone about Kemya, or what you've been doing here," I say when she drops her hand. "I know that would be just as dangerous for me as anyone else. All I care about is knowing the shifts will stop."

She doesn't comment on that. The corners of her mouth tighten, and she says, "Jeanant had another message for me?"

There's something hopeful in the question. Jeanant was her mentor. From the way he talked about her, the messages he wrote, they were close friends too, if not more. And then he disappeared from her life seventeen years ago, without even telling her where he was going. All I have for her is some vague impersonal advice that's still about his mission. Suddenly I feel twice as awkward.

"Yes," I say. "He said—he wanted me to tell you—to be careful, when you rebuild the weapon. To make sure you have the right moment before you try to destroy the generator. He thought … he moved too quickly, and that was why the Enforcers caught on."

She seems to be waiting after my voice falters. "I'm sorry," I add. "That was everything."

Her face hardens. For a second, I think she's going to hit me. Then she says, "Ah," with a soft release of breath, and the moment passes.

"He was the best of us," she says. "You're lucky to have met him." And I can hear it in her voice, as plainly as if she's said it out loud: she loved him. All at once, I'm ashamed of how scared of her I've been.

I knew him for less than an hour, when you add it up. She was with him for years. My regrets are nothing compared to her grief.

"I know," I say.

She turns her head away as if she's tired of looking at me.

"Thank you," she says, "for assisting Win and passing on Jeanant's last message. We won't keep you from your life any longer." Then, to the others: "We should head out before the Enforcers have time to break this code as well. Isis, you'll contact Britta?"

Isis hurries to a corner of the room, pulling a small device out of her sleeve. Win clears his throat. "If it's all right, I'd like to be the one who takes Skylar home. I'll just need to use one of the other cloths."

"Yes," Thlo says, all business now. "Of course, but be quick about it." She catches my eyes once more. "I do mean that thank-you. And we appreciate your discretion."

She hands him the cloth she was using and swivels to face the others without another word. They gather around her. Then it's just Win and me again.

32.

There's an instant, as we whirl away from the polished office space, where I squeeze my eyes shut and try to prepare for a present I don't recognize, that I might not even be a part of. As if I'd notice blinking out of existence if it happened.

I'm still there when we come to earth in a sheltered driveway a couple blocks from my house. I can't quite feel relieved yet. I keep my eyes on the sidewalk as we hurry down the street in silence, not wanting to see the way things might have changed, how much more *wrong* it might feel than those few twinges the last time I came back.

I remember my parents and Noam, Angela and Lisa, Daniel and Jaeda. My impressions of them all feel normal, right. But would I even know if their roles in my life have been rewritten since before I was born?

The spare house key is in its usual hiding place. I step inside onto the burgundy mat beside the narrow plastic shoe rack. My purple jacket with the melted mark on the sleeve from my first encounter with Kurra hangs where I left it. The savory smell of last night's stew lingers faintly in the air, mingling with the cedar scent of the hall cabinet. Through the kitchen I can see the amber leaves of the maple in the backyard.

I suck in a breath, too choked up to speak. It's all okay. I'm here. I traveled around the world and back and forth through centuries of history, and my life is just where I left it.

Maybe humans were never supposed to live on this planet. Maybe we all belong back with Win's people on his cramped space station. But I can't imagine any place other than this being *home*. It's ours now.

Standing there, the last two days feel like a dream. It hasn't really been days at all—maybe half an hour since I first vanished from my room upstairs. But it's been a very long and exhausting dream. The numbness from the Enforcer's blast to my shoulder has faded, and Win retrieved a bandage from the office that's wrapped around my ankle, sapping most of the pain away with its cool touch, so all I feel is tired. The longing rises up inside me to wobble to my bedroom, crash onto my bed, and sleep for about a week.

Win coughs softly where he's standing just inside the door, which reminds me that I can't walk away quite yet. I turn to him, and the side of his mouth curls up in a half smile. He's still so vividly present and real against the muted lines of the hallway. But this world won't fade anymore, now. Together we've made sure the experiments, the shifts and rewrites, will come to an end.

I want to say something like that, something profound, but what actually comes out of my mouth is, "So, Darwin?"

A ghost of a blush colors his cheeks. "I didn't name myself," he says. "Blame my parents. And I'd *really* prefer if you stuck with Win."

There's a lot I want to ask about naming your kids after historical figures from a completely different planet, but it's obviously a sore spot. And I guess it shouldn't matter to me. Very soon I'm never going to see him again to call him by any name, and he'll feel like a dream too.

An ache wells up inside me. I didn't realize until this moment how hard it was going to be to watch him leave. How do you say good-bye forever to someone who's been there beside you through the most horrible and amazing things you'll ever experience; whose life you've saved, and who's saved your life; who's seen you fall apart and stayed to help you put yourself back together? He's been my constant companion for the last two days—and eleven centuries. I don't know if I can call him a friend and yet at the same time *friend* doesn't seem to cover half of it.

"Thank you," I say. "You kept your promise. Here I am, safely home."

"Thanks just as much to you," he says. "I'll do everything I can to make sure you stay safe. We'll be back to take down the time field as soon as we possibly can."

"Do you think …" I start to ask, and then I remember there's no way it'll be *that* soon. Not this month, not this year. As soon as they possibly can is sometime at least seventeen years from now.

"In the future, in your present time, it hasn't gotten that much worse here, has it?" I blurt out instead.

"You don't need to worry about that," he says. "Earth will still be fine. And because of you, there won't be any more harm done to it."

I nod, trying to let his words sooth my nerves. "And then the planet can start to recover."

"Recover?" he says.

"Start … binding itself back together again," I say, motioning vaguely.

He hesitates. "Oh. Skylar, I didn't mean to make you think— The damage that's been done, it isn't something that can heal."

I stare at him. Noticing again the faded quality of the hall behind him, a mark of that damage, sends a chill over my skin. "It isn't?"

I should have guessed. A recording of a recording of a recording. You can't bring back the detail once it's lost. Maybe I just didn't want to let myself think it.

"The planet will still be completely sustainable," Win says quickly. "And some of the environmental issues, they should settle down in time as everything … adjusts. I'm sorry."

"No," I say. "It's not your fault. It's the opposite of your fault." I set my hand against the wall. No matter how it looks, it still feels perfectly solid. Perfectly real. "I guess it doesn't really make a difference anyway. This is normal to us now. What really matters is that we'll be free, that it won't get any worse."

I repeat the words to myself, willing them to sink in. Earthlings are a resilient bunch—I've seen plenty evidence of that. We'll survive. We always do.

"I'd say I'll come see you again, when we make it back, but I don't think there's going to be time for side trips," he says.

And, seventeen years in the future, in Win's present, he'll still be the eighteen or nineteen he looks now and I'll be … thirty-four. The ache in my chest expands. I clamp down on it, my hands balling. I shouldn't be keeping him, even now. He has to get back—Thlo told him to be quick. But I haven't said what I need to. I don't know the words to express it all.

Forget about words, then.

I step forward, reaching for him, and he meets me halfway, wrapping his arms around me. My head tips against his shoulder as I hug him. He squeezes me back, one hand brushing over my hair. He smells like the places we've been to together: like newspaper ink and green jungle, snowy marsh and summer trees.

"Skylar," he says, his voice rough. I ease back. He holds my gaze, his eyes bright in the dim light in the hall, but whatever he was going to say, he can't seem to find the words either.

"You stay safe too, okay?" I say.

His smile returns. "I'll work on that. And … thank you again. For everything. I'm glad I got to know you."

"Yeah," I say, and anything I might have added sticks in the back of my throat.

That smile is the last thing I see as he pulls the folds of the time cloth around him and wavers out of sight. I stand, watching, until I'm sure he's no longer there.

"Good-bye," I murmur to the empty hall. I didn't even think to say that.

I'm back to my life, my real life. A restless urge to make sure everything in the house is as it should be pierces the momentary melancholy. I turn and head down the hall.

Everything isn't as it should be—not quite. There's a framed photograph of a Spanish-looking city in the dining room that sparks a tiny vibration of *wrong*, and when I blink I see the kitchen cabinets in robin's egg blue instead of mint green. An afterimage hovers over the soap dish in the upstairs bathroom, of all things, of something … rounder? The whisper of *wrong*ness passes as quickly as the image fades.

I creep into my bedroom last, and rotate on my feet, braced for another twinge. My gaze catches on the photograph from my junior-year camping trip. I move toward the desk, studying it. Me, Lisa, and Evan, with Angela out of sight behind the camera.

The space around us looks too empty. Is someone missing? But it's always been the four of us—

Bree. The name slithers through my head, and my stomach clenches. A grinning face as we jog through the park. Rich laughter as we joke over bowls of tofu curry. Dark ringlets shaking as we safety pin a dress mishap while the thrum of school dance music carries through the restroom door.

The flashes of memory dart away before I can grasp them, leaving only pale ripples in my mind.

She's gone. Something I shifted, or something the Enforcers did, in the chaos we made of Ohio—it took her away. The loss stabs through me, even though I hardly remember who she was.

She meant something. I liked her. She's gone.

I tear my eyes away from the photo, sinking down onto the edge of the bed. What have I done? Maybe it was just a tweak to her life, some minor change that meant she ended up at a different school, or in a whole different city.

Or maybe I've erased her completely.

What could I have done differently? I don't know.

The echoing *wrong, wrong, wrong* reverberates through me. I drag in a breath, and make myself think of digging up the box by the log, slamming into Kurra, watching Win place every item I helped find into Thlo's hands. I fought for that girl. I stood up to the people who are truly responsible for every shift, every *wrong*ness. I won.

Mostly.

The feeling of loss fades, along with the wisps of memory. Who am I mourning? It seems suddenly distant.

I tip over, setting my head on the pillow. Exhaustion washes over me again, and this time I don't fight it. Sleep is one place no *wrong*ness can reach.

• • •

For a few minutes, when I wake up in the thin early morning sunlight, it feels like a perfectly normal day. I'll get up, head to cross-country practice, sit through my classes. Coach will bark at anyone who ran over their previous time, the teachers will review the homework and assign more, the halls will be full of the usual raucous chatter. Beautifully, amazingly normal.

Then I go downstairs to grab breakfast.

"Busy day yesterday?" Mom says as I come into the kitchen. She yawns, holding the kettle under the tap.

I freeze. "What?"

"Whatever you got up to, you must have really tired yourself out," she goes on in her usual breezy voice. "I called your name a couple times when dinner was ready and you didn't even twitch. I thought if you were that far out, you probably needed the sleep."

"Oh," I say. "Yeah." Dinner. All that jumping—morning to evening to afternoon—I'd lost any sense of schedule.

But I can't exactly say that. "I, ah, I guess I didn't get enough sleep the night before. I stayed up kind of late getting an essay done. And we ran a hard practice yesterday morning."

Mom nods as if this all makes perfect sense, which I guess it does. Except it's not true. These are the first words I've spoken to Mom in what feels like days and I'm spouting lies.

The wonderful sense of normal starts to recede with a knot in my gut.

My stomach seems completely aware that it missed dinner. It grumbles as soon as I open the bag of bread, with a pang of hunger that shoots right through me. I have to grip the counter for a second, afraid I'm going to puke. Not that there's anything in there right now to throw up.

Two days of Traveling, give or take, and all I've eaten was a bag of trail mix and a few bites of pecan pie.

I manage to gather myself before Mom notices, and pop two slices of bread in the toaster. When she ducks out, I make myself two sandwiches as I wait for the toast—one for lunch and one for right after practice. I feel like I could eat five breakfasts, but if I fill up too much before the run, I really will puke.

I'm gulping down bites of toast slathered in peanut butter when Mom comes back in, holding a spiral-bound book. When she flips it open, I realize it's one of Noam's sketchpads. I stop chewing.

"I started thinking, after we talked the other night," she says, her eyes on the book. "Maybe we've gone too far, boxing all Noam's things away as if we're pretending he was never here. It might be nice to have a couple of his pictures framed, put up in the house. What do you think of this one?"

She presents a colored pencil drawing of a vine creeping down a latticework fence, one bright red bloom in the midst of the pointed leaves. It's one of his more polished pieces, only sketchy around the edges, the shades of green bringing out the textures and shadows so the vine seems to emerge from the page.

I swallow the sticky lump in my mouth. "It's great," I say, and it is. But I have to tuck my hands under the table and press my fingernails into my palms to hold back the tears that want to spring into my eyes. Imagine what he could have done, if Darryl hadn't— If those boys from school hadn't—

Mom keeps flipping through the sketchpad, oblivious. And I remember nothing's changed for her. Noam is still as distant to her, a memory from twelve years ago, as he was to me when we talked on Tuesday.

She doesn't know. In her mind, he could still be wandering the world out there, alone, or with new friends …

"Skylar?" Mom says, and I realize she's looking at me now. "If it bothers you, honey, we don't have to do it."

"No," I say quickly. "Of course, it's fine. It's a good idea."

She smiles and wanders back into the hall, maybe trying to decide where to hang the pictures. The rest of my toast catches in my throat going down.

They need to know. She and Dad—it isn't *right* for them to have nothing but that uncertainty—it isn't right that Noam's life trailed off without any acknowledgment. It isn't right that Darryl and the other boys never had to own up to what they did.

I have to figure out a way for my parents to find out. I mull it over as I clean up my dishes. Noam's yearbooks are in that box upstairs. I could find Darryl's full name—and maybe Babyface's and his tall friend's too, if their photos look enough like they did in person. That would be a start.

I think maybe I can work out a plan while I run. The rhythm usually helps me sort out my thoughts. But a half hour later, as I'm pounding along the paths in the park, a different sort of uneasiness drifts over me. There's a hollowness in the team, in the space around me, even though Marie's running with me like she often does. A sense of something missing, so hazy it slides away from me whenever I try to latch onto it, only to slink back the moment I let it go.

Is there a shift, something about the park, about us? I can't pick out any specific vibe of *wrong*ness. It's just not exactly *right*.

I manage to tune it out during calculus and Spanish. But when I walk into the cafeteria and Angela waves to me from where she's sitting with Lisa and Evan, it rises over me again. The table is too empty.

Of course it's not. I sit down and the four of us fill the space, just like always. Still, the apprehension won't stop niggling at me. I glance over my shoulder a few times, half expecting to see someone standing there, waiting for us to notice. It's just the usual cafeteria crowd.

"So, I think it's time we start making winter holiday plans," Lisa declares, and Angela grins.

"You can never wait long, can you?"

"Didn't we—" I start, and hesitate. I was going to say, *Didn't we talk about that yesterday?* But we didn't, did we?

I try to think back to our conversation in the pie shop, but the memory is slippery. I asked Lisa about the battle, I remember that. And … the rest is a haze. I picture the four of us, sitting around the table: Lisa by the window, Evan on one side, and Jasmin, who's been hanging out with us sometimes since we all had English together last year …

A whisper shivers through me. *Wrong.* The image blurs. I blink, but I can't seem to focus on anything in that moment.

Around me, the conversation has veered off in another direction.

"You're all *coming* to the dance, right?" Angela says.

"Of course," I say automatically, and Evan mock grumbles, "I don't think I was given a choice," and Angela and I giggle as Lisa punches his shoulder. The whisper slips away, but the vague uneasiness remains.

"You've got to ask someone to dance," I tell Angela, trying to bury it. "Time for a new crush."

Her cheeks flush and her gaze darts toward Teyo, a few tables over … with the sophomore girlfriend he hooked up with last month. A chill tickles over my skin.

"We'll see," Angela says, turning back to us.

"If you don't pick someone, I'm going to do it for you," Lisa announces. Angela squeals in protest. And I just breathe.

Everything's okay. Win and Thlo and the others are speeding back to Kemya to assemble Jeanant's weapon, and everything here is perfectly, perfectly fine. Nothing's felt *really* wrong, after all. I'm just being paranoid, psyching myself out.

My pulse keeps thrumming in my head. My fingers itch for my lost bracelet. But it wasn't helping that much anyway, in the end. I think of bringing the weapon parts to Thlo, a beam exploding the generator over our heads …

Not for seventeen more years.

I can't quite shake it off. My nerves are still buzzing when we get up to head to our next classes. "See you," Angela says, turning down the hall toward her geography room, and the uneasiness bursts into a sudden panic.

"Ang—" I blurt out.

She pauses, looking back. "Yeah?" she says. That oh so normal worry line crinkles up in the middle of her forehead. It should bother me that I'm worrying her, but somehow I'm relieved to see it.

Be careful, I think. *Stay safe. Don't disappear.*

It's not as though she could help it, though, could she? Who knows what shifts the Kemyate scientists above us will make in the next seventeen years? In the weeks or months or years it takes after that for Win's group to find the right moment to take down the time field generator? All our lives are going to be rewritten hundreds, maybe thousands more times …

I open my mouth, those fears prickling through me. All I can force out is, "The dance. It's going to be great."

She smiles. "Thanks," she says.

I hurry off to physics. A sweat's broken over my skin. I concentrate on the rows of lockers, the numbers on the doors, my desk there in the middle of the classroom. An aimless drone of apprehension hums in my ears. I grit my teeth as the teacher starts to write on the board, and close my eyes. *Three times three is nine. Three times nine is twenty-seven.* I picture the numbers in their steady spiral, winding around me like armor.

No matter what the Travelers and the scientists playing with our planet do, they can't shift that. They can't stop three times three from equaling nine—

Or can they?

It's an absurd idea, but the moment my mind's latched onto it, I can't shake it. I make myself open my binder and copy Ms. Cavoy's notes, but it's still there, in the back of my head.

I don't know. I did so much, I fought so hard to protect everyone I care about, and I still don't *know* whether a single one of us is really safe.

I'm never going to know. Seventeen years from now, I can start wondering if it's happened yet, if the fishbowl around us has been shattered and the watching figures in their satellite have finally gone home, but there'll be nothing to tell me for sure. I can't help; I can't hurry it along; I can't do anything but wait, like one more clueless goldfish.

I did my best. More than anyone else on Earth could ever imagine. So why do I feel like something horribly important has slipped through my fingers?

Physics passes in a fog. I stumble through the recitations in Spanish, ones I'm sure I knew by heart a couple days ago. Finally, the clock ticks across the last few minutes toward final bell. Bags rustle as my classmates pack up their books, ready to be done.

It's not done, I think. I stare out the window, over the school's courtyard to the street beyond.

How am I going to get through another seventeen years feeling like this?

I suppress a shudder, and narrow my eyes. The interlocking stones of the courtyard. Seven bikes chained to the rack. A green van rumbling by. Maybe, if I can just absorb every movement, every detail in my view—

All at once, the frantic buzz inside me quiets.

Win's outside. Standing on the other side of the street beside the bus shelter, turned toward the front doors, as if he's meant to be there.

The bell rings. Without any conscious thought, I'm moving. Snatching up my backpack, shoving in my notebook as I'm rushing for the door. When I hit the stairwell, I'm running. Down, and out the front doors, and across the road, toward the smile that splits across Win's face when he sees me.

"You came back," I say, breathless, as I come to a halt in front of him.

The first few students are ambling out the school doors behind me. Win draws back behind the bus shelter, and I follow.

"Yes," he says, and then, in a rush, "This might sound completely ridiculous, but I thought there was a chance, and I can still bring you back so you haven't lost any more time here, and—"

"*What*?" I interrupt. The hum that's filling me now isn't apprehension. It's anticipation. "Win, just ask."

"I talked to Thlo," he says, slowing down. "Just now, after you left—it hasn't been long for us, but I came today so you'd have had time to think. She's approved it. You've helped us so much already, and I thought … maybe you'd want to come back to Kemya with us. To see Jeanant's plan through to the end. We can make it work."

He still hasn't actually asked anything, but the question is obvious. The remains of my anxiety wash away. This is it. This is what I needed. I couldn't deal with being back because I'm not actually done fighting: for the planet, for my parents, for Angela and Lisa and Evan. I don't have to be.

I don't care if I have to go to the other end of the universe to do it. I'm going to see that generator burn. I'm going to know it really is done, for good.

Nothing has ever felt more *right*.

"Yes," I say.

"Yes?" Win repeats.

"Yes, I'll come."

"Oh. Well." He breaks into a grin so wide it's dazzling. "Then we should get going. We've got a galaxy to cross."

He holds out his hand, and I take it.

ACKNOWLEDGMENTS

I have to acknowledge, with gratitude, the books and authors that helped me figure out my own rules of time travel (as unscientific as mine may be): *Physics of the Impossible* by Michio Kaku, *Time Traveler* by Dr. Ronald L. Mallett, and *Black Holes & Time Warps* by Kip S. Thorne.

Many thanks to the Toronto Speculative Fiction Writers Group, who got the story on the right track; to friends and critique partners Amanda Coppedge, Deva Fagan, and Jenny Moss, who helped me take the book from early draft to finished novel; to my agent, Josh Adams, who found the trilogy not one but two homes; to my editors, Miriam Juskowicz and Lynne Missen, who guided me in bringing Skylar's story into better clarity; to everyone at Amazon Skyscape and Penguin Canada who has helped bring this book to life; and to my family and friends for their continuing support, and their patience and understanding when I'm deep in the writing cave.

THE ADVENTURE CONTINUES IN

THE CLOUDED SKY

1.

My first doubt about leaving Earth comes five seconds too late for me to change my mind. Win's Traveling cloth hurtles us into a round peach-toned room lit by glowing lines that lace the ceiling. "This is the Travel bay," he murmurs to me as we step out. The other interplanetary rebels, the ones I encountered just a day ago by my time and less than half an hour by theirs, are already standing scattered through the room. Thlo, their leader, nods to the curvy woman with crimson-streaked curls—Isis, if I remember right. Isis taps a band around her sinewy brown wrist.

"Stell," she says, "hit it."

A trembling spreads through the floor. And it hits *me*: I'm on an alien spaceship, on a course across the galaxy. I'm already farther from home than I've ever imagined being. When we reach our destination—the space station orbiting the devastated planet of Kemya—*my* planet will be a speck so small it may as well have disappeared. I'll have journeyed hundreds of times farther than any human-made object has ever gone.

Any *Earth*-made object, I amend as I hug myself. Because the "aliens" surrounding me are as human as I am. Humans whose true home is Kemya, who populated Earth with their settlers thousands of years ago and let us forget our origins as generations lived and died. They wanted us to forget, to remain unaware while they used our planet as a vast experimental terrarium, shifting our history and watching the impact echo across the timeline without any concern for the way those shifts were degrading the fabric of our world down to the bonds between our atoms.

Several pairs of alien human eyes are watching me now. Win moves forward, his hand on the side of my arm. "You weren't properly introduced before," he says quickly. "Isis is the one I told you about who handles the tech work. Mako and Pavel have been with the group since Jeanant's time—Mako's specialty is finding resources and Pavel's is, ah, information gathering, you'd call it. And you've talked to Thlo ... and Jule."

An edge has crept into his voice. Jule, who spent most of our first meeting taking jabs at Win, raises his eyebrows at the two of us, his smile baring teeth bright against his dark skin. "Hey, Skylar," Isis says with a bob of her curls. Mako, a lanky woman whose caramel hair matches her complexion, glances over me as if unimpressed. She turns to murmur to the slightly pudgy man whose face has remained dour throughout the introductions—Pavel. Thlo motions the two of them and Jule over to her, emanating authority despite her short stature in the set of her broad shoulders, the cool tone of her voice.

I scoot closer to Win. He's the only one here I really know, now that we've spent most of the last three days together, whisking through history and around my world to find the pieces of a weapon this group's former leader left behind. The weapon that will destroy the time field that allows Kemyate scientists to alter Earth's past, and stop their experimenting—and its continued deterioration of the planet—for good.

I have to remember that. The people in front of me aren't like other Kemyates. They're risking their lives to free Earth.

Abruptly, the lights go out. The floor shudders, and I stumble. My body feels oddly flimsy. There's a little less gravity on Kemya than on Earth, Win mentioned before. They must keep the ship the same.

Win's hand tightens around my elbow. A high voice pierces the darkness from somewhere above, speaking in Kemyate.

"The satellite's directing a sensor sweep this way," Win murmurs by my ear, the familiar British lilt to his English steadying me. "We're going into minimum power mode so it doesn't 'see' us, until we're out of range."

The research satellite over Earth houses not just scientists and Travelers but also the Enforcers, the Kemyate police who'll shoot us down if we're spotted. I wait, legs locked, heart pounding. The floor has settled back into the gentle trembling I noticed before. The voice above makes another announcement. The darkness is so dense I can't make out even the outline of Win right beside me. I wish I were close enough to touch a wall, to remind myself that the space around us is not as vast as it feels right now.

I wish I had the slightest idea what to expect from this place.

Win is just saying, "It shouldn't be much longer," when the voice above peals out, this time sounding cheerful. A second later, the lines on the ceiling gleam back on. I blink in the sudden glare.

Mako and Pavel head straight out, Jule sauntering after them. Thlo looks at Win and me, her near-black eyes as impenetrable as the earlier darkness.

"I'd like you to adjust to the ship before we discuss the logistics of your stay," she says to me. "We'll talk further after first bunkdown."

I nod.

"Try to stick to the job you've been given," she says to Win dryly. Win has let go of my arm, but I feel him tense as she strides out of the room.

"Is she still upset that you disobeyed her orders?" I ask. Win wasn't assigned to track down Jeanant's weapon himself, just to keep watch. And he was never supposed to reveal their mission, or anything else about Kemya, to an Earthling like me. Never mind that the two of us accomplished more in those few days than the rest of them had in weeks. They might not have retrieved even one piece of the weapon if he hadn't risked asking for my help.

"She's happy with the results," he says, swiping a hand through his jagged black hair. "I'm not sure she trusts that they were a result of quick thinking and not dumb luck."

"It was a lot of initiative to take all at once," Isis remarks from where she's lingered by the doorway.

Win shrugs, but his deep blue eyes are pensive. Thlo didn't mention what his current job is, but I'm going to guess he's on babysitting duty. I drag in a breath, the crisp air leaving a faint mineral taste in my mouth. I don't want him to regret inviting me to help see their mission through.

"So, here I am," I say. "Give me the tour?" I'll be more useful once I have some idea where—and what—everything is.

"Of course," he says, shaking himself out of his thoughts.

"I'll help show you around," Isis says. She smiles, but the analytical sharpness of her gaze as it slides to me reminds me of Win when we first met, when he saw me as more of a scientific curiosity than a person. "We should get to know each other," she adds. "You're going to be staying with Britta and me when we reach Kemya."

Her accent is thicker than Win's or Thlo's, giving her English a staccato rhythm. It takes me a moment to absorb what she's said.

"Staying …" I hadn't thought that far ahead. I haven't had time to.

Isis's cheek dimples. "I assume that's all right?"

"Yes. Thank you." I'm not sure how big an imposition it is, letting me into her home. From what Win's said, there's not much room on the space station, which has been his people's entire world since a technological accident poisoned their planet ages ago.

We step past the Travel bay's doors into a narrow hall with one of those thin glowing lines running the length of the arched ceiling. The walls are the same peach tone as in the bay, the floor a silvery gray, spongy under my feet. "This is what we'd call a, ah, scrounging ship," Win says. "Mainly used for gathering resources in the atmosphere, on asteroids … Not the fastest, but a decent cover for sneaking out here."

His gold-brown skin seems dulled in the artificial light. I can't help thinking of the way he basked in Earth's sunlight. Those last few moments with me, hurrying to my house to pick up a few things before we jumped to the ship, they might be the last he's truly *outside* in years.

Then he sneezes. Okay, so there are a few things he won't miss about Earth, our cold viruses among them.

"Where do people on Kemya think you all went?" I ask.

"Thlo arranged a project that has us scouting and conducting experiments in a different part of the galaxy," Isis says. "We've made sure all the official records reflect that." She's stepped closer to me now that we're in the hall, just a sliver too near to be comfortable by Earth standards. Win used to get in my personal space too—it must be a Kemyate thing. I suppose when your living space shrinks, your sense of personal boundaries might too.

"Thlo could arrange a trip across the galaxy just like that?" I say.

"She's on one of the councils—the groups that make all the decisions about what happens on Kemya," Win explains. "She has a lot of influence when we need it."

"In public she pretends to be completely supportive of the current policies, so no one suspects anything," Isis says.

She waves open the first door we come to, and then the next, and the next. "Recreation bay, to keep fitness up. Supply room. Cafeteria. Laboratory. About three-quarters of the ship you won't see, because it's cargo hold."

I catch my lungs clenching every time a new space opens up before us, my mind cataloging the details as fast as I can take them in. Seven doors down this hallway—strange cylinder as wide as the spread of my arms—rectangular table with ten beige stools around it—screens and lights and geometric patterns etched on walls. I'm so overwhelmed it takes me a minute to figure out why my body's instinctively bracing. I'm waiting for a *wrong* feeling and the jolt of panic that would come with it. Those feelings struck most often when I experienced something new: new people, new music or movies … new places. Leaving me shaking and chilled and an inch from an emotional breakdown. It's been a long time since I let myself take in so much "new" all at once.

But I'm okay here. I know where those feelings come from now—the inescapable sense that something isn't as it should be was a real impression left behind when one of Win's fellow Travelers made a shift to Earth's history. It's not even possible for a shift to happen now that we've left the time field behind. As long as I'm off Earth, the *wrong*ness and the panic attacks can't reach me.

Huh. I've wanted my whole life for the *wrong* feelings to stop. Turns out I had to leave the planet to get that.

The hall forks ahead of us. "Cabins," Isis says, nodding to the left. "There are a few empty ones to pick from, but they're all the same. First, why don't you meet the rest of the crew?"

The door at the other end of the hall opens into a chamber about the size of my bedroom at home. A vast screen covers the wall opposite us, speckled darkness overlaid with floating orange-lit boxes and Kemyate characters. Three consoles with attached seats form a triangle in front of it. Mako sits at the one in the back, caramel skin tinted green by the display she's peering at, which is projected into thin air over the ridged top of the console.

Two unfamiliar figures glance over at me from the consoles at the front of the room. Isis motions to the woman first and then the guy. "Britta and Emmer."

Emmer raises a hand in greeting. He's so tall his body seems to have been folded into the seat like an origami figure, topped by blunt-cut auburn hair. Britta's tan face lights up as she smiles, though the smile is directed more at Isis than me.

She's as slight as her colleague is tall, and could do an accurate impression of a porcelain doll if it weren't for the tattoo that frames her delicate features, weaving in and out of her hairline like a spidery vine.

"This is Skylar," Isis says with such brevity I assume the two have already gotten a basic explanation of who I am. "Emmer's our spacecraft expert, making sure the ship stays in one piece. And Britta's our primary pilot—we couldn't have made it here without her."

"I'm sure you'd have found someone else somewhere who knows how to point a ship in the right direction," Britta replies in a chirpy voice I recognize from the Travel bay speakers. Isis rests her hand on the other woman's shoulder. When Britta reaches up to squeeze it, I remember Isis saying I'd be staying with the two of them. From the way Britta lit up when Isis came in, they're more than just roommates. So I'm imposing not just on a couple of friends, but the privacy of an actual couple.

"The satellite never got a hint the ship was out here?" Win asks.

"We stayed out of sensor range until we got your signal," Britta says. "And kept far-side, working around the pulses in solar energy. The Enforcers switched their usual sweep when I didn't expect it, but we responded in time."

She flicks her fingers toward the console. The airy display in front of her blinks to show a sphere that must be Earth, surrounded by a complex matrix of curved lines and dotted waves, and a reddish streak I guess is the ship's course. I can't read the characters scattered across the diagram, but the configuration strikes a chord of recognition.

"You had to adjust because of the planet's magnetic field there?" I say, pointing to a dip in the course line. Britta's eyebrows leap up.

"That's right," she says. "You've done a little interstellar travel before?"

My face heats. "No, I just—physics class, and I've done some extra reading. I like understanding the math behind how things work."

Britta aims a grin fully at me this time, but it feels overbright. "Well, it's about time we had a real numbers—what's the word?—geek on board." She drops into a mock whisper. "These two techheads, they'd toss theory down the chute and spend all day just playing with circuits and sockets if they could."

"It's not as much fun if you can't hold it in your hands," Isis says with a playful nudge.

"Yes, but you'd have nothing to hold if people like me hadn't calculated how to make your tech work in the first place," Britta returns. "The real power's up here." She taps her head, her amber eyes sparkling. I get the feeling this is a well-worn topic for the two of them. Then her voice takes on the same overbright quality as her grin. "You stop by sometime and we'll chat velocity and magnetics and all that," she adds to me.

As if I'm going to keep up with a professional who's been zipping around the galaxy. "I'm not sure I have a grasp of the concepts at this level," I say.

"Everyone starts somewhere," she says. "You can't help the limitations you've had."

Growing up on a degraded planet with feeble technology. As gracious as Britta's obviously trying to be, I bristle inside.

Win must catch my reaction, because his fingers brush my hand. When I glance at him, his mouth is tight. He used to be the one making thoughtless comments like that. But his attitude changed, and quickly, as he got to know me. I can hope everyone else's will too.

Before Win can say anything, Emmer redirects the conversation, in a low voice that almost disguises his eagerness: "You met Jeanant." "Yeah," I say, and my throat closes up. Jeanant, the leader Thlo was second in command to. The man who traveled all this way alone to try to save both our peoples. The man who died before my eyes yesterday and two hundred years in my planet's past. I search for something to answer that eagerness. "He'd be impressed by how much you all have done."

Emmer relaxes in his seat, looking pleased. Britta clicks her tongue to get his attention.

"Grain cluster in 6-5. Time to get back to work. See you all later!"

The three of us step back into the hall. "She did mean that, about coming to talk with her," Isis says. "But I think it's best if you don't just wander into the navigation room. It might look, to Thlo …"

"Like I didn't care if I was distracting them?" I suggest.

"Yes," Isis says, sounding relieved that I understood. "It's going to take a little time for everyone to adjust to you being here."

"But Thlo wouldn't have agreed to you coming if she thought there'd be any trouble," Win puts in.

We wander into the hall of cabins. "The … toilets are the last rooms on the end," Isis says, and then points to the first door in the row. "Why don't you take this cabin? It'll be easy for you to remember which is yours. We'll program it with your sequence and vocals …" She types something into a glassy panel beside the door. "Press your thumb here, and say, 'Open.'"

A glowing circle appears on the panel. I touch the slick surface with my thumb. A prickle darts over my skin. *Sequence*—is it sampling my DNA? "Open," I say. Isis taps the panel again, and the door hums into the wall. On the other side is a tiny room half-filled by a set of bunks.

"Bed," Isis says, as if I couldn't figure that out. "Desk." She pushes a spot on the wall opposite the bunks and a thin slice of the surface peels away to jut out at a perpendicular angle. "Computer." She waves her hand in front of the wall on the other side of the door, and a rectangular pattern of light blinks on.

"We can set it to display in English for you," Win offers.

"Of course." Isis ducks into the cramped room. Win leans against the doorway, covering a cough, as I sink onto the lower bunk.

It can't have been more than an hour since he met me outside school and asked if I'd carry on this mission with him—I doubt it's even five o'clock in the afternoon by my time—but I'm suddenly exhausted. Nothing, not the walls or the floors or the beds or the desk, is quite like the ones I'm used to. And they all have that faint edge of extra *there*ness, that I can feel even more as I rest my palms on the dense bunk padding. The difference I can sense between how solid all this Kemyate equipment is compared to my Earthling body with its atoms decayed by thousands of years of shifts.

"There you go," Isis says, stepping back from the computer. "Is there anything else you need? I'm not sure what you're used to." She looks suddenly concerned, as if she's brought home a puppy and realized she's not sure she has the right food.

"I'm good," I say.

"I can show you some programs you might find useful," Win says. "Or—"

"I think I'd like to take this in on my own for a bit," I interrupt. "Oh," he says, looking taken aback. "All right."

My uneasiness is making me rude. It's because of Win I'm getting

this chance at all. Because he was brave enough to take a chance on me, when just talking to me went against every rule he'd been taught. I scoot forward on the bunk so I can grasp his hand. "Sorry," I say. "It's just a lot all at once."

His expression softens. "No, I should have realized. If you want me—Anything you need, just ask. My cabin's three doors down. Convenient, right?" He smiles at the allusion to our shared knowledge of the way I've multiplied by threes to help my mind cope with the shifts. For an instant, holding his gaze, I don't want him to go anywhere.

"Come on, Win," Isis says. "We have to take care of the Traveler equipment."

He squeezes my hand and lets go. "I'll come by later so we can get dinner?"

"Sounds good," I say.

He bobs his head and slips into the hall with Isis. The door closes automatically, and I'm alone. I look at the smooth panel, suddenly picturing the front door of my house. I have the urge to make some sort of gesture, the way I used to click that lock open and shut three times to reassure myself everything was safe and secure. My hand's already lifted before I catch myself. I was trying to keep myself safe and secure from the *wrong* feelings, and those aren't here. Fidgeting with this door isn't going to change anything. My little symbols of protection seem empty now that I know what the *wrong*ness is, and that it was completely outside my control.

I lie down, testing the bunk. A small slant rises up to meet my head in place of a pillow. There's no blanket around, but a hum arcs over my body, forming a layer of warmth against my skin as if the air has been shaped into an invisible duvet.

It should be soothing, but instead it's just one more alien intrusion. I sit back up, reaching for my backpack. I didn't bring much—Win said it'd be easier for me to blend in wearing Kemyate clothes, carrying Kemyate tech. But I couldn't stand the thought of leaving without a few reminders of home. My MP3 player. My tattered copy of *Flowers for Algernon*, which I expect to hold up to a few more rereadings. And two photographs: the most recent one I could find with Angela, Lisa, Evan, and me all together—an extra copy of the one a yearbook staffer took of us kicking our legs while perched on the railing by the school's back door—and one of me with my parents, the last time we went on a family hike in the state park just outside the city.

I snap bits of sticky tack from the packet I brought and fix the photos to the wall between the bunks. My friends and family beam back at me, and the tension inside me starts to release. *This* gesture feels meaningful. It's funny to think no matter how long I'll be out here, the way Win can hop through time, I'll be back before they know I've left.

I'm here for them, facing all these unknowns for them. And for me. So that I can come back knowing that no scientist from beyond the stars will ever make another change to our history, ever rewrite another life out of existence.

As long as I hold on to that, I can handle anything.